D1736414

ℰ ciela

Ciela Norma AD

ISBN: 978-954-28-1299-9

Ludmila Filipova

Translated by *Angela Rodel* and *David Mossop*
Edited by *Angela Rodel*

CONTENTS

Each scene from the novel is based on an actual historical fact, an extant artifact, or a real place. Readers eager to follow the clues on their own can visit the unique **Virtual Museum of Traces** *at the novel's website* www.parchmentmaze.com, *containing thousands of photographs from Moscow, Bulgaria, Burma, the Vatican, Berlin, Greece, Rome, and Thrace collected by the author in her four years of research. The clues are organized by location.*

Each chapter in The Parchment Maze *opens with an excerpt from a mysterious manuscript's missing final pages, so the reader can find his or her own way out of the puzzle.*

PROLOGUE

In January 2008, restoration work began in one of Rome's first libraries, located at the start of Europe's ancient road, the *Via Appia Antica*. An unfamiliar manuscript whose existence surprised historians was discovered in the process. They estimated it to be around two centuries old. Interestingly enough, it had no author or title, only a catalog number. There was a sign resembling a meander[1] or part of a maze engraved onto its leather cover with the word "The Taenarian Gate" in the center. To include it in the new card catalog, the archivists gave it a name: *The Parchment Maze*. Its contents were a curious jumble of artifacts, clippings, pictures and texts, some of which seemed to have been added to the manuscript long after its creation. On first reading, the various topics did not seem to be related. However, a more careful study of the text revealed that the various pictures and artifacts were clues to the manuscript labyrinth. Although each reader could find his own way out of the manuscript's tangle of words, no one could unravel the very mystery behind it, likely because the manuscript had no beginning or end – they had been destroyed. The final inky scrawl hung unfinished on ***page 406***. The librarians kept the manuscript's old catalog number so that it could be found. They knew every manuscript was created so as to be discovered eventually…

[1] The meander is one of the most widely-used symbols in the world. Today most people refer to it as the Greek Fret; however, it is thought to have appeared more than 8,000 years ago in the Central Balkans and to have been used by the first civilization using a primitive writing system to encode information into signs.

THE INCORPOREAL ONE

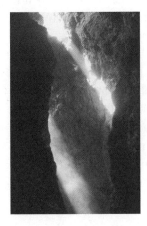

Page 407 began with a picture from **The Devil's Throat** cave and the following quote:
Orpheus mourned her to the upper world,
And then, lest he should leave the shades untried,
Dared to descend to Styx, passing the portal
Men call Taenarian. Through the phantom dwellers,
The buried ghosts he passed –
… he swept the strings, and chanted:
"Gods of the worlds below the world, –
… the music made the pale phantoms weep: –
[Orpheus and Eurydice] climbed the upward path, through absolute silence,
Up the steep murk, clouded in pitchy darkness…

From Ovid's *Metamorphoses*, Book X, "The Story of Orpheus and Eurydice"

Along the Path, Devil's Throat Cave, Rhodope Mountains, 1944

No one knew what the world above was.
He touched the face chiseled into the stone before him – the face of the first to descend from the upper kingdom. This man had come to them, here below, restoring their hope that the human race was not irreversibly lost among the shadows. They had called him Orpheus.

The man gave them music as well as hope that there would come a day when they would be able to go back home. In exchange they gave him the Knowledge they had gathered and brought with them here from their world. And then they showed Orpheus the way back.

Now he glanced back at the impenetrable darkness of his world one last time and started up towards the exit. He climbed slowly, as the path was steep, as well as damp, dark and narrow. Sharp stones cut into his feet despite his calluses. He had been climbing for hours. But he couldn't go back. Nor could he stop. So he gave up on thinking of Up and Down and instead concentrated his thoughts and strength on moving forward – step by step along the wet rock.

The narrow stone furrow led him to a river, and the river to a spacious cave, which was nevertheless much smaller than his world. He continued crawling upwards until he reached the stairs and started climbing. There was even a railing to hold on to, but he had no idea who had made it. No one had ever spoken of them. No one had ever returned from Above. Would he?

Step by step, he trudged onward. The infernal roar of cascading water silenced his thoughts, while icy steam soaked and numbed his pale body. Then a warm light bathed him. He wanted to believe that the Upper World had finally changed, that the Seven Stars prophesying the End had gone back to their places, that he would go home again. They would be waiting for him – the same way they had waited for all those who had never returned.

Although they had lost many of their men, they would not stop sending them. Because they knew that if they ever gave up hope of going back to earth, they would cease being human. The story of what had happened had been passed on by word of mouth for thousands of years, down to the present day.

"Will I ever see them again?" he thought, knowing the question was pointless.

It was the same with death. You don't know where it will lead you. Maybe nowhere. Maybe Heaven, maybe Hell. So instead of wasting time on fear, savor the unknown, revel in solving the eternal human riddle that has puzzled all the generations that have gone before you. There's no use in getting distracted by fear or excitement.

He saw the tunnel in the distance, at the top of the stairs, next to the White Cypress, which was bathed in pure light. He had heard about it in legends and tales.

He could feel the light creeping over his skin, soft and warming. He trembled as it began to sear him. His eyes could not see. Not yet. They had taught him that his body's senses needed a few hours to adjust. And his eyes would be able to see, although mainly in the dark.

The desire to learn what had happened before the First Ones had left the earth drove him onward. He had been preparing himself for this day his whole life – the moment after which nothing would be the same.

Life was different here. The trees grew upwards, instead of down. And their leaves were colorful, not drab as in his world. Countless animals killed and devoured other animals. Every living creature was desperately fighting for survival. The farther on he went, the more he realized that for one to live here, another had to die. A strange world.

He heard sounds, different from animals' howls. It was like speech but in an unfamiliar language. Besides words, there were screams, moans and cries of pain.

A rumble, deafening and terrifying – he saw flames, and in the flames – people. "The legend was true," he thought. "Flames were still on earth."

EIGHT SUNS

Page 408 *began with a clipping from a German book. Beneath it the caption indicated in small letters that this was Friedrichshain,[2] one of Hitler's three bunkers. At the end of the Second World War a fire broke out in the control tower and spread throughout the entire building. The conflagration's cause is still unknown. Numerous works of art were forever lost to the flames. Today the world knows about them only from photos and descriptions included in different museum catalogs compiled before 1945.*

East Berlin, 1945.

… Eight suns will shine and scream the truth
That Heaven in Hell may be on earth…

These were the last lines Georg read on *page 408*, the final page of the manuscript. The title had caught his eye – *The Parchment Maze*. Yet the book made no sense to him, so he tossed it into the corner.

The match he was holding turned black and went out. Darkness surrounded him once more.

"Heaven?" the boy whispered almost inaudibly.

---

[2] The Friedrichshain Flak Bunker.

14

His dry, calloused fingers felt around for the matchbox. Two matches left. The thunder of bombs exploding had stopped. Maybe it was all over, he thought. He pricked up his ears, but heard only the distant wailing of sirens and the muted roar of the wind like a tank creeping across the sky.

Georg struck a match and its light filled the concrete cell, illuminating its dry, gray ugliness. There were two hastily cobbled-together wooden chests in front of him. The boy was leaning against a towering stack of file folders and scientific reports printed on thousands of loose sheets of paper. For as long as the matches in the matchbox had lasted, Georg had tried reading the letters that covered the paper. Millions of ink symbols, silently marching along in lockstep. Most of the pages also bore the stamp CONFIDENTIAL and the signature of the Führer.

The boy didn't want to steal the words, he was just trying to kill time. In any case, the pages mostly contained dull theories about "a new race and an old religion." And the most interesting thing in them was a story about some kind of *Solar Code*. Of all the signs accompanying the text, Georg recognized only the swastika. It was drawn by hand, with its vertices numbered one to eight with Arabic numerals.

On his second day in the concrete cell, Georg opened up one of the chests after clawing out the bolts with his fingernails. It was full of books and stone tablets covered with obscure hieroglyphics. At the bottom of the second trunk he found a small stone amulet with a cross, seven stars and other details carved into it. It hung from a leather strap. Georg lifted it out carefully. He thought it might be something valuable. But the light from the next match showed him that it was just a miniature engraved stone. Nevertheless, he squeezed it in his fist. He wanted to believe that the small cross would bring him closer to God, who would notice him. Even nonbelievers expect someone to be watching over them.

The bunker was full of Russians. Their strange language echoed through the cold walls. The boy silently grasped the stone amulet and prayed that the enemy would not discover him.

The second-to-last match flickered and died, like his memory of recent days. He had only one match left. It was quiet outside. Even the sound of the sirens and the wind had faded away. He swallowed noisily, as if trying to dislodge something stuck in his throat, to make sure he could still hear.

He felt along the hollow wall with his fingers. When he found a place where the paneling was loose, he pushed against it with his shoulder. The gray pasteboard panel crashed to the floor, sending a cloud of dust billowing through the air. Georg coughed and stepped out of his hiding place.

He could barely make out the moon through the smoke-filled sky. Like a gigantic apparition, it threw its silvery blue glow on the towers of the Friedrichshain Bunker.

The boy listened attentively. Snatches of Russian floated in from outside. "They've left guards," he realized.

"Sergeant Alexeev, we've loaded about ninety pictures," a bass voice said.

When Hitler had realized that a Russian invasion of Berlin was inevitable, he had ordered that all precious artworks be hidden in the bunkers. Georg had been left to guard part of the Führer's personal archive that had been built into one of the Friedrichshain towers.

The boy peeped through the hole in the wall that served as a window. Outside, two soldiers were loading wooden chests into a military truck. Others were standing guard, smoking nervously.

"They've conquered us!" the boy thought. He had received clear orders: he was to burn the manuscripts if Russian soldiers captured the bunker. Georg grasped the matchbox more tightly. He hesitated – as soon as the flames lapped at the paper, the Red Dogs would sniff him out. But it was his duty! Everyone had a duty – and what distinguished people was whether they ran from it or remained true. The Führer had said that his archive must never fall into the occupiers' hands.

He struck the last match. The flame danced in his pupils. He hesitated again for a moment before dropping the lighted match into his hiding place. The paper twisted, white flames spitting black soot like tortured shades from Hades.

Georg dashed down the stairs, deaf to everything except his own hysterical panting. He saw a door and opened it. The coast was clear. The feeling of freedom coursed through his body like water flowing into the hollow veins of a wilting plant. The boy ran towards the river.

"Halt!" a stern voice shouted behind him. "Halt or I'll shoot."

Georg turned around. The bunker looked like a gigantic black crow in the night, perched in an ash-white meadow. A cloud of smoke surrounded it, a whirlwind that threatened to sweep it away at any moment. Both towers were in flames.

Three soldiers were chasing him.

"Shoot!" one of them shouted.

"But he's just a boy!"

"The Fascist has no age!"

The river was his salvation. He clutched the talisman with the cross so tightly that his palm bled.

The man who had given the order raised his rifle. The muzzle tracked the boy's skeletal figure, which jumped to the left and right trying to dodge the bullets. Georg had almost reached the water when he felt the lead ball pierce his body. He fell lifeless into the cold water.

"Drag him out of the mud!" the Russian officer barked to one of the soldiers.

The officer searched Georg's body. He noticed the clenched fist, pried it open and saw the amulet. He studied it in the light of the fire.

The Son of God crucified on a cross. Seven stars above him arranged in an arc. A moon below them. At the bottom – the words *Orpheus-Bacchus*. The Russian decided it was some kind of tasteless joke. He put the amulet in his pocket and kicked the emaciated corpse into the river. The flames danced on the dark water's smooth surface, fiery tongues leaping wildly to the rhythm of screams and sirens.

The fire engulfed the whole building. The soldiers tried to put it out but failed, so they loaded whatever they could onto their trucks and started for Moscow.

THE FORGOTTEN CHATEAU

*Clippings from a daily newspaper were glued to the upper right-hand corner of **page 409**. They showed a photograph of the towers and gates of a castle overgrown with weeds. A note was scribbled next to it: "A group of experts were sent on an urgent mission to a desolate Alpine chateau near the Swiss-French border." According to the article accompanying the photo the castle was deserted but "full of secret treasures."[3]*

Swiss-French border, March 1, the present

Frozen rain whipped their faces mercilessly. The pearly eddies pelted the six figures trudging through the snowdrifts. The wind crashed against them and rebounded into oblivion. The trail had long since disappeared, so the guide followed the tall metal posts jutting out above the snow to mark the path.

Hours had passed since they first started looking for the castle amidst the mountainous white waves. Their trek towards the Swiss-French border took them across the Alps at an altitude of 1,200

---

[3] The fictional description of Chateau Jacques is inspired by G. Milkov's investigation published in the Bulgarian newspaper *24 Hours* as a serial piece run in a few issues during November 2007. The articles describe the obstacles the group of experts had to overcome in order to assess the cultural treasures bequeathed to Bulgaria by the castle's late owner. All names are changed in the novel.

meters. After reaching the peak, they began to descend towards French territory.

A narrow footpath blanketed with deep, pristine snow led to Chateau Jacques. There was also an old waggoners' trail, but that was on the French side of the border.

Vera Kandilova plodded along silently behind her father. The cold wind and lashing rain had dulled her consciousness. She had even stopped shivering. She had wrapped her head in a plastic bag, leaving only a crack so she could see her father's back. Vera quickened her pace and caught up with him.

"Did we really have to hike in this weather, for God's sake?" she asked weakly.

"Vera, remember that *you* decided to come with us," the professor replied sharply. "We all came voluntarily. There are precious artifacts in that castle and God only knows what's disappeared already!"

She fell silent. Her father was right. Vera was the one who had asked to come along. She thought a visit to the castle would spark some new interest that would wash away the muddle of the present. Lately she had spent a lot of time alone. Feeding the ravenous phantoms of her unrealized ambitions was growing ever harder. Whenever she felt them nearing, she tried to smother them with work and study.

When the hikers had begun that morning, the sun had been shining from a lavender sky. Here in the mountains, however, it felt as if Hell had opened its maw through a sliver of moon to swallow up the earth.

Vera felt exhaustion gnawing at her limbs. She just wanted to let go of everything and collapse into the snow. She kept walking. Perhaps because everyone else was still moving forward. The group gave strength to the individual. Nevertheless, Vera started to lag behind and eventually everyone passed her up. Her father turned around a couple times to make sure she was still there. Regretting his sharp comments, he waited for his daughter and threw his arm around her shoulders.

"Dear, do you want to go to the exhibition in Moscow?"

"The one in March? At the Pushkin Museum?" Vera cheered up. "Are you kidding me?! It's every archaeologist's dream!"

"Well, I won't be able to go," he replied morosely. "You can take my spot."

Vera stopped short, as though her feet were nailed to the ground. Her amazed eyes followed her father. Gestures of this kind were not in his nature.

"Look! I can see the lights!" the guide shouted, pointing into the gaping gorge. Indeed, a few pale, yellow dots quivered down below, like electric fish on some unexplored ocean floor. These signs of civilization reinvigorated the group. Vera clutched her father's elbow, feeling her feet sink into the snow. With great effort, she managed to pick them up and keep walking.

At the castle's wooden gates a man huddled in a brown overcoat greeted them. The hood kept half of his face hidden from their sight. Holding a lantern in one hand, he looked like a jailor from a Dumas novel – time and progress seemed to have skipped over this desolate pocket of the Alps. The man introduced himself as Monsieur Marten, Chateau Jacques' caretaker. The guide had already warned them that he was an eccentric. He spoke little and almost never to other humans. He had held the key to the castle for years. Monsieur Marten announced that they would have to wait until the morning to look around the uninhabited castle. The exhausted and freezing hikers silently blessed him for not inviting them in.

The Bulgarian group had booked rooms in a nearby hotel. The guide, whom the embassy in Geneva had hired to take them to the castle, stayed with them for the night to make sure everything was in order.

The group had dinner in the hotel's basement tavern, where they were the only customers. The innkeeper deigned to make a fire, repeatedly mentioning that he was doing this only in their honor. Apparently he hadn't had any other visitors for months. He served them homemade bread speckled with suspicious brown spots and onion soup with a thick, dry skin on it – and promised to be better prepared for their meals the next day. He circled the table, stealing glances at the group. Obviously eager to quiz his visitors, the innkeeper visibly wracked his brains for a conversation opener, eventually settling on:

"Cold night for hiking, huh?"

He tried to look somber, probably hoping this would hide his obvious penchant for sticking his nose in other people's business. The foreigners answered with polite and highly unsatisfying smiles, so he tried again.

"We don't get many tourists at this time of the year in the Alps. Where are you headed?"

"We've already arrived, thank God!" replied Hristo Kuzmanov, the only one of the group who spoke French.

"Here?" the innkeeper asked, confused.

"We've come to the chateau."

The innkeeper grew pale, as if someone had pulled a plug and drained his blood. He carefully studied the guests one by one, starting with Vera, who was busy removing the hard skin from her soup and wiping it onto a napkin. Then he eyed the old professor. The two other people next to him had said they were some kind of scholars, although they looked more like hungry mice in wet clothes. At the far end of the table a blue-eyed young man who had introduced himself as a reporter was chatting with the sun-burned guide.

The blood slowly returned to the innkeeper's face.

"You mean the Bulgarian's chateau?" he asked, noisily dragging a chair from the neighboring table and sitting down at theirs. He took their surprised glances as his cue to go on.

"Since he died five years ago, no one's been in there," he whispered, glancing around furtively like a conspirator from the Three Musketeers. He leaned towards the middle of the table, sweat pouring from his face. "Monsieur Marten has been looking after the place by himself."

"The caretaker, yes, we've met him," Kuzmanov replied and moved closer to the innkeeper.

Kuzmanov, the director of the Ethnographic Museum, had studied history in Paris, grooming himself for a stellar career worthy of his rocket-fuelled ambition.

"Monsieur Marten is an odd duck. He doesn't mix with any of us locals. Sometimes he gets the strangest visitors… foreigners. Are you friends of his?"

"We are a group of experts sent by the Bulgarian government. The owner of the castle left all his possessions to the state. Ever since, however, there've been endless legal wrangles over the inheritance with the deceased's family," Vera's father offered this explanation. Unlike the others, he wasn't whispering.

"I knew he had died," the innkeeper replied curtly. He spoke English with a thick French accent. Then he shouted to the bartender, "Bring us a jug of red wine!"

Intrigued, he decided to stay at the Bulgarians' table a bit longer.

"And who won the case?" the innkeeper asked.

"The state. The will was indisputable." Kiril, the journalist, jumped into the conversation.

"Hm, really? You must know that there were some scary times at the chateau"… the innkeeper explained. "The villagers say there were ghosts. But I haven't seen any. What worried me the most was… the brotherhood," he said these last words so quietly that they had to read his lips.

"What brotherhood?"

"Don't you know? This region was one of the largest centers for the medieval heretics known as Cathars." Then he added loudly, "They supposedly still exist today in some secret organizations."

The innkeeper was eager to bombard them with everything he knew on the subject. He explained that the Cathars had appeared in the tenth century and that their beliefs had spread throughout Europe, but that their home base was in France. He even regaled them with Cathar theology: the sect had preached that since time immemorial there had been an ongoing struggle between the principles of darkness and light, between spirit and matter. They upheld the basic idea of dualism and shared the Bogomils' belief in reincarnation. What made the deepest impression on Vera was the fact that the Cathars believed that the sun was the Devil and that the Devil was actually the Creator.

"I've heard of them," Kiril boasted, picking up the scent of a good scoop. "But what did the owner of the castle have to do with them?"

"All kinds of people used to come here. To see the Bulgarian," the innkeeper replied. "Strange people. And their music made your blood run cold…"

"Rituals?" the reporter asked with a smile. "Did you ever see them?"

"No, that was impossible. They would lock themselves in the basement. All you could hear was the music."

The innkeeper got up and put the chair back at the neighboring table.

"I don't suppose you'll be here long?" he asked in the same cold tone he had greeted them with.

"A week, perhaps," Kuzmanov replied.

The innkeeper picked up the jug of red wine and took it back to the bar. Vera watched him. He was short and plump, like a Greek amphora. His body wobbled like a corkscrew, requiring no small effort to walk in a straight line. He reached the bar and ducked behind it.

Vera lit a cigarette, deeply inhaling the smoke. She closed her eyes to savor it. Exhaling a misty thread, she leaned back in her chair. She didn't smoke often, only when she was enjoying herself in company or very lonely.

"Hope you don't mind," she said to Kiril, who was sitting next to her watching the wafting coils of smoke.

"No problem. I'm used to it."

"My father said that this mysterious chateau owner died of cancer…"

"A great way of covering your tracks."

"What tracks?"

"I looked at his medical records. The tumor was only in the early stages. But isn't it strange how he suddenly decided to change his will completely and sign it in the hospital? Five days before he died?"

"Interesting," Vera said and stubbed out her cigarette.

She looked at her watch – it was almost midnight. Vera finished her wine and looked back towards the bar. The innkeeper was wiping it with a greasy cloth, not taking his eyes off the foreigners for a second. The bar looked as if it had been crafted years ago. It was made out of a single piece of solid wood lined with large stones along the base. In the centre there was a drawing of a king tightly grasping his gilded throne. Beneath it, a Latin inscription read "Rex Solaris" – The Sun King.

THE AMULET

Page 410 began with a sketch of the Orphic Amulet. At first glance it seems to be Christ crucified. Next to the drawing in small letters there is a note, "In 1945 a mysterious medallion disappeared from the Friedrichshain Bunker. This medallion has given rise to many academic disputes today. The object is made from engraved hematite. It measures 14x19mm. It is known that the archaeologist E. Gerhard acquired it in Rome at some point before 1867. It was subsequently purchased by the Berlin Museum in 1904 and is included in the museum's catalog under number 1164." The famous historian Eisler (1921) was the first to publish an academic article about it. He wrote, "It is remarkable for the history of religion, since Christ is depicted in Orpheus' place, rather than the reverse."

Berlin, March 2, the present

It was a quiet, clear day. Dr. Franz Werder reached the last bend in the path. The summit of the hill was already visible amidst the branches of the trees. His sneakers pounded the footpath winding through the man-made hill in Friedrichshain Park. The mound itself had no name. It had appeared in the middle of the city about half a century earlier,[4] like the hunched back of a huge green monster.

The cool morning breeze blew Werder's gloomy thoughts away. He squinted as rays of sunlight darted amidst the trees and shrubs around him.

Werder jogged here every morning. The more he pushed himself climbing the hill, the more satisfying he found the rest of his day. The time he spent in the park breathed life to his otherwise monotonous routine as a bookworm burrowed among the artifacts and archives at the History Museum.

The ruins of the Friedrichshain Bunker

[4] In 1945, following Hitler's orders, the Friedrichshain Flak Bunker was used as a bomb shelter. It was completely demolished during World War II; one of Berlin's most beautiful parks was subsequently built in its place. The debris from the bunker is piled under a high hill in the center of the park. Observant visitors can still spot enormous concrete slabs, remnants of the bunker, at the top of the hill. A more careful inspection of the surroundings reveals the presence of mysterious staircases, parts of walls, columns and bars among the shrubs.

Just before reaching the plateau at the summit, Werder saw the gaping hole that split the concrete wall at the top of the hill in two. Younger visitors had no idea why the wall was there at the top of the mound. Franz Werder was one of the few who knew that fifty years ago this had been the site of one of Hitler's three bunkers. The steep hill had been created to hide its ruins from the citizens of Berlin forever.

All that was left of the burned-out control tower was one wall, cracked in half by bombs. Now it stood there harmless, covered in graffiti. Yet every time Franz saw it, an invisible hand tightened around his throat. He heard the distant cries and explosions, the never-ending dirge sung by the wind and the rustling leaves.

His cell phone rang, but he hesitated to pick up. His morning jog was his time for himself, his secret escape from the city and its people. He looked at the screen. The director of the museum was calling – and he didn't call often.

"Werder here."

"I'm calling to notify you about your upcoming trip." The director didn't waste time with chitchat.

"What trip?"

"You're going to Moscow. Our Russian colleagues kindly informed us at the very last minute about an exhibition."

"What exhibition?"

"'The Age of the Merovingians – Europe without Borders,'" the director said with a chuckle. "Works acquired by Russia during World War II will be on display. I don't think it's an accident that we weren't informed any earlier." After a short pause he added, "The exhibit opens in five days at the Pushkin Museum. You've got to go. We might be able to get back some of our stolen pieces."

"What do you mean five days!? I've got a trip planned…"

"Before I forget," the director interrupted.."The Bulgarian Archeological Museum has called three times, looking for you. Some grad student… Vera Kandilova is insisting on getting detailed information from your department about the Orpheus Amulet. You supposedly promised to send it to her."

"Oh, yes… I did promise. She is doing research on Orpheus."

Franz Werder started back down the winding path, lost in thought. He recalled that this same woman had called him before. She had explained that she was studying the connection between Orphism and Christianity. He had promised to help. She was extremely persistent. Strange, he thought, the interest in the miniature artifact had increased inexplicably recently. People from all over the world had been asking about it. Last week he'd received a letter from Columbia University and even from National Geographic.

He was home before he knew it. He lived at 9 Buschingstrasse, close to the park. He took a cool shower. The thought of going to Moscow had reinvigorated him. Escape from habit has a strange way of bringing us back to life.

THE SOLAR CODE

Page 411 began with the outline of a sun drawn in charcoal. Beneath it were several hieroglyphs, followed by a handwritten text: "Since antiquity, people have believed that the Sun God was born on December 25th after the longest three nights of the year. Most pagan gods were born on this date. Orphism is one of the most popular Sun-cult religions. It is a long-forgotten fact that Dionysus, himself the son of a god, was also born on this day, along with the divinities Osiris and Mitra. Although Jesus Christ was also born on this solar birthday, the solar cult is nevertheless a taboo topic in Christianity."

The Roman Catacombs, March 2

The man was dressed in a black habit with a tight white collar around his neck. Beneath it hung an iron cross that swayed over his chest, keeping time with his steps. His eyes peered through a pair of thick, frameless glasses. His blond hair flecked with platinum-grey strands and ruddy cheeks betrayed his Germanic roots.

The priest was in no hurry. His dark silhouette melted into the blackness of the night. He was walking along the paved path through the verdant gardens covering the miles-long subterranean labyrinths of the Roman catacombs. The pathway led to the Via Appia Antica, considered the oldest and longest road in Europe. The ancient stone walls lining it were decorated with marble bas-reliefs, the remnants of ancient buildings. The ruins of a nameless castle rose on the green slope beyond them.

As he walked along the path, Herbert often thought of how transient life was compared to human civilization, which never died. Quite to the contrary, civilizations left their mark for later generations to find. They inspired imaginative theories, aroused curiosity, filled history books and fed archaeologists' ambitions. Even as the stone remnants of old civilizations crumbled, the metamorphosis of civilization as a whole continued, incorporating earlier ideas within its very foundations. Herbert loved trying to find his way through their labyrinth. Today, however, he wasn't thinking about them. Terror gripped his whole being.

Despite his slow pace, he reached the end of the path, which came out near the small church, Domine Quo Vadis. The church was a major tourist attraction. Beyond its high wooden gates lay a marble slab with two symmetrical footprints in it, not unlike those from Hollywood's Walk of Fame. The creamy white stone itself was enclosed under iron bars which tourists crowded around to marvel at the sight. The tour guides told them these were Jesus's footprints. According to Catholic legend, Christ's feet sank into the stone when St. Peter saw Him after the Resurrection and asked Him where He was going, to which Christ answered: "I am going to Rome to be crucified again."

The slab was just a human attempt to materialize the traces left by the incorporeal, Herbert mused. He crossed the pavement in front of the church and continued on up the narrow street. The entrance to the San Domitilla Catacombs was just a few steps away.

He turned his key in the rusty lock and pushed the door open. Herbert crossed the courtyard and his shadow slid over the windows of the Basilica.[5] Herbert found the silence and darkness unnatural.

---

[5] The Basilica in the Catacombs of San Domitilla is thought to be the first underground basilica in Europe. Its last story rises above the ground, looking like a one-story building.

The closed doors of the Domine Quo Vadis Church

He had never come here at night. "But what does light matter in the catacombs?" he thought. He took out a flashlight and started down the steep steps leading into the ancient manmade mole-hole. "I've been working here for years," he thought. "I must be the only person who knows the way to the southern tunnel. That must be why the stranger came to me. Or perhaps he knows about the old manuscript."

When he reached the altar of the subterranean basilica, he struck a long match and began lighting the candles one by one. Flickering shadows performed a spectral dance on the walls and Herbert's face.

"Are you sure you recognized the symbols from the Solar Code?" the stranger with the elongated, strangely colored eyes had asked him pointblank yesterday. He was an expressionless, cold man. Herbert had seen others like him.

The previous day he had taken the stranger to the San Callisto Catacombs and pointed out a side room located opposite the sarcophagus of Pope Miltiades,[6] as the stranger had requested. The dark cell was called the Four Seasons Burial Chamber. The painter had depicted the endless cycle of life after death. A young man holding an Orphic lyre[7] and singing surrounded by animals[8] was clearly visible in the picture. The tourist guides didn't mention Orpheus. They were not supposed to direct visitors' attention to heretical scenes like this one.

"How long has the cross been under the sarcophagus?" the stranger asked.

"Since the second century A.D."

The man with the colorful eyes took a picture of the fresco with a tiny camera. Herbert observed him with curiosity. He was the strangest man the priest had ever seen. Not only his eyes were different, but also he was very tall, covered with hat and sometimes in the darkness Herbert could swear he could see kind of luminosity around his hands.

Then the man requested that they go to the Catacombs of Santi Marcellino e Pietro, which were officially closed to civilian visitors. Herbert could sense a trap, yet couldn't deny any of the stranger's wishes. Only death could stop him now. What he felt could only be understood by someone obsessed with the thrill of discovery. He often regretted the day he'd gone to the library at the beginning of the Via Appia Antica, looking for a manuscript referred to in one of the historical books he'd been reading at the time. He thought it must be a mistake, but as soon as he said the name aloud, the librarian

---

[6] The Catacombs of San Callisto are most famous for the fact that thirteen Popes from the third and fourth centuries were buried in them. Miltiades was the final one (he died in 314). He had African origins.

[7] It is thought that this fresco was painted by Thracians who went to Rome looking for work more than seventeen centuries ago. Many of them were buried in the catacombs.

[8] This fresco is one of the most popular works of art showing the connection between Orpheus and Christ. The animals depicted around the Thracian poet come to symbolize his transformation into Christ and other later deities.

disappeared into a narrow corridor and returned a few moments later with a book called *The Parchment Maze*. In its pages Herbert found the question whose answer he was still looking for today, seeking clues that would lead him to the Solar Code that had been used – as well as hidden – thousands of years ago. The manuscript ended unfinished on ***page 411***. From that moment on Herbert knew he couldn't share what he had seen with anyone. Yet the coincidences between what he had read and what he had discovered at catacombs were so numerous and inexplicable that they left him torn between the suspicion he was imagining things and the hope that someday someone would come and search for the code. And then Herbert would likely learn the answer. But years had passed and no one had come looking for it. Until today.

Now, despite the sensation of impending doom that accompanied his presence, the man with the strange eyes seemed to be the only one who could quench the historian's torturous thirst for knowledge. He'd finally learn whether he had truly decoded the symbols on the walls or just imagined them.

They went to the Catacombs of Santi Marcellino e Pietro. Herbert showed another fresco to the stranger. Once again it pictured Orpheus with a lyre in his hand. There was a tree beside him, from which a peacock[9] gazed at the singer.

"You're probably Thracian, right?" Herbert tried to start a conversation. "I don't know what a Thracian should look like, but…"

"Why are you talking about the Thracians?" the stranger interrupted.

---

[9] The peacock is one of the fundamental early Christian symbols. It signifies the Resurrection, as Christians believe its flesh is the only natural flesh that doesn't rot. The lyre was a symbol popularly used at the time of the painting to indicate the connection with Orpheus and his teachings. Some scientists believe that the combination of Christian and Orphic symbols can be ascribed to the ignorance of the painter. Others argue that the mixture is the result of a wise revelation.

"You're looking for traces that lead to Orpheus. A lot of Thracians were buried here, you know. Thousands of them worked in the Roman Empire."

The stranger was silent.

"Some people say that Constantine the Great was also a Thracian. Did you know that? They say he ordered that the Gospels[10] be written. The task was assigned to an unnamed subject, also a Thracian. Given all that, it's impossible for there to be no connection between Orphism and Christianity."

"You're not a believer," the stranger said. He spoke perfect Italian.

"I've been a priest for ten years. But I've been a historian for twenty-five."

The chilly air brushed its lips against Herbert's back and made him shiver. All these years he had never gotten used to it.

Pieces of white marble were visible, embedded in the stony vaults of the Basilica, some of them thousands of years older than the rest of the walls. They immediately attracted attention, conspicuously white against the brownish-gray surface. More careful observers could spot names and symbols written on them. Most were seals of ancient companies and undertakers, which people today found mysterious and even magical.

---

[10] According to official sources, in 325 A.D. Constantine the Great presided over the first Ecumenical Council in Nicaea at which only four of the Gospels were recognized as canonical: those written by Mark, Matthew, Luke and John. All the others were declared heretical. The church searched for and destroyed copies of the heretical works for centuries, persecuting anyone who dared to disseminate them. In 1945 in a monastic cemetery in the vicinity of the Egyptian city Nag Hamadi some villagers accidentally found ancient manuscripts written in Coptic, including the Gospel of Philip, which has been assumed to be lost and which tells about Christ's wife. Constantine the Great, a Thracian born in Naissus, passed the Edict of Milan, which acknowledged Christianity as a religion equal in rights to the other religions professed in the territory of the Roman Empire. During the subsequent centuries, most Thracian cities had well-organized Christian communities and actively participated in religious life.

The more the darkness of the catacombs swallowed Herbert, the more he felt suffocated by fear of the unknown. He tried not to think about it and went over his tasks in his mind. Tomorrow he had to send the photos he had promised to an archeologist named Vera Kandilova. They had been exchanging emails for months. She had explained to him that she was researching Orpheus and had learned about the frescoes in the Roman catacombs that show an ideological connection between Orpheus and Christ. Herbert helped his colleagues whenever he could. He believed that the point of knowledge was passing it on to people.

He heard footsteps. Herbert raised his head. The shadows of the candles' flames leapt on the damp domes. The stranger was coming.

LEGACY FROM ANOTHER WORLD

*On **page 412** there was no picture, but instead a reference to the link between the modern image of Orpheus and the ancient sage from the legend of the "secret underground world" and the "nocturnal earth." It was also said that much of the evidence had been lost due to human ignorance. Only the initiated can interpret the surviving evidence correctly. "Logical questions remain open, including how the religion that people have associated with Orpheus's name since ancient times came into existence, what it was like, and who Orpheus really was. Orpheus was mentioned for the first time in the sixth century B.C. and was described as brilliantly famous."*

From Orpheus the Thracian by Valeria Fol, 2008

Early in the morning, the rays of sunlight caressed Vera's face. The tattered old lace curtains hanging over the windows were little obstacle to the sun, whose dancing stripes trickled into the darkness of her room.

Vera's sleepy gaze slid along the surfaces of the hotel room, as if trying to figure out whether her soul had already left her dreams and descended into her earthly body, ready for another day.

The rays of sunlight frolicked like playful rabbits on the ceiling. As a little girl she used to play with mirror reflections, trying to be like the other children. Eventually, however, she got sick of pretending to be like everyone else and started liking herself instead.

She pulled on a pair of ratty jeans, a shabby blue sweater and a faded jacket. She knew she would be working in cave-like conditions. Then she went down to the restaurant but found it empty. People didn't seem to eat breakfast anymore. Some didn't have the time, while others lived under the delusion that this would help them lose weight.

A plump waitress informed her that they had only coffee and croissants for breakfast.

"Do you want some, mademoiselle?"

Vera studied the woman's lace apron and puffy sleeves with interest before answering, "Yes, please."

She opened her notebook and numbered the page: *118*. Then she jotted down the ideas that had come to her during the night.

Vera had almost finished her master's degree in archaeology at Sofia University. Her father worked in the Department of Prehistory at the National Institute of Archaeology. Unlike him, she preferred to delve into subjects connected with the Thracians and antiquity – perhaps precisely because he wasn't so interested in them.

Professor Kandilov had left Vera and her mother a long time ago. When Vera was seven, he had started babbling incoherently. He began mumbling that he had lost himself, that the monotony of his days suffocated him, that he needed to breathe and reawaken his senses, that he missed the excitement of discovery, that life was too short to spend it trying to satisfy society's illusions, that everyone had the right to pursue their lost happiness. With these words, he left for Moscow, where he had been invited as a guest university lecturer. When he came back he rented an apartment in the suburbs. Vera visited him on the weekends but could hardly stand being there, usually counting the minutes until she could leave. She didn't understand either of her parents. Which is why when she grew up, she started imitating both of them in everything she did, eventually finding herself deep in the same quagmire.

Ever since her mother had died of an agonizing illness a few years earlier, Vera had focused on her thesis to drown the pain.

During the long sleepless nights, however, the work grew so vast that rather than being a thesis it had turned into an idea for a research book. None of her fellow students had written anything on the subject. She had dedicated most of last year to writing and research, believing that the main theme of her work was so scandalous and unexpected that the book would finally launch her out of her father's orbit and make her a factor to be reckoned with in her own right. In her free time, Vera played at being fiancée to a man named Kaloyan. She had almost no time to dwell on what had not yet happened.

The main topic of her research was the idea that the story of Jesus, the son of God, was older than Christianity – preceding it by at least a couple of millennia. The most ancient roots she had dug up so far were the concepts of Orphism.

The search for new evidence soon became an obsession, probably initially kindled during the hot summer nights she had spent as a child with her grandmother in Pazardzhik.[11] The elderly woman believed she was a Thracian princess, descended from an ancient family. At twilight they would both go to the hill by the city, trying to catch the distant echo of Orpheus' song.

Vera added a full stop and smiled. One-hundred and eighteen pages should be enough to convince readers that Orphic ideas were at the root of Christianity. At least, this was what she had set out to prove. Yet in the process, the nagging feeling arose that she still hadn't discovered the most important thing: Who was Orpheus really? And how had he come to learn all the things that his followers repeated?

That was something no one knew – which was why the question was never asked. And there seemed to be nothing before Orpheus.

An hour later, the group gathered in front of the hotel. Kuzmanov brought gloves, masks and flashlights. There was no electricity in the castle. According to the embassy report, it had been years since anyone had entered most of the rooms and basements.

---

[11] A small city in central Bulgaria.

Monsieur Marten phlegmatically unlocked the gate. He was wearing a bright red slicker. Despite the fact that it wasn't raining that day, he had the hood up, as if expecting a downpour. Vera instinctively raised her eyes. The sky was a pleasant, bright blue with the faintest of clouds.

The door squealed. The experts followed the caretaker down a gloomy corridor. Professor Kandilov suggested that they go exploring in pairs so that no one would be left alone.

"Afraid of ghosts?" the reporter joked.

"Afraid of having no alibi if anything disappears!" the professor answered.

Kiril and Vera were paired up. They were given instructions to examine a number of ground-floor rooms and the basement. Kuzmanov stayed with M. Marten.

Vera started down the stairs confidently. Before parting with the daylight, she looked at her watch. "It's eleven o'clock already." Kiril followed her. He was an observer on the expedition and every now and again he would mutter something into his voice recorder. His job was to report everything he saw for a daily newspaper. When nothing in the castle's interior particularly impressed him, he watched Vera's fluid movements. She in turn strode bravely ahead, as if unaware of the possible dangers lurking in an abandoned castle known as a hideout for eccentrics. She suddenly started flailing her arms to brush away the cobwebs sticking to her face.

She had a flashlight strapped to her forehead like a miner. She wore her hair in a long braid. Her slender body swam in the faded jacket, which was a few sizes too big.

The cold darkness engulfed them like the setting of some unfamiliar fairy tale. There was no natural light in the basement. The beams of light from their flashlights flickered and chased each other along the walls. Anemic climbing plants grew from each crack in the plaster – undisturbed by humans, they had spread their tendrils onto the dusty walls and ceilings. The rooms were filled with all sorts of objects piled on top of one another. It was as if Chateau Jacques had been built with a single purpose – to serve as a warehouse.

"Wow. It probably takes a few lifetimes to collect so much junk," Kiril remarked in amazement.

"Or rather, what sort of life would you have to live to collect all this?" Vera replied tersely.

Her voice was filled with sadness. She remembered her own grandfather. When he died, they had found his home similarly full of both precious stuff and worthless junk. Every object had a history. Her grandfather hoarded things to compensate for the insignificance of his existence. The piles filled the emptiness, giving their owner the sense of creation. Vera and her mother didn't have enough space to keep his grand collection, however. Her father had just left for Moscow. So the two women invited over some junk dealers, who divided the boxes between themselves and carted off the history of a man's life.

Vera was absorbed in carefully inspecting the randomly scattered objects. It was obvious that some of them had great cultural significance, while others were just remnants of a life now relegated to the past. Now and then she stopped to run her fingers over a dusty volume or a painting, or lifted figurines and turned them around. Then she jotted a number with some kind of description into her notebook and took pictures of some objects with the heavy camera hanging around her neck. The light-haired reporter observed Vera in silence.

"Why would a girl like you want to become an archaeologist?" Kiril broke the silence.

"You mean a blonde like me?"

"I mean a young and... beautiful woman."

"Perhaps for that very reason. Because no one expects it." Vera replied briefly. She even didn't smile or look at the journalist.

"And what do you do in your spare time? Do you collect bones from rotting bodies and number them?" Kiril laughed, trying to neutralize the creepy surroundings with humor.

"No. My father's the one who's interested in bones."

"Isn't he frightened of retribution by the souls he deprives of their eternal rest? Why do archaeologists think they have the right to other people's bones and possessions?"

The young journalist had grown interested in the subject ever since he had seen two crates of eroded bones in one of the offices at the Archaeological Museum. The thought that some day someone could be studying his own remains horrified him.

"Listen, I haven't taken anyone's bones… But I can tell you that the thrill of discovery makes the fear of retribution fade into insignificance."

Having uttered these words, Vera went into a small room, as narrow as a pantry, measuring no more than six square feet. There were no windows and the walls were not plastered. There were naked wires hanging down from the ceiling. On one bare brick wall there was a single, crooked three-story bookshelf, hanging precariously on a couple of nails. The shelves looked unstable, but luckily only one dust-covered black book lay on them. It was so old that the creases on its spine were worn down to threads. Vera took the book down and looked at the leather cover, where the title was written in golden letters:

The Christian Catacombs of Rome
First Edition.[12]

Her fingers traced the gilded title. Then she carefully turned the pages. They were filled with numerous bookmarks. A red one in the middle piqued Vera's curiosity and she opened the book to that place and skimmed the text.

"This is amazing," she exclaimed.

"What?" Kiril asked.

"The frescoes. Look." Vera pointed at one of the photos. "I have the same book and all these images of the Orphic Christ are described in mine, too, on page 103. But," she turned the page, "look here. I've never seen this fresco from the Catacombs of Santi Marcellino e Pietro. Interesting… And below it someone has

---

[12] The first edition of *The Christian Catacombs of Rome* can still be found in libraries in France, Germany and Italy.

written a note referencing *page 412* of some manuscript… I don't understand."

Kiril was looking at her, rather confused.

"It might be another edition of the same book."

"Yes, this is the first one, and mine is the second."

"So maybe the authors decided it wasn't that important and left it out of the second edition to save space. That's understandable enough. I do it every day in the newspaper."

Vera's irritation with Kiril's reasoning showed plainly on her face.

"Actually, this might be the most important fresco in all of the Roman catacombs."

"What's so important about it? I've never heard of an Orphic Christ."

"Just look at it!" She pointed to the first image. "The man in the cloak is holding a wedge in one hand and the lyre of Orpheus in the other."

"Is that Orpheus?"

"Well, the lyre is his symbol, but the hat he has on is definitely Mithras'."

"The Persian god?"

Vera glared at him for interrupting her before continuing.

"The bird in the tree is a dove, one of the obvious Christian symbols of that time. Like the fish. In the picture below the connection is made even more conspicuous with the inclusion of the lamb." She pointed at the next image. "The lamb follows the Good Shepherd."

"Wait. What connection are you talking about?"

"The painter was obviously trying to depict the transformation of Orpheus, Christ and Mithras into one another."

"But what do those three gods have in common?"

Vera didn't reply. She sat on a dusty crate turning page after page. She stopped to take photos of some of them: first, she made sure the focus was perfect and then, holding her breath, she snapped a picture.

"I've never heard of such a connection. How do you know these things?"

"It's the topic of my book," she answered without lifting her head.

"You're writing a book?"

When Vera saw his eyes fill with the expected amazement, her face glowed with a reserved smile.

"A research book. With lots of pictures – to make it more… understandable."

"So what's the topic?"

"Serious enough to change the world."

"Oh, that's a bit ambitious, don't you think? Is it a secret?"

"It's too early to announce it to the media."

"I'll keep it to myself, provided you promise to give me the first interview… Some day!"

"Deal. I'll need the media coverage…"

Kiril sat down next to her on the cold floor, resting his chin on his knees. Vera proudly explained her theory to him.

"Now I can see why no one wants to publish it," Kiril said smiling. "But why would anyone steal a religion instead of simply becoming its follower?"

Vera took her eyes off the pages and bitingly fixed them on the reporter.

"It's not that simple. Imagine you are convinced that the religion in question is a source of invincible strength. In that case, it becomes dangerous in the hands of the enemy and invaluable to you."

"Yeah, I think I've heard about incinerated Orphic books and Thracian texts obliterated from stone tablets. Wasn't the Pythagorean School even burned down because of the books stored there?"[13]

---

[13] Pythagoras is believed to have been a follower of Orphism. Dr. Rositsa Dankova writes: "Still, we want to remind you that the philosophical school Pythagoras founded, despite the fact that it was not in Samos, completely followed the Orphic tradition, which G. Krastev connects with the Huns and the

"More than once. History tells us that as soon as the conspirators acquired the power of Orphic Knowledge, they started hunting down and killing off the enlightened. They destroyed all sources of their teachings, leaving in existence only the ones they had rewritten themselves. Gradually a widespread religion disappeared and another rose from its ruins."

"That's a good story," the reporter smirked. "But what is this power you're talking about? Some kind of Holy Grail?" He laughed again. Vera threw another scowl at him and sank her nails into the black cover.

"I don't know. Some secret. Knowledge about something... The truth was kept and passed on only among members of the enlightened Orphic society."

"The Orphic Mysteries?"

She nodded before continuing to page through the book, like a hen rooting through ashes.

"So how did you come upon this idea?"

"Everything started two years ago when I saw a picture of a stone amulet on the cover of a book in my father's office. What impressed me was the strange mixture of symbols in the amulet's engravings. There was a moon, seven stars arranged in an arc, a crucified man, two large wedges at his feet and a caption about Orpheus. Intrigued, I opened the book, but the author didn't say anything about the amulet. So I searched the Internet and found out that the stone in question had disappeared in a fire at a German bunker during the war. In the process, however, I came across a related scholarly discussion: *Orphism as the basis for Christianity*. After extensive research on the subject, I decided to write a non-fiction book about it. People love religious scandals."

"Hmm. I had no idea Orpheus was so popular. I thought he was a singer."

Bulgarians. The Pelasgian Orphism existed long before the rise of the Greeks, whose religion is characterized by Neanderthal elements. Pythagoras, in fact, is an Orphic who precisely followed the Pelasgian and Etruscan traditions."

"You've just got to know where to look. Even Shakespeare wrote about the transformation…"

Impressed, Kiril took the old book about the catacombs and paged through it. There were photographs of original subterranean Roman frescoes. Some of them showed signs of erosion while others had been almost completely destroyed by human hands.

"These are the most well-known images of the Orphic Christ from the San Domitilla Catacombs," Vera pointed. "They depict Orpheus the way Christ was depicted in early Christianity – as the Good Shepherd. But Orpheus is in the center of the eight-pointed star."

"The eight-pointed star? What's its significance?" Kiril interrupted.

"I don't know for sure... But I imagine that at some point there must have been an important text beneath Orpheus' feet which has since been destroyed by vandals."

"But couldn't the transformation you're talking about just be a mistake?"

Vera looked at Kiril irritably. For a moment, she even regretted telling all this to a journalist.

"It must have taken a lot of courage on the part of the artists to show the connection…"

Suddenly they heard a man's distant voice, as though carried on the wind from a rocky mountain top. It was calling Vera's name. The damp stone walls distorted the sounds, giving them a mysterious resonance and rusty echo.

"Are you in there?" the voice asked from outside.

Vera stood close to Kiril and whispered, "We'd better not tell anyone what we saw here."

"But I think it might be important." He looked at her, puzzled.

"Well, if they don't find it themselves, they don't deserve to know… I want to use it in my book."

The door opened and Kuzmanov rushed in.

"What's going on here?" Kuzmanov shouted. "Your father's out of his mind with worry!"

"Wow, he actually noticed I wasn't there? Now that's what I call a miracle. C'mon, let's go," Vera snapped.

She bent down, picked up her notebook and flashlight, and went up the stairs. She wore the determined expression of a person prepared to do whatever it takes to reach her goal.

METAMORPHOSES

Page 413 began with the following text:

"The transformation between Orpheus, Christ and even Mithras is depicted in hundreds of murals, sculptures and antiques. An example of this is the monument found in the cemetery of Ad Duas Lauros in Rome. The figure of Orpheus is depicted amongst the scenes suggesting a commonality between the Thracian sage and the New and Old Testaments. The scenes are arranged in the form of a cross" (The Christian Catacombs of Rome, *Schnell and Steiner, page 103). Certain specialists claim that at one time there was a text in the fresco beneath the feet of Orpheus reading, "Eight suns between Heaven and Hell..." But this text no longer exists. The surface of the fresco has been severely damaged.*

Subterranean Rome

"Herbert?" A male voice broke the damp silence and interrupted his thoughts.

It was him – the man with the strange eyes: colorful, silent, more elongated than is typical for a Caucasian. But he didn't look Asian, either. He was just different. He had a tall muscular build, simple clothing, an inconspicuous short haircut, and skin so white and pale that he looked like someone from the north. Or even a ghost. But in the darkness he always was covering his body and his head with hat as if he was hiding something.

In the catacombs

"Let's go," he said abruptly.

Herbert raised his large flashlight, one of those with rubber casing to protect it in case of accidental blows. Sometimes parts of the tunnels collapsed. But Herbert had never considered the fact that only his flashlight had such a protective shield.

They walked for nearly thirty minutes through the cold labyrinths of the catacombs. The light from the infrequent lamps illuminated a ghostly mist of pearly drops, turning them into a cloud of transparent flies swarming through the black void. The dampness crept up the walls, feeding the thick moss growing on the stone ceiling. When moisture touched the volcanic stone, it sparkled in the shining slivers of silica that dotted the magma, glittering like a gold mine.

"Why are you here?" whispered Herbert.

He always whispered in the abandoned cemetery.

"People waste too much time thinking about what's possible," the man replied.

They were walking towards the southern-most point in the catacombs. Herbert raised his hand to show him the third fresco.

This one also depicted Orpheus, now amidst a flock of sheep.[14] The stranger knelt down and photographed it. It was all too popular in academic circles, so apart from photographing it, there was nothing else he could do.

"Do tourists come here?" the man asked.

"No… they're not allowed."

"Good."

The stranger stood up and the two men walked on slowly. In this tunnel, the air was stale and the floor uneven. It had not been ventilated for years. The stranger bent down and picked up a human bone from the floor. He raised it to his eyes for a closer look.

"People are believers when it comes to those close to them and non-believers when it comes to anyone else," he said conclusively, still examining the bone.

He blew the dust off it and placed it into one of the holes in the wall. Once a believer had buried his relative here for the peace of his soul and his family. And then another believer had dug it up, the stranger thought.

"The tourists usually steal them, you know," Herbert said, surprised by the stranger's gesture. "They put them on their knick-knack shelves as souvenirs."

"I'm not a tourist."

They continued along the narrow tunnel. There were holes carved into the walls at regular intervals. They resembled bookshelves that could fit about twenty thick volumes. Rome's earlier residents would put corpses in them and seal them with a slab of white marble. The smaller holes were meant for babies. Now all were empty, black and bare. Six rows of holes from floor to ceiling on both sides of the tunnel, as far as the eye could see. Around every bend in the tunnel the holes began again.

---

[14] One of the most famous frescos in the Catacombs of Domitilla picturing Christ/Orpheus (or the Orphic Christ). The harp that the young man holds in his hands symbolizes the song and speech of Orpheus, while the flock of sheep is among the most popular symbols of Christ as the Good Shepherd.

Herbert stumbled and fell. His hand caught the edge of one of the holes carved into the wall. His eyes sank into its darkness. He felt unwilling to go on.

"One hundred thousand..." he whispered.

"Keep going."

"One hundred thousand human bodies were buried in this catacomb alone. Isn't that terrible? So many bodies!"

"People die," the stranger remarked coldly. "Others are born."

"People will never accept death. It's like loneliness – always there, but you never surrender to it."

"Stop chattering."

"I'm afraid, too," Herbert went on. "I even became a priest. People will do anything to try to deceive death."

The stranger closely followed the black-robed man, who couldn't stop jabbering excitedly.

The narrow tunnel finally came to an end in a wide hall. The plaster was still well-preserved, but where it had eroded you could see the fragile cinnamon earth, like a deliberate reminder that everything is transient.

"Fourth century," Herbert quickly explained.

Two burial chambers were situated under the dome of the ceiling. Besides the eroded spots, there was not a single centimeter of the walls and ceiling not covered in colorful frescoes dominated by shades of saffron. This was a painstaking effort on the part of the painters to emphasize their belief in the majesty of the Gods and saints who cared for the dead.

"All this effort... People working strenuously among dead bodies decaying in the cold and dirty air. Just to dress reality in illusions," Herbert whispered in a monotone. "When we experience the greatest doubt in the journey of our souls, we most insistently tend to our graves. The effort gives us the feeling that we are close to our desires."

"It has always been so."

"But man would do anything to believe that the end is not in the ground. Heaven is a beautiful illusion that the millenniums have turned into a truth."

"You are wrong, the truth has almost been erased," the man replied and then added, "Now be quiet."

The priest took a few silent steps and then began whispering again. "The catacombs are one of the most popular attractions of Rome. Aren't you interested in their history?"

"No."

After ten minutes, Herbert pointed to the ceiling. Orpheus was in the center of an octagon. Next to him, like the points of a star, were scenes from the Old and New Testaments.

"The artist is unknown," Herbert commented. "Most scholars believe that the connection between David and Orpheus is deliberate. They both exerted power over souls by means of speech and song.... but I don't know anything about the octagon."

"Step back," the man interrupted.

He examined the mural carefully, running his fingers over it. Beneath the feet of the Thracian sage there was an inscription in tiny letters and reference to *page 413* of a nameless book scribbled at its end. The stranger took a short-handled pick from his sack and struck the plaster containing the text.

"What are you doing?!" the historian cried.

"Step aside. I still need you."

He struck the image once again, removing several solid chunks of plaster. They fell to the floor, sending up a cloud of dust. Frightened, the priest jumped back. He could have run away, but he didn't.

The man hesitated for a moment, wondering whether or not to strike the ceiling with his pick, but he stopped. There was no point. Pictures of the fresco already existed in a number of history books. But without the caption it could be understood only by those enlightened to its secrets. He put the broken pieces of plaster in a sack, which he slung over his shoulder. At that moment Herbert thought he saw again the strange luminosity around the hands of the pale man. He wiped the white dust off his face with his sleeve and said hoarsely:

"Now I want to see the triple divinity."

Herbert stood up and walked on. They said nothing. Only the sound of their heavy footfalls could be heard, echoing through the tunnels. The only light in the tunnel came from their flashlights. They reached the very end of the catacomb where there was no electric lighting, nor any signs for guides. The air was heavy with dust and strange smells. Herbert illuminated the vault above one of the burial chambers. There Orpheus was depicted in Mithras' military helmet, playing his harp for a lamb and a peacock.

"Kneel!" the stranger ordered. A badly-tattooed, eight-cornered meander was visible on the taut sinew of his neck.

Herbert recognized the symbol. He knelt. His hands were trembling and he dropped the flashlight.

"You can't erase history," he whispered.

"Are these all the images that contain the encoded symbols?"

"Yes…"

"How can I be sure that you're not lying?"

An icy chill sliced through Herbert's body.

"I can't lie." The historian raised the iron cross hanging across his chest and showed it to the man with the elongated eyes.

"You are not a believer." The stranger smiled.

Then he turned back to the mural and struck it with his pick, first destroying the fresco and then the text below it. The plaster collapsed into dust, leaving nothing in its place but soft volcanic rock.

"You can destroy artifacts, but not history," said Herbert helplessly. He was no longer whispering.

"Turn around."

The aging historian obeyed. Words didn't matter anymore. The cold shivers were gone. His body was numb. But the waiting had been worth it. So many years… perhaps the Hidden Ones had survived. He would never learn the answer, though.

A single gunshot rang out.

The stranger gathered the remaining pieces into his sack and walked back the same way they had come in.

DOPPELGANGERS

Page 415 *began with a table consisting of two columns with twenty-two identical symbols in each one. The caption next to it read: "The first column contains Cretan Linear A and the second shows 8,000-year-old symbols found in the Balkans. The table was composed by Harald Haarman, from the University of Helsinki who discovered more than fifty common symbols between the alphabets of the extinct central Balkan Atlantis and Mycenaean Linear A. According to him the significant number of parallels excludes the possibility of accidental coincidence. The eminent Latvian archaeologist M. Gimbutas also defines the pre-Thracian hieroglyphs as 'the linear symbols of Old Europe,' hinting at their possible origins."*

From R. Rudgley, British anthropologist

"They weren't Cathars," Kiril whispered as he followed Vera through the forest of cobwebs.
"Pardon?"
"I've read enough to know that the residents of the deserted castle had nothing to do with them."
Vera didn't reply. At the end of the underground corridor there was a flickering light resembling a road sign to the Upper World. Vera caught a whiff of the pungent smell of dust mixed with the aroma of paper and mold. She walked confidently ahead of everyone

else. No sooner had she climbed the last steps than she saw her father bent over a box, meticulously arranging small brown objects in it.

"Vera, there you are! We searched the whole castle for you!" the professor shouted.

"Well, they found me. And did you find what you were looking for?"

When he heard the sarcasm in her voice he turned back to arranging the clay objects, disfigured by time, in the box. He was concentrating so hard on not damaging them that he looked like a watchmaker whose slightest flinch might destroy the mechanism's perpetual motion.

Kuzmanov was behind Vera, but when he saw her father, he announced loudly:

"Professor, I found another one!" He handed Kandilov a clay tablet as wide as his palm. Symbols, perhaps hieroglyphs, looked as if they had been carved into it with a fingernail.

"Very unusual. It's unlike anything we've found up to now, isn't it?"

The professor nodded. An expression of excitement crept over his face. He looked at the scratched square of baked clay, touching it with latex gloves, hardly able to believe that it was real. Then he looked at Vera and shared: "We just found something very unexpected – rare prehistoric objects."

"Where?" She asked, surprised.

"Mostly under the stairs. But some of them were scattered around the house. Like this tablet, for instance."

Vera peered into the cardboard box where her father was still carefully arranging his finds.

"They can't be real!" she exclaimed.

"Why not?" Kiril looked at her in surprise.

"Those same artifacts are on display in the Vratsa[15] museum in Bulgaria. They're some of the most important Neolithic pottery objects ever found."

---

[15] A town in western Bulgaria.

"Really? But what makes them so special?" Kiril asked with curiosity.

"The symbols on them," Professor Kandilov replied as he straightened up, stretching his back to pop the vertebrae into place. "Vera's right... these objects are quite similar to those found in 1969 in the village of Gradeshnitsa. They are almost 8,000 years old. Some academics believe that the hundreds of ancient pictograms on them are evidence of the first primitive form of writing found in the world."[16]

Impressed, the reporter switched on his tiny voice recorder and moved closer to the professor.

"Last year I was at a press conference," Kiril recalled. "It was organized by an American who claimed that he had read the 'Testament of Orpheus' written 7,000 years ago and published a book about it. The book also contained some references to the clay objects from Gradeshnitsa. He claimed to have deciphered the messages using Egyptian hieroglyphs."

---

[16] In 1969 the famous Gradeshnitsa Tablets were found in western Bulgaria along with hundreds of clay figurines and pots. Another internationally renowned object was unearthed in central Bulgaria: the Kranovo Seal, another clay tablet covered in pictograms. Historians unanimously agree that the signs are a form of proto-writing. Some of them even call it "the writing system of the first civilization, which mysteriously vanished." Similar items were found in Serbia (Vinča) and Romania. The finds quickly attracted international attention. Historians and linguists from all over the world discussed the resemblance of the signs to those of the first Minoan/Cretan writing system. The German Assyriologist Adam Falkenstein finds similarities between the tablet discovered in Romania and those discovered in the Sumerian city of Uruk (dating from 3,000 B.C.). A number of scholars believe that the Balkan signs are similar to Egyptian and Mesopotamian hieroglyphs. **But precise results from radiocarbon dating show that the tablets are thousands of years older than the first known human civilizations in Mesopotamia.** The discussion about their exact dating is still open, though most scholars now believe they first appeared around 5,500 B.C. (*Lost Civilizations of the Stone Age,* Richard Rudgley, p. 99). Bulgarian scholars generally accept the idea that the signs are pictograms that encode ideas and religious messages. Scholars from Western Europe are trying to prove that this is actually the oldest writing system in the world.

Vera stared at her father. She knew that this topic always annoyed him.

"You're talking about Dr. Gaid,[17] right?" The professor interrupted him angrily. "He's neither a historian nor an archaeologist, and even less of an American. His real name is Gaidarski and no one in academic circles takes him seriously."

"Be that as it may, it's still a sensation!" Kiril said excitedly. "Just imagine, the first alphabet and civilization cropped up in Bulgaria of all places!"

"Don't jump to conclusions, my boy. These signs are not a writing system. Besides, we are not talking about Bulgaria, but ancient Thrace."

"Don't expect my father to talk to you about sensations!" Vera intervened. "But I can tell you one. The signs you see are supposedly actual letters written by the first civilization. Don't laugh, that's been proven. But the curious thing is that in the fourth millennium B.C. it disappeared for no apparent reason."

The professor took a roll of transparent, tea-colored paper from his bag and wrapped the clay objects in it. Then he carefully placed them in the box and after a long pause added,

"Personally I'm more interested in how these replicas got here."

"Why do you think they're replicas? What if the ones on show in the museum are copies of these here…"

The same thought had occurred to Vera. The figurines looked completely authentic. But it wouldn't be the first time someone had replaced a museum exhibit with a forgery. The clay tiles were extremely valuable in European scholarly circles, even though Bulgarian academics preferred to ignore this.

"I would appreciate it if you didn't write anything in your newspaper about what you have seen, for the moment at least," the professor concluded dryly. "If you're right, it's all the more

---

[17] Also known as Stephen Guide, a Bulgarian-American from the Institute of Transcendent Analysis, Long Beach, California.

important that no one but us knows about these finds. They must be examined first."

It was then that Vera first made the connection.

"I knew it," she whispered quietly. "The knowledge must be even older than Orpheus. But whose idea was it, then?"

She said the words so quietly that no one heard them. They were for her ears only.

THE MAN ON THE CROSS

In the top right-hand corner of **page 416** *there was a photograph from the Berlin Museum's pre-1945 catalogue. It was marked as exhibit No.1164. Beneath it was the following text: "The amulet depicts Orpheus-Bacchus crucified, hanging from the cross in Christ's characteristic pose. The base is a cylindrical seal of unknown origin dated to 300 A.D. The cross is crowned with a crescent, the sign of the lunar god Menos, who appears at midnight in the mysteries of the Thracian god Sabazios. The seven stars of Pleiades are engraved above the cross to symbolize Orpheus' lyre. For this reason, the Christian cross itself bears the significance of the old cross with equal arms – itself a symbol of the main star from Orion, the so-called Nocturnal Hunter, or in other words the sign of Dionysus."*

From *Ancient Thrace* by Al. Fol, K. Jordanov, K. Porozhanov, and V. Fol.

Dr. Werder was looking for a place to park his green Citroen. He found a vacant spot on a narrow side street just opposite the entrance of the Pergamon Museum, across the Spree River. Before getting out of the car he placed his official parking permit on the dashboard. His slender, stooped figure strode towards the Bode Museum.

The street was deserted. He stopped in the middle of the road and put on his checkered cap. He thought it gave him a mysterious and youthful appearance. His gaze was fixed on the museum's impressive cupola. It was the symbol of the Kaiser Friedrich Museum, as it had once been called, and was built where the Spree

Bode Museum is where Dr. Werder worked and where the Orpheus Amulet had been housed until it disappeared in 1945.

and Kupfergraben Rivers met, forming a triangular island. Most impressive was its entrance with its marble floor and its splendid basilica in the style of a Renaissance Florentine church.

Werder quickened his pace. He didn't want to make the director wait. The latter was an impatient man, sometimes given to shouting and threatening people with dismissal. That's what he had heard, at least. The doctor had not personally seen him enraged because he had always been meticulous and punctual. He greeted the uniformed guards and continued along the corridor.

The museum had just opened and there was a profound, tense silence in the hallways, broken only by his footsteps. They followed him as though stuck fast to his shadow, echoing through the high vaulted ceilings. The eyes of hundreds of gods and saints from early Christian icons and sculptures followed his every move. The scholar didn't return their glances. Although he'd been studying them in infinite detail for years, he felt that seeing the sorrow and tears etched on their faces was not a good way to start the day.

"I haven't forgotten about the broken window. I thought tomorrow…" Werder hurried to explain to the director as soon as he entered his office.

"Sit down and close the door."

The director opened a metal wall safe. He took out a sheet of paper and a sealed envelope. He handed them to Werder and said, "Read this."

The small print forced the historian to bring the page closer to his eyes. The words were written in Russian, but spelled phonetically in Latin script, as though they were meant to be spoken rather than read.

Twenty-five years ago, Werder had gotten his PhD in Moscow, so he knew the language quite well. He read: "An anonymous person is seeking a buyer in Moscow for an object with the description you have given. The Pushkin Museum among others are interested in the offer. No official information has been published because of an attempted burglary… "

There was no signature.

"What object do you think it refers to?" Werder asked.

"You won't believe it… The small amulet with the Orpheus inscription, which used to be part of your department's collection until sixty years ago."

The director took a couple of paces and then collapsed into a leather armchair. Without looking at Werder, he continued. "Last year I made some unofficial inquiries about it. If that object exists anywhere in the world, I want to get it back and put an end to all the speculations about it and us."

"When did you receive this message?"

"Three months ago."

"And?"

"That's it…. I still don't know who's trying to sell it or whether it's still for sale."

"Who's the source?"

"It's best you don't know." The director opened the sealed envelope. "Yesterday we received an invitation from the Ministry of Culture in Moscow." He gave it to Werder, adding, "This is what I mentioned this morning. Either the Russians are up to something or they're overconfident. For the first time since the Second World War, they're actually going to officially display what they looted from our museums. What impudence!"

"Perhaps they're trying to legitimize their possession of the extremely valuable items?"

"There are a dozen or so objects that I would do anything to get back to Germany. We'll pay for them if we have to. But first we need a clear picture of what's going on in Moscow. That's your job at the exhibition."

"I…I'll do my best," the historian replied rather unconvincingly.

"By the way, there's been another publication about the amulet – the PR department sent me a copy."

He began to noisily leaf through a thick folder and when he found the page he was looking for, he said, "I don't know what they see in that amulet. There's always someone nosing around and writing nonsense."

"Probably because if it really proves to be from the third century, coming from what is now Bulgaria, it might cast doubt over accepted views of the 'man on the cross.'"

The director stood up and threw the folder down onto his desk. Then he went to the window, striking a pensive pose. He lit a vanilla cigar and blew a thread of smoke towards the pane.

"I don't understand," he continued. "Why would people want to nose around in our most precious illusion and hack away at its roots? What if they succeed? What will we do afterwards with our overwhelming fear of death? Our faith in God, Heaven and Hell seems to be the only thing that makes our stay on earth meaningful."

"There was a time when people couldn't find the answer to any questions without reference to God, while today the only questions we can't find the answers to are about God. This just seems to be human nature. We can't live without poking our noses into something."

"You know, Werder, every Sunday people go to church with their families. I do, too, because everyone does. But ever since my hair has started graying, I've made plans to actually believe in it. How else can I face my final days? Just remember that without the miracle of Christ, even your department wouldn't exist," he said the last words slowly and emphatically.

"That's not really true... If we ever abandon our faith, the same forces that are today trying to denounce Christ would then be fighting to resurrect him, more fervently than ever. Now they are trying to restore the cult of Orpheus because thousands years ago, he was erased from the face of earth because of Christianity's ambitions. And that is exactly the miracle we need to restore our faith... We most likely have to destroy it first!"

"And that may very well happen soon."

The director stepped away from the window and sat down at his desk. He rested the cigar on the brim of a crystal ashtray and opened the folder once again. As he put his index finger on a sheet of paper, his face lit up and he said, "Just listen to how this new Internet article ends: 'Therefore, at the end of my study I dare state that the Orphic amulet today has its own internal logic, which is not self-contained but rather to be understood within the context of some other secret teaching. And since we have not been enlightened to that knowledge, the logic of the hematite relief is hidden from us.[18]'" He raised his head to look at Werder and added, "Has anyone asked you for information about the amulet?"

"Almost every month someone sends an inquiry. I'm not hiding the meager information we have about it from anyone –

---

[18] L. Tsonev's research study about the Orphic amulet is one of the well-argued works on the topic.

or the contradictory sources and interpretations,[19] for that matter. Some scholars today even think that we are not talking about one amulet only, but at least two, even three."

"If it still exists, the amulet must be in Moscow now.[20] We've got to get it back. And that will be your task."

"I'll do what I can…"

"The Pergamon Museum and its Babylonian street already attract huge flocks of tourists. They all want to see the ancient Egypt exhibits. Maybe this amulet will rekindle the interest in our exhibitions, too – especially the Early Christianity collection. If it's so popular when missing… imagine what's going to happen when it's finally found."

"But I don't know anyone in Russia."

"I've arranged for the Russian special services to help you. Scandals aren't in Moscow's best interest."

"But the object might be in a private collection already."

"That's what you need the special services for."

Dr. Werder left the director's office deep in thought and walked along the sunlit marble corridor towards his department downstairs.

As soon as he got to his office, he checked his e-mail. Just a habit. The actions we repeat often turn into habits sooner or later, shaping our days, filling them. They repay our loyalty by giving us the feeling that we are not wasting time.

Having made sure that nothing significant had happened in his virtual mailbox in the Internet universe, Werder set about his daily

---

[19] Some sources include Freke and Gandy (1999); Campbell (1968); Eisler (1921, 1925); Al. Fol, K. Jordanov, K. Porozhanov and V. Fol, *Ancient Thrace*, published by Europa Antique and the Institute of Thracian Studies at the Bulgarian Academy of Sciences, Sofia (2000).

[20] The details surrounding the disappearance of the amulet are based on an account from Dr. Mitka, departmental director at the Bode Museum. She explained how dozens of precious objects that were stolen from the Friedrichshain Bunker by Russian soldiers and transferred to Russia appeared for the first time since their disappearance in 2007 at the exhibition in Moscow.

tasks. He regretfully noted in his planner that he had to postpone his trip to Rome. He was planning to visit a library on the ancient *Via Appia Antica* near the Roman catacombs, to search there for a mysterious manuscript called *The Parchment Maze*. It was cited in an old Christian almanac kept in the archives of the Bode Museum. Werder was skeptical about its supposed contents, so he had decided to see if the manuscript really existed.

Then the historian completed the list of the department's artifacts that had been lost during the Second World War. He even found a map of Moscow and printed it out. He looked at the red-blue cobweb of streets and boulevards, dissected by a darker and thicker line through the middle – the Moscow River.

CLUES IN CLAY

Page 417 began with The Flight:
"In the process of migrating (abandoning their lands),
the people who left the Central Balkans gradually began
to lose the material symbols of their identity through
which we recognize them (namely, ceramics). However,
they managed to preserve over the years that which
is most difficult to lose – their beliefs and religious
concepts. Their descendants took these nonmaterial
traces with them to even the most distant places where
they established new settlements. The religious traditions
of the new arrivals combined with those of the locals
and were perhaps even subject to influences from the
regions of Asia Minor, the Middle East and Egypt.

Professor Ana Raduncheva[21] on the disappearance of the
Chalcolithic[22] population from the ancient Balkans, in her
Doctoral Dissertation Summary, **1999, p.43.**

Night in the Alps appears as the deepest black – undoubtedly
because no electric network of artificial lights crisscrosses the
mountain peaks, preventing darkness from falling, as in the city.
In the mountains, night's veil cloaks the earth, covered only by the
star-strewn sky, as though an artist had spattered it with a brushful
of silver paint. Yet even these countless stars cannot illuminate the

---

[21] Professor Raduncheva has spent twenty-five years researching the
vanished Eneolithic civilization, which she calls the first and most-developed in
Europe, or the "Golden Age" of human culture.

[22] "Neolithic" refers to the period between 6200-4900 BC. It was followed
by the Chalcolythic Era (also known as the Eneolithic Era), which lasted roughly
until 3800 B.C.

66

This is the so-called "clay tablet" from Gradeshnitsa, famous for being the world's earliest known written work. It dates back to approximately 5500 B.C. and is the oldest such artifact found to date. Similar tablets, but with fewer symbols, were found in Serbia and Romania. The signs on it are considered one of the first proto-writing systems in the world. Ten centuries later, other such writing systems arose in Mesopotamia and Egypt.

forest. The moon alone casts ghostly shadows, which flit between the tree branches, playing tag with the hoots of owls and the distant howls of dogs.

Only two windows in the hotel near the chateau were lit up. One of them was Vera's. She couldn't sleep after everything she had seen that day, yet despite her excitement she felt a heaviness gnawing at her. In Sofia she had gotten used to seeking out solitude, but here the emptiness was an invisible needle injecting her with lethal poison. As if loneliness were a witch disguised as someone familiar so you don't chase her away, but when far removed from everyday life, she strips down to the bone, inciting terrible fear.

Vera opened the fridge and took out a small bottle of wine in the hope that the alcohol would dull her consciousness. After a dozen or so sips, she wrinkled her nose and put the bottle down. The bitter liquid flowed through her body. She had never been able to get used to the acrid taste of alcohol – then again, who drinks the stuff for the taste alone?

She took the camera out of her bag to look at the pictures she had taken of the clay objects they had found that day. She compared them with the photographs of those excavated in Gradeshnitsa, which she easily found on the Internet.

"Perfect copies," she thought – if they were forgeries, that is. They were identical, down to the most minute details. Vera knew that if anyone was more excited than she was about this discovery, it was her father. These prehistoric pictograms engraved in clay, the oldest yet discovered, were one of his favorite subjects. Yet unlike her, he couldn't afford hasty interpretations – or enthusiasm. "He's missing out on the euphoria of discovery," she thought. Still, he wouldn't risk his reputation on account of some clay pictograms. His entire academic career revolved around official recognition and respect from fellow members of the guild.

Professor Kandilov was wary of flash-in-the-pan sensations. He remained loyal to the facts, as dull as they might be.

Vera had heard stories about Bulgarian treasures stolen from the country during the communist era. Supposedly, certain famous artifacts had been secretly replaced by perfect copies, with the fakes remaining on display in Bulgarian museums to this day. However, the only people who knew about this were former secret service agents.

The clay objects they had found today proved that the items discovered near Gradeshnitsa and Karanovo were more valuable than Bulgarian scholars had ever imagined. The pictograms and hieroglyphics engraved on them could challenge accepted theories about the appearance of the first written alphabets, as well as the course of civilization's development as a whole. This claim was so extreme that it frightened historians, rather than intriguing them. Thus, even though the symbols on the ancient ceramics and stones found in the Balkans were exceptionally clear and systematic, most historians preferred to see them as random decoration.

However, decoration normally aspires to symmetry and repetition – and precisely this is what the clay signs lack. Even the way they were engraved shows that the writer began with large, ornate symbols, but in the end, realizing he was running out of space, he made the symbols smaller and more cramped to fit the message in. However, the most interesting thing about the ancient Balkan symbols is that they are the oldest known signs in the world. Several centuries after the inexplicable disappearance of the Balkan civilization that created them, the symbols seemed to have been revived with the appearance of the Egyptian and Cretan civilizations, as though the traces of the First People had been carried to the east and south. Yet no one knows how and why this happened.

When the clay objects were first discovered in the Balkans, academics from all over the world were sure that this was an advanced form of writing brought from the Middle East. However, once carbon dating tests were carried out, the graphic symbols on the objects turned out to be much older than anything previously known. Since this starkly contradicted everything categorically accepted as the truth, historians rejected the obvious. And the symbols languished in museums, undeciphered and forgotten.

Vera finished her glass of wine but still couldn't stop the incessant buzzing of her thoughts. She put on her jeans and went out into the hushed corridor. The silence was more intense than the noise of the city. She hesitated to turn the light on, as she didn't want anyone to know she was there. She left her door open a crack to light the way and crept down to her father's room. As she approached it, she slowed her pace and listened. Light seeped out from under the door. She knocked hesitantly.

"Can I come in?" she asked, poking her nose around the door.

The professor was just getting off the telephone – obviously with someone in Bulgaria, as he had wished them "goodnight" in his native tongue before hanging up. His face was anxious.

"Has something happened?" Vera asked, trying to look curious rather than worried.

"Problems at the museum… I don't seem to have any luck with clay tablets these days."

Vera took his words as an invitation and stepped into the room, closing the door behind her.

"Does it have anything to do with the ones we found today? Are they real?"

"No… it's not that. Let's talk about it later. I've got work to do now."

The professor put on his glasses and went over to the desk where he had placed a handful of chocolate-colored figures. The rest of the objects were still in the box on the floor. On the corner of the desk there was a tall microscope, a magnifying glass, a soft brush and a jar of chemicals which he used to carry out a few simple scientific tests.

"Are they authentic or just very good forgeries?" she asked insistently.

"I'll have to do some more research on them… it's quite possible they're originals."

"Are you serious? How could that be?"

Vera stepped closer. She hesitated for a moment, then, despite the knot she felt in her stomach, she looked at her father. Ever since she was a child she had been scared of catching his eye whenever she expected to see traces of anger there. And even a hint of his stern gaze would cause her to freeze up.

70

A clay model of a Chalcolithic dwelling from 7,000 years ago. It is from Gradeshnitsa Culture and has several meanders inscribed on it, while its entrance is paved with the Egyptian hieroglyph for "ark" (according to the linguist Dr. Stefan Guide).

Yet now his eyes seemed softer than she had ever seen them. So she took the final step towards him. She bent over the figurines and examined them carefully. One of the objects resembled something like a jewelry or candy box with tiny legs. Next to it there were two tablets with asymmetrical grooves and a few ritualistic statuettes of wide-hipped women.

"More meanders," she whispered.

"What's that?" The professor didn't understand.

"The clay design you're looking at… The meander is the most frequently used symbol on it, just like on the other objects we saw at the chateau."

"So?"

"Sometimes you don't need a microscope to see the obvious."

Vera continued looking over her father's shoulder, studying the details of the "model dwelling" as scholars liked to call it. She examined the curves of the clay figure twisting around its axis, then stepped back and whispered, "Can't you see the sign?"

The professor looked at her questioningly. Vera pointed out to him the repeated rectangular spiral and added, "It must mean something. It can't just be there for decoration… Look at where it appears. And on the tablet with the symbols it's quite clear that it's one of the written signs."

Vera didn't tell her father the real reason she wanted to discover its meaning. The same symbol was repeated on the clay tablet that her father had kept for years at the Archaeological Museum. About the same size as the one now sitting here on his desk, it also appeared to be prehistoric. The main difference, however, was that the other tablet was a personal gift to him from a famous Bulgarian antiquities collector who had decided that it was too ordinary for his treasures. They called it the "Nameless Tablet" because no one knew where and how it had been discovered.

Yesterday Vera saw the same symbol depicted on the signet ring of the chateau caretaker, Monsieur Marten. Only then had she made the connection between the symbol on the prehistoric vessel, the sign on the ring and the image of Orpheus.

"Why are you so interested in it?" the professor asked her.

She hesitated for a moment. "I've seen it in ancient art, too, mostly in scenes with Orpheus and Dionysus."

"You're very observant. In fact, this symbol, the meander, appeared for the first time during the Neolithic Period precisely in the Balkans. But no one really knows what it meant at that time. It might symbolize the sun or the spiral of the eternal beginning and immortality. I don't know."

"Could it possibly be evidence of the birth of Orphism? The sun and immortality of the human soul are its fundamental tenets."

"Vera, what is this nonsense – Orphism in prehistoric times?" Blushing, she lowered her eyes as he went on. "The meander is very common in ancient cultures, but is mainly used as decoration. You can see it in a number of ancient hieroglyph systems. Almost everywhere it has the meaning of 'protector.'"

Vera wondered how her father could possibly miss the obvious connection even as he himself was saying it out loud. But she didn't want to get into an argument.

"Perhaps the survival of this fundamental symbol through time is a clue that its creators have not completely disappeared, as scholars thought. They've merely managed to hide from The End... At the very least," she added, "the symbol could be used to name the first civilization. Academics have wondered what to call it for years now. How does 'The Meandrites' sound to you?"

The professor ruffled his beard and took off his glasses again. He smiled gently and said, "Better than nothing... But before you call them the First Civilization, you'll need quite a bit more evidence."

"Are there any older traces of civilization?" she asked indignantly. "Just because the Balkans today are synonymous with poverty and crime doesn't mean that we have to close our eyes to persuasive artifacts proving the existence of the first advanced human culture in the world... Precisely on the Balkans. You know yourself that there are seven, even eight-thousand-year-old clues in the Central Balkans that prove its existence. What's more, ancient Thracians were the first people to mine gold, they made the first gold jewelry and developed a basic writing system. Salt was also discovered there, to say nothing of the proto-Thracians' mathematical and astrological knowledge. The calendar they created became the basis for the ancient Bulgarian calendar, which UNESCO has declared the most accurate in the world!"

"Yes, but why would all this knowledge crop up precisely in the Balkans and nowhere else?"

"I found good argument reading a *National Geographic* study about soil fertility. The article said that since the dawn of humanity the highest concentration of 'exceptionally fertile soil' has been here in the Central Balkans.[23] This was a precondition

---

[23] According to the article, which appeared in *National Geographic*, September, 2008, only three percent of the earth's surface can be categorized as "exceptionally fertile," while of this, 1.3 percent of the highest concentrations of such soil can be found in the Central Balkans.

for advanced local evolution. For me, the important thing isn't whether they were the first, but why, after all they knew and accomplished, did they suddenly destroy their own temples and traces and just disappear one day.[24] It's as if they were fleeing from something…"

Orpheus playing a seven-stringed lyre. The decorations beneath him are most often bands of meanders, crosses and V-shaped symbols

The professor laughed. "Vera, you can't just hide an entire civilization."

"Of course you can't! I meant only the last of them! It's as though the earth just swallowed them up."

Professor Kandilov put his glasses back on. He picked up a thin brush and began cleaning the body of a Mother Goddess clay figurine.

---

[24] There are still no archeological facts indicating what caused the Eneolithic population of Ancient Thrace to unexpectedly leave its lands in the fourth millennium BC. There is no evidence that it was killed off, nor any clear traces of where it may have gone – only speculations.

"I'll include this sign in my thesis," Vera said. "It might just make things more interesting..."

"Aren't you writing about Orpheus?"

"Yes, but just imagine that the meander connects the Chalcolithic culture from the Balkans with Orphism and Thracian civilization. The symbol plays a leading role in both."

"Don't be ridiculous," he laughed. "There's a hiatus layer[25] of a millennium between them. The Chalcolithic people disappeared without a trace, scorching their own lands, which remained unpopulated for more than eleven centuries... There's no power on earth that could have created a link between them."

"But it sounds good, right? I might be able to link the ancients with the secret that transformed Orpheus from a singer into a sage and prophet. In any case, nobody can explain how he learned everything he knew. What if he found the Meandrites' hidden messages and deciphered them?"

Her eyes roamed over the clay figurines' contours, but she wasn't looking at them. Some irresistible torrent was sweeping her imagination down fanciful paths. She had been working on the idea of Orpheus for years. However, until now she had not realized that the Thracian poet's image was always accompanied by a ribbon of repetitive meanders. She had given even less thought to just how old they might be. That evening she decided that the coincidence between the symbols was just too striking for her wild imagination to have invented it. Instead, she began to suspect that the meander was Orpheus' secret symbol.

She was suddenly jerked back to the present by her father's laughter. "So you think Orpheus revived the Hidden Knowledge of the extinct Chalcolithic civilization!"

---

[25] A "hiatus layer" is a subterranean layer offering archeological evidence that for an extended period of time a given region shows no trace of human habitation. Precisely such a layer has been discovered in Thrace, indicating that after the disappearance of the Chalcolithic Balkan civilization, no other people lived in the area for more than 1,000 years.

He was peering into his tea cup. Reassured that it wasn't empty, he swirled it and drank down the dregs.

"Why not? There is evidence that Orpheus studied in Egypt[26] and that he had been in the Kingdom of the Underworld, whatever that means, but right after that he brought great knowledge to the Thracians and became a prophet."

The professor screwed up one eye to look through the microscope. Making a concerted effort not to tremble, he said, "Vera, history is not a game."

"You never praise me, no matter what I do!"

"Don't expect me to help you prop up your illusions. Your idea about a link between the Thracian poet and Christ is scandalous and inadmissible. And now you want to get yourself mixed up in some global conspiracy about an ancient civilization…" Her father was getting more and more furious. "Not a single self-respecting historian will back you up. You'll destroy your own reputation before you've even established it. And mine, too.

"Say whatever you like. My idea is sensational – and I've just come up with a way of making it even better. And it's completely based on facts!"

"Vera, don't commit professional suicide… Reputation is everything in archaeology."

"Reputation? And what about the truth? You said so yourself – these are artifacts!"

"I don't want to argue. You're far too headstrong. Just remember that it's easy to deceive yourself about the 'truth' because people always see what they're looking for. Humans can't resist coming up with reasons, explanations and connections between facts. In astrology, a handful of stars might make a constellation, but in science a handful of signs doesn't make a civilization."

---

[26] According to Diodorus Siculus (a Greek historian from the first century BC), in Egypt Orpheus completed his training in the fields of theology and religious cults. "This information must be seen as an encoding of the worship of the Sun God, who became the leading deity in Egypt towards the middle of the second millennium BC," (Valery Fol, *Orpheus the Thracian*, 2008).

The professor avoided encouraging young scholars who espoused extreme positions so as to further their own careers. He was irritated with his daughter for rushing to link up contradictory facts in illogical yet intriguing combinations. To his mind, they sounded so improbable that he preferred to put them down to pure coincidence.

"But if we accept that the Meandrites didn't leave our lands," Vera persisted, "perhaps some of them managed to hide themselves away somewhere… in secret… And that's why we have hundreds of stone engravings in Bulgaria with ancient symbols we still haven't deciphered."

The professor poured himself more tea from the porcelain teapot and gave a strained smile. Vera stared down at his beat-up, thick-soled shoes and his shabby beige pants so favored by her father and the entire older generation of archaeologists. They were held up by a worn-out, fraying belt. The professor topped off the ensemble with a baggy eyesore of a blue sweater that he always wore on cold days. At that moment, acute fondness for the elderly man washed over her.

"The similarities in the signs might be due to parallels in the societies' development during comparable historical periods. In any case, there are thousands of examples of Sumerian and Egyptian writing, while only ten examples from the extinct Meandrite civilization with its undeciphered pictograms have been found," he added curtly.

"Actually, there may be more for all we know…. Just imagine how many artifacts may have been destroyed or stolen by thieves and collectors! We even saw several in the basement of the chateau today… And you yourself told me that there are at least six tablets with symbols from Chalcolithic cultures in private collections. Weren't you given one as a present? Didn't the famous archeologist Professor Ovcharov get one as well? Others will turn up, you'll see."

The professor was silent, hesitant as to how to answer.

"The Nameless Tablet has disappeared," he told her quietly. "Before I even got a chance to catalogue it."

"What do you mean, 'disappeared'?" Vera asked him and pearls of sweat appeared on her forehead. She tried to look surprised, but her efforts only gave her away. She didn't dare look at her father – any outside observer would have immediately realized she was hiding something.

"I got a call from the museum," he replied, "just as we were leaving the embassy to go to the chateau. Someone took it from the display case in my study."

"But how? Did they take anything else?"

"No, only the tablet."

A woman's scream shattered the nighttime silence. It came from the forest – the only house in that direction belonged to the caretaker. Vera pressed her nose to the window to see what the commotion was about.

Tense voices buzzed in the corridor. A clamor arose outside in front of the hotel. The professor and Vera ran down to the ground floor. The innkeeper was already standing at the door holding a hunting rifle. Most of the Bulgarian group was gathered outside, talking excitedly.

"Did you hear it as well?" the innkeeper asked.

Vera and her father both nodded.

"I heard just one scream, then nothing more," he added, frightened.

"Let's go see what's going on!" Kuzmanov suggested. "I swear it sounded like a scream."

"There are ghosts in these parts."

"And do they make trouble?" Kuzmanov didn't believe in phantoms – although he would have loved to meet one.

They all ran together towards Monsieur Marten's house. When they arrived, the front door flew open, revealing Marten's wife standing there with a suitcase in her hand. She eyed them fearfully, then silently pointed to the upper floor of the house.

"This is one of those nights when I miss being in town," she announced angrily, as if someone had demanded an explanation.

She darted toward the pick-up parked in front of the house. She threw her suitcase into the truck's rusty bed and gunned the engine.

Meanwhile, the innkeeper had barged into the house. His tense footsteps echoed on the wooden floors and shook the entire structure. He reappeared a few minutes later.

"All clear," he declared.

The group headed for the forest. They divided into pairs and disappeared into the maze of paths and trees. Vera stayed with her father. Their shoes crunched on the freshly fallen snow, while the silence magnified the echoes of distant voices and the crackling of broken branches. Occasionally they heard drunken shouts from the inn. Vera grasped her father's arm for support. They both tried to protect their faces from the prickly branches.

Finally they came out onto a well-trod path. As the professor pointed his flashlight down it, Vera jumped with fright. A silhouette loomed in front of them – and was heading straight for them. They stood frozen to the spot, not daring to breathe. The shadow took on the shape of a husky man. A face appeared – that of Monsieur Marten. It was expressionless, cold and pale, half-hidden in the hood of his coat. He stared at them as he drew closer. The professor shined the flashlight in his eyes.

"No point this at me!" Marten shouted in broken English.

"What's going on here? We heard a scream!"

"Sometimes forest talks," the caretaker replied unperturbed. "No go any deeper into forest. You get lost."

Vera and her father had no idea how to react.

"Give me flashlight. I show you the way back." As Monsieur Marten reached out for the flashlight, his arm peeked out of his sleeve for a moment, revealing a tattoo on his wrist. Vera only caught a glimpse, but she was sure that it was a blue meander framed by an octagonal star. She had never seen the two symbols combined before.

She glanced at her watch. It was already past one o'clock.

COLLECTORS

Page 418 began with the history of Babylon, which was founded by Nimrod (Genesis 10: 9, 10; 11:1-9). From the very beginning, the city symbolized a rejection of the new God and a challenge to His Will. The Tower of Babylon was a monument to apostasy, a citadel of revolt against the Keeper of the Heavens. The prophet Isaiah depicts Lucifer as the unseen king of Babylon (Isaiah 14:4, 12-14). The founders of Babylon intended to create a kingdom that would be completely independent of God. For this reason God decided to destroy the tower and cast its builders far and wide (Genesis 11:7, 8). The people suffered many trials and subjugation by foreign rulers.

Rome, the night of March 4

They met out in the open. When they were in Paris they used the eighth bridge over the Seine. Not even the tramps went there, since according to local legend it was the domain of strange shadows. They always chose windy, rainy nights when people covered their heads with hoods and umbrellas, so nobody can suspect their covered bodies and faces. They knew how they are different from people and learnt to hide their luminosity, skin and shapes. They chose times of the day when angry winds roared over the river, drowning out their words. They would whisper and read replies on one anothers' lips. Their modus operandi was rarely improved upon and never violated.

In Rome they used the Santoni family's castle and estate. The Santonis were an old Florentine clan who had moved to the city of the seven-headed serpent in the middle of the sixteenth century. Carlo Santoni founded an organization modeled after a brotherhood that had first appeared in Florence in 1200 and whose original purpose was to help the sick. Its black-hooded members also accompanied condemned prisoners to their executions and saw that they were properly sent off on their journey to the other world.[27] Santoni had broken away from the earlier fraternity in protest over some of its members' abuse of power. In Rome he used his family inheritance and rebuilt the organization in accordance with his own beliefs.

The Santoni Castle was located on a large estate on the outskirts of the city. High walls and iron gates protected its enormous green grounds. A guard was always stationed at the entrance ever since neighbors had poisoned the watchdogs. The local inhabitants exchanged terrifying stories about the castle. They were frightened by noises which they believed were part of secret rituals accompanied by strange music. Some even claimed to have seen dark shadows and ghostly emanations beyond the castle walls.

Today, two silhouettes entered the gates at dusk, passing beneath the eight-pointed star which gathered the last of the sun's fading rays.

They met in the inner courtyard, surrounded by ancient stone statues and tall, thin cypresses. Their shadows were unnaturally elongated and shimmered among the lily pads on the lake's surface.

---

[27] In the past, a similar mission had been carried out by a brotherhood known as *S. Giovanni Decollato* (St. John the Baptist), which had existed since the beginning of the 13th century. Evidence can also be found in documents from the Synod called in 1257 by the Bishop S. Cavalazzi (1250-1270), at which the decision was made to dissolve the brotherhood due to abuses committed by some of its members during public appearances. Prior to 1497, few documents about the organization exist. Their primary function was to help the sick, but they also accompanied condemned prisoners to their executions wearing black hoods and were responsible for funeral rites. In 1579 the Roman brotherhood joined the Florentine organization, receiving equal rights and privileges. It is assumed that some members later split off and formed their own, smaller organizations.

Dressed in long, hooded cloaks, the two figures did not seem to notice the heavy drops of rain pelting their heads and splashing into the water, forming circles on the surface. A mist suffocated the dusk like a gray sponge, choking off even the moon-lit breeze.

"I'm concerned about the manuscript," the Incorporeal One began.

"What about it?"

"A man, an eminent German historian, went to the library last month to look for it. He spent all day studying it... Perhaps it's time to change its storage place."

"Why don't we just take it? Temporarily."

"No, it's the only way back," the Incorporeal One replied. "Anything could happen to us, we can't allow the return path to close."

"So then rip out the first few pages. There are too many clues there."

"I will do so," the figure said from beneath his hood and fell silent. "But that's not all... An antique dealer in Burma is again trying to find a buyer for a golden tablet. It fits the description." He stopped to take a breath and continued in a lower voice. "They say he's an Englishman, one of those who has gone so native that he refers to the Old Continent as 'abroad.' General Hultau personally passed me this information."

"Is the tablet still in Burma?" the other shadow asked.

"Yes. Ancient texts are inscribed on both sides of it."

"The general will never forget what we did for him. How did he learn about the antique dealer?"

"The Englishman comes from a family of former colonial administrators. He tried to sell the piece in Europe but had problems with documentation... He must need the money," the Incorporeal One mused.

"Do you think it could really be the missing link? In Burma?" The other shade wondered aloud.

"We must investigate!"

"There's nothing we can do. Burma is ruled by a harsh military dictatorship."

"Our general will sort it out for us. If we can't get the golden tablet out of the country, we'll have to destroy it... I've already sent Ariman there."

"You're letting your very best agent go back?" The other shade's voice was tinged with fear. "He'll put two and two together..."

"He won't. Ariman has no past. He has no memories. He is simply a machine."

"Your best machine." The other voice melted away into the rumble of the pouring rain.

"If it is indeed the missing tablet, it must be destroyed as soon as possible! And recorded in the manuscript. And then we'll have no more use for our machine..."

"They are not yet ready to know."

THE MAENADS

Page 419 *began with Dionysus' words from Euripides'*
Bacchantes
Where a chorus of Maenads sings Orphic verses:
"Oh! happy that votary,
when from the hurrying revel-rout
he sinks to earth, in his holy robe of fawnskin,
chasing the goat to drink its blood,
a banquet sweet of flesh uncooked,
as he hastes to Phrygia's or to Libya's hills..."
The dance of the Maenads on the mountain slopes
was considered an escape from the burden of civilization
into the world of nonhuman beauty and freedom, of the
wind and the stars.

Vera woke up early with a headache and sore shoulders. She had an apple, yoghurt and coffee for breakfast. The tavern was empty again today – only the cigarette-drenched air hinted that people had been there the previous night. The innkeeper was resting his head heavily on the bar, fighting back persistent yawns, stretching his jaws like a Bengal tiger. The scent of last night's dinner wafted from the kitchen.

The mountain guide entered the smoky room.

"You're late!" Vera greeted him.

"Well, as far as I can see, you're the only one ready."

"Exactly – they're all waiting for someone to round them up. You could be that someone."

They had summoned the guide urgently to take the journalist, Vera and her father back to the embassy in Geneva. Professor Kandilov had to return to Sofia to organize an investigation into the theft. The Nameless Tablet was one of the most valuable artifacts he had come across, as it bore symbols from the vanished Balkan civilization. Some scholars even believed that such tablets were the key that would answer the complex question of how Egyptian and Sumerian civilizations were able to make such sudden progress out of nothing. Since no adequate explanation existed, all too many shysters pointed to this as proof of extra-terrestrial influence. The professor zealously promoted the idea that civilizations followed a natural evolutionary path and that the pottery clues from the Balkans could support this – Vera was indeed correct that they were the earliest such artifacts. But her father could not admit this publicly without jeopardizing all that he had achieved.

The innkeeper came over to Vera, his jaws stretching into another cavernous yawn. He stared coldly at the young woman and then fixed his eyes on the mountain guide.

"You're here already?" he asked with a tone of displeasure. He took a damp cloth out of this pocket and wiped the table top.

"We've got a difficult mountain crossing to make. A good breakfast is crucial," she replied.

Vera looked at her wristwatch with curiosity to see where the hands were. Her watch had the habit of hiding under her sleeve, but the simple act of glancing at it always gave her the sense that whatever she was waiting for was just about to happen.

"I've got a flight to catch this evening," she declared to the guide and left the restaurant.

Vera, her father, and Kiril said goodbye to Hristo Kuzmanov, who was staying behind to make an inventory of everything the state had inherited at the chateau. When the guide explained that the forecast promised good weather, they decided to return along the same path through the Alps.

The sun warmed them as they followed the horizon, while the thick spruce forest buffered them from the wind. The only sound was the crunching of their boots in the snow. The mountain path wound through the white, fluffy eiderdown. The sun's rays reflected off the pearly drifts, making them sparkle.

Vera put her sunglasses on to shield her eyes from the bright light. Again, she had let the others pass her up. Her gaze wandered over the imposing ridge of blue-grey peaks, which made her realize how ridiculous the stifling, everyday problems of her urban life were. After reaching the path's summit, they began climbing downward. Small patches of dense greenery began to appear, hinting at meadows hidden beneath the thick covering of snow. As if in step with their descent, a handful of white clouds appeared in the sky, chasing their own shadows and flitting over the mountain peaks. The narrow path wound through the pristine Swiss countryside. Through the distant haze, they caught sight of red-roofed mountain cottages huddled one on top of another.

Monsieur Marten's face popped into Vera's head. His unexpected appearance in the forest the previous night had scared her half to death. What had brought him out there in the middle of the night? He must have been there before they had even heard the scream. And when he saw Vera and her father he didn't want them to go any further into the woods – supposedly for their own safety. But she had heard the scream quite clearly – or was it someone sobbing? Marten seemed to be hiding something, he was always silent and avoided human contact. He even refused to let them take his picture – it was a miracle that the reporter had managed to snap a shot of his back. Monks and members of secret brotherhoods hid themselves from the rest of the world in just the same way.

Vera also recalled his tattoo. She tried to remember whether she had seen that combination of a meander and an eight-cornered star somewhere else, but drew a blank. She had seen a star within a star or an eight-pointed star with an equilateral cross, but not together with a meander. People don't just go around tattooing any old thing on their wrists, yet she couldn't make sense of it. In the end she decided that it didn't matter, since she would never see him again anyway.

She caught up with the others, who were in the middle of a conversation.

"Do you think you could get up to the chateau with a truck?" the professor asked the guide.

"From the French side, yes. Through Gex."

"You'll need more than one truck to haul out all the stuff accumulated over the years in all those different rooms."

"I heard you discovered something very valuable," the guide pried.

"How did you know? We only spent twenty-four hours there," the professor exclaimed in amazement, hoping the mountain guide wasn't referring to the clay figurines.

"You forget that we all know each other around here... Everything belongs to the castle," he said curtly and hurried on ahead.

The professor took this as a reproach for having taken the finds. He was perfectly aware that he had no right to do so. But after the loss of the precious tablet from the Sofia museum, these artifacts were the only ones that might support his theory.

"I can't allow such a treasure to lie rotting in a damp castle," he said in his defense.

The guide didn't answer. He didn't even turn around.

A small cloud floated between the sun and the earth, casting a shadow over the mountain path and the four figures wending their way through the maze of peaks and valleys.

"Vera, it's your turn," Kiril turned to her after completing a solo rendition of a Macedonian folk song.

"My turn for what?"

"Your turn to sing. That's what we said, right? We've each got to sing a song to help pass the time."

"That's what you said. I didn't agree to that," she replied coldly.

Vera slowed her pace, hoping to fall behind.

"You're always such a loner!" The reporter wouldn't leave her in peace. "Come on, there's no one around to hear you except for the mountains. Sing something!"

"I hate singing. I don't know any songs."

"Everyone knows at least one verse of something," the professor objected.

Vera scowled. She knew it would be more ridiculous to dig in her heels – she ought to just sing something and get it over with. She looked at the sky and tried to come up with a melody. Her lips moved and she began to sing "Little White Cloud" quietly. Gradually her voice became stronger and louder. The professor smiled and slowed down to hear her. Soon he was shoulder to shoulder with the journalist.

"What a marvelous voice… Your daughter sings very well!" Kiril said this as if obliged to mention it – as if the professor didn't know it already.

"She never sings. I can't believe she agreed," Kandilov replied.

And the little white cloud released the sun from its embrace.

By Their Eyes

Page 420 spoke of trafficking in antiquities. In Europe this practice reportedly began in the early twentieth century. Objects of value were smuggled around the globe and sold to the highest bidder. Some treasures reached the other side of the world – but never had a chance to gain notoriety as priceless artifacts, since they merely gathered dust on display in some millionaire's mansion or were locked away in a safe. Certain items that could change our understanding of human history could suffer such a fate. But "could" doesn't necessarily mean "will." In their search for more and more valuables to feed global demand, traffickers continue to excavate sites in the Balkans almost every day, dreaming of finally striking it rich... Someday...

Burma, Inlay Lake, 8 PM local time

At this hour the chilly air begins to descend from the mountains and melt into the heat, bringing with it the scent of the approaching night. The dusky curtain falls like ash over the lake and the houses until the shapes lose their outlines. Lights flicker in the grey haze, while the amorphous silence sharpens all sounds. The infinite indigo sky covers the land, swallowing up the day.

The boatman rhythmically punted the gondola over the muddy river bottom with a long pole, helping it along with his leg. His fluid movements revealed years of experience. His bony foot pressed the pedal attached to the rudder, his sinews rippled beneath his skin like ropes. His eyes focused mechanically on the foreign man's tattoo, on the left side of his neck, just below the line of his short hair. The boatman had never seen such a design.

 It resembled a rough spiral or a river wound around its own axis, ending in a snake's head. But this was no ordinary snake, but a fire-eyed serpent. Above its head hung a crescent of seven stars.

He took the pole out of the water and cleaned off the weeds wrapped around it. Then he lay it down in the boat. The small man with the straw hat bent down and quickly jerked the outboard motor's starter rope. The popping noise filled the night air.

The foreigner man stood motionless in the front of the boat. He didn't turn around, even when the reeking cloud of gasoline smoke enveloped him. He stared straight ahead as though searching for something. The prow of the boat crawled through the water, creating ripples and causing the reeds on the riverbank to sway. Swarms of frightened fireflies chased the purple glow, like footmen escorting the sun's final glimmer. Enormous mountainous ridges hunched in the distance, wrapped in misty cobwebs. At their feet the golden domes of ancient Buddhist temples sparkled.

The man with the tattoo wiped droplets of water from his face. The cold night wind pierced his body, which the sun had warmed during the day.

Ariman had done his research and knew the exact location of the Englishman's house. He would find it easily amongst the others. The local people lived on the water as in Venice. Instead of streets and cars they had canals and gondolas. The lake was famous throughout the country for its enormous tomato gardens, which didn't grow in soil like everywhere else in the world but in the center of the lake. It was a brilliant idea on the locals' part – to use every scrap of arable land available, and then some. They wove baskets which they filled with seaweed and planted their vegetable gardens in them.

Dusk faded into night. The gondola floated past an empty market. During the day it was so noisy that you couldn't hear your own voice, but now it was deserted. Here and there a lone boat loaded with souvenirs floated homewards. The water was quiet and calm. The reflections of infrequent lights from the windows glittered onto the water's mirror-like surface. A black cloud threatened to devour the moon in its smoking jaws.

At this moment, Ariman could sense within himself a soulless emptiness. An unfamiliar sensation. It growled in his throat, yet also contained a hint of something sweet which stopped him from hurrying to shake it off. Since his arrival in the country the previous evening he had felt strange and vulnerable. It was his first time there, yet the place felt less foreign to him than anywhere else he had been. Perhaps because of the silence and the simplicity of the local lifestyle. Or perhaps because the strict discipline of the ruling junta made him feel at home. Or perhaps because of those eyes....

There was something about the local people's faces that he recognized. Like the first day of a warm autumn – very familiar, very different and sweet, because you know how fleeting its beauty is. He looked into their eyes, examining their shapes, colors, expressions. They were almost like his, he thought. The broad smiles the people constantly wore on their faces captivated him, almost as if he had been hiding away a few such grins deep in his soul his whole life. And he had only spent one night in the country.

Ariman could see himself in them, yet they were very different from him. They were extremely small, wiry and emaciated, with sunburned skin. Their faces were flat and their eyes narrow. He, on the other hand, was almost twice as large as the locals. His skin was a pale white and his body muscular and strong. His nose was straight, his eyebrows thick… anyway, it didn't matter. He was leaving tomorrow. And before that, he would erase all memories.

The lake hotel's water garden

The boatman knew very few words in English. He couldn't ask the foreign man where he came from or what he was doing there. He knew only that bad times were ahead. Rumors were flying that the junta was preparing another crackdown on the monks, who still steadfastly opposed them. Much blood would be shed. Everyone except the foreigners feared for their lives.[28]

The man ordered him to stop. The boatman tied the gondola to one of the docks next to a lotus-filled garden with lily pads and long-legged herons.

The foreigner got out and tossed some money at his feet. It was a generous tip.

---

[28] Several months later, in September 2007, a violent revolution broke out in the country. The military junta slaughtered thousands of monks and threw their bodies into the jungles.

MADMEN AND ILLUSIONS

Page 421 began with a quotation from Shakespeare:
ANTIPHOLUS OF SYRACUSE:
Am I in earth, in heaven, or in hell?
Sleeping or waking? mad or well-advised?
Known unto these, and to myself disguised!
I'll say as they say and persever so,
And in this mist at all adventures go.
COURTEZAN
Now, out of doubt Antipholus is mad,

The Comedy of Errors by William Shakespeare

Geneva, March 5

After trudging along a rocky path through the Alpine peaks for more than two hours, the four hikers arrived at a paved road where a jeep was waiting to take them to the Bulgarian Embassy in Geneva. Exhausted, they piled into the car. Vera reluctantly sat next to her father, expecting him to start lecturing her again at any moment.

However, the thought of going to Moscow cheered her up. Her work in Sofia could wait – as could her problems. She would use the time now to think, to try to make sense of the confused jigsaw puzzle that was her life, before the pieces scattered out of control. From a distance she could see the shapes more clearly, while in the middle of them she felt lost.

Sometimes she felt that the most exhilarating parts of her life were her expectations about future events, painstakingly embellished with the characters and outcomes of her own choosing. Vera was experienced enough to know that none of what she imagined ever came true; nevertheless, life without such expectations would be nothing but a vicious circle. Even if nothing ever happened and she were left only with her illusions, at least they were life's most beautiful side.

The professor was silent. He sat unmoving in the car, his chin in his hands, staring out the window. Even though Vera was irritated with him, she couldn't help but sense that she had said something to upset him. She decided to break the silence – and spent a few minutes wondering how to begin, since his eyebrows were moving together threateningly, forming a prominent outcrop over his nose.

"Will you let me take pictures of the clay artifacts?" she asked, twisting her lips into a timid smile.

"Why are you so interested in them?"

"Because… the symbols engraved on them might be the oldest form of writing in the world. Just imagine if they really are different from the originals in the museum!"

The professor crossed his arms soberly. His expression remained anxious.

"There are prehistory experts who will look into that," he replied coldly.

"But what if these objects disappear as well?" she added, although the moment she uttered the words she regretted them.

Her father took off his glasses, closed his eyes and rubbed his furrowed brow. He may as well have been trying to rub out Vera's line of thought. She scowled. Months ago when she had been planning to steal the Nameless Tablet from the museum, she had never imagined that her father would take it so seriously. But she still didn't blame herself, since as far as she was concerned the whole thing was nothing more than a game. She believed that people decide for themselves when to grow up – perhaps when they forget how to play games anymore and start taking everything too seriously. In any case, being grown-up wasn't a matter of counting years. Since for Vera, thrill-seeking was the name of the game and things were still somehow make-believe and fixable, she figured she was allowed to remain in a world where everything was possible. Now, however, she realized that for her father, what had happened was no joke. It turned out that the world had at least two dimensions: the one made of her expectations and the other of everyone else's rules.

The road wound through icy gorges and rows of bluish peaks stretching back toward the horizon. Vera took her notebook out of her bag, capturing her wandering thoughts and letting them take shape on the paper. She often did this to scribble out unwanted thoughts with a mere wave of her hand. But the curvy road got in the way of her emotional exorcism – after about ten minutes she began to feel carsick, so she snapped her notebook shut and announced decisively: "I'll show you that the myth of Ark of Orpheus is not just a legend."

The professor sighed without taking his eyes off the wreath of mountain peaks.

"That's enough nonsense about arks, Vera" he said indifferently. "Archeology has only one thing in common with Indiana Jones. You know what that is?"

"What?"

"The fact that Indiana Jones calls himself an archeologist."

"Why don't you ever encourage me?" she asked angrily and turned towards the window. "Mom would have."

Kandilov stole a glance at his daughter. He could either get angry or try to understand her. He wanted to discover the reasons for her behavior. The most likely source of her stormy temper was that she had still not gotten over the loss of her mother. She hid her feelings behind the angry mask of an irresponsible young girl. So fragile and small, she looked as though she had never grown up. To him, she would always be the little girl who yanked at his hair through the bars of her crib. He took her hand uncertainly and squeezed it.

"Vera, I don't want to argue. Why don't you tell me about Kaloyan?"

"There's nothing to tell, really. We're getting married in October."

"Oh! Well, that's news! You didn't tell me!"

"I'm telling you now."

Kandilov turned to better see her face. She resembled her mother, but there was something else, something different, unfamiliar – that was his daughter. Vera had changed a lot since the death of the woman who had raised her. She had turned from a happy-go-lucky little girl into an insular and stubborn woman, bordering sometimes on rude. She had become merciless, most of all with herself. Her vulnerable, love-starved soul was locked behind stone walls of unrealized ambition and perfectionism. She was like an animal caught in the jaws of a trap, not made of iron but of her own feelings. And the more she tried to free herself of it, the more strongly it held her.

"As far as I can tell, this fact doesn't seem to have changed your life in any way," he noted.

"Why should a wedding change things? I like my life. And I like myself."

"That's the problem. When people are in love, they usually want their lives to change."

"You don't like Kaloyan, do you?"

"I've had dinner with him twice. I haven't really had the chance to get to know him. How long have you been living together?"

"We haven't been living together recently. We decided not to… before the wedding."

"You know best."

The jeep reached the centre of Geneva and stopped in front of the Bulgarian Embassy.

The chief secretary came out to greet the new arrivals with a rehearsed smile. He gave Vera and Kiril plane tickets for Sofia, adding, "Professor Kandilov, you'll have to stay the night here. Your flight to Moscow is tomorrow."

"Actually, I have to return to Bulgaria. There's been a robbery at the museum," he replied in a steely tone.

"I'll go to Moscow in your place," Vera whispered and smiled faintly, as if she hadn't dared believe until now that she would get to go to the most important archeological conference of the year.

Vera put her bag into the car that would take her to the hotel where she would spend the night before catching the first flight to Moscow.

"I'll see you in Sofia next week!" she told the group matter-of-factly and went to get in the car.

The professor tried hard not to show his disappointment. He didn't expect much, perhaps just a "thank you." Sometimes Vera could be unbearable. She picked fights with his every word and ridiculed his efforts to get close to her, as though she considered him the root of all her troubles. In order to avoid these tense exchanges, they hardly ever spoke to each other anymore. But that was no solution. He hoped that everything would pass with time and that a day would soon come when Vera would be the little girl he remembered before he went to work in Russia.

"Time passes quickly, Vera. All that remains are the seeds you plant in those few fleeting moments," her father said in reply.

He waited. Realizing she would not make the first move, he moved closer and touched her shoulder.

"I'm late," she shouted and ran towards the car.

The professor watched her. Before she got into the car, Vera stopped and looked him in the eye, as though once again regretting her coldness.

"I don't like being told what to do. You know that," she said in apology. "And anyway, I have no grand plans of becoming a professor."

Kandilov snatched his suitcase away from the chief secretary who had leaned over to help him with it. The professor personally carried it to the other car, bound for the airport. He had to use both hands to lift it, stooping under its weight. It was full of the clay artifacts that had to get to Sofia intact.

THE GOLDEN TRACE

*The text on **page 422** stated:*

"Dozens of ancient clay, stone and gold tablets are known to exist in private collections. Most of them have never been examined by scholars. Among them are a number of tablets found near the village of Gradeshnitsa dating to approximately 5500 BC, as well as others from Karanovo and Tartaria in Bulgaria and Vinca and Lepenski Vir in Serbia. They are thought to be traces of the First Civilization. The similarities between them as well as their dates indicate that they were left by a Balkan Eneolithic civilization that seems to have mysteriously disappeared. Some historians call it the 'Golden Age' of human history, since many important cultural developments arose during this time.[29] Although more than 400 artifacts with ancient symbols have been examined, they are still considered insufficient evidence to be officially accepted as messages in the first proto-script bequeathed to us by the First Civilization."

Burma, midnight

Ariman had been hiding in the house's shadow for several hours, sitting motionless in the wooden boat he had rented at the canal's mouth. He was camouflaged among the stilts rising out of the water to support the Englishman's home. The house seemed to be the

---

[29] A quotation from "An Ancient Civilization That Once Occupied Bulgarian Lands Speaks," on Bulgarian National Radio, on February 23, 2008.

sturdiest in the neighborhood, as if flaunting the fact that the man's father had been a wealthy colonialist. Ariman's eyes stared blindly into the black water. Eventually he heard steps coming from the shore. It sounded like a man stumbling.

Ariman peeked out of his hiding place and caught sight of a drunken man. He recognized the thin, hunched-over figure, whose long legs looked more like stilts themselves than limbs. He had blond, almost ginger-colored hair and a ruddy complexion. His eyes bulged like blue marbles behind his thick glasses. The Englishman staggered, dragging his feet along the path. He was so close that Ariman could follow his every movement. As he stepped onto the wooden boards of the platform, he coughed up thick phlegm and spat it into the water before going into the house.

Dawn was breaking, yet the dark clouds blanketing the sky didn't allow a single ray of light to reach the ground. Ariman took one last drag on his strong cigarette and stubbed it out on the edge of the boat. He didn't normally smoke. Yet when he entered the village he felt the need to stifle the screaming voices within himself. The place had a strange effect on him – it made him look for answers to questions he had never asked. He had been taught that questions are a weakness, just like fear, memories and intimacy. So he never permitted them.

He had bought the cigarette from the villager who had given him the boat. The boatman licked the edge of a square piece of paper, sprinkled it with sawdust and tobacco and rolled it up.

Ariman heard a child's voice from inside the house, followed by the command, "Go to bed!" Ariman waited a few more minutes. A child shouldn't have to witness this. Then he left his hiding spot, crept through the shadows alongside the wooden house, jumped onto the platform above and grabbed the door handle. He opened it quietly, holding his gun in his other hand.

It was quiet and dark inside. He went up the wooden staircase – he knew all the bedrooms were upstairs in these village houses. The boards creaked beneath his feet. When he reached the top he found a large open room. He entered and saw a mattress on the floor, heaped with entangled bodies. Ariman pressed the barrel of his gun to the Englishman's head and whispered, "Get up!" The man began helplessly flailing his arms, trying to scream. Ariman grabbed him by the collar and yanked him out of bed. The tiny woman next to him leapt up like a frightened fawn and scurried into the corner where the little boy was sleeping.

"Where's the golden tablet?" Ariman demanded.

"What... tablet?"

The stranger pressed the gun's muzzle to his throat. The ginger-haired man spluttered and began struggling again.

"Where's the tablet?" Ariman repeated.

"I haven't sold it... The local antique dealers want to know what the symbols mean..." he coughed violently. "Damn symbols... they're afraid of them. I only want two hundred dollars for it."

His breath reeked of cheap whisky. A red spider web of blood vessels veiled his eyes, while the lids drooped with exhaustion.

"I asked you where..." Ariman repeated, unmoved.

"Here, it's here... I wanted to sell it, but it's just junk. My father always thought it was valuable, so he kept it hidden." The disappointment rang in his voice. He hiccupped and rolled over.

Ariman grabbed the drunken man's shirt and pulled him closer. He stared coldly at him. Only now did the Englishman's whiskey-soaked brain register that there was a dangerous stranger in his house.

"What do you want from me?" He trembled.

"Why did your father hide it? Who was he hiding it from?" The question was unnecessary, yet Ariman asked it anyway.

"I told you... he thought it was valuable. He brought it with him from Europe," he said proudly. "He said he bought it from a private collector but always kept it locked in the safe. I can't sell it." He pondered this for a moment, then added, "Do you want to buy it?"

"Who have you shown it to?"

"Just a couple of antique dealers. My family needs money, but no one wants it. It's not from around here. I have to sell it in Europe."

Ariman looked around. The scuffed wooden floor. The huge room with simple furniture. And in the corner, the tiny woman. She was a local and looked frightened. Huddled into a ball, she held the little boy tightly in her arms. He couldn't have been more than five years old and was very thin. He was breathing quickly, not daring to move. "The boy shouldn't be here!" Ariman thought. His arms felt weak, as if the child had drained their power. He couldn't take his eyes off the tiny figure. He was neither Asian nor European, a half-breed.

Ariman himself had been called a half-breed as a child. He had heard the other kids taunting him. They didn't like his eyes... because they were different.

He looked into the mirror across from him. Foreign eyes in a foreign body. Ariman had always been different, always a foreigner. He didn't know who he was – and he didn't search, didn't ask. Discipline and order had given him everything he needed. If there was anything else, he didn't want to know about it.

"Daddy!" the little boy shouted.

Ariman looked away from the mirror and stared at the Englishman.

"Worthless drunk!" he whispered hoarsely. "Is that what you want the money for? Give me the tablet!"

The inebriated Englishman froze.

"But it's all I have left from my father!" he moaned.

Ariman pointed the gun at his head.

"Where is it?"

"Stop, Daddy! No!" the little boy screamed. His mother was squeezing his sinewy body in her arms.

Ariman once again felt the weakness in his arms. The little boy's voice was rekindling memories that his conscious mind had skillfully hidden.

"Where is it?" the intruder demanded.

"Under the bed!"

The Englishman turned to his wife and ordered, "Bring it to me!"

The woman put the little boy down. She walked barefoot over to the mattress on the wooden floor and felt around underneath it. The Englishman was shaking all over. She found something wrapped in handmade paper.

"Open it!" the gunman ordered.

The woman unwrapped the package. She, too, was surprised at the thin golden tablet, and eagerly ran her fingers over its surface. It wasn't very big, about four inches square and completely covered in strange hieroglyphics. She looked at her husband, her eyes filled with questions and reproach. Her face still showed traces of *thanaka*, the local cosmetic paste made from tree bark, which further emphasized her terror.

The woman gave the gold tablet to the stranger. She approached him slowly with her head bowed, like a Japanese geisha. He took it from her, wrapped it up again in the flowered paper and put it in his pocket. The woman ran to hide the little boy in her arms.

The stranger pointed the gun at the Englishman's head again. "No witnesses," he told himself.

Just then the little boy wriggled free of his mother's arms and rushed over to his father. He wrapped his arms around his legs and howled, "Daddy, daddy!"

"No witnesses!" Ariman repeated to himself to stifle the screams. But the little boy was pummeling his legs…

For a moment he saw darkness. And a stranger. The man wanted to hurt his mother. Did he do it? She was screaming. Someone grabbed his hand and led him away from there… the memory disappeared. It evaporated from his mind like someone else's recollection. He didn't know what had happened to the woman.

Ariman's arms fell to his sides, the gun pointed at the floor, as though no longer under his control.

He leapt out the window onto the rough wooden terrace and climbed down into the canal. He got into his motor boat and lost himself in a forest of lotus leaves. The rippling water made them look like dozens of black wings, flapping bodiless across the surface.

Somewhere in the distance he could hear a song. A light glowed from the window of one of the wooden houses. A mother was singing a lullaby to the child cradled in her arms. To his astonishment, Ariman recognized the song. His hand lay motionless on the outboard motor, powerless to start it.

The boat drifted amidst the tangle of rushes. He strained to hear every note of the song, feeling a lump forming in his throat. He didn't understand the language, yet he knew the words. He remembered them from somewhere.

> ...*Please bring me a froggie from the Meiktila River*
> *My little one speaks only of this.*
> *Please bring me his froggie,*
> *With its wide eyes and small body,*
> *Bring it back from the distant shores of Meiktila*[30]
> *To sing my little boy to sleep...*

The woman's voice disappeared amidst the birds' cries and the wind's hum.

Ariman's eyes glistened in the morning chill. He couldn't remember the beginning or end of the song. He didn't even know the name of the woman singing it. He couldn't hear the name of the child being rocked to sleep with it...

He started the motor. The boat putt-putted along the canal, its symmetrical wake rocking the reeds. The blossoms of the lilies and lotuses swayed in rhythm until they lazily unfurled their petals to soak up the sun's weak light. Brilliant white herons hopped from one foot to the other. The early-rising villagers began preparing their boats for the new day.

---

[30] This is one of the songs that mothers in Burma have used to lull their children to sleep since time immemorial (the excerpt here is only a small part of the full text). The song tells of one of Burma's most famous lakes, Meiktila, a favorite spot for all the country's kings. Today the lake faces serious ecological threats.

THE STOLEN GOD

Page 423 began with a quotation, "When Paul came to Athens, he took advantage of an altar inscribed by some superstitious person to the still dreaded although long-forgotten 'unknown god' of the place, in order to persuade by a clever rhetorical stratagem the 'pious' Athenian people, that they were already worshippers of that unknowable and 'wholly hidden' god of the Jews, whose true worship had only not yet been revealed to them by any prophet."

**From Orpheus the Fisher by Robert Eisler of the
Austrian Historical Institute, 1920, p. 56**

"You haven't told me what your book is about," Professor Kandilov reminded her.

Actually, you've never asked me, Vera thought to herself in her sleep.

"I'm glad you're finally interested. My book searches for the roots of the Orphic god, who, known by many different names over the centuries, has a more than four-thousand-year-old history. In fact, I'm now convinced that it's much longer than that."

"So you're recycling the well-known theory that the first Christians adapted an already existing faith for their own religious purposes?"

"Not just that. My question is: if the Christians borrowed their belief system from the Orpheans, then who did the Orpheans take it from? Historically, they cropped up out of nowhere in Thrace – right where the Meandrites had vanished two thousand years before. For centuries after their disappearance no one dared enter their lands. Actually, you're the one who got me interested in this hidden ancient civilization…"

"Hidden?"

"Well, since we don't have any evidence that they were killed off or destroyed, their culture must be hidden," Vera replied. "I find it curious that the Meandrites and the Thracians not only shared the same geographical homeland, but that they also revered a single God in similar ways – monotheism is considered a high level of development for any society. They worshipped the sun cult, the Holy Mother and the Son of God. I'm beginning to think that even Orpheus wasn't the author of this eternally recurring story, but that he himself borrowed it from somewhere, from someone else. I want to know who started it."

"Is it worth playing around with two religions?"

"Religions don't exist any more – only the sensationalistic exploitation of human hopes and our desperate need to believe in immortality. And in any case I'm not just comparing two religions, but studying eight religious concepts."

"And why are you doing this?"

"I told you – because of the need for an answer."

"I think it stems more from your need to rebel. You haven't forgiven me for leaving you. So now you see me as the embodiment of conservatism and rules in the academic establishment."

"You left her to die. Alone."

"No one told me she was sick."

Vera opened her eyes. She had been dreaming – and now the roaring of the airplane's engines filled her head, in chorus with the loud snoring coming from the seat behind her. Here and there, small shards of light shone from the ceiling above the seats where minds wandered sleeplessly while bodies leafed through magazines.

A stewardess was standing at her lonely post at the end of the dimly lit aisle. She stared into space while scenes from her life flipped through her head like filmstrips. The other stewardess prowled along the rows of firmly fastened-in passengers, on the lookout for troublemakers.

Vera glanced out the window. On her side of the plane, the sky was blossoming orange and purple, while on the other side she could just glimpse the sun scurrying beyond the horizon.

Three hours of timelessness. That's what the flight to Moscow was.

Funny how you start hearing the thoughts buzzing beneath your scalp when you're cut off from the earth, locked in a juddering metal box in the sky. Looking down, you glimpse the vortex of events and people frozen in a moment of eternity.

"Did I really say all that to him?" Vera was horrified. But no, it had been a dream. The professor hadn't asked about her ideas. And he never praised her. Vera doggedly kept her distance from him – because deep down she knew that she grasped at his words like a drowning man clutching a rope.

She looked at her watch. They would be landing in Moscow in thirty minutes.

Vera lay back in her seat and closed her eyes again. She was having trouble shaking her father's persistent image from her thoughts today. The moment they had parted yesterday, she realized she had been very cold to him, as if she had written him off as a parent entirely. Now remorse was gnawing away at her.

The plane shuddered. Vera's eyes flew open. They had hit a heavy patch of turbulence. The "fasten seatbelt" sign flashed on above her head. Tightening her belt, she tried to stay calm.

"Poor Dad!" she said to herself. "I keep waiting for him to find the right words to get me past my anger. But maybe he's the one who needs me…"

Her thoughts were interrupted by the pilot announcing their descent into Moscow.

LOOKING INWARD

Page 424 began with the verse:
"Enjoy experiencing that
which you have never before experienced!
From a mortal you are transformed into God!"

Verse from an Orphic text engraved on a golden tablet
from the Timpone Grande burial mound in Thurii, Italy.

Ariman hired a car to take him to the airport in Bagan. The trip took five hours even though it was less than 200 miles. The roads were dotted with potholes and in some places the asphalt had disintegrated entirely. They hadn't been repaired for more than a century – since the British colonialists had created the country's first transport network.

The road wound through mountain peaks echoing with the whine of chainsaws and the roar of trucks that lumbered along the roads like herds of dinosaurs with hundreds of tree trunks in their bellies. The poor villagers cut down the jungle to sell the timber to the whites, who made furniture, paper and other goods.

The mountains gave way to endless rice paddies that seemed to stretch off into the sky. Their steely-grey surfaces were dotted with millions of bright green tufts, which exhausted blackened fingers harvested grain by grain. Thanks to these precious white seeds, nature's generosity and human charity, Burma's extremely impoverished citizens managed to survive. Low levies divided the rice paddies into squares and also served as bridges allowing the villagers to gather the electric-green shoots. Hunched over with their pant legs rolled up, dozens of men and women waded like storks in the leaden marshes, as the white herons watched over them.

The car drove past a crowd of people wrapped in ankle-length shawls, all carrying something on their heads or shoulders – baskets of fruit, vegetables, dry grass, water. Some women were carrying children as well. Their faces were heavily daubed with *thanaka*. Despite the day's suffocating heat, they held their heads high and smiled at the strange foreigner in the car when their eyes met. At first Ariman hesitated. They had forbidden him from making contact with people. It was an unnecessary weakness, a distraction him from the mission that gave his life meaning – so they had taught him. But he soon began smiling back. They didn't know who he was. No one anywhere knew. He was always alone, like a ghost. However, in this country he realized that he had never asked why. Worse yet, he also realized there was no answer.

He saw three emaciated little boys wrapped in saffron robes. Ariman had gotten out of the car and was bending down to take a drink of water from a deep tub. The young Buddhist monks were carrying jugs filled with food gathered from the village to take to the monastery where they lived. One of the boys approached Ariman and offered him something from his dish. No one from the world of men had ever offered him anything.

His eyes glistened, his lips trembled. He wanted to thank the little boy with all the words bubbling up inside him, he wanted

Buddhist temples in the Bagan Valley

to give him something in exchange, but realized that besides the golden tablet in his backpack he had nothing else. The boy saw the tears in the man's eyes and ran away, frightened. Ariman regretted this display of weakness. He splashed cool water on his face and eyes and got back into the car to continue his journey to Bagan.

The road threaded through a thicket of spires – thousands of Buddhist temples underpinning the sky with their white stone and golden domes. The car stopped at the airport just outside the city. Ariman thanked the driver and paid him. He tossed his bag over his broad shoulders, clenching the sinews in his neck.

His telephone rang. There was only one person who could reach him here: the Incorporeal One.

"Where are you?" a familiar voice demanded.

"I'm about to fly out of Bagan," Ariman said, then added in a choked voice, "I completed my mission."

"Good. Now take the flight from Bangkok to Moscow."

"Today?"

"The first available flight. You'll find instructions in the safe at the airport."

"The usual combination?"

"The usual combination."

COMEDIES AND ERRORS

Page 425 *began with the following words:*
"In the Orphic religion, 'Once fallen, the soul cannot return to its true home,
the highest heaven, until after ten thousand years, divided into ten periods of a thousand years each, each period representing one incarnation and
the period of punishment or blessedness which must follow it.' The theme of wandering that is so prevalent in Orphic theology is also very much a theme of the play. The title of the play, A Comedy of Errors, can be read as "A Comedy of Wandering," since the word 'error' comes from the Latin errare, 'to wander.'"

Mather Walker, analyst of the works of William Shakespeare.

The plane dove sharply into the downy abyss. Vera watched anxiously as the aircraft plunged through the dense cloud layers.

The kindly looking stranger sitting next to her began fidgeting when he felt the plane descending. Best that he remain a stranger, Vera thought. She pressed her forehead to the glass and concentrated on the unfolding view. Only window seats allowed for privacy on a plane, hence the reason they were so fought-over. People ran from solitude in order to find it.

The city swam out of the haze. Moscow had always sounded so mythical and magnificent to Vera. At last she would see and experience it. But for some reason she felt fear rather than excitement.

After grabbing her last suitcase from the baggage claim, Vera followed the colorful crowd towards the exit. Her small frame bent under the weight of her bags. She stopped for a moment and set everything down on the floor. "What the hell am I doing?" – this worrisome thought flashed through her mind. She quickly stifled any misgivings with the argument that this was not the most appropriate moment to reconsider her plan. Somewhere out there, the director of the Bulgarian Cultural Institute was waiting for her with a sign reading, "Vera Kandilova." She would probably be surprised by how young Vera was – until she remembered who Vera's father was and who really should have been there in her place. Then the director would take her to the hotel to prepare for her lecture.

A few days earlier, Vera had called the director to let her know that she would be coming to the archaeological conference instead of Professor Kandilov. They had managed to get her an express visa and even suggested that she give a lecture on a subject of her choice at the Bulgarian Cultural Institute. They had already arranged for her father to meet with a select Bulgarian and Russian audience. When the institute staff realized Vera was also an archaeologist they insisted she come in his place and give a lecture, so as not to disappoint the guests.

After thinking it over briefly, Vera decided this would be the ideal opportunity not only to pad her resume, but also to test-drive her theory in public. She had used her free day in Geneva and the speedy Internet connection in a small café near the hotel to develop some of the new ideas which had come to her during the expedition to Chateau Jacques. Giving a lecture to a small circle in Moscow was the safest way to feel out public opinion. If her hypothesis was too extreme, she would get the message – without the criticism being reflected in the media or in academic circles.

Following the throng of people, Vera walked out of the cavernous arrival hall that echoed with unfamiliar languages and thumping luggage. She looked all around, hoping to spot a sign with her name on it while trying to hide her uncertainty. She had not warned them that she didn't speak Russian.

She finally saw the sign – and the diminutive woman with a fake smile standing behind it. The woman's hair was piled into an enormous 1960s-style beehive, cemented in place with a thick sheen of hair spray. A rainbow-colored face with blue and black highlighted eyes peeked out from beneath it.

Vera stared at her hands. Her fingernails were cut short and not manicured. She put down her suitcases and quickly pulled her disheveled hair into a pony tail after fishing an elastic band out of her pocket. She had not had time to put any lipstick on. The woman with the large bun and garish makeup began waving at her. Only then did Vera smile and walk towards her.

"Oh, are you Ms. Kandilova? You're so young!" the director sputtered.

That's what they all say – Vera thought and replied in her own defense: "I only look young!"

The woman smiled even more broadly in response, almost cracking the makeup around her eyes. She tucked the sign under her arm and grabbed one of Vera's suitcases. They walked together towards the exit, pushing their way through the dense crowd.

Outside they were met by a wine-colored Peugeot, which almost buckled under the weight of luggage and travelers. They fought their way through the Moscow traffic for three hours before the driver and director finally dropped Vera at the reception desk of the Bulgarian hotel behind the ambassador's residence.

Hidden Treasures

*This text was in the top right corner of **page 462**:*
"Few manage to follow the trail of symbols. Human logic is such that people rarely admit that they might not know that which they think they know. For this reason there are clues that do not need to be hidden – human logic can't even recognize them. Even faced with categorical evidence, people still refuse to admit that it was not the great Egyptian or Mycenaean Cretan civilizations which heavily influenced the Thracians but rather the predecessors of the Hidden People of Thrace, who millennia earlier had carried their knowledge to the south and east. A few of them vanished into their native lands, while others fled, pursued by the forces of Hades. Because when the Seven Stars are aligned in a crescent, the wind dies, the sun takes flight, the ashes glow and the shadows return..."

Source: scribbled out.

Moscow

Her room number was 909.

The key, gummed up by scotch tape, got stuck in the lock. Vera pulled the handle towards her to see if the key would turn more easily. The door creaked and opened.

She dragged her suitcase through the door. The wheels rumbled over the dusty carpet.

Vera found herself in a small room. To the left, a cheap desk stood snoozing, bare wires sticking out of the wall above it. To the right was the bed covered with a woolen, hand-woven Bulgarian blanket. She switched on the lights in the bathroom, which gleamed white and bare. There wasn't even a trace of used soap in the sink.

She went over to the window. The faded curtains gave off a whiff of time and untold stories. The cold winter air whistled into the room through the wide crack under the balcony door. In the distance she could see a deserted, puddle-soaked playground surrounded by enormous drab buildings. Like huge parallelograms with windows for people to live in. Above them, grey clouds strangled the sky.

For years she had dreamed of coming here. The thought of everything she had lived through as well as everything she hoped for had kept her going. But now she was beginning to come to terms with reality. Her expectations had turned into sandcastles that the sun had dried into dust. And in her heart there was a gnawing emptiness, as though someone had set up a sticky net to trap any wings searching around in the darkness. Reality always differs from our expectations – but the later we realize it, the better. Without hope, we are lost.

Vera was shivering with cold. She wrapped herself in her coat and found a towel in the bathroom to stuff under the balcony door to stop the draft. She huddled on the floor, hugging her knees to her chest. She leaned her back against the barely warm radiator and stared at the wall in front her. A wave of fear suddenly overcame her, that shapeless fear which imperceptibly creeps under the fingernails and seeps into the flesh. Especially when the walls close in and the air fills with silence – a moment later the dust of wild crocuses envelops you . Robbed of the strength to remain within yourself, your only salvation is to go to sleep or take off running blindly.

Vera picked up her cell phone and scrolled through the contact list. When she found the name she was looking for, she dialed the number.

114

"What time do you finish work?" she asked.

"Six-thirty."

"Can I see you today? Please say yes!"

"How about eight o'clock at the Hotel Metropol?"

"See you there."

Vera hurried out of the Bulgarian Embassy onto the wide street. It was empty except for the lone soldier in front of the residence. She started waving at passing cars. The woman at the reception had explained to Vera that in Moscow almost no one uses taxis – if you need a car, you simply stand at the edge of the road and flag one down. Almost every car doubles as a private taxi. Vera couldn't believe it, but gave it a try anyway. A few short minutes later, a shiny white Lada pulled in front of her. She showed the driver the address she wanted to go to. He nodded and said, "1,000 rubles." Vera hadn't yet realized this was far too steep a fare for that distance.

They were silent the whole way. The driver didn't bother wasting his breath. Neither of them had any idea who the person sitting next to them was or whose life they had casually intersected at that moment in time. They crossed the Moscow River. Vera had never seen such a wide river cutting through a city and found it unbelievably beautiful. As the car drove along its banks, she watched the dark coil meekly following the stone channel the megalopolis had relegated it to. The granite walls hugged the water, while the wide bridges' black shadows sliced through the flowing current at every kilometer. A lone ship sailed downstream, its passengers huddled under the awning. On the deck, the Russian flag flapped in the icy wind.

The white Lada stopped in front of the Karl Marx monument. The driver pointed at the beige building to the right, a simple edifice adorned with decorative trim, mosaics and stained glass. An elegant sign reading "Hotel Metropol" hung next to a propagandistic mosaic:

The dictatorship of the proletariat is capable of liberating people from the oppression of capital. – V. Lenin.

Vera gave the driver two 500 ruble notes and angrily opened the door. She didn't see the puddle and splashed into it – but didn't care too much about muddying up her shoes. She crossed the street and entered the hotel's revolving door. The warmth engulfed her body. She snapped her umbrella shut, leaving a trickle of water on the fine marble floor of the lobby.

A scowling security guard gestured for her to put her belongings in a plastic box and walk through the metal detector. Such scanners were everywhere in Moscow, even at the entrances to shop, museums, hotels and larger restaurants. Another uniformed security guard rummaged through her bag. Then he asked for her ID and hotel registration card. Vera showed him the invitation to the upcoming academic conference at the hotel and the man let her in. She left her wet coat in the cloakroom and went up the red-carpeted stairs to the foyer on the first floor.

It was sparkling, spacious, bright, and sumptuously decorated. On both sides of the staircase rose tall, gilded lamps, each topped with a cluster of brilliant bulbs. The unexpected change in décor made her eyes swim, lost in the details. Crystal chandeliers hung from the ceiling like giants' crowns encrusted with diamonds. The hall glowed with gold leaf, wood carving, granite, and white, green and red marble. Sharply dressed staff and bellboys rushed every which way. Even the marble underfoot shined so brightly that Vera hesitated to step on it for fear of slipping.

However, what most impressed her was not the hotel's opulence, but rather the whiff of tsarist grandeur spiced up with hints of a centuries-old history. The time-honored hotel had given shelter to so many figures from the past that it was almost a history museum itself.

After her eyes adjusted to the splendor, Vera continued on. Across from the long reception desk, there were a few tables, all occupied. At one of them sat a thin man in his fifties with graying hair and a thick beard. He was talking on his cell phone, yet the moment he saw Vera he waved. She went over to his table, her face lit up with a broad smile.

"Looks like they've beefed up security here. They must be expecting some very important guests," Vera commented as she shook the man's hand.

"Oh, that's actually quite normal. Muscovites constantly live under the threat of terrorist attacks. Is this your first time here?"

Vera nodded.

"Someone should take you on a tour of the city."

"Work first, play later…"

"So you finally managed to make it here!"

"I really wanted to – but things almost didn't work out as I had planned."

"Don't expect too much from the conference. In my opinion it's just for show," the bearded man confided. He had been the Bulgarian radio correspondent in Moscow for years. He lived in the embassy hostel and knew the city better than his hometown of Sofia.

"What do you mean?"

"A gesture to demonstrate the rekindling of Russian-German relations. They were quite frosty thanks to all the artwork stolen during the Second World War."

"I heard that many artifacts which haven't been seen for years will be on show. And that some of them are Bulgarian in origin."

"Are you interested in anything in particular?"

"Come to my lecture tomorrow and you'll find out. So, I take it you're interested in history?"

"It's just a hobby of mine."

"Here's the stuff you asked me for." Vera took some printed-out pages from her bag. "But don't let my father find out you got them from me."

"Thanks! This'll be very useful for my research."

"Tell me more about the exhibit."

"The press conference was today." The correspondent slowly sipped his beer, enjoying Vera's impatience. "The museum hinted that besides the German works, there are also Bulgarian treasures in the Russian archives. And one of the conference's focuses will be the treasure of Khan Kubrat. But there will also be other gold treasures belonging to Ancient Bulgarian nobles that Bulgarian scholars have never seen before."[31]

"Just think how many other artifacts exist that we have no clue about!" Vera exclaimed.

"Well, you'd better take pictures of them, since they'll soon be hidden away again."

"Do you think they'll ever be displayed in Bulgaria?"

"That was my question today. The organizers said that depends on the Bulgarians' initiative. In any case, the focus here will be on 700 objects taken from German bunkers during the war. They've been squirreled away in museum archives for the past sixty years."

"Do you know what exactly they are?"

---

[31] In March 2007, the Pushkin Museum opened a unique exhibit entitled "The Merovingian Era: Europe Without Borders." The exhibit's 1,300 items included the golden sword and scabbard of the founder of Greater Bulgaria, Khan Kubrat. These rank among the most important artifacts from the famous Malaya Pereshchepina hoard – the largest treasure from the seventh century AD, found in Eurasia. The Pushkin Museum exhibit also included other artifacts from this treasure, such as several richly ornamented clasps, jewelry and silver goblets, as well as golden treasures belonging to Ancient Bulgarian aristocrats that were previously unknown to Bulgarian scholars. One hoard, known in academic circles as the Borisovo Burial, found near Gelendzhik on the northern Black Sea coast, consisted of golden jewelry and warrior's armaments. During the seventh and eighth centuries, this area was the southern border of the Khazar khanate. The exhibit also displayed a unique find from the village of Morskoj Chulek along the Sea of Azov, which researchers believe to be the burial site of a prominent noblewoman of Bulgarian descent. Precious Byzantine jewelry belonging to an Ancient Bulgarian nobleman was also on display. This treasure was discovered in the Krasnodar Region. (*As described by Professor Nikolaj Ovcharov, a Bulgarian archeological expert who was one of thousands of visitors to the exhibit.*)

"In all, the Russians supposedly have almost 800 German pieces. Six hundred of them have been restored recently. Tomorrow the exhibit will include objects from Antiquity and the Middle Ages."

"Why do the Germans put up with this?" Vera asked in amazement.

"What do you expect them to do? They can't exactly declare war." He sipped his beer and continued. "This isn't the first time it's happened. There was another exhibit in 2005 called 'The Archaeology of War: Return from Oblivion.' They showed the first part of the collection, which had been amassed by the Berlin Museum since 1698. As far as we can tell, the Russian army carted it out of Berlin bomb shelters after the war."

The correspondent smiled, his eyes vanishing into two slits. The subject clearly amused him. However, he sensed that the young archaeologist was looking for something more specific.

"A lot of priceless works were taken during the war. Are you interested in anything in particular?"

"I'm looking for previously unknown artifacts, scenes and fragments showing the mythological heroes Orpheus and Dionysus."

"There was something... You'll have to check, Ms. Kandilova."

"Please, call me 'Vera,'" she said, certain that he would never actually do so.

For the next few moments, neither of them spoke. The correspondent took a few more sips of beer.

"What a cold, gloomy city," she said finally.

"It only looks that way," he replied. Seeing that she expected more, he added, "Don't pay attention to the veneer. Dig beneath it... Vera."

The correspondent constantly watched the other visitors at the hotel and sipped his beer. He hadn't ordered anything else. Moscow was an expensive city – and the Metropol was one of the most expensive hotels. The Bulgarians who lived here only shopped in certain stores and usually did their entertaining at home. They rarely allowed themselves the luxury of dining out.

He stared at Vera as if trying to read any final questions in her face, then said: "It's time for me to be going. I can give you a ride back, if you'd like."

"It's still early. I'll stay a while," she replied decisively.

"Well, have a good night, then."

He shook her hand, smiled politely and headed for the exit. Vera looked around. She was the only woman sitting in the armchairs in the foyer. This didn't bother her – she preferred male company.

Misunderstood

Page 427 was about the other world.
"Don Quixote believes in a reality he has read about in books. This reality is generally called Chivalry. A careful reading reveals the Chivalry of Don Quixote is that of the Quest for the Holy Grail. An understanding of the Grail Quest shows it dealt with the trials, ordeals, and adventures of Initiatism. Initiates are people who have escaped, or are escaping from the shadow world. Ordinary people have only heard about these people in books. Initiates undergo certain trials and ordeals that enable them to develop latent inner faculties that move their lives from the 'shadow world' into the real world. Compared with their world the life of ordinary man is a life of madness in a world of illusion. But to ordinary man accounts of their world are tales of imagination by writers of fiction, and people who think they are real are mad. Dionysus was thought to bring madness because he symbolizes the introduction of the elevated 'self' into the lower world."

Source: Mather Walker

Vera looked at her watch and felt relieved. It was already ten-thirty. The day had flown by, but it was still too early to return to her cold room. She looked around.

It was too bright here. She walked around the foyer, examining it like a museum exhibit. And every detail deserved her attention, preserving within itself a glimpse of eternity.

At the far end of the room she noticed an elevator. The doors were covered in exquisite stained glass, while a resplendent crystal

121

chandelier hung from the ceiling above it. As she got closer, she spotted another smaller room next door. Drawn by the dimmed lighting, she went in.

The room, finished in rich mahogany, was almost empty. In the center stood two antique tables surrounded by leather armchairs. A pair of blackish-red columns framed the U-shaped marble bar. Above its shortest side, a built-in clock ticked away, its hands tirelessly racing around with time in furious pursuit.

Vera sat down on a high stool beneath the clock and ordered a whisky. A single. She lit a cigarette and exhaled the first drag with pleasure. Her eyes followed the bartender's every move. He was expertly pouring beer into large glasses and scurrying around behind the bar. Her thoughts were occupied with the forthcoming exhibit and the opportunities it offered. The ominous feeling that had seized her in her gloomy hotel room had faded.

Her gaze unwittingly stopped on a male figure on the right side of the bar. When she had sat down at the bar she hadn't noticed anyone. The stranger seemed to be sunk in his own thoughts. Most likely a foreigner. The elongated shape of his pensive, cold eyes was unusual for a Caucasian, while his skin seemed unnaturally pale for his dark hair and muscular body. His eyebrows furrowed forbiddingly. An old scar ran from his hair line down his forehead. He was not looking at her. Or the bartender. The only thing he seemed to want was to isolate himself in timelessness.

When Vera realized she wanted the man to look at her, she felt ashamed. Loneliness had the habit of making people addicted to other people's attention. Yet was it really loneliness if you sought out the isolation yourself? Perhaps only in the physical sense. Because while loneliness was pitiful, solitude was somber yet revitalizing. Vera enjoyed hearing her own thoughts in a haven of silence. She deliberately avoided noisy parties, which only underscored her inability to enjoy herself in generally accepted ways. She was always the one who stood out as different, but when no one else was around, this was less noticeable.

This is the bar at the Hotel Metropol in Moscow, where Ariman and Vera meet for the first time.

The heaviness in her chest gradually eased, erasing the traces of her disappointment, perhaps due to yet another shattered illusion. Time would wash it away. The problem, however, was that Vera was finding it harder and harder to trust anyone...

When Vera had met Kaloyan, he seemed like someone she could live with. Although she knew next to nothing about him, she decided that he fulfilled most of her criteria. At that time she still believed that she had to do things in a particular order to reach her goal. And so she followed her plan step by step – getting to know Kaloyan was part of it. Perhaps she had finally grown up now that she was gripped by the fear that her whole plan had been a mistake. And that any order in life existed in her head alone. No matter how many times she rearranged the pieces, she always ended up with a meaningful – albeit different – picture.

In time, Vera and Kaloyan got to know each other in intimate detail, but their everyday life disintegrated into habit. Bit by bit, they gnawed away at their carefully constructed future. The magic imperceptibly vanished amidst the days and months, the annoying habits and dirty socks, rehearsed phrases and repeated demands. Their love for imaginary images broke down in reality.

Their relationship had reached the point where everything about him irritated her so much that all she tried to do was avoid him.

She didn't miss him, only the lost illusion of eternal union. Because this time she realized its absolute impossibility. The ever-recurring tremor was fleeting, so it must be used wisely, sparingly, never entangled with the human need for eternity. People want desperately to believe that love and desire are beyond time's grasp, but wishes don't change facts.

The bartender dropped a glass, shattering it into a thousand invisible fragments. Startled, Vera jumped up from her stool. A couple sitting at a table at the far end of the room took this as their cue to go, leaving the bar nearly empty.

Vera hesitated a moment, then turned to the stranger and asked him in English: "Are you here for the conference?"

The man looked at her. His face showed no surprise or pleasure at her interest in him.

"I shall probably stay," he replied coldly without relaxing a single facial muscle.

His eyes held hers without a trace of unease. They were the strangest and most colorful she had ever seen. He didn't ask her who she was, where she came from or why she was alone. He looked back at the wall and sipped his drink intently, as if carefully studying it.

Vera glanced around for some movement in the room to distract her, but they were alone in the small space. The night air carried the barely audible melody of violins, all but lost in the auburn glow of the lights. The silence only sharpened the awkwardness she felt.

"I guess we haven't found the most happening bar in Moscow," she commented.

"That's the way I like it," the man said in a quiet, husky voice.

"I suppose you've only just arrived, too?"

He nodded. As if nothing mattered except the spot he was staring at. He took another sip from his drink with the same exaggerated concentration as before.

"Is your room too small as well?"

He didn't answer right away, then seemed to decide that silence would be too rude. "My room is fine."

"There are dark evenings when everything seems different. Have you ever noticed? The exhaustion is oppressive, without bringing you any rest."

"I'm not afraid of the dark."

"If you saw my room, you'd know what I mean."

A barely perceptible smile flitted across his lips. Vera noticed it but couldn't decipher its meaning.

"You don't like talking."

"It's not something I do often," he replied nonchalantly, without looking at her. He picked up his glass and finished his drink.

He'll order another one, Vera thought. *His coolness is an act.* She also tried to pretend she wasn't interested in his actions. The man took some money out of his wallet and stuffed it in the glass along with the bill.

"Are you staying at the hotel?" Vera quickly asked him.

"I haven't decided yet."

The man got up from the bar.

"Good night!" he added stiffly.

Then he looked away and walked towards the lobby.

THE REMNANTS OF HISTORY

Page 428 *had a photograph of the Orphic amulet from the 1909 Berlin Museum Catalogue. Despite its poor quality, the photo nevertheless offered proof of the amulet's existence. "Freke and Gandy's 1999 book contains a well-known 'green' photograph, in which a half-tone image of the original engraved stone amulet is shown in green. This raises a number of questions: (i) The object is greenish, indicating it is not hematite at all; (ii) cracks are visible in the object, which seem to suggest that it is made of ivory. In fact, hematite is fragile and would crumble if fractured in such a way; (iii) the engraved relief is depicted as raised, while from the 1909 catalogue we know that it is carved; (iv) in addition to everything, the image is decorated with an unfathomable wealth of chiaroscuro."*

Analysis of the amulet by senior research fellow L. Tsonev.

Muffled footsteps, slamming doors and snoring from the neighboring rooms were getting louder as daylight started to seep through the curtains. Someone coughed, a moment later a toilet flushed. A window opened and someone whistled the street a serenade. Outside in the hallway, the elevator marked comings and goings with the metallic clattering of its doors.

Dr. Franz Werder's first night in Moscow had not gone spectacularly well. He had registered for the conference at the last minute, so the only room his secretary had been able to find him was in a small hotel near the museum. Most of the conference attendees were staying at the Metropol where the sessions were being held. However, the director of the Berlin Museum refused to shell out for the exorbitant prices of Moscow's more acceptable hotels.

Werder heard a knock at his door. He had ordered his breakfast in the room since he didn't know when the car would arrive for him.

The insistent ringing of his telephone had awakened him. He recognized the anxious voice of the German minister of culture's chief-of-staff. So Minister Norman was here, too. It was the first time since the Second World War that such a high-ranking German statesman had been to Moscow for a cultural event. The minister's presence gave the media good reason to search for hidden agendas behind his visit to the museum.[32] German historians knew perfectly well what was missing from their museums and treasury bunkers. Over the years, they had organized a number of unofficial visits from Berlin to insist that the objects be returned. However, Russia's unfailing reply was that it was still gathering the necessary information. The truth was that sixty-two years after the end of the Second World War, hundreds of priceless treasures which had disappeared from Nazi Germany and were officially considered lost were hidden in archives in Moscow. The Russians did not dare put them on display for fear that the Germans might claim ownership.

Berlin's hard-line stance on "returning the trophies" had softened as Germany's economic interests in Russia grew – and finally changed completely when it came out that Russia's missing Amber Room might have been discovered in Germany.

---

[32] This once again refers to the exhibit "The Merovingian Era," which featured unique artifacts from the little-known period of the fifth to the eighth centuries AD. During this period, the barbarian Merovech founded the Frankish kingdom of the Merovingians, centered in what is now Belgium. This exhibit reunited for the first time in sixty years the more than 700 objects from German museums that now belonged to Russian collections following the so-called "transfer of objects of cultural value after the Second World War" (*Chavdar Stefanov, correspondent for the Bulgarian National Radio in Moscow, March 15, 2007*).

"I thought you'd already gone out!" the woman exclaimed in relief.

"At this time of the morning?" Dr. Werder had just glanced at the clock – it was barely seven o'clock.

"Minister Norman insists that you come to the meeting as an expert."

"What meeting?" The historian woke up.

"At the museum… a high-level, closed-door meeting. The minister received a letter last night and is putting a team together." The woman sounded out of breath and flustered. "He insisted you come."

"When?"

"Nine o'clock at the Pushkin Museum. A car will pick you up soon."

Franz Werder finished his breakfast and pushed the cart with the leftovers outside his door. He brushed his teeth again, combed his halo of hair and stood at the window waiting for the car.

The telephone rang again – the reception desk informing him that the car had arrived. He took his coat and left the room.

The traffic on the boulevard was flowing in the same direction as the river. Still half-asleep, Werder followed its twists and turns. For a moment, it reminded him of the river that surrounded the museum in Berlin – except the Moscow River seemed wider. The car turned near the recently restored Church of Christ the Savior – one of the wonders of Moscow, whose history was no less fantastic than its architecture.

The historian opened the window to enjoy the sight of the gleaming cathedral. The golden dome shimmered in the reflected sunlight. However, the icy wind made him retreat to the warmth of the car again.

The car stopped at the entrance to the museum. The driver opened the door for the scholar.

"They're expecting you," he said, pointing to the path through the courtyard.

Werder buttoned up his coat, not because of the cold, but rather to shore up his faltering confidence.

The silver firs and bushes were white with the fresh snow that had fallen overnight. The path had obviously just been swept. There were no visitors at the museum, since it was closed to the public on Monday. The heavy silence and perfect stillness gave the classical building a ghostly look. The towering rows of marble columns at the entrance resembled soldiers resigned to their duty – pensive, invincible, summoned by eternity.

Franz climbed the steps to the entrance. When he reached the ticket office, a museum employee directed him down the right-hand corridor. His ears caught the echo of distant voices, their serious tones floating from nearby rooms. As he passed beneath the vaulted remnants of a Catholic church, he heard someone calling his name.

"Dr. Werder! How good of you to come!" The minister smiled politely, yet looked anxious as he approached. Beads of sweat lined his brow.

He shook Werder's hand mechanically and resumed his conversation. There were three other Germans in the room, two of them obviously security guards for the high-ranking guest. Werder didn't recognize the other man, who was speaking to a small group of Russians and an elderly woman, the director of the Pushkin Museum. Werder had seen her at academic conferences. When their eyes met they nodded to each other. She approached Werder and in broken English invited him to sit down in one of a dozen chairs in the center of the room.

"Strange meeting," he thought to himself as he took his seat. With the exception of the silent security guards, the participants in the meeting had gathered in two groups. Their whispered conversations brought the shadows of the room's frozen statues to life. Echoes faded into the gloom. Two enormous iron horses ridden by metal knights flanked the murmuring circles. They looked so real that Werder half expected steam to billow from their nostrils and their hoofs to clatter on the marble floor. Opposite them, a naked Apollo waved to the horsemen with his broken arm. At the end of the room, two stone sarcophagi lay undisturbed. The frosted-glass ceiling above them illuminated the room with a fan of white light. The sign near the entrance beneath the church's arch read "The Italian Room."

In the hallway, the sound of marching boots grew louder. A uniformed Russian officer entered, slightly winded. He went over to Mr. Mihalkovich, the director of FACC,[33] and announced in a steely voice: "The artifacts have been arranged. The security systems have been disarmed. The guests may enter."

At that moment, the minister sat down next to Werder and whispered, "I want you to let me know which objects are the most valuable to Germany." He paused, then added, "And I want your guarantee that they really do belong to the Berlin Museum. Mistakes are unacceptable!"

"What on earth is going on here?" Franz asked excitedly.

"I'll explain later. For now just walk along with me and try to avoid any misunderstandings."

At that moment, the Russian officer left the room in another clatter of boots. His grey-green figure darted beneath the vault above the Golden Doors, like the ghost of a military maneuver from a century earlier. Werder trembled with excitement when he recognized the famous *Zolotie dveri*, the multi-faceted entrance

---

[33] The Russian Federal Agency for Culture and Cinematography.

arch from the St. Maria Church. Built in 1230, it had served the faithful for many centuries, yet here it was today, scorched and destroyed, adorning the Italian Room of a museum in Moscow. The delicate decorations on the smoke-stained stone depicted the "Adoration of the Virgin Mary." In one of the scenes, the Virgin Mary gives the baby Jesus a heavenly apple, symbolizing the redemption of original sin.

The officer stopped beneath the arch to wait for the visitors to catch up with him, seemingly indifferent to the tons of history hanging directly above his head.

Werder followed the minister closely, involuntarily eavesdropping on his conversation.

"I'm sorry, but the collection will not be allowed to go to Germany," the FACC director replied, his voice calm and dispassionate. "From here it will go to St. Petersburg. Then it will be returned to the archives."

A smug smile danced across his face. He couldn't hide his satisfaction at tweaking the Germans' noses. Even though the war was already several generations behind them, the deep-seated animosity between the two nations still lingered.

"But the German people have a right to see it. Seven hundred artifacts belong to the Berlin Museum. German scholars created the collection over many centuries," the minister interjected.

"We mustn't allow ourselves to get too sentimental. Just imagine if the Iraqis asked you to return Babylon Street[34] or the Egyptians demanded their mummies. Artifacts from the war belong to Russia by law."

---

[34] During the war in Iraq, the few remaining remnants of the legendary Babylon were seriously damaged. According to a report by a keeper at the British Museum, John Curtis, during 2003 and 2006 the city's ruins were fundamentally damaged – for example, the street paved 2,600 years earlier was destroyed when heavy military vehicles were driven over it. The Pergamon Museum in Berlin has a life-size reconstruction of this street, which reportedly incorporates many authentic materials, decorations and architectural elements excavated from Babylonian ruins and transported to Germany.

"According to your law! It's..." the minister almost said "absurd," but diplomacy prevented him. Instead, he quoted the law itself, "Are 'transferred objects of cultural value' really 'not subject to return'?"

"You have omitted to note that the law only refers to *Nazi* property," the Russian corrected him. "We have already returned a collection of paintings to the Hungarians. A private collection..."

"In return for a hefty infrastructure contract. Vested interest, perhaps?"

"Your sarcasm isn't helping. I invited you to today's meeting to try to reach a peaceful solution to the problem. In March of next year, President Putin will pass a law returning six disputed stained glass windows to Germany. The Soviet Army also transferred them to Russia at the end of the Second World War."[35]

"That's news to me!" The minister was genuinely surprised. He tried to conceal his excitement by nodding nonchalantly to Dr. Werder, who was pointing to an object in a glass case and making notes in his notebook. If the stained glass really was returned to Germany while he was still in office, his name would go down in history. "So why are you telling me? I would assume that information is still confidential."

"That's right. I'd like to offer you a deal."

While the two senior statesmen continued their tense exchange, Dr. Werder followed them in silence, excitedly inspecting the remnants of history locked beneath the alarmed glass cases. He felt as if he had stumbled across a precious time capsule, which, like a black hole, had gobbled up everything poured into it. Some of the artifacts had languished in Muscovite cellars for decades. Others had been assumed lost, so now their historical value had skyrocketed. If it were up to him, he would take everything back to Germany. The academic world had been searching for many of these objects for years, expecting them to leap out of some forgotten trunk. Their rediscovery would force

---

[35] On March 28, 2008, the Federation Council passed a special law signed by Vladimir Putin in which Russia officially returned to Germany the stained-glass windows from the St. Marienkirche in Frankfurt an der Oder, brought to the USSR after the Second World War.

scholars to rewrite the dusty histories now filling library shelves. Yet Franz knew that it would be impossible to take everything.

"I'm listening," Norman replied almost inaudibly.

"As a token of our good will, we might be able to add a few more artifacts to the law on the six stained glass windows… objects of particular value to you. There are a total of 947 pieces exhibits here. But the public only knows about 700, so I don't think anyone will notice if 250 of them disappear."

"Which 250 do you mean?"

"That's for you to say. The pieces that no one suspects even exist are right here before your eyes!" Mihalkovich gestured to the display cases. "Most of them were taken from private collections. Unsurprisingly, many soldiers and officers pinched a trophy or two here and there during the war. Fortunately, we have been able to purchase many of them."

"What do you want from us?" the minister asked anxiously.

"You know. The Amber Room and the *Graf Zeppelin.*"[36]

"Even if we had them, it wouldn't be an equal trade."

"You haven't seen everything yet!" Mihalkovich replied, rubbing his chin.

At that moment, Werder was staring rapt at one of the display cases, completely forgetting the high-ranking officials. His eyes were keenly studying an unprepossessing piece of reddish stone. Norman went over to him to ask him what it was.

"This is the Orphic amulet!" he whispered, as if fearing that his voice would break the spell and cause the vision to vanish. "It can't be! Yet it really is. I didn't think I would ever see it…"

---

[36] The German news magazine *Der Spiegel* reported that the wreckage of Hitler's aircraft-carrier, the *Graf Zeppelin*, discovered off the shore of Poland, could spark another Russia-German spat. According to sources at the German Defense Ministry, the *Graf Zeppelin* was Russian property and thus Berlin had no rights to it. At the war's end, the German warship, which was never actually used in battle, became one of the USSR's trophies. Present-day Russia has the legal rights to the ship, one of the biggest military legends of the twentieth century, according to the magazine (*Der Spiegel* 2008).

"What amulet?" Norman asked, confused.

Werder gestured to the minister to follow him to the other side of the glass case. He had no idea what the Russians knew about the miniature. If they had any inkling of its value, they would never return it.

"This is one of the most disputed and sought-after artifacts from the Bode Museum," Werder whispered in excitement. "You can't begin to imagine…"

"That's quite enough!" Norman interrupted. Any unnecessary excitement would raise the object's price. The minister turned to the FACC director and casually pointed at the case, "Put this medallion on the list."

"You have said nothing about our proposal," Mihalkovich persisted.

"As far as the ship is concerned, consider it done. But we do not have the Amber Room."[37]

"Our intelligence indicates that much of it has been discovered during excavations near the Czech border."

"That's just a rumor. Nothing has been confirmed," Norman replied drily.

---

[37] In 2008 in the village of Deutschneudorf in Saxony, an amateur German archeologist excavated nearly two tons of precious metals thought to be part of the Amber Room stolen from Russia by the Nazis. In 1716, King Friedrich I of Prussia gave the Amber Room to Peter the Great. It was installed in the Winter Palace in St. Petersburg, then moved to Tsarskoe Selo in 1755. During World War II, Hitler's forces transported the Amber Room to Königsberg; its subsequent fate remained a mystery. Some time before its rediscovery, *Der Spiegel* reported that elderly residents of Deutschneudorf remember how on April 9, 1945, a colonnade of military trucks appeared in the village, soldiers blocked off the area, and trunks were lowered into one of the abandoned mineshafts. The whole operation took two days. The English newspapers the *Times* and the *Daily Telegraph* claimed that special technology has shown that the valuables lie twenty meters underground (*from P. Stamenova*).

WHAT IF THE CROSS ISN'T A CROSS?

Page 429 *began with a string of cryptic symbols and the words: "The followers of the secret science of Kabbalah are united by the belief that God created the world with his Word and thus the correct interpretation of biblical texts may lead to a profound understanding of the deep truths of creation."*

The International Kabbalah Center, from On the Book of Zohar.

And the Word is in symbols and words. When read correctly, they can bring you closer to God. And when traced back through space and time they decode the path to and metamorphoses of the First Word..."

There were no blinds here either, so Vera woke up early again. When she heard the exhausted flapping of fishtails in the sky , she opened her eyes and got out of bed.

The director of the Cultural Institute arrived at 8:30 sharp in a small minivan. Vera and three Bulgarian journalists who had arrived to cover the conference were already waiting for her in front of the hotel, shivering in their winter coats. Despite the morning sun, the dense fog made the air a cobweb spun from millions of tiny droplets. The thick grey sky hovered close to the ground, its ashen dome lopping off at the fifth floor the two diplomatic skyscrapers next to the embassy.

The director waved to them into the vehicle. Vera thought the woman's hairstyle was more restrained today, even attractive. Vera, for her part, had painted her nails. The group got into the van and set off for the museum.

For more than two hours they suffered through "the ordeal," as the director facetiously called Moscow's traffic jams. The minivan eventually pulled up to the Pushkin Museum. Today was the exhibit's official opening, while the academic conference would begin the following day. The Bulgarian group sprinted through the galleries as if racing. Their schedule was hectic, made more so by the director's repeated reminders that time was pressing. They paused longest before a gold treasure thought to be Bulgarian.

Vera lost them in the antiquities hall. She had stopped to examine a red-figure bowl decorated with a scene of Hermes seated on a rock holding the baby Dionysus in his arms. Orpheus was often depicted in the same pose. Beneath the figures was a row of symbols that most scholars dismissed as "decorative." Although Vera had seen hundreds of vessels decorated with similar bands of meanders and crosses, she only now realized that they might have a hidden meaning – or at least the meaning she was looking for. She found herself in one of those moments when mute objects don't just speak, but scream, so quickly and loudly that you can't follow their logic. Vera whipped out her notebook and hurried to jot down her own racing thoughts. She copied down several combinations of symbols.

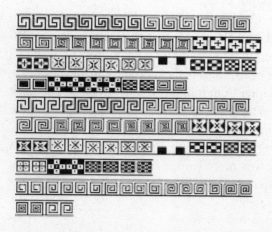

Various types of crosses and meanders found in ancient art

The bowl's pattern consisted of groups of three meanders broken up by squares with equilateral crosses inside them. The equilateral crosses were made up of four light and five dark squares.

The numbers hinted at the formula $5 + 4 + 3 = 12$, which, according to Orphic beliefs, represents the annual cycle. Every third cross, however, had five light squares against a background of four dark ones. Vera quickly calculated: three meanders plus five light squares or three dark crosses plus five light crosses equals eight. The equilateral crosses, also known as "eight-pointed crosses" were quite common in the ancient world and the Middle Ages. Yet until now Vera had never realized how ubiquitous they were in Orphic scenes. Why had the artists used eight-pointed, equilateral crosses? she wondered. And where the crosses were not eight-pointed, they were intersecting lines like a plus-sign, four-pointed with a dot in each of the four corners. Four plus four again equals eight.

Could these numbers mean anything? she asked herself excitedly. Why had she never thought of this? Moreover, the pattern of symbols varied from object to object, yet the diversity could not be attributed to the different schools that had created them. Could they be codes pointing to a cipher kept hidden from the unenlightened? Or was her conscious mind merely trying to imagine into existence evidence for the theory she had come up with in Switzerland: that the meander might be the symbolic link between the Meandrites and their descendents – whoever they might be. Perhaps it really was no coincidence that the ancient meander sign reappeared in Thrace along with Orphic images and themes.

At that moment, Vera realized that she could use the Meandrites' surviving ideas to figure out what had become of their civilization. In prehistory, ideas were captured in symbols – symbols that lived on, even while undergoing metamorphoses. If you trace the path backward through all those transformations, you should logically arrive at the original idea. Vera paged through her notebook – earlier she had copied down the Meandrites' most commonly used symbols, the ones on the artifacts discovered near Gradeshnitsa, Karanovo, Vinca, Lepenski Vir[38] and Tartaria.[39] The most frequently found symbols included the meander, the equilateral cross, mirror-image pairs of hooks joined at the base, the swastika, the spiral of eternity, the circle with a dot in it (a symbol of the Sun), and the anatomical heart, among others. And it was precisely this group of signs that made up the borders edging Orphic scenes in later art.

After another hour in Moscow traffic, the Bulgarians arrived at the Mausoleum. This stop stirred up the most excitement among the young, first-time visitors to Moscow – perhaps because it is the only place in the world where you can see a real mummy not hidden under layers of bandages or eroded by millennia. Lenin's diminutive mummy was such a huge tourist draw that the few lamenting the fate of his wretched soul remained voices in the wilderness. Who cares about a single soul's rest if millions line up to see his embalmed body? A body withered onto bones, like the emaciated corpse of a child with a reddish beard.

The minivan stopped at the entrance to Red Square. The passengers snapped open their umbrellas against the falling snow and quickly darted towards the square.

Vera fell behind once again, since the mummy didn't interest her. The snow alternated with icy rain. Her umbrella was useless against the wet eddies whipped by chaotic winds.

Once they reached Red Square, the group headed for the iron railings around the Mausoleum. The wet cobbles, lit up by flashing cameras, glistened like the night sky. Despite the terrible weather, tourists tirelessly snapped photos, recording their brief moments in the square for posterity.

None of the Bulgarians group noticed that Vera was still back at the square's entrance, studying the startling architecture with its

---

[38] In Serbia.
[39] In Romania.

millions of fiery red bricks. To the left, a small church huddled in the corner of the famous square, its blue-red exterior and golden dome hardly noticeable. Vera would have passed it up as well if she hadn't noticed the equilateral crosses lining its windows.

Intrigued, she went up the steps and slipped through the door of the Orthodox church. Inside, the low ceilings created a sense of comfort and warmth. The entrance opened onto two corridors. One led to the main nave where a priest was monotonously chanting a prayer, while the other encircled the sanctuary.

The shuffling crowd swept Vera down the right-hand corridor. The whispering, the movement and the heavy scent of incense swallowed her up.

"Excuse me, do you have a pencil?" a voice asked her in Russian.

Vera whirled around. A small woman in a headscarf was holding out her hand expectantly, like a beggar asking for a piece of bread. Vera mechanically waved her away and shuffled along with the crowd. One colorful icon caught her eye, then another and yet another. She felt the saints' eyes smiling on her from the walls, despite her impious behavior. The candles filled the air with smoke, making her lightheaded. She stood still for a moment, her body slicing like a knife through the stream of whispering, kerchiefed women. In Russia, all women were expected to cover their heads in a church.

The murmuring mass of women was stronger than Vera, she felt herself being drawn into the large nave. She felt a heaviness in her chest, while the thought gnawed at her: "Can they tell I'm not a believer?" She wondered whether she should go back to the little booth selling candles, but decided against it. Was it her fault that she didn't believe? She didn't want to become one of the herd, following along with everyone else without looking for a reason. She didn't believe, yet she was searching for the truth – which was much more difficult than simply lighting a candle and crossing herself in front of the smiling icons.

The heaviness suddenly turned to fear, freezing her to the spot and paralyzing her thoughts. She quickly turned around and pushed her way back toward the entrance, searching for the small woman, one of the many head scarves. Vera recognized her faded overcoat and tapped her on the shoulder. The woman had been watching her intently.

"Just a moment," Vera mumbled in Russian and rummaged through her purse for a pen.

Despite the snow outside, Vera felt herself sweating. The woman stood still and silent, her eyes growing wider and more demanding. Vera's fingers finally found the cold thin instrument, her trusty tool for the preservation of thoughts. She pressed it into the woman's hand.

The woman's smile revealed a row of rotting teeth. She tightened her headscarf and turned to the little desk against the wall and wrote her sick daughter's name on a scrap of paper. She limped towards a shabby box in the central nave and shoved the note into the slit onto a soft nest of hundreds of other pieces of paper. Then the woman sat down at the back of the church to wait for the priest to read the name of her child in his prayers, so it would be heard by God. During this whole time, her daughter would be home alone, waiting for her mother to return.

Vera didn't wait for her pen. As she turned to go, the first icon in the hallway caught her eye – teeming with dozens of miniature scenes from the New Testament, its brilliant colors were impossible to miss. But what grabbed Vera's attention was the decoration around the border. One of the symbols she had copied from the antique bowls in the museum was repeated here as well, hundreds of times. What had led her to this Orthodox church on Red Square today? Did some higher power want her to make a connection between the symbols?

Vera studied the pattern of symbols framing the myriad New Testament figures and scenes. One sign was constantly repeated – the equilateral cross with dots in each of the corners.

There it was again: a four-pointed cross + four dots.

The same sign divided Orphic symbols in ancient Thracian and Greek art. But was she making too much of the coincidence?

Was her own imagination – or worse yet, her own overwhelming desire for an answer – causing her to see nonexistent connections? Perhaps it was precisely because the answer always seemed to elude her that her conscious mind was looking for a way to twist the facts so as to outsmart it.

How was today different than any other day? Why should she suddenly see something that had existed for centuries? Why hadn't it happened yesterday or during the years she had studied every inch of the Archeological Museum in Sofia? Vera felt as if someone were laying out a labyrinth of meanings, leading her in an unknown direction from one hour to the next. Perhaps the maze had always been around her or in  her, but she could only now recognize its outlines. Perhaps this was the way people for millennia had invented the stories they believed in …

The woman with the headscarf tapped Vera on the shoulder and thrust the pen into her hand. She crossed herself quickly several times in front of the icon Vera was looking at and continued on her way. Vera followed her into the central nave as if hypnotized. Before going in, her gaze once again froze, this time on the colorful symbols painted on the arch leading to the sanctuary. The step-like arch had many layers, each decorated in a repeating pattern. She stopped trying to explain what was happening and just gave herself over to it. The ceiling swam with four of the Meandrites' most common symbols. Only now did she realize their significance to history and various civilizations.

They had first appeared in the earliest Neolithic-Chalcolythic culture on the Balkans, then later resurfaced in ancient mythology and Orphism. And now here they were – in an Orthodox church! Was it possible that the three religious and philosophical worldviews shared a hidden connection through the millennia? Or was it just that people were people regardless of the time or place, and these signs were simply inherent to the species?

Two years earlier, when Vera had begun collecting materials for her book, she had realized that her main argument was clearly exaggerated and artificial. She had focused on the secret link between two of the most popular religions in the world – Christianity and Orphism – since she thought the topic would easily lend itself to expansion. Hundreds of scholars around the world had written about it, but the idea was new to the general public. She also realized that at least half of her arguments had been whittled down to the bone and made to fit neatly in place with each other like a jigsaw puzzle. But then she saw the link with the mysterious disappearance of the Balkan civilization, which she called the "First Ones" or the "Meandrites." This gave the story the harmonious finale she had been searching for.

Yet something happened that she hadn't been expecting – with every new bit of evidence, the coincidences snowballed. If yesterday she had thought she controlled them, today she realized that the facts and coincidences had begun controlling her.

Everything had changed after her trip to Chateau Jacques. The proof she had never been looking for had begun appearing – leaping out before her eyes, insisting that she notice it. It was too indisputable, too categorical and unfamiliar for her to have imagined it. The clues logically followed one after another in the perfect order.

The stream of kerchiefed women kept dragging her along. She felt like an animal trapped in the middle of a stampeding herd. Struggling to keep her balance, Vera made her way to one of the columns of the archway. She leaned against its sturdy base and took out her camera. "Are they real?" she wondered. How was it possible that she, a mere student, who had gotten away with skipping so many lectures and courses scot-free thanks to her father's influence, had now glimpsed something that had been invisible to millions of eyes? Something long obscured, something fighting against time to avoid discovery. Yet it had burst into her mind unexpectedly.

At the beginning of her research, Vera had shored up the chaotic aspects of her theory with well-accepted scholarly concepts. When her argument seemed sufficiently original and streamlined, she would add in invented elements, thus transforming it into a notion that was logical yet unfamiliar to venerable academic circles. This little dose of fiction was crucial to avoid her theory being rejected from the outset; Vera had learned that scholars feared the unfamiliar and preferred keeping silent rather than admitting their uncertainty. Yet now, with every newly appearing sign, her idea was convincingly proving its existence – even the invented elements of it.

It was as if something or someone had permitted her to see the invisible: encoded messages in decorative patterns from prehistory, antiquity and the present day. The cipher was perfectly clear. It was so simple, yet so imperceptible. Her first thought when she saw the cross alongside the Orphic symbol was that it was merely a coincidence. However, this was not the usual Christian cross symbolizing the crucifixion – such an explanation was impossible, since the image had been created centuries before the story of the crucified Son of God was born. The circles in the four corners most likely symbolized the sun, which was at the basis of Orphism. One circle for each of the seasons.

What could the same pattern mean when used in every detail of an Orthodox Church? It could be seen in the decoration of the walls and the icons. Perhaps it was another clue that had survived through the centuries, albeit with its meaning altered in accordance with the tendencies of the culture it served. The cross was just the latest symbol borrowed into modern civilization – however, other civilizations had used it for more than 8,000 years.

Eight, eight, eight … it buzzed in her head like a fly. Vera hated talk of the Masons and Templars and dismissed stories about them as shallow sensationalism. However, their symbols were appearing to her uninvited. The Templars' symbol was known as the eight-pointed cross, while the eight-pointed star was a Masonic symbol. This detail disappointed her and for a moment the numeral lost its magic. Everything seemed to lead to them – but she didn't want them in her story.

The symbols Vera was pursuing were different – they dated back more than 7,500 years. What could have happened then to cause the first written signs to appear?[40] And why precisely in ancient Thrace? This was exactly the same time when certain scholars argue that the Great Flood deluged the lands around the Black Sea. The same time when the Meandrites' civilization arose in the Central Balkans. The Ancient Bulgarians described this time as the beginning in their calendar, which is considered the most accurate in the world. These coincidences could not be accidental.

This was The Beginning. From there, the first religious and philosophical concepts most likely began their development, preserved down to the present day in symbols and hidden messages, yet constantly modified by society's changing needs. Involuntarily, Vera recalled the axioms of the Word and God:

---

[40] Scholars still disagree as to the dating of the oldest symbols from the Balkans. In recent years, most have accepted the view that the artifacts date from around 5500 B.C. (*Lost Civilizations of the Stone Age*, R. Rudgley, p. 99)

144

In the beginning was the Word.
And God was in the Word.
And God is the Truth.
The Word is preserved in written symbols,
images and numbers...
In the Word is the truth, the path to God and the Beginning...

Ideas have always been transmitted through symbols.

Vera crossed herself – not because everyone was doing it, but as a subconscious reaction to her insuppressible excitement. She took a step back and squatted down to photograph the decorated column and archway. The camera quietly clicked. She looked around for witnesses to her transgression. Fear clouded her mind. She knew that photography was forbidden in the church.

The throng continuously pressed through the archways, like grains of sand trickling through an hourglass' waist. No one even for an instant suspected the significance of the colorful decorations that had captured Vera's attention.

She searched through her bag and pulled out a copy of the *Book of Symbols*. She had planned to quote from it at the lecture that evening. She opened to the page entitled "Cross." She stared at the entry's opening sentence: "The cross is one of the most ancient and widespread symbols in the cultural history of humanity. Its earliest images appear at the end of the fifth and the beginning of the fourth century BC..."

"That's absurd!" she whispered. "They're just grasping at answers."

She snapped the book shut. Only one week earlier, she had described in her notebook a number of carefully formed variants of crosses created by the Meandrites 5,000 years before Christ. A crucified man was even depicted on one of them.

Someone in the crowd bumped into her, sending her camera crashing to the floor. She looked around, frightened of being scolded for taking photographs of God's traces without permission.

Vera grabbed her camera and ran outside. She only now remembered the group she had come with and the director with the big hair, which was, in fact, quite tame today. She had last seen them hurrying towards the mausoleum.

She ran across the iron-gray Red Square.

They were still there, taking pictures in front of the red pyramidal temple containing the decaying body of Lenin.

In the Bowels of the Earth

Page 430 began with a tale about vanished traces, followed by the quotation:
"What makes the Thracians more unique than other nations is their belief in immortality, which we today call Thracian Orphism. Even in ancient times this created an enormous impression on observers and as Herodotus wrote about the Getae, they were immortalized. The Thracian people's and kings' belief dominated their lives and historical conduct. The question logically arises about the appearance and nature of this belief, which has been connected with the name of Orpheus since ancient times, as well as the question: who is Orpheus?"

From Orpheus the Thracian *by Viktor Fol, p. 22*

At this time of the day the sound of flapping fishtails, carried bodiless on the wind, had already died down. Yet there was still hope that tomorrow they would again swim up from the bottom of the abyss of the skies.

Vera was sitting on a chair next to the piano in the reading room, not daring to lift her eyes from the white pages covered in black letters. This made her look engrossed in her lecture. But she wasn't reading the words, she knew them by heart. She was trying not to look at the audience filing into the salon of the Bulgarian Cultural Institute in Moscow. If there were only a few people, she would be worried that her lecture had not sparked much interest. If the audience was large, on the other hand, all those pairs of eyes staring expectantly would paralyze her. She hated public appearances, because even the most sought-after eyes multiplied and became terrifying.

Vera had always found speaking to groups difficult. Her voice died away in her ringing ears and her thoughts evaporated, while her heart thumped in her chest and her body jittered. There were people who enjoyed being the center of attention, but she was not one of them. She tried to convince herself that the audience was just a collection of absolutely harmless eyes.

She couldn't resist the urge and looked up – just in time to see the ambassador and his wife walking over to her. Vera leapt from her seat and offered him her hand.

"Your Excellency, it's a honor to meet you! Thank you for the invitation."

"Hello, Vera, just call me Vladimir," he replied with a wink.

She looked at him, flustered. She almost said, "I can't," but decided that would sound naïve and ridiculous.

"My father… he wasn't able to come."

"That won't matter as long as your lecture is interesting. I must admit, 'The Ancient Traces of Orphism' sounds intriguing. Natalia and I will sit in the front row and say a few words…"

"Thank you!"

"There's no need to thank me," the ambassador hesitated for a moment before continuing. "You father, Professor Kandilov… must think about you a lot. It's difficult to live far away from your children… I understand him very well."

The professor and the ambassador had known each other since 1989, when they were young and moved in the circles of the political nomenclature of the time. People from that social stratum had preserved a sentimental sense of camaraderie during the turbulent years of political transition. They belonged to a common family, devastated by a typhoon that had flung refugees to all points of the compass.

The ambassador took his wife's arm and led her to the front row, next to the stage. Vera gazed after him, her eyes roving over the people taking their seats in the room.

148

An audience is most terrifying the moment you first have to get up and open your mouth. Once you pass that point of no return, it gets easier. Vera quickly subdued the shaking in her body and the uncertainty in her voice. She got so carried away by the subject matter that she completely forgot about the audience.

"There just might be more people in the world than we have realized," Vera argued passionately. "Recent discoveries provide new clues about the disappearance of an Eneolythic civilization in Thrace. While Bulgarian academics stick to safe theories, Western scholars have made audacious claims that the first primitive writing systems arose in the Central Balkans. And the proof is in our museums. We have evidence that in addition to letters and numbers, they were the first to discover gold and salt. They also created a calendar and medicine. They believed in rebirth and a single god. They built amazing stone temples, altars and tombs. Even the complexity of their funerals is surprising: men were buried face up, while women and children under eighteen were buried in a fetal position, confirming their belief in eternity. Textbooks have no name for them, but I call them the Meandrites, or the First Ones, since they are the earliest civilization we have evidence of. For some reason unknown to us, they disappeared, burning their temples and altars. In the fourth millennium, during the transition between the Chalcolythic and Bronze Ages, something happened in the territory of modern-day Bulgaria. We still don't know what that was. We only know that after the disappearance of this advanced ancient civilization, no other human culture lived in our lands for more than 1,000 years."

"How can you be sure that a small group of this disappeared civilization didn't remain in Thrace?" an audience member asked.

"One bit of proof comes from ceramics," Vera replied confidently. "As Professor Vasil Nikolov says, 'Ceramics are trendy.' They mark the appearance of a new culture and a new generation. After Thrace lay uninhabited for an entire millennium, the ceramics from new settlements were different than the earlier types. Unfortunately, the shapes become simpler and cruder. These new ceramics indicate that completely different people appeared during the Bronze Age. It is as though the Meandrites disappeared into the bowels of the earth. We have no information suggesting that they died out. And they vanished without a trace until the era of Orpheus. We don't know why, but the era of Orpheus witnessed a cultural renaissance and a renewed belief in the solar cult. The Thracians returned to the caves and rock temples, rediscovered exquisite gold-working and begin using the secret, ancient symbols of the First Ones. Another cause for amazement is the fact that several centuries after the disappearance of the Meandrites, the Egyptian and Cretan civilizations appeared. Surprisingly, their religions and cultures show a number of similarities with the vanished civilization, including their written symbols and solar cult. Moreover, one of the Cretan alphabets known as Linear A[41] uses almost forty percent of the disappeared civilization's symbols.[42] As you know, symbols and pictograms contain ideas.

---

[41] Linear A was a writing system used by the ancient inhabitants of the island of Crete. It was discovered in 1900 by Arthur Evans. There is also Linear B, which was deciphered in 1952 as an early form of Greek. Linear A has yet to be deciphered, despite the fact it has been partially transcribed using phonetic values from Linear B. Although the two writing systems share common symbols, the language behind Linear A remains unknown. The language has tentatively been labeled "Minoan" and is thought to have been spoken on Crete before the Mycenaean invasion around 1450 B.C., although this has not been proven.

[42] Maria Gimbutas was one of the first archeologists to posit a connection between Linear A and the symbols from the first Balkan civilization. The researcher H. Haarman of Helsinki University developed a chart that revealed the 100 percent correspondence between more than fifty symbols from the prehistoric Balkan civilization and Linear A, which developed later. Demonstrating the same phenomenon, the British anthropologist Richard Rudgley claims: "We must ask whether there are other links between the prehistoric symbols from the Balkans and those from other regions of the world. We can make a similar comparison with the symbols that appeared on ceramics and other artifacts in the Aegean world, primarily in Egypt, Troy and the Aegean island of Melos… But that would mean abandoning the idea that the 'high civilizations' that appeared 5,000 years ago in the Middle East were the first to develop writing systems. To the contrary, they were beaten to this achievement by the 'barbaric' prehistoric tribes of Old Europe" (*The Lost Civilizations of the Stone Age*, pp. 103-109).

The Egyptians' hieroglyphic system also has symbols used by the First Ones. They are assumed to have a similar meaning."

"Amazing!" cried two elderly women in the second row, who began whispering excitedly to each other.

Vera continued her presentation, changing the slide on the computer. A new image appeared on the screen: the meander.

"Do you recognize this symbol?" she asked.

"The Egyptian hieroglyph for 'temple,'" a young Russian Egyptologist called out from the front row. He had introduced himself to Vera only minutes before the lecture and mentioned that her father had taught him pre-history at Moscow University.

"Correct!" She smiled at him. "It later became the Egyptian letter 'X.' The spiral is also the symbol of immortality, the path toward perfection and eternity. All ideas fundamental to Orphism."

"Speaking of Orphism," the Egyptologist interrupted, "did you know that in the Northern Cretan dialect this symbol is pronounced *efrei* or *orfei*, depending on the region?"

Vera fell silent, unsure of how to respond. At that moment she was conscious only of her own stunned expression and the insufferable silence. Yet no words came to her. Her answer was that she had not come across this fact but that it confirmed her every word. Could it possibly be true? So it turns out that what

[meander symbol]		One of the most widely used decorative motives in
[meander symbol]	ervei erfei orfei	Temple , shrine (Coptic Bohairic Grammar, 6.3 Vocabulary 6)
[meander symbol] **h**		The Egyptian hieroglyph for "temple," "shelter," and "protector" The hieroglyph was later used for the letter "h" (in Cyrillic alphabet this is the letter "X", in Latin - "H")

she had been calling the "Orphic" symbol because it accompanied the Orphic messages and images was actually pronounced *orfei*! That was an enormous clue! The symbol which encapsulated the ideas of Orphism and which followed the deity through artwork, eras and religions also bore his name. And in an Egyptian dialect no less, the civilization which was the Meandrites' successor and which Orpheus revived in Thrace – the very same Orpheus who was believed to have studied in Egypt.

"You're right… that's very interesting," she said finally. "There is a similarity."

Vera flipped through the images on the screen, struggling to conceal her excitement. She showed them pictures of vessels, amphora and bowls with depictions of the Thracian singer. Each object had a band containing a pattern of uninterrupted meanders and crosses. Vera noted the dating of the symbols.

Silence followed, which was soon broken by a question from the rear of the hall.

"But if the symbol you're talking about really is connected with Orpheus, are you suggesting that he lived in the sixth millennium B.C.? The entire world knows that if he did exist, it was in the thirteenth or fourteenth century B.C."

"What if the entire world is wrong? What if we are just repeating the same mistake over and over again? There is no categorical evidence that Orpheus lived at precisely that time.[43] People have the extraordinary ability to believe what they want to

---

[43] "According to Pausanias (who lived in the second century A.D.), there were even two Orpheuses, the more ancient being Orpheus the Thracian, the more recent Orpheus the poet-singer. Herodotus also mentions two Orpheuses, the one who sailed on the *Argo* and Orpheus the Singer," writes V. Fol. From an inscription from the city of Paros, we can conclude that the "historical Orpheus" lived in the fourteenth century B.C. This date coincides with that given in the Suda Lexicon from the tenth century A.D. This conclusion can also be drawn from several vague legends, as well as from the oldest extant fresco of Orpheus dating to the thirteenth century B.C. However, in this work, Orpheus appears very dark-skinned, almost African. In any case, these traces do not provide sufficient evidence to prove when exactly the wise man, poet and king Orpheus lived.

believe. Take the legendary city of Troy, for example. Every year thousands upon thousands of tourists visit the village where the ruins of Troy supposedly are. Yet not a single stone there provides categorical proof of this."

"So you believe that the tenets of Orphism are more than seven thousand years old?" the journalist clarified, obviously impressed.

"It's possible... just examine the pictograms left by the Meandrites."

"Why do you think this ancient civilization disappeared?" he asked with curiosity.

"There are a number of hypotheses: natural disasters, the Great Flood, invading hordes of Indo-Europeans or barbarians, religious reasons, cataclysms... But the truth is that we just don't know. The prehistoric inhabitants of Thrace took their most valuable possession – their knowledge – and scattered in different directions. Some of them no doubt remained... hidden," Vera stopped for a moment, as if hesitating, then added, "Perhaps that's the connection. If Orpheus indeed lived in the fourteenth century B.C., there is much evidence suggesting that he was the one who revived the Orphic beliefs of the people who had lived millennia before him. And that he was the cornerstone of the teachings, knowledge, religions and philosophies that are still alive today. Yet how could one person have learned all that? The previous millennium had been a knowledge vacuum, as empty as the land itself. I believe this is an important question. Some scholars claim that he gave writing systems to the Thracians and the Greeks. Others argue that he studied in Egypt with Moses and then passed on his wisdom to the Thracians, as Moses did to the Judeans. But this gives rise to yet another question: where did the Egyptians suddenly get this knowledge from?"

"No scholar is perfect!" the Egyptologist chimed in. "If we do not bravely admit that there are gaps in our knowledge of history, there is no way we can ever get closer to the truth."

Vera had been waiting to hear exactly these words.

After the lecture many people stayed behind to congratulate the young archaeologist, including the ambassador. He also praised Vera, albeit rather restrainedly since he had not understood much of the lecture.

"What led you to choose Thracian archaeology?" he asked her as they were leaving.

"It wasn't too difficult… All the legends and folk tales from our lands, the ancient symbols and myths about Orpheus, Eurydice, the young god Dionysus and the Lower Kingdoms are beautiful and thought provoking. But when I tried to explain them to myself the ideas got so mixed up…"

She was lying to him. It was better to lie than to admit that her choice was an attempt to escape the stifling shadow of her father's authority. She had always been interested in prehistory, but that was his turf. So she had had to choose a subject for her master's degree from a different field, any field, as long as it was sufficiently distant from her father's area of expertise. Vera needed space of her own where she could be good enough to overcome the phantom of his influence. But her passion for prehistory constantly echoed in her mind like the voice of a man drowning in a storm. Her thoughts were being dragged in unexpected directions, back into the little-understood epochs. With her current subject matter, the ancient past was once again looking for an opening through which to burrow its way back into her life.

UNDECIPHERED MESSAGES
FROM THE HIDDEN ONES

Page 431 began with a quotation from a leading Bulgarian archeologist, Professor Nikolaj Ovcharov: "What is most remarkable in both discoveries (from Perperikon[44]) is that they are the remnants of a writing system of a now vanished civilization. The Great Cretan Mycenaean culture (which appeared in the third millennium BC) was discovered by the eminent archaeologist, Arthur Evans, who conducted the first major excavations in the main city of Crete.... Linear A is still undeciphered and can be read only phonetically. It was connected with a cult and created to be read only by certain people."

**From Perperikon: The Civilization of the Rock
People, p. 98-99.**

"This alphabet (discovered in Pliska on stone tablets of unknown origin) was very complex, yet was used. It has many similar shapes that are barely distinguishable. It must be read with great attention."

**From The Alphabet of Pliska,
Cyrillic and Glagolitic by Professor V. Yonchev.**

When the guests had left the cultural center, absolute silence once again reigned in the old Muscovite building. The dull roar of cars on the boulevard replaced the buzzing of human voices.

---

[44] The ancient Thracian city of Perperikon is located in Bulgaria's Eastern Rhodope Mountains. The megalithic complex is thought to have been an important sacred site.

The cultural center was located in a spacious two-story house more than a century old, with fanciful architecture reminiscent of a castle. Its high ceilings were elaborately decorated with biblical scenes, while in one of the first-floor rooms, an elegant wood carving hung overhead. The director asked Vera to wait so they could leave together. Vera took advantage of the opportunity to take pictures of the frescoes and the wood carving, which would soon exist only on film. Rumors had it that the center had been sold to a Russian entrepreneur who was in a hurry to demolish it and build a shopping center in its place.

Vera went up the stairs and walked down the hallway. With every step the light grew dimmer and the hardwood floor creaked, as though the building itself was groaning. At the end of the hall she reached a wooden door standing slightly ajar. A thin stripe of light shined through the crack, the only source illuminating the corridor.

Vera reached the door and opened it carefully, not knowing what she might find. The first thing she saw was a huge wooden desk, its sides decorated with exquisitely carved lions' heads that fiercely watched over small drawers ideal for locking away secrets. Besides the desk and a matching bookcase, there was nothing else in the room to catch her eye.

Vera went over to the bookshelves. The millions of printed words consigned to eternity on the books' white pages drew her attention like a magnet. Her eyes mechanically scanned the titles and authors. She noticed a white book about letters. Its whole cover swam with symbols from the Glagolitic[45] and Cyrillic alphabets.

---

[45] The **Glagolitic alphabet,** also called *Glagolitsa,* is the oldest known Slavic alphabet, most likely created in the ninth century AD. The name was not coined until many centuries after its creation, and comes from the Old Slavic *glagolъ* „utterance" (also the origin of the Slavic name for the letter "G"). Since *glagolati* also means "to speak", *glagolitsa* is poetically referred to as „the marks that speak".

She opened the glass doors and pulled the book out. As she hungrily paged through it, her eyes fell on a forgotten symbol. Her breath caught, while her heart began to pound impatiently. It was a cross, another equilateral cross. Yet in this small book it was "A," the first letter of the Glagolitic alphabet. Vera was irritated with herself for not making this connection sooner – and she regretted skipping that epigraphy course on the Ancient Bulgarian alphabet and writing systems, which she had deemed too boring and trivial at the time. Instead, she had gone with her father on excavations to Nesebar.[46] He had arranged for her to get a passing grade at the end of the semester.

The book's glossy pages contained photographs and illustrations of Ancient Bulgarian letters and inscriptions discovered in the medieval cities of Pliska and Preslav.[47] The author repeatedly noted that the symbols carved into the stone blocks had not yet been dated, nor was it known who had written them. Most of the inscriptions were undeciphered. Some contained elements of Cyrillic and Glagolitic, while others resembled symbols used by the Meandrites. There were photographs of several stone columns, tablets and amulets decorated entirely in this nameless symbolic language.

"Perhaps some of the First Ones fled towards the sea," Vera thought. The Thracians were afraid of the open sea, but perhaps the people before them had not been. The next moment she decided she must be imagining it all. Perhaps she had reached that inevitable point at which the discoverer becomes obsessed with his own fantasies and starts making things up just to prove

---

[46] Nesebar is an ancient town on the Bulgarian Black Sea coast with a rich history and well-preserved archeological sites. Originally settled by Thracians, it became a Greek colony known as Mesembria in the sixth century B.C.

[47] Pliska, located in northwestern Bulgaria, was founded by Khan Asparukh and served as the capital of the First Bulgarian Kingdom between 681 and 893 A.D. Preslav, also in northwestern Bulgaria, was the capital of the First Bulgarian Empire from 893 to 972 A.D. and one of the most important cities of medieval Southeastern Europe.

his theory. Her maniacal pursuit and interpretation of clues about a long-lost civilization might just be a symptom of the serious illness that strikes hundreds of researchers. Eventually the desire to find the answer becomes so overpowering that it anesthetizes all remnants of sensible thought. You reach the stage where you find proof wherever you look. Even the greatest scholars fall prey to it – and history repeats their delusions until they find their way into textbooks as the truth.

Vera knew the symptoms well. As a young man her father had always seemed infected by this disease until one day the fever burned him up inside and he became a cautious academic, trusting books more than artifacts or his own eyes. Vera had promised herself to stop as soon as she felt the first symptoms. She had assumed it would be easy – if it were ever necessary at all.

The pages of the book whispered hysterically beneath her fingertips. The mysterious nameless symbols marched across the pages as if animated by a brilliant artist.

"But these symbols are real. I'm not making them up. And the coincidences are tangible. Anyone could see it, as long as they know what to look for," she told herself to stave off her doubts.

This "necessary knowledge" was exactly what made the connections. It led to the truth by recognizing the clues – or else paved the path to illusion. At the end of the first century, St. John had written his *Book of Revelation*, and since then thousands of believers and scholars had been trying to understand the exiled martyr's message, the hidden text within the text. The majority saw his writings as a complex cipher for the Apocalypse, the return of Christ and God's brilliant plan for revenge against Evil. Behind the letters and words, they looked for secret encoded messages. A minority considered the *Revelation* twaddle, the invention of a desperate old man who sought revenge on Rome and thus punished it with his only weapon – words. Despite the fact that not a single one of his prophecies had come true, people continued poring over its pages to discover hidden truths. Indeed, the human drive to sniff out secret messages and rediscover the world over and over again is insatiable.

Vera preferred to believe this was not a matter of concern for her.

Holding the book in her hands, she sat down in an armchair in the library. She couldn't stop turning the book's pages as if spellbound.

She reached page thirty-five, which showed the Module-Figure. This brilliant creation by Constantine the Philosopher[48] had always intrigued her – however, this historical invention was all but ignored by contemporary scholars. The figure consisted of a circle symmetrically divided by eight rays emanating from its center. The eight triangles formed in this way were in turn filled with eight circles

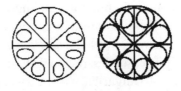

"Eight, eight, eight…" Vera whispered.

She recalled that the Constantine the Philosopher had based the Glagolitic alphabet on the Module-Figure, with each symbol being a part of the whole. The first letter "A" was the equilateral cross from the center. In the beginning was the Word. The Ancient Bulgarians' alphabet also began with this same "Word," but how was this possible, since their writing was invented before they were converted to Christianity?

---

[48] According to Professor Vasil Yonchev's academic works, the Module-Figure was invented by Constantine the Philosopher, who used it to create the Glagolitic letters at some time before 863 A.D. The outlines of the figure were taken from older unnamed written signs. "The Module-Figure is a philosophic-graphic synthesis of the symbol for the universe, made up of the basic elements: air, earth, water and fire" (Professor Svetlin Rusev).

What Vera saw when she turned to page forty made her realize that she had at last found the clue she was looking for.

"Finally!" she whispered, running her fingers over the red images.

The first of the two symbols on the page resembled the numeral "1," while the other was its mirror image. This was the first time Vera had seen a sign similar to those carved on the chests of the clay figures from Gradeshnitsa, the symbol she had mentioned in her lecture. Although she was not sure of its meaning, she supposed it signified something like "the organ of the soul" or "the wings of the soul."

Vera looked at the explanatory caption beneath the symmetrical figure, which read: "Runes carved in stone at Pliska."

She felt a chain tighten around her neck and leapt up from the chair. There must be another book about letters, something more detailed, since this one only hinted at an answer.

At the end of the shelf she saw a larger book with the Module-Figure on its cover. It was entitled *The Pliska Alphabet, Cyrillic and Glagolitic* by Professor Vasil Yonchev, one of the foremost researchers of Ancient Bulgarian writing systems. Vera grabbed the tome and feverishly flipped through it. On page seventeen she found what she needed: "The Main Letters of the First Pliska Alphabet and Their Sounds."

There were the two symbols again, side by side. The author noted that they were the Ancient Bulgarian letters "la" and "ra." It was almost too fantastic to be true – they not only resembled the two symbols on the figurines' chests, but were also placed next to each other in exactly the same way in this book. But what could they mean?

As she read, Vera kept telling herself that if she could trace the metamorphoses of these basic symbols, she could find the path back to the First Ones, to the Meandrites.

The two mirror-image runes, joined in a V, were found not only on the clay figures, but on everything meant to be preserved. Vera felt as if she had stumbled into a maze of meanings whose only exit was the answer. Could the Ancient Bulgarian alphabet possibly be connected to the Meandrites' Eneolythic symbols? Scholars still did not know who created the alphabet; they only knew that it was very complex, well thought-out and ancient.

Vera continued reading page seventeen:

> *Whose alphabet was this? The people who created it must have had a nation state and a strong government to be able to create an alphabet and introduce literacy. It was clearly not used as a direct basis for the Greek alphabet, yet like Glagolitic, which is based on the Pliska alphabet, it begins with an equilateral Greek cross. And this means that the alphabet was created for a Christian or converted people.*

> **From *The Pliska Alphabet, Cyrillic and Glagolitic* by Professor Vasil Yonchev**

"But as far as we know, this alphabet predates the Bulgarians' conversion to Christianity," Vera mused. Besides, wasn't the "Greek equilateral cross" or "Gammadion" a perfect copy of the cross found 4,000 years earlier in the culture of Gradeshnitsa?

Most people think too linearly, believing that less familiar things must have been borrowed from more familiar, better-known sources. To argue the opposite sounds absurd. It is much easier to say that the letter "A" in the Ancient Bulgarian alphabet was taken from the Greek cross under the influence of Christianity, rather than suggesting that a vanished ancient civilization had bequeathed its symbols and the hidden messages in them to future generations.

The author noted that one of the main letters found in the stone slabs at the Ancient Bulgarian capital, Pliska, was read as "Ra" or "Re" when a small triangle jutting out to the right was added on top of it.

Was it possible that the symbol drawn near the clay figures' hearts could mean "Re" or "Ra"? In Egypt, Re was the "real name

161

of God the Creator" and the "God above all Gods." The word *religion* is even thought to come from this root. Today, however, the god was more commonly known as "Ra."[49]

"Are you coming?" a woman's voice called insistently from the ground floor. "The car is about to leave!"

The voice yanked Vera's soul back from timelessness, hurling it with a painful thud onto the creaking floorboards. She couldn't take her eyes off the book. She had found the answer that had eluded her for so many years. Discovery was always like magic, a hundred times more powerful than even the instinct for self-preservation.

"What are you looking for?"

Vera glanced up. It was the director, her hair more bouffant than ever. But her face was calm, even tired.

"I don't really know," replied Vera. She didn't have the strength to think up a more plausible response.

"You have that glow of discovery about you!"

"I'm just curious…"

"Curiosity means you're looking for something."

The director plodded into the room and sat down next to her. She looked over the top of her glasses and smiled. Vera was overwhelmed by the urge to share her discovery with the woman.

"Two weeks ago I knew, I really did. But the symbols and accidental clues started taking me in an unexpected direction. There are traces everywhere. I feel like someone…"

"Looking for a snowflake in a snowstorm. I know."

Vera looked at the director in amazement and added: "In the beginning the clues all pointed out the path of the symbols'

---

[49] Egyptians have called the Sun God Ra (or Re) since ancient times. Ra was also believed to be the protector of all Egyptian gods who bore the title "Son of Re." The name Amun (Amon) was combined with Re as Amun-Re (Amon-Ra). In this form, the name means "The Hidden One" or "The Invisible One" (from Teodor Lekov's *The Religion of Ancient Egypt*). With time, the pronunciation Amon-Ra became dominant; hence, in the present day the Sun God is more commonly known as Ra.

metamorphoses, but now things are going in so many different directions that the logic has gotten completely jumbled."

"Perhaps because there isn't any logic. Nevertheless, there is a path to every truth. Some truths are so old and intertwined with our very being that they are undetectable."

Vera hesitated, then asked, "Can I take this book?"

"I have absolutely no need for it." The director stood up and looked at the bookcase, finally adding distractedly: "Just fill up the hole up with something else. Empty spaces bother me."

Afterwards they slowly walked down the dark corridor together and out to the waiting car.

BEFORE YOU LOSE
YOUR WAY

Page 432 began with a fairy tale and ended with the quotation:
"Beauty and the Beast is a fairy tale which, like a wild flower, appeared so unexpectedly that it gave rise to a sense of wonder that we had not noticed until that moment. The sense of mystery inherent in such a story is a universal application not only of the most important historical myths but also of the rituals where the myth is expressed or from which it might be extracted. The type of ritual and myth suitably representing this psychological experience is well expressed in the Greco-Roman religion of Dionysus and the religion of Orpheus which followed it. Both religions promulgate ritual enlightenment known as 'mysteries.'"

From "Orpheus and the Son of Man" in Symbols in Art **by Carl Jung, 1964, p. 134**

Absorbed in her own movements and the thought of how she must look from the outside, Vera quietly followed the hostess to the restaurant. As she passed under the high archway, she was drawn into the music and light and forgot her self-consciousness. Perhaps due to the décor's exaggerated elegance, the centuries-old stained glass windows that seemed to float in midair, and the blinding brilliance of the crystal chandeliers, she felt like an extra in the ballroom scene on the sinking *Titanic*. The hall looked enormous, like a glassed-in tennis court encased in high gilded ceilings and heavy, cascading wood paneling. Glistening yellow columns rose from the floor, their crowns of branches glittering with hundreds of tiny lights. The centerpiece of the red-carpeted room was a marble fountain.

At the far end of the hall, a group of musicians in white played as black-and-white clad waiters carried gleaming trays of drinks and hors d'oeuvres among the tables. Smiling faces, excitedly awaiting the evening's entertainment, had already staked out most of the tables. The cream-colored tablecloths were laden with appetizers, alcohol and soft drinks. The organizers had done their very best to provide an unforgettable opening night for the conference.

Vera awkwardly picked her way through the noisy tables, her usual gracefulness having deserted her. She struggled against the weight of the eyes fixed on her, cursing people's eternal fascination with anything that moves. Her gestures were tentative, as if at any moment she expected one of the waiters to ask what she was doing there. Although she normally never bothered with make-up, this evening she had made the extra effort. She had even carefully styled her hair and manicured her nails, assuming that most of the women would be dazzling this evening. Her long platinum hair was gathered into an elegant twist at the nape of her neck. She was wearing a simple black dress with fine embroidery on the neckline that accentuated her petite figure.

Vera stopped in the middle of the room and looked around. The guests included famous history and archeology professors. She also spotted several representatives of the most exclusive art dealerships, including the deputy director of Christie's. They had once invited her to work as an expert consultant with them. While the attractive and prestigious proposal had tempted her, the prospect of losing the freedom she had found in the dust of excavations had scared her.

She looked at her invitation – seeing her father's name on it brought her swiftly back down to earth, reminding her that she had not yet earned her place in these circles. She was the only one who knew this, however.

The pearly card indicated that her seat was at Table 18. Suddenly the lively music gave way to a gentle waltz. Vera continued more confidently to her place, following the numbered place cards. The tables were arranged like a chess board, each one with ten place settings. Bouquets of red roses stood in the center of each table.

Three men and an elderly woman were already seated at Table 18. Vera approached gingerly, as though expecting to stumble at any moment. Three of her tablemates were huddled together, already deep in lively conversation. The other man was sitting alone at the opposite end, looking the other way as if searching for someone in the crowd. His face was unnaturally pale against his dark hair and stubble. He was dressed in expensive black tails and a bowtie.

Vera found her father's seat – right next to the solitary guest. There was no card with his name or title at his place. Vera sat down carefully and placed her small evening bag on the table. She heard the man next to her turn around. Their eyes met, yet his gaze expressed no surprise.

"You!" exclaimed Vera.

It was the stranger she had talked to at the Metropol bar. The man who had left as unexpectedly as he had arrived.

He wore the same aloof expression, but a shadow of melancholy flitted through his steely eyes.

"Last night… you sure left quickly," she murmured.

"I had to go."

The man hurriedly turned his back on her, once again staring in the opposite direction as he had been before Vera arrived. She followed his gaze, expecting to find something interesting. But besides starry-eyed strangers, she saw nothing. Her eyes drifted back to the man, his pale skin. He had the arms and shoulders of a soldier who put his body through daily drills.

"White or red wine?" the waiter repeated his question, bending over her with two bottles.

Vera looked at him, flustered. "White, thank you."

She took out a pack of cigarettes, placed one between her lips and quickly lit up. Her eyes involuntarily traced the sinews in the

166

man's muscular neck. His hair was cut short. A black tattoo caught her attention, a little beneath his hairline, to the left. It looked like a snake coiled into a meander, crooked and jagged as if inked by an amateur. To distract herself, she counted the vertices. Eight. A crescent of seven dots hung above it.

She had seen them somewhere before.

On the Orphic amulet – right above the cross and the mysterious moon. Although the amulet dated from the Middle Ages, academics still had no idea what it symbolized. She herself was also seeking an explanation in her book. Perhaps her father was right that the passion for discovery was infectious. It begins as a harmless virus that surreptitiously overwhelms your consciousness until it becomes a full-blown obsession. It changes you, steers you, dominates you, blinds you until you see only what you are looking for. The object of pursuit becomes the pursuer. But her father had never told her how to cure it.

"Seven stars?" she whispered.

The stranger turned abruptly toward Vera. His eyes examined her face as if seeing her for the first time. He had a sharp, straight nose. His eyes were yellowish grey, almost the color of sand and shaped like drops of water about to fall. The kind of eyes that gave nothing away, yet whose intensity made your whole body shudder. You want to get away from them, while constantly seeking their gaze.

"Do they bother you?" His voice was low and husky.

"I've seen them somewhere…"

"In this world, there's nothing we haven't seen."

Vera regretted broaching such a personal subject with the stranger. "Sorry," she whispered.

The man didn't reply. He stood up and walked towards two Russian officers who had just entered the restaurant. Their puffed-up chests were decorated with colorful ribbons and medals.

"Who is that man?" an elderly man with a German accent asked Vera. She hadn't noticed him sit down on the other side of her.

"I didn't ask," she replied distractedly. *I've seen them before… but not with the meander*, she thought. Then she turned to the elderly man and introduced herself, "Vera Kandilova. Archeologist."

She offered her hand to the man, whose thick glasses magnified his eyes unnaturally without distorting their kindly gaze. His forehead wrinkled anxiously, while the fringe of hair encircling his balding head quivered slightly.

"Dr. Franz Werder," he said. "I'm a historian at the Bode Museum in Berlin."

"What's your area?"

"Early Christianity and Byzantium. And yours?"

"I'm interested in Thracian archaeology and Orphism."

The doctor said nothing for a few seconds then exclaimed, "Well, what do you know!"

At that moment the stranger with the tattoo returned to the table and sat down next to Vera. She caught his scent but didn't turn around, not wanting to let on that she had sensed his presence.

"Are you familiar with the subject?" she asked the historian.

"Somewhat… I even had a brief encounter with it today."

"What do you mean? Did you see something at the exhibition?"

"You could say that… One of the most frequently discussed artifacts with the image of Orpheus, but… I shouldn't really talk about it. Why are you here? Excavations or the conference?"

"The conference. I'm gathering material for my book."

"Oh!" he exclaimed, almost with disappointment. "You look too young and pretty."

"Is it wrong for young, pretty women to write books?"

"It doesn't happen very often. What is your topic?"

"A vanished civilization and a great deception by the Church."

"How did you come up with that?"

"Anger, I guess."

"I beg your pardon?"

"When I was studying archaeology back in Bulgaria we had lectures about Thracian contributions to the world since the most ancient times. The problem is that we Bulgarians know about them, but the world doesn't…"

"You mean the computer, yoghurt and the Bogomils?"

"See what I mean?"

"That was just a joke! I know you gave the world Hristo Stoitchkov as well." The historian grinned to show the young lady he was kidding.

Vera shook her head as if shaking off uninvited thoughts.

"Hundreds of academics are studying the oldest traces of civilization, which were discovered precisely in the Balkans. Yet they don't officially acknowledge their ancientness, since that threatens to shake up the status quo and the globally accepted notion of the great eastern cultures and the barbarian, uneducated tribes of Old Europe. But did you know that barbarians in Stone Age Thrace used a complex writing system with eighty symbols two thousand years before the Egyptians did?"

"I understand what you're saying about the development of human civilizations, but what does God have to do with it?"

"I'm not opposing God, just exposing plagiarism. The story at the root of the New Testament was copied from the oldest story known to mankind. The story studied by Orpheus, the wise man from the Rhodope Mountains. But he didn't write it, either. The problem is that the Bible fails to mention that the events it describes took place several millennia before Christ. And since that time the story has been retold about many Sons of God… Do you know what I read in an encyclopedia?" He shook his head, so she continued, "'The Bible can be seen as a record of human history. One of the world's most ancient books, it preserves the wisdom of the ancient peoples of Mesopotamia, Egypt and Greece. The New Testament and Christianity connect us with the Greco-Roman world, and in such a way become part of the foundations of modern European civilization.' Don't you see? There's not a single word about the achievements of the Thracian civilization that was at least 5,000 years older. And not a word about the great teacher Orpheus, who told the story of the Bible

169

centuries before it was written. That's the sort of thing that makes me angry."

"Don't you think you're overstating things a little?"

"See what I mean? You think it sounds absurd. Which is completely understandable. We contemporary Bulgarians have such a bad name and are so apathetic about our own heritage that even we think our achievements are ridiculous."

"But as far as I know, there isn't any direct evidence that Orpheus was anything but a mythical figure…"

"Of course, because he was savagely killed and all traces of him were destroyed."

"So who murdered him?"

"The oracles of Dionysus," she replied categorically. "The religion Orpheus professed was different from the mass religion of the time. He opposed bloody sacrifices, eating meat, senseless orgies, drunkenness, and instead taught knowledge, love, literacy, belief in a single God, immortality and the aspiration to perfection. And his influence was so overwhelming that it threatened the power of the oracles who governed the masses with rituals and prophecies. So they tore him to pieces, just like Dionysus is killed in their stories, to demonstrate their god's strength over heretics. And in order to destroy the myth about him, they said that women had killed him. They burned his books, which we nevertheless have evidence of even today. The Greeks, who coveted Orpheus' power, wrote down all sorts of rumors and stories about him from the popular religion. However, the true Orphic secrets were kept only for those enlightened to the mysteries. Then the Christian Apostles recycled the stories that had earlier been recycled about Orpheus. And so on…"

Franz Werder scratched his nose uncertainly, hesitated and said, "Christians don't tear each other apart, unlike the Thracians."

"Really? So why, then, are the relics of the saints dismembered and carried to all points of the earth by their worshippers? And why do Christians take bread and wine in order to eat the torn flesh of the Son of God, just like the Titans devoured Dionysus?"

"Be careful with such topics! You're still young but one day you'll realize… Faith must be safeguarded. It mustn't be studied in a laboratory. What's important isn't its chemistry, but its power to redeem us. From ourselves. From life. To lead us towards the inevitable painlessly… That's what I've learned during a life time of curating crosses, icons, frescoes and altars."

"I, on the other hand, have always wanted to know the truth."

Franz Werder sipped his wine and straightened his glasses.

"It's not your fault," he said. "Communism is to blame. It turns out that fifty years is quite enough time to erase a people's faith in its God."

"Communism has nothing to do with it." Vera gave him an ambiguous smile and fell silent. There was no reason to continue a pointless conversation that was on its way to becoming an argument.

Her gaze drifted over the kaleidoscopic swarm of people in the room. Then she turned so she could see the stranger next to her out of the corner of her eye, without showing her curiosity. His face was frozen in an emotionless expression, his gaze mute in its solitude, staring into the soulless crowd. He seemed to be searching for the invisible, yet resigned to the flow of expected and occurring events.

Vera couldn't help herself and turned toward him. He sensed her movement. Their eyes met. His were like a pair of glowing coals, different from the other eyes, which melted into the excitement of the festive evening. His were indifferent to the visible and tangible, ignoring it and losing themselves in the current of movement and lights. She had never seen colorful irises like his. His features were not perfect, yet something about his pale face attracted her.

The people sitting at her table began to stir, pairing off and heading towards the dance floor. Only then did Vera start listening to the music. The musicians were playing Tchaikovsky's graceful waltz from *Swan Lake*. Vera felt awkward, sensing that the elderly German would invite her to dance. She decided that this was her only chance, so although she had never done anything like it before, she turned to the stranger and asked: "Do you dance?"

"No."

"So you refuse to accompany me to the dance floor?"

"I don't dance," the man repeated, giving her a cold stare.

Yet a moment later, Vera felt that he might just smile at her. So she insisted.

"If you agree just this once, I'll be the only person who knows."

He stood up and offered his hand. He led her straight towards the waves of dancing couples. Vera could see nothing but the stranger's back and head, as he was very tall with broad shoulders. When they reached the crowd of rhythmically swaying bodies, he stopped and took her hands in his. Without speaking they joined the sea of dancers. It was as if he knew the steps but had never danced before. Vera sensed his breathing, while the closeness of his unfamiliar body unnerved her so much that she lost track of the music and felt disoriented in space and time. It was then when she felt something like light electricity from his skin, but she decided it's just an illusion.

Disquieting thoughts washed over her. She regretted inviting him.

"I don't know your name," she said quietly.

"Ariman."[50]

Vera couldn't hide her smile as she exclaimed, "How on earth did you get a name like that?"

The man didn't seem to hear her. He didn't even deign to glance down at her. He continued moving to the general rhythm, looking as if he were doing something extremely unnatural to him. Like someone lost, his eyes stared into the clumsy throng of chattering and laughing dancers. The only sign that he was real and not an incorporeal image came from the flexing of his tense muscles, which Vera could sense under her fingers on his shoulder.

---

[50] Name of the Devil or Satan used in Ancient Persian.

The music stopped briefly, in anticipation of a new tune. The crowd froze and began to disperse. The man let go of her as unexpectedly as he had taken her hands a moment earlier. Without saying a word he walked towards the exit.

Vera stood where he had left her, gazing at the receding figure, as if waiting for him to turn around. But he didn't.

He simply disappeared into the crowd.

Deflated, Vera returned to the table, glancing expectantly at the restaurant's wide-open doors all the while. An untouched glass of wine sparkled ruby red in the empty place to her right. She was irritated with the waiters for not removing it, as if they knew that the one it was meant for would return. She didn't blame them, it was her fault for allowing herself to notice a stranger who hadn't even glanced at her. She hadn't even found out who he was. She only knew his name – Ariman. What kind of name was that?

It didn't matter.

Vera turned to Dr. Franz Werder, who was excitedly discussing the upcoming exhibition with his neighbor. She couldn't muster up the strength to curl her lips into a smile or to join a conversation that did not interest her. She might have even gotten up and left at that point if she hadn't heard the historian whisper something about the Orphic amulet – one of the most controversial pieces of evidence of the transformation.

TWINS

Page 434 *began with an account of Elizabeth's immaculate conception of her son John the Baptist: "When she praised God for the gift of her son, Elizabeth said, 'So much did God do for me in those days when he looked upon me kindly, taking away men's scorn.' In the sixth month after this event the same Angel Gabriel who had come to Elizabeth was sent by God to Nazareth to announce to the purest Virgin Mary that she would be the mother of the Savior Jesus Christ. The Holy Virgin asked: 'How can that be, as I have not known a man?' The heavenly messenger answered her: 'The Holy Spirit will come upon you, and the power of the Most High will overshadow you. So the holy one to be born will be called the Son of God. And behold, even your kinswoman Elizabeth has also conceived a son in her old age; and she who was called barren is now in her sixth month.'"*

**From: Lives of the Saints, Synodal Publishers, Sofia,
1991, edited by Parthenii, Bishop of Leucius and
Archbishop, Dr. Atanasii (Bonchev).**

Making her excuses to the other guests, Vera took her bag from the table and headed for the exit. A few taxis were waiting outside the hotel. It was the only time she had seen a real taxi in the city – this strange, mythical megalopolis, overflowing with universal emotion, history and hidden longings.

The boulevards glowed pale yellow under the street lights, which were shining like thousands of orange moons in the cloudless

174

night. There were no people, only a few cars speeding along the glistening, damp asphalt.

Leaning back into the seat of the cab, Vera hurried to fish her notebook out of her bag, hoping it could snap her out of her mood. She opened it to the last page, which contained the symbols she had stumbled across today. She examined them carefully, one by one. She focused on the last two, the mirror-image hooks. Side by side, this pair was the most frequently used symbol in the ancient culture of Gradeshnitsa. They were normally drawn like this:

Even the first time she saw them on the chests of the ritual human figurines, she had realized the symbol was not random. The Meandrites also used it on ceramic vessels that held precious contents, as well as on pictographic tablets and their altars. It seemed to symbolize a protector or a connection to God and eternity. Whatever the meaning, it was clearly important, since the symbol was on the figurines' chest. Next to the heart.

Deciphering this symbol could unravel the snarl of secrets encoded in the ancient hieroglyphs. However, this sign did not have an analogy in any later writing system – or at least Vera had not previously seen anything that could be even a distant parallel.

So when she came across the mirror-image Bulgarian letters next to each other she could hardly contain her excitement. "More clues," she thought and shivered.

Perhaps the symbols whose meaning she had been searching for in Egyptian and Cretan civilizations had been preserved in some transmuted form in Bulgaria – along with their ancient message.

The symmetrical pair of symbols were called *La* and *Re*, yet these syllables held no meaning for contemporary people. In order to understand them, Vera would have to trace their metamorphoses back to the beginning. Starting with their current meaning, she would have to travel back in time.

The first thing that popped into her head was the significance of the musical notes *la* and *re* in Greek mythology. The seven notes corresponded to the seven planets known to the ancients. *La* was the symbol for the Moon, while *Re* stood for Mars. "Perhaps the symbols stand for male and female," Vera mused.

Her thoughts collided, digging for the answers buried beneath the symbols. Yet she felt no need to run, because unlike people, symbols couldn't hurt her.

"*La* and *Re*, the Moon and Mars," she whispered to herself. But the Red Planet held no significance in the prehistoric religion based on sun worship. One of the signs had to be tied to the fiery disc in the sky.

Vera got out of the taxi in front of her hotel and watched the car disappear into the fog. Her high heels tapped rhythmically on the asphalt as she walked past the guardhouse and headed towards the glassed-in entrance. Even before going in, she felt a heaviness in her chest and a blackness dissolving into her veins. She had felt this way the first night in her hotel room. She tried not to read too much into the feeling. She got in the elevator and leaned her head against the polished wall.

Suddenly it came to her. She remembered where she had seen one of the syllables before. Sublime bliss washed over her, the inimitable intoxication of discovery – everything tangible and fleeting dissolves into eternity, while the senses, hunger, health, air and desire lose all meaning.

Vera impatiently unlocked the flimsy door and immediately opened the suitcase in the middle of the room. She rummaged through her clothes and pulled out a thick volume entitled *The Religion of Ancient Egypt* by Professor Teodor Lekov. She turned to the "Glossary of Terminology" at the back of the book to look up the meaning of *Re*.

"Re: the primary Egyptian divinity, God the Creator and personification of the Sun. His name means 'The Exalted One.' In addition to signifying the deity, the same word is also used in the

Egyptian language to mean 'Sun,' 'day' and 'light'… The cult of Re gained popularity during the ancient kingdom (in the Fourth Dynasty and thereafter), when kings adopted the title of 'Son of Re'… Re's role as the supreme deity was maintained during all periods of Egyptian history…"

Her mental gears lurched into motion so quickly that their grinding filled the silence. The newly assembled jigsaw of thoughts started to fall apart until the same invisible hand that had been pointing out signs all day reappeared to put them in order. The syllables suspended in the void took on meaning – yet to decipher them completely Vera would have to be even more dogged in her search.

Perhaps the sign "Re," which had been preserved in Bulgaria, also symbolized God the creator. This wasn't totally left-field; for thousands of years the proto-Thracians, and later the followers of Orpheus, believed that the Sun was the creator. Moreover, Egyptians wrote the word for "god" with a hieroglyph resembling the Slavic symbol "La" – the mirror image of "Re," which also meant "strength." Taken together, two signs expressed the strength and wisdom of God.

But where could the ancient Bulgarian pronunciation "La" for the mirror image of "Re" have come from? Vera knew sleep was out of the question until she had come up with a satisfactory theory. She tossed the book onto the bed and began pacing up and down the room in agitation. Her thoughts feverishly wandered through the chaos of symbols and words. She knew that it would turn out to be something extremely simple in the end. The way various civilizations encoded their ideas in symbols was not complex. The majority of symbols were not intended to conceal anything from anyone. On the contrary, when ancient peoples chose pictograms, they looked for the clearest possible expression. However, as her father always said, to guess the hieroglyphs' meaning today, you had to think like their creators. And this was particularly difficult for modern man, as he is irreversibly different and distant from the First Ones.

The note "la" symbolized the moon in many ancient mythologies. She figured this would be a good place to start. For the ancients, the moon was the "Night Sun."

"That's it!" she whispered, snapping her fingers. "The Night Sun! The mirror image of *Ra* – or *Re* – his nocturnal twin!"

This idea was widespread among sun cults. In Orphism, for example, followers believed the sun god had a twin who stood in for him at night – fire. In the Dionysian cult, his symbol was the moon. The twins' most recent names, preserved down to the present day, were Apollo and Dionysus. We can only guess what their original names were.

Vera sat down at the shabby desk and lit a cigarette. Satisfied with her explanation, she jotted it down.

The idea of twins was preserved longest in Orphism and in the religion of ancient Egypt.[51] The god of light and his dark twin most probably embodied divine unity and omnipotence. The idea that shadows lived could also be found in such belief systems. Moreover, the mirror was a key symbol in both the Orphic and Dionysian mysteries. The ancient Thracians' mirror-image deity deceived the Delphic sages to such an extent that for a long time they could not distinguish between the real god and his double. However, the Delphians coveted the power the solar god granted his followers. Since they could not distinguish between the god of light and the god of darkness, they introduced a strict system of worshipping the dark god Dionysus for six months and the light god Apollo for six months.[52]

---

[51] The ancient Egyptians believed that the supreme deity Re (Ra) had a twin who appeared at night. Since ancient times, Ra has been the Sun God. According to legend, every day he is reborn in order to bring the sun to the earth. Every day he passes through twelve gates, which symbolize the twelve hours of the day. After the twelfth gate the god dies and is transformed into the god Auf, whose task is to pass through twelve gates in the underworld and to bring the sun to the lost souls of the night. "Osiris was often called the nocturnal sun. The pair is also known as *Bauifi* (The Two Essences) or *Chauifi* (The Two Twins)," Professor Teodor Lekov, *The Religion of Ancient Egypt*.

[52] From Herodotus, as well as a series of Orphic poems, we know that in Delphi, Apollo and Dionysus were worshipped in turn for equal periods (R. Eisler, *Orpheus the Fisher*, p. 11).

178

The twin was the explanation for everything. It was also why the pair of runes were mirror images.

> And the great care of goods at random left
> Drew me from kind embracements of my spouse:
> From whom my absence was not six months old
> Before herself, almost at fainting under
> The pleasing punishment that women bear,
> Had made provision for her following me
> And soon and safe arrived where I was.
> There had she not been long, but she became
> A joyful mother of two goodly sons;
> And, which was strange, the one so like the other,
> As could not be distinguish'd but by names.

The Shakespearean quotation about Antipholus and Dromio leapt uninvited into Vera's mind, followed by the recollection of the icon she had seen that day in the Pushkin Museum. The image of the Madonna holding two blond babies in her arms, absolutely identical like twins, hung prominently in the hall. Vera had been so surprised that she had noted down the name of the icon: "Madonna with Jesus and John the Baptist."

Vera turned on the shower and waited for the hot water to reach the top floor of the hotel. She recalled her conversation with Kiril at Chateau Jacques. Then, although she had known the basic facts, she had not been able to put together their meaning as clearly as today.

"So, are you trying to prove that Christianity, too, is just the latest in a long line of metamorphoses?" Kiril had asked her. "But Christ doesn't have a twin!"

"Oh, yes he does! Except that the modern Christian, who only knows about Easter eggs and Christmas presents, isn't too familiar with him. In fact, St. John the Baptist is considered Jesus' theoretical twin. He was conceived supernaturally, just as the Virgin Mary and her son Jesus were: immaculately. And it is no

179

*"The Madonna with the Christ Child and Saint
John the Baptist" by Raphael*

accident that John the Baptist was born exactly six months before
his twin[53] – on June 14, the summer solstice. Precisely six months
before Christmas and the Winter Solstice."

"I've never heard that Jesus had a twin."

"It presents a bit of a problem for the Christian reworking of
the story. The church has been trying to erase this detail for so long
that people have forgotten about it. Leonardo da Vinci himself was
vilified for depicting Jesus and John as twins."

---

[53] "When the Unsetting Sun of Justice – our Savior – deigned to light up the
world and descended from the heavens and took root in the pure virgin womb, at
the same time St John the Forerunner, His Morningstar, had to be born by a barren
woman. As a herald he had to precede the coming of the Lord," *The Lives of Saints*,
translated into Bulgarian from the Church Slavic *Cheti-Minei*, or the *Great Menaion*.

Vera got into the shower, the soft water caressing her skin and refreshing her senses. She got out and wrapped herself in a white bathrobe. The hotel room filled with thick steam.

She stood in front of the mirror above the sink, watching her own image swim amid the phantoms and visions of past millennia. It was as if someone had just switched on the light. She studied her own face as though she had forgotten it. She had handsome features, smooth skin dotted with pale freckles, straight platinum hair and tired grey eyes – always alone in the reflection.

She switched off the light and walked over to the window. As the colorless image in the glass melted into the depth of the night, the meaning of the other symbol suddenly appeared. On the clay figurines' chests, the symmetrical pair of signs frequently merged into a single symbol, linked with a line at the bottom, similar to the Egyptian *Ka*. The hieroglyph resembled two hands raised in prayer, connected at the base by a horizontal line. The dictionary of Egyptian terminology said that it could be translated as "double," "spirit" or "strength," but that it is above all associated with the Creator's energy, which flows from Him to all creation and which serves as a common thread throughout all generations since the moment of Creation.

It was precisely *Ka* that united the symbols *Re* or *Ra* (the Sun) and *La* (the Night Sun) on the ritual figurines' chests – right where the organ that housed the soul was, according to the Meandrites. In the same place, but on the other side, they had depicted the heart. It is not by chance that people today believe that the soul lies in the heart.

Vera leaned against the wall and closed her eyes. The explanation sounded convincing enough for her to allow herself to go to bed. However, the powerful thrill of an apparent discovery always blinds the mind to its own madness. And when the details all fall perfectly into place, the mind readily accepts its own musing as the only possible explanation.

THE LONG-AWAITED ONES

Page 435 began with a quotation from
The Egyptian Book of the Dead: *"You [the heart] are Ka in my body" – that is, the heart is the channel through which Ka acts upon the human body.[54] Another quotation from the same source followed: "it is a closely guarded secret that must not be shared with anyone, not even one's closest family members: brothers, sisters, mother or father. And it must be studied in this life, not only as a ritual element."[55]*

Ariman had gotten up early, before dawn. The heavy curtains hid him from the moonlight and the electric glow of the billboards in the square. He didn't turn the lights on. He wanted to be sure no one could see what he was doing. In expensive hotels someone was always watching – especially in the most luxurious rooms. He had tried to find the camera the first night, but hadn't been able to.

The darkness did not frighten him. Over time his eyes had grown so used to it that they could make out shapes. He double-checked his luggage, making sure he hadn't forgotten anything. All his senses were on high alert. He had only slept for two hours.

He went into the bathroom and shut the door. Only then did he turn on the light. He looked around, searching for anything forgotten. He again checked for hairs and red stains. He had washed off the Russian's blood in the sink. He had been one of the security

---

[54] From Teodor Lekov's *The Religion of Ancient Egypt*.

[55] This quotation was provided by the team that shot the documentary film *The Truth about Orpheus*.

guards at the Pushkin Museum. Ariman had had to kill him after they had stolen the amulet from the glass case and left the museum. In exchange for a hefty sum, the guard had agreed to show him to the vault and disable the alarm. He had seemed reliable and might not have betrayed Ariman, yet he would have always been a living clue to a very closely guarded secret.

Ariman had thrown his body into a dumpster and returned to the hotel.

No clues. No memories.

He turned off the light and went back into the room. Everything seemed to be in place. He opened his bag and looked for the small box, as if needing to make sure that he really had taken the amulet from the museum. It was there in his backpack, along with the inscribed golden tablet wrapped in paper.

He left the hotel room. It was already growing light. The billboards' kaleidoscopic reflections danced on the windows of the hallway, the green silk wallpaper and filmy drapes turning them into shadows.

Ariman paid his bill, Put on his baseball cap and left the hotel. He continued down the street. Female giggling echoed in his ears. He turned around. Two women, walking arm in arm, were whispering and tittering. His tendons grew taught. He stepped aside to let them pass, while they looked him over. The redhead even turned around a few times after they had passed him.

His breath came fast, filling his chest with a searing pain. They can all see it, he said to himself. They could all see that he was different. No matter what he did, no matter what he wore, even if he hid his face and eyes and only came out in the light, so as not to stand out in the darkness, they could always tell that he wasn't one of them. Their eyes followed him, as if he were a stain on a white wall. When they could sense that he wasn't one of them, they kept their distance, as if he were covered in black grease that would soil them. As if he were diseased or would humiliate them in front of society if they got close to him. They say that people are genetically programmed to run from snakes and spiders, to recognize the devil in human skin. Could they possibly see the devil in him as well?

He shoved the earphones of his MP3 player into his ears and turned it on. Depeche Mode's "Enjoy the Silence Live" came on. Ariman cranked up the volume and hurried on his way. Tiny droplets of sweat ran down his neck. He anxiously rubbed the scar where the cut-out tattoo had been, right below his hairline. He had gotten it as a child. Perhaps as a sign that he was different. He pulled down his cap and covered his hands with gloves, so no one could see the strange radiance around them.

Vera rolled over in bed and opened her eyes sleepily. She got up slowly, her head heavy. She had had more to drink than usual last night and gone to bed late. She wasn't used to it –and never would get used to it. Books, dictionaries and paper lay scattered by the bed. She had read until late, finally dissolving her excitement in a bottle of wine.

She went over to the window. As she opened the curtains, the bright light made her squint. She retreated to the bathroom and turned on the shower. She tried to recall what had happened the previous evening. Dancing with the stranger… Why had he left again? Unexpectedly, just like the night before that.

Although Vera realized that nothing could ever happen between them, the memory of him nagged at her, while the thought that she might see him again filled her with impatience. She knew that he was just a chance traveler, appearing out of nowhere, only to return there once again. We meet dozens of such people every day. Yet some of them leave traces, raising questions that make us come alive. They inspire the logically inexplicable sensation that wild crocuses could bloom, even in the dark. And that life is not as preordained or foreseeable as we thought it was yesterday.

Her sadness was strangely sweet. Because it had happened to her before, she knew how fragile and fleeting the experience was, so she didn't hurry to snuff it out. Perhaps precisely its transience gave it such insurmountable beauty. It would always remain so, like the pale flame of a solitary candle that gives no warmth, but burns only to revive hope.

The shower's heat began to make Vera feel ill. She turned off the water and went to get dressed.

Damn these scattered illusions.

"I've spent my whole life hungering after them!" she thought. Everything revolves around that sense of anticipation. But when the euphoria dies away as it does after every discovery, you realize you've lost the most precious thing, the thing that set everything in motion: the thrill of expectation, the as-of-yet-unlived dreams. Only at the moment when you reach what you've been hungering for do you realize that it is the most terrible prison for the soul. Some people stop there. Others manage to free themselves from the cage and again take flight. But can you really fly when you know there is no sense in landing? And if there is no landing, can there even be flight?

That is what had happened with Kaloyan.

Vera forced herself to have breakfast, although she had no appetite. She felt as though she no longer needed to eat or breathe.

She looked at her watch. It was past eleven. She had missed the first two lectures. She wasn't interested in the third, but she decided to go all the same. It would help her avoid thinking.

THE SUN PEOPLE

Page 436 stated that Christ the King was the son of God the Creator. From time immemorial the Thracians had believed that the sun was God the Creator's son, born every year on December 25. When Egyptians worshipped God the Creator, they called him "Re" (Ra), while their kings bore the title "Sons of Ra."
The Egyptian kings built "sun temples" to reflect their own solar nature, just as the oracles of the cave-dwellers and the First Ones thousands of years before them had built stone temples to the solar cult.

Vera entered the dazzling foyer of the Hotel Metropol. She sat at one of the tables and ordered a latte to kill the ten minutes left before the end of the second lecture. She was in no hurry to enter the hall where she would spend the rest of her day.

She heard a persistent buzzing and reached into her purse to pull out her cell phone. Not recognizing the number, she hesitated for a moment. Curiosity got the better of her, however, so she answered.

"You've infected me with your stars and secret messages," an enthusiastic male voice exclaimed.

"Who is this?"

"It's Kiril," the voice replied. After an awkward pause, he added: "From the Chateau Jacques…"

"Oh, Kiril!" Vera suddenly remembered the reporter. "Sorry, I was thinking about…"

"Do you have an Internet connection there?"

"I'll have to boot up my laptop."

"Check your email. I've just sent you some photographs."

"Give me a second."

She took out her computer, set it on her lap and switched it on. She had a few new messages. She clicked on the message from Kiril, but had to wait, as the attached files were very large.

"So what's going on with you?" she asked him in a business-like tone.

"I was in Varna, for work."

"What sort of work?"

"I was writing an article about the Solar Villa at Euxinograd.[56] It's finally been refurbished so that this year the president can enjoy his vacation undisturbed by squeaking doors, falling plaster and dingy walls."

"What made you think of me?"

"The Solar Villa," Kiril laughed. "I was strolling around, looking for a good angle to shoot from. I climbed a few steps that led to the top of a small cliff overlooking the sea. Right in front of Ferdinand's Royal Villa…"

"I know the place… the sundial."

"Exactly."

"I've been there myself. It's wonderful."

"But you didn't see anything there?"

"Such as?"

"The symbols. You didn't pay any attention to them. Have you opened the pictures yet?"

"Not yet," Vera was losing patience. She could sense that Kiril had found something interesting.

"Stars… When I saw them, I thought it was a strange coincidence. It reminded me of what had happened in the Chateau Jacques, but this time it wasn't a castle, but a royal palace. The sundial stands right in front of the central bell tower. Beneath the iron pointer there are two eight-pointed stars inside each other.

---

[56] The Bulgarian royal summer palace built on the Black Sea coast in the late 19th century.

The first is plain, not filled in, while the second has decorations engraved in the iron – just like what we saw in Switzerland."

Vera didn't answer right away. She had just opened the photographs and was examining them very closely. In the first picture she recognized the sundial, which she had seen in the Euxinograd gardens. Yet she had never looked closely at the symbols before. On the iron surface she could clearly see two interwoven eight-pointed stars, right below the pointer.

The sundial near Varna

Kiril had taken the next photograph from the sundial, looking towards the palace. Vera could see the Bulgarian flag waving proudly atop one of the towers, high above the trees that fanned out like sails. In front of the sundial there was a white sand garden with two parallel paths leading from it. Vera decided that they, too, must symbolize something – if only she could figure out what. Perhaps they hint at duality, mirror images, paths... Kiril's insistent voice interrupted her thoughts.

"Are you still there?"

"I was just looking at the pictures... You're right about the stars. It's amazing how we see symbols that have always been around us only when we're ready for them."

"You infected me with your crazy theories. I'm surprised at myself... I stood there for hours counting the corners, every single stone and beam, searching for a message. Just look how the stone slab under the sundial's iron face is octagonal. Just like the stars."

Vera bit her lip in amazement. The octagon was quite striking, as though it hid some coded meaning crying out to be deciphered.

"But that's not all," Kiril continued. "The small enclosure around the sundial is also octagonal."

Vera counted the corners of the fence – it was indeed eight-sided.

"I couldn't help but notice. That story about the fresco from the catacombs stuck in my mind..."

"What story?"

"The fresco you showed me with Orpheus, where he's in the center of an octagon. When I got back to Sofia I looked up the meaning of the symbols in some dictionaries. I found only one thing: In early Christianity baptismal fonts were shaped like that, with eight sides. Orpheus in the middle of a shape associated with christening... it seemed interesting to me. It must be another clue to the connections you're looking for."

"I'd forgotten about that... you're right, baptismal fonts all had eight sides to begin with and then they started changing for no reason, right around the same time as the cross began to be imposed as the symbol of Christianity."

"I thought the pictures might be of use to you. They seem to fit in with your research."

"Thank you." Vera could have said much more, but she preferred to say nothing, so as not to let on her excitement over the discovery.

A fresco from the Roman catacombs:
Orpheus in an octagon

Although the telephone was still pressed to her ear, Vera was no longer listening to the reporter. She was staring at the sundial, sketching imaginary figures in its outline. She examined its stone base very carefully. It was made up of four columns in the shape of an equilateral cross – the obligatory form for all medieval Christian church foundations. So the octagon was in the center of an equilateral cross. Kiril was right about it being the same symbolism as in the Roman catacombs where the cross was clearly connected with the sun, Orpheus, the octagon and Christ.

Why were these signs so meticulously depicted on a sundial in front of a royal palace? A perfect symbolic system had been bequeathed to posterity on a cliff above the sea, poised at any moment to tumble into the waves and be swallowed up by the salty water. The Roman frescoes were also hidden from the eyes of the unenlightened, buried in the catacombs' ancient tunnels. Where else had these symbols been etched? Until now, Vera had not realized their significance.

A fresh stream of words flowing from the receiver reminded her that Kiril was still on the line.

"I sat on the bench in front of the sundial and thought for a long time. I couldn't leave without figuring it out. Then it came to me: the octagonal star on the sundial, above the Solar Villa, to the east of the palace... could only symbolize the Sun. Even the decorations in the painted star show it. It's so simple!"

"Too simple," Vera replied coldly. "Kiril, I have to go. The lecture is about to start. Thanks for thinking of me and sending the pictures of the sundial. I'll definitely use them..."

THE LABYRINTH OF SYMBOLS

Page 437 was filled with symbols. Someone had written beneath a row of crosses:

"The same can be seen when comparing the crosses. The 7,500-year-old Gradeshnitsa culture used five types of crosses, engraved on tablets and vessels of baked clay.

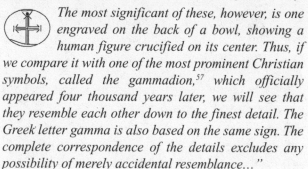 *The most significant of these, however, is one engraved on the back of a bowl, showing a human figure crucified on its center. Thus, if we compare it with one of the most prominent Christian symbols, called the gammadion,[57] which officially appeared four thousand years later, we will see that they resemble each other down to the finest detail. The Greek letter gamma is also based on the same sign. The complete correspondence of the details excludes any possibility of merely accidental resemblance..."*

"...the Meringovians, also known as the 'long-haired kings,' were the Franks' first ruling dynasty," a deep bass voice filled the conference room of the Hotel Metropol. "From the fifth to the eighth century AD, they are thought to have founded one of the earliest medieval states in Europe. Their name comes from their founding ruler, Merovech."

At that moment Vera heard someone calling her. The quiet whisper came from somewhere behind her.

She waited to hear it again before turning around. Inches from her stood a thin-faced, light-haired boy, his dove-like eyes watching her

---

[57] Its name comes from the Greek letter "gamma" (*The Book of Symbols*, Svetlozar Vlaykov, p. 112).

closely. He couldn't have been more than twenty. The hotel's black and red uniform hung on his scrawny frame. Vera remembered seeing him checking passes at the entrance to the hotel. She nodded, then the boy explained to her in Russian that a gentleman wanted to talk to her.

The boy looked down at his feet while he spoke, as if trying to hide something – perhaps curiosity or excitement over an easy tip.

"Where?" Vera instinctively looked around.

"Outside, near the main entrance to the hall," the boy replied. "A foreigner."

Vera felt her stomach seize into a ball – not from fear, but from uncertainty, impatience and amazement all at once. She wasn't expecting anyone. Except perhaps that man…

It must be him. She was sure that they had both felt something last night, while they were dancing. He couldn't leave just like that without a word. It must've been a game. He was trying to make her wait for him, think about him, wonder where he might be. Because he knew that the most exciting presence is absence. She had played the same game, but that didn't lessen its effect on her. So the guy was smart. Good.

Vera got up and nervously headed for the exit. Before opening the door she straightened her jacket and brushed the hair off her forehead.

"Oh, you?" she exclaimed in surprise as she stepped out of the hall.

She tried to hide her disappointment at seeing an elderly man with a fringe of salt-and-pepper hair standing in the corridor. Wire-rim glasses cut across his round reddish nose. It was Dr. Werder, the historian from the Berlin museum, who had been sitting on her left the previous evening.

"Could you spare me a moment?" he asked hesitantly, clearly flustered at having taken the unusual step of calling her out of the lecture hall to talk. He was hunched over slightly, his eyes roving the marble floor for some distraction from his awkwardness.

"Aren't you interested in the lecture? It's on early European history," she broke the silence.

"I myself could tell you a lot about our esteemed lecturer's subject matter."

Franz Werder caught Vera's puzzled look and became even more flustered. He added: "What do you think the connection could be between faraway Russia and the kings who founded Western Europe's feudal system?"

Vera thought it best to wait for the answer.

"Surprising as it may seem, the reason lies in some of the many treasures taken from Germany in 1945 by the Russians."

"I didn't know," Vera fibbed.

They casually walked towards the lobby bar.

"It's my understanding that your museum also holds quite a few confiscated treasures… What are the Russians up to?"

"It's no accident that the exhibit is in Moscow." He fell silent. He had already said too much.

Vera brushed a stray wisp of hair from her face. They walked up a wide staircase with heavy marble banisters, so exquisite that it seemed painted into the white space. The fine carpet covering the snowy stone muted their footsteps.

"Is there anything I can help you with?" Vera asked.

"A symbol… I urgently need to learn its meaning."

"Why are you asking me?"

"You said you were a Thracian specialist," he hesitated for a moment and scratched his nose. "From everything you told me last night about Orpheus and Christ, I decided there's something you ought to know… I haven't told anyone else."

"What are you talking about? I'm just a student. There are plenty of experts here who…"

"I'm not speaking as an employee of the Bode Museum. The answer interests me personally," he added quietly. He looked around as if checking for eavesdroppers. "Why don't we sit down and have a cup of coffee?"

Vera nodded. They walked over to the armchairs in the black and white foyer. The doctor pointed to a free table. They sat down in silence and waited for the waiter. Vera distractedly watched the faces of the people coming and going. Franz Werder reached into his jacket pocket and took out a crumpled sheet of paper.

"Take a look at this symbol," he said, handing it to her.

Vera unfolded the sheet and froze in amazement. Yet she did all she could to hide her astonishment.

"This is a meander," she whispered.

"An eight-sided one!" he exclaimed. "But I doubt you think that the meander is just a pretty decoration! What you told me last night made it clear that you know more... I'm convinced it has another meaning, perhaps one too important to be recognized by just anybody."

"But why are you so interested in this symbol?"

Franz Werder looked around nervously to see whether anyone at the adjacent tables could hear him. He scratched his nose again, which was turning purplish. He slid forward in his armchair and began quietly.

"I saw it in on a book... on a manuscript, to be exact. There was nothing on the cover except this sign and a few words that I can't recall offhand. It has no author, no title, even though it is listed in the card catalogue. The manuscript mentions many things, including Thrace."

"What manuscript are you talking about?"

"I'm still not certain... Do you recognize this symbol?" he persisted.

Vera nodded conspiratorially. She wasn't sure whether she should share all the details she knew with him. She hesitated a moment before declaring: "OK, let me show you something interesting."

She got up and walked towards the front entrance of the hotel. The doctor followed her. They walked out into Theater Square. It was snowing softly. The dusty blue sky hung low over the heads, while fine snowflakes whirled around their faces. They landed on their coats like white moths, melting into the still-warm cloth.

When they reached the square in front of the Pushkin Museum, Vera said, "Now you can see and figure it out for yourself."

After checking their passes at the entrance, the curator let them into the exhibition without any questions. Vera went straight to the Antiquities Gallery, which contained artifacts from Troy, Ancient Greece and Thrace. The corridors were packed with visitors crowding around to get a closer look at the golden objects on display.

"I'll tell you what I know… because I haven't met anyone else looking for this symbol." Her gaze was confident, even defiant. "The meander allowed me to trace two of the paths. The other symbols later proved these paths really do exist."

"What paths?"

"Why don't we sit down?"

A red leather sofa beckoned from the rear of the gallery. The museum staff must have put it there for tired tourists to catch their breath before continuing their endless sprint around the sites of Moscow. As luck would have it, the couch was free at the moment. Werder followed Vera and they sat down facing each other.

"I'm all ears!" he said with curiosity.

Vera told him about the mysterious disappearance of the Meandrites, who were so advanced that it had taken later civilizations thousands of years to catch up with them. She told him how they had vanished without a trace in the fourth millennium BC, while their abandoned lands stood deserted for centuries after their disappearance.

"A number of academics have tried to prove the link between the vanished civilization and later Egyptian and Mycenaean civilizations," she added. "I found their arguments convincing. I also began finding traces of them in other later civilizations around Thrace. I assume that certain offshoots of the Meandrites must have survived, fleeing in various directions and carrying their knowledge with them. I figured that by tracing the paths of their symbols and the ideas they preserve, I would be able to reconstruct the original signs."

"But what does this have to do with the meander?"

"The symbol you're asking me about… is one of the Meandrites' most important symbols. It can be used to trace the hidden civilization's path."

"If I understand you correctly, you believe that the meander is a trace leading back to them?" The historian adjusted his glasses and stared expectantly at Vera.

"It is one of the key symbols in their religion," she continued. "Like the cross for the Christians. That is clear from the places where they used it: on the body of the Mother Goddess, on vessels, amulets and houses, like a hieroglyph."

"Sounds interesting…" Werder paused. He rested his chin in his hands, deepening its cleft. He pondered the possible connection between this mysterious civilization and the manuscript he had seen in the library in Rome. Unable to make sense of it, he asked, "But how is it possible to trace the path of a civilization that was lost so many millennia ago through a handful of symbols?"

"These are the primary symbols they used to encrypt their messages. Take a Christian symbol, for example – the cross. From the appearance and the frequency of its usage you can see how Christianity spread, since the cross is the leading sign of this cultural and religious community. Others avoid using it, just like we avoid using the swastika or the crescent. If you study the metamorphoses the cross has undergone, you can see how the idea transformed into a symbol and a message over the past 2,000 years. It's a signpost, just like the meander, the 'symmetrical hooks,' and other symbols which were like crosses for the Meandrites."

"Fascinating," Dr. Werder muttered, shaking his head.

His glasses slipped down his nose, squeezing his nostrils and causing him to snort. He pushed them back in place with his index finger. The movement helped him focus his gaze on the black ceramic bowl in the first show case.

"Will you tell me more about the book where you saw the symbol?" Vera pressed him.

"I doubt it's very important," he mumbled. "I happened upon it in Rome."

"Is it Italian? How old is it?"

"As I said, it's not important."

Dr. Werder's unwillingness to give her any details made Vera suspect that he was trying to hide something. Her insistent questioning was most likely giving him reason to believe that his secret was more important than he had imagined. Sometimes feigning disinterest is a better tool for untying a reluctant tongue than curiosity.

Vera stood up and gestured for Werder to follow her. She went over to the second showcase and pointed out two antique bowls. "Take a look at the artifacts in here. The symbol you're asking me about always accompanies Orphic scenes. If it's not in the decorative border, then you'll find a series of stylized 'V' decorations, or, as I like to call them, 'symmetrical hooks.'"

"Orphic scenes? What are you getting at?"

"Orpheans followed a set of teachings that existed at least 1,500 years before Christ – but I suspect that it is far more ancient than that. Scholars think that if Orpheus really did exist, he was probably the religion's most eminent prophet and missionary." She was reluctant to share any more of her ideas, but Dr. Werder's expectant gaze tempted her into continuing. "I have proof that the Orpheans somehow became the first European followers of the Meandrites."

"How can you be so sure?"

"Many of the details of their teachings coincide, as do the symbols they used. I've collected all the Orphic scenes found in ancient art and put them in an electronic archive. I myself was amazed to see that the meander always accompanies them, in complex combinations with other familiar prehistoric symbols, no less. Look at this scene, for example."

Vera pointed to the center of a red-figure bowl. The sign beneath it read: "Ancient *krater*. The original belongs to the Jatta Museum's Fenicia Collection." Werder carefully studied the motifs on the bowl, which were united by a scene of six gods and animals from ancient Greek mythology, all surrounding Orpheus

and gazing at him. The singer was dressed in luxuriant regal robes, while the gods around him sat listening. The names above each figure made it clear who was who – although the Thracian sage with his seven-string lyre was unmistakable.

Vera pointed to the eye-catching plethora of meanders adorning Orpheus' robes, all identical to the symbol Werder was looking for. The most curious part was that in contrast to Orpheus' numerous meanders, no other figure on the bowl wore a single one.[58]

---

[58] The scene described can be seen in *Helenic Orphic Evidence* by M. Yordanova-Aleksieva, p. 263.

THE IMAGINARY TRUTH

Page 438 began with a table containing the most frequently occurring symbols among the two hundred or so signs that the vanished Thracian civilization used during the fourth millennium BC.

"Most of these symbols were widespread and are still in use today. Western academics such as Haarman, Gimbutas and others are convinced that the ancient European symbols form the basis of the linear writing system of Crete. Modern studies show that they were one of the fundamental elements of the ancient Greek writing system. For the moment, at least, no one has deciphered the writing system of the disappeared civilization – not even the relatively late Cretan linear alphabet. Their deciphering will remain a dream until another new bilingual Rosetta stone is discovered."

From *The Lost Civilizations of the Stone Age*
by Richard Rudgley

Vera was pleased to see her words causing Franz Werder's ruddy face to wrinkle up in amazement. Perhaps her assumptions were much closer to the truth than even she had expected.

"Look, all artifacts with Orphic messages have these symbols," she continued, pointing one after another to the ceramic vessels in the display cases.

"Couldn't these strings of symbols just be decoration?"

"Here's the crucial thing. If you look carefully, you'll see for yourself that the symbol isn't just painted randomly any old place. I even think that it might be the key to a cipher. Look at the scenes and the decorative borders below them. Each group of meanders is separated from the following ones by an equilateral cross. Sometimes there are pairs of meanders, sometimes groups of three or four, even up to five. The crosses are also different in terms of type and structure. You can see that, right?

Werder didn't reply. He scrutinized the bands of symbols as if wanting to convince himself of Vera's words. He slowly shifted his weight from one foot to the other, while his hands fidgeted behind his back. Nodding silently in front of the display cases, he looked like a stork hunting for frogs.

"If this really is a code," he began, carefully weighing every word, "what do you think it might conceal?"

"Orphic messages, perhaps. Or the Meanderites' ideas, more likely."

"So, if we assume that this knowledge has been handed down, who are the Orpheans' successors?"

"Christians," Vera blurted out, then her face froze as though she had just dropped a bomb and was waiting for the explosion.

The symbol X
in a Thracian tomb

"Christians?" he exclaimed, a hint of disappointment in his voice. He thought about mentioning blasphemy, but refrained.

"For now I can only tell you about the symbol… I'm still researching the other topic. But do you think it's just a coincidence that the Orphic symbol was used in Egypt for the letter 'X'[59] and the word 'temple'? You can easily link this to the word for 'Christ,' as well. What's more, three thousands years ago the Thracians decorated their temples with the letter "X."[60]

"How did you think to link these three cultures?"

"I realized it at a deserted chateau in Switzerland…"

"At Chateau Jacques?" he interrupted and made the sign of the cross.

Vera looked at him thunderstruck, as if no one else had the right to know about that place.

"How did you know that was the place I was talking about?"

"I read the name in the manuscript… It's part of the maze."

Vera looked at the historian in confusion.

"Never mind… Tell me more about the symbol. Please!"

And his "Please!" sounded so desperate that Vera managed to swallow her anger at his reticence and continued. "Despite the disappearance of the Meandrites, the meander survived and spread to the south and east, its meaning gradually began overlapping with that of the cross, since the two symbols were frequently used in combination."

"Interesting theory. The meander and the cross," Dr. Werder thought to himself.

"It's a natural law that every combination of symbols or letters becomes simplified and synergized over time. So gradually all that was left of the combination of the two signs was the equilateral cross – simple and convenient. It later became a symbolic guardian for the new era. Eventually the lower arm of cross was extended to its widespread, contemporary form."

---

[59] "In the original of the novel is used the Cyrillic letter "X", which is "H" in Latin"

[60] This tablet can be seen in the Bulgarian National History Museum.

202

"So the main trace of the vanished prehistoric civilization today is the Christian cross?"

"You don't believe me, do you? Look, I'm just following the symbols' messages. Very few of us realize that they preserve ancient ideas from the time when legends and reality were one..."

Vera was certain she had interpreted the symbols correctly. She had spent more time on them than anything else in her whole life. Today, however, she herself was no longer so sure that the connections she was talking about existed. She spoke mechanically – to forget what she didn't want to think about. Perhaps that was why she allowed the German scholar to glimpse the secrets she had so zealously guarded. It was as though she wanted to understand whether her theories were true or just the product of her consciousness' flight from reality. Today some important part of the overall argument was missing. And that made all the difference.

Vera tried to fight off the hubbub bombarding her from all sides – people, too many people, with their whispering, talking, squeaking shoes and annoying guffaws. They swarmed like ants between her ears as she struggled to figure out what had changed since yesterday.

Vera and Franz wandered around the gallery with ancient treasures for hours. They stopped at every exhibit and commented on it. She told the historian almost all her hypotheses, because he was listening. Some he accepted, while others he rejected.

"Have you ever suddenly seen something that had always been right in front of your eyes?" she asked.

"Sometimes I see details I want or expect to see."

"My father says the same thing... There are no coincidences, no fate. Everything is insinuation."

"He must be a wise person."

"You don't believe me... That's fine, you don't have to."

They had reached the last display case when Vera stopped once again and looked at one of the red ceramic vessels decorated with figures. Her eyes blazed triumphantly, seizing on another piece of evidence.

"Look at the band of symbols on this bowl," she showed him. "The message is clear. In the middle of the crosses there is an ancient symbol for the sun: a dot in a circle, also known as the 'Crucified Sun.'"

The historian tried to follow the young woman's thoughts, watching her eyes and the movement of her lips, then examining the ancient scenes her fingers pointed to.

Groups of foreign tourists constantly stampeded through the galleries like hunted prey. They had come to see the gold. People are always excited by the thought of gold treasures. Sometimes they are interested in silver, too, but very few stopped to look at the fired clay pots that mesmerized Vera and her German companion.

And so they came to the last red-figure bowl. The sign said it was from the fifth century BC. It featured a scene of the young god Dionysus with the Devil next to him. In ancient Greek mythology he was known as Pan, an evil mountain god who lived in a cave and frightened people with his terrifying appearance, giving rise to the word "panic." A white creature with angel's wings fluttered on the other side of Dionysus. Beneath them was a prominent band of meanders and crosses.

"Dr. Werder, you know more about Christianity, will you tell me how the Devil and the Angel came to be?"

The historian thought for a moment before replying. "They are mentioned in the Old Testament." His hollow tone hinted that he was unsure of what was behind the question.

"As far as I know, the Christians borrowed the image of the Devil from the cave-dwelling goat-man, Pan. And he appeared in around the thirteenth century."

"It had never crossed my mind that their images are completely identical…"

"See, there you are again!" She interrupted, her eyes gleaming. "Pan crawled out of his cave at the same time as Orpheus appeared."

"Perhaps he followed him up from the black depths of Tartar?" The historian laughed and then explained, "That is, when Orpheus was returning from the Underworld."

Vera didn't find his joke very funny.

"I didn't mean to offend you," he continued. "I'm not familiar with the period. I suppose that some being, a prototype of the Devil, has always been in our heads. Like God himself."

Vera's face grew serious, as if she were trying to dig something out of her memories. The gleam in her eyes faded into the shadow of wandering thoughts.

"I have to go," she said suddenly. "I don't want to miss all the lectures."

This was far from the truth, but had she spoken it – even to herself – it would've sounded pathetic. She wanted to return to the crowds at the Hotel Metropol. The crowds would fool the sense of loneliness which had been stifling her the past few days – and which was now joined by a feeling of loss.

Vera and Werder walked in silence towards the museum's exit, which poured the noisy crowds out onto a quiet street. It was thankfully free of traffic and zombified tourists gaping at unexpected visions. Only a handful of pedestrians rushed like ants in various directions, going about their business.

They walked towards the boulevard, keeping a decent distance from each other. They would try to catch a taxi or trolleybus to take them back to the hotel.

Yet before they managed to melt into the lively stream of Muscovites on the main drag, an engine roared behind them, followed by squealing brakes. Startled, Vera whirled around and instinctively clutched Werder's arm. A red van with Russian license plates stopped next to them. It was the only vehicle on the quiet street. The doors flew open and three men leapt out. They were dressed in grey, wearing dark hats and sunglasses. It all happened so quickly that Vera didn't have time to take it all in.

The men rushed towards them without hesitating and without saying a word, as if following a well-oiled plan.

"Run!" the historian shouted. But two of the men had already grabbed Vera. The other one was going for the doctor, who did nothing to defend himself. The men gagged them and shoved them into the back of the van.

The tires skidded over the wet snow and spewed gray clumps of ice as the van peeled out. The masked men tied the prisoners' hands and forced them to lie face down. The van drove quickly, constantly swerving to the right and left as if running an obstacle course. It was a rough ride; the van shuddered and shook at every bump in the road. One sharp turn sent them rolling into the side of the van. The men with the dark glasses pulled them back to their places, pinning them down with their feet and leaving them in tortuous anticipation of the next blow.

They were on the road for a long time, almost two hours. They were likely stuck in traffic most of the time, since the van almost stopped moving now and then. Only the engine growled threateningly, like a wounded animal ready to make its last stand. Vera could hardly breathe from terror. She was trying to follow the turns in the road, in a desperate attempt to figure out where they were going. If nothing else, this helped her to avoid thinking about what lay ahead. She had read about dozens of kidnappings, but now, lying on the floor of the old van, she seemed to be watching herself from the sidelines, unable to grasp the fact that this time she was the victim.

They seemed to cross the Moscow River twice. She could tell by the van's rhythmic juddering as it passed over the joins in the bridges' panels.

At last the vehicle stopped and the fear of the unknown now became more terrible than their present predicament.

The two men guarding them got out first. They opened the doors wide and took the captives out. The third man, who had been driving, also approached them. No one said a word. Vera looked at the historian. Half of his face was contorted into a terrible grimace, while the other half was hidden under a thick layer of masking tape.

"What is going on here? What do you want from us? For God's sake, this is a mistake!" he had shouted before they stuck the tape over his mouth.

Werder's face was dotted with sweat, like a glass jar filled with icy liquid. His glasses were knocked askew, hanging diagonally across his face.

The men led them through a scruffy forest of young trees towards a crumbling wall splashed with colorful graffiti. It was about six feet tall and topped with barbed wire. Beyond the wall was a derelict, three-storey building.

Vera caught a whiff of stagnant water and looked around. They were only a couple of yards from the Moscow River, which now looked much wider than it did from the bridge. The muddy water lapped at the frozen shore. On the opposite bank she could see docks, cranes, abandoned warehouses and rusting ships.

They passed through the corroded gates. The top of the fence curved outward and a coil of barbed wire crept along the edge like a huge millipede. Vera anxiously looked around for other people. It was deserted.

The building they were approaching seemed to be an old warehouse or abandoned factory. Its high windows were blackened with dust, cobwebs and mold. The white plaster walls were crumbling, erasing the graffiti sprayed on them.

Heavy rain clouds hung above the city.

Before they went in, the driver took off his hat and glasses and smoothed down his dark hair with his hand. He made a sign to the other two, his expression angry and cold.

He was the last person Vera had expected to see at that moment. Her heart thumped furiously, while her hands and feet went numb. It was Ariman, the stranger she had danced with at the restaurant the night before. She followed his eyes as though hypnotized, expecting to catch his gaze. But he was either too angry to notice anything or was deliberately avoiding her. After glancing around in all directions, he ordered one of the men to take the doctor away.

"Don't you recognize me?" Vera whispered.

He turned to look at her with cold indifference.

"What are we going to do with the woman? We don't need her. She's just a witness," the man holding her arms asked in Russian.

"We can't let her go," Ariman replied angrily. "Take her up to the room."

The man jerked her sharply around the side of the building and through a low doorway. A dark concrete corridor engulfed them in its cold, damp embrace. They came to a narrow spiral staircase, as in a lighthouse, which took them up to the second floor. The man opened an iron door and pulled Vera in. He wordlessly surveyed the room, as if daring her to find a way to escape the airtight space. He did not take off his glasses or hat, but Vera could see a few stray locks of blond hair.

The small windowless room had two beds. The crumpled sheets indicated someone had slept there recently. The man shoved her down onto one of the beds and quickly left the room, turning the key in the lock behind him.

ANYTHING BUT A DREAM

*The first lines of **page 439** had been erased, leaving the following lines:*
"But the dream does not end here. The woman added, 'At some time later the bull was pierced with a golden arrow.' Now in addition to Dionysus we can see another proto-Christian ritual in which the bull plays a symbolic role. Mitra, the Persian sun god, also sacrificed a bull. And like Orpheus, he expressed the desire for eternal life of the spirit which triumphs over the primitive animal passions of man. And the ceremony of secret enlightenment gives peace to the soul."

From *Symbols in Art* **by Carl Jung, 1964, p. 143.**

Vera must have fallen asleep waiting in the dark room for the door to open. A distant rumbling, like something heavy being unloaded on the floor below, awoke her.

She was lying on the one of the beds. She had rolled a black sweater she had found on the bed into a ball to use as a pillow. It bore the faint masculine scent of the man who had recently worn it.

She sat up on the bed, the worn-out springs creaking like rusty hinges. Her head felt heavy. She didn't know what time it was or how long she had slept.

Thirsty, Vera got up from the bed, standing still until her eyes got used to the dark. Feeling her way through the blackness, she walked in the direction of the door. When she reached the cold wall, she ran her fingers over it to find a light switch. Her palms became entangled in cobwebs, which she quickly wiped back on the wall. She eventually found the switch and flipped on the bulb hanging from the ceiling.

She turned around and saw that she was locked in a bare concrete box. A paint-spattered board stood on four legs in the middle of the room. Scattered on this makeshift table were several crumpled plastic cups. There was also a pile of antiques catalogues, maps and photographs of places unfamiliar to Vera. There was also a sink. Rubbing her dry lips together, Vera turned on the tap. She tried the water, but it tasted rusty.

Vera went back to the door and tugged at it, even though she knew it was locked. She leaned against its frigid surface. She could feel her heart beating hysterically, while the breath she sucked in couldn't seem to reach her lungs. She wanted to start screaming and not stop until her air ran out.

She still didn't know where she was or why and at whose command.

She looked for her cell phone, surprised to find it still with her. She hastily took it out of her pocket and tried Kaloyan, the first number on her list of missed calls. She mechanically dialed the number but there was no signal – either they were out of range or something in the building was jamming it.

A chair with a wicker seat stood next to the table, so old that the bottom was stretched like a basket. Next to it was an army green backpack. Vera hesitated for a moment, then untied the string at the bag's neck. She reached inside, hoping to find some clean water or food. Her fingers plunged into the crumpled clothes. Hearing something rustling at the bottom of the sack, she put her hand in deeper and found something flat and wide wrapped in paper.

She listened for foot steps. Hearing nothing, she took the object out of the bag. It was wrapped in newspaper printed in an Asian script. She quickly opened the package. Her whole body shook nervously as her ears struggled against the silence to pick up the slightest sound. She imagined that someone might come in at any second and find her rummaging through the backpack.

From between the paper's folds something bright yellow caught the naked bulb's light. Vera stopped shaking and forgot about listening.

In her hands she held an exquisite gold tablet. Her eyes feverishly traced its engravings. About four by five inches wide and approximately half an inch thick, it was made of two thin plates put together. It had no front or back; instead, both sides were covered with deep lines grouped into signs and arranged in rows of symbols and letters lost to modern man. Vera recognized some but not others.

She examined the tile in amazement, turning it over to inspect both sides. The engraved gold surfaces resembled the famous Orphic tablets found in Italy, Greece and Bulgaria. However, such artifacts were normally as thin as parchment and engraved only on one side, primarily with Greek letters.

Vera recognized some Greek symbols here, too. Yet on the other side there were hieroglyphs larger than the letters. She tried to discover the meaning of the rows, arranged like beads on a string.

A noise came from the corridor, like the sound of a metal door closing. Vera jumped, so startled that the tablet slipped from her fingers.

She quickly snatched it up and started to hide it in her clothes, but then she realized what might happen if her captors caught her trying to steal the precious tablet. Frightened by her own imagination, she took out her cell phone and snapped pictures of both sides, then hurried to put it back, like a child who has found a forbidden toy.

The steps in the hallway got louder and closer. Vera tried to wrap the gold object back in the newspaper, but her fingers felt as soft as putty and refused to obey.

The footsteps came to a stop as a key turned in the lock. Vera whirled around at the sound. A figure emerged from the darkness of the corridor. Ariman.

He was dressed in military fatigues. The visor of his cap cast a shadow over his face, making him look even more severe than he had that morning.

Vera held her breath, as motionless as an ice statue. She was still holding the gold tablet and newspaper in her hands. She felt the crushing weight of his furious gaze, his frowning, cold face. She instinctively took a step back. Without saying a word he followed her. He came closer until he was only inches away, all the while fixing her with eyes clouded with rage. He took the tile from her, raised his hand, hesitated for a split second, then struck her across the face.

Vera fell to the floor, feeling heaviness rather than pain. The shapes before her eyes became shadows, which in turn faded into a cloud of dust and glittering gnats. Seconds passed before she realized where she was, as if surfacing from a terrible nightmare.

She felt a stinging pain in her cheek. She touched it, lying helplessly on the floor and waiting for whatever came next. Her eyes followed his outline as her terrified mind screamed, "Who is this man?"

Ariman turned towards the door and closed it. He propped his fist against the frame, resting his forehead against it with his back to Vera. His head was covered with baseball cap. He stood like that for almost a minute – as though someone had slapped his face, not Vera's. He now seemed to be hesitating whether to get on with the inevitable or fight it to the last.

Vera watched him in disbelief, not daring to move.

Ariman finally turned around. He went over to the girl's crumpled body and carefully lifted her arms. Then he tied them – so tightly that she let out a muffled cry.

He didn't react. He didn't seem to have heard. When he pulled her to her feet, she meekly obeyed. They left the room and went back down the dark staircase. All she could see were stairs, concrete and rusty iron. The walls were damp. They walked past a narrow window. Moonbeams seeped through the dirty glass.

Ariman quickened his pace. The stairs led to a peeling door that resembled the bulkhead of a ship, just large enough for a person to fit through. He opened it and turned on the light. The fluorescent tubes began flickering and hissing from the high ceilings like angry ghosts.

Vera looked around. The room looked like a deserted harbor warehouse. Piles of abandoned junk, broken machines and remnants of furniture towered in the corners. The floor was covered with timeworn green linoleum, while the acrid smell of mold and marsh water hung in the air.

Ariman squeezed Vera's upper arm and led her into the room. She felt the floor creak under their feet. "It must be wooden," she thought.

Suddenly she saw human legs sprawled motionless on the floor, sticking out from behind a pillar. As they approached, she recognized Dr. Werder.

"Sit down!" Ariman ordered in a low voice.

"How long are you going to hold us hostage?" Werder asked quickly, as though he hadn't seen his captors in days.

The man didn't deign to look at him. His eyes met Vera's, but quickly looked away. He turned around and left the room. Before closing the iron door, he turned off the droning bluish lights.

"Who are these people? What do they want from us?" Franz Werder whispered.

"I don't know."

They fell silent. From a distance they could hear the roaring of the river, carried to them on the snowy wind. Rhythmic drops of water marked time in the incorporeal darkness, falling on an old sheet of tin that rattled and danced to the drumming.

"Did they want anything from you?"

"Yes, actually… They made me identify and date an object," Werder replied hesitantly.

These words took his thoughts several hours back. The memory was so clear that he could still feel the blows to his body and face, like a whirlwind of steel balls coming at him from all sides. He had raised his hands to shield himself. The men were sure he was hiding something and were determined to find out what.

They had asked him again and again whether the stone amulet was the original or a fake. Was it the same one that had disappeared from Hitler's bunker in 1945? But Franz Werder kept giving them the same answer: he had never seen it, except in a black and white photograph in an old Bode Museum catalogue. He suggested they find equipment so that he could carry out some elementary tests. The men agreed and again locked him up in the warehouse.

"What was the artifact?" Vera asked.

"A nondescript medallion that supposedly shows Orpheus crucified on Christ's cross. I saw it the other day in the museum vault."

"So it really does exist!"

THE CRUCIFIXION

Page 440 began with the words:
"Plato, who propounds the teachings of Orpheus and his rituals in the Dialogues, says the following in The Republic:
'They will tell you that the just man who is thought unjust will be scourged, racked, bound, will have his eyes burned out; and, at last, after suffering every kind of evil, he will be crucified.'"

Plato, The Republic **II, 361E**

Thin scalpels of light flicked through the boarded-up windows, dissecting the darkness and illuminating the cloud of dust and flies whirling around in the void.

Vera opened her eyes. She recognised the outlines of the junk heaps cluttering the warehouse. She heard the familiar rhythmic tapping of drops on the dancing metal sheets. Only the nauseating smell had disappeared – probably because she had gotten used to it. Just as the nose grows desensitized to scents, supposedly a person can get used to anything.

"Another day here!" she thought, her entire body quivering in anguish.

She felt Dr. Werder fidgeting anxiously. He sounded like a giant caterpillar writhing on the other side of the concrete pillar.

"There's got to be a way," he muttered, "I have to get out of here. This rope is so tight!"

Vera also felt the ropes chafing her wrists and cutting into her skin.

"Let's try to loosen them," Werder continued. Talking seemed to calm him. "They'll be back soon – for me!"

The historian fell silent and stopped moving. Only his tense breathing could be heard, fast and labored. Vera could see the damp, warm cloud of his breath wafting from behind the pillar and cooling in the darkness, sliced by the thin shards of light. The cold felt like centipedes crawling all over her body.

"Why is the Orphic amulet so important to these people?" she whispered.

Werder didn't answer. His breath was the only sign he was still there.

"Is the man crucified on it really Orpheus?" Vera continued.

"That's what it says on the stone."

"I've always wanted to know the truth…"

"There is no truth. It's just a piece of stone with an image of a crucifixion and an inscription 'Orpheos – Bakkikos.'"[61]

Vera fell silent, hearing a distant scratching and rattling sound. It was coming from the darkest part of the warehouse, but seemed to be getting closer. She drew her legs up close to her body, despite the pins and needles racing along them. But the rustling disappeared, so she assumed she must have imagined it.

"Crucifixion is just a metaphor," Dr. Werder explained. "It symbolizes an agonizing public execution."

-----

[61] The 1909 catalogue from the Berlin Museum offers the following description of the amulet: "Christ, dressed in a tunic, is crucified on a cross anchored to the ground by two symmetrical wedges. A half-moon rests on top of the cross, with an arc of seven stars arranged above it. This item is notable for the history of religion, as Christ is depicted in Orpheus' place, rather than vice-versa…. Beneath the cross' horizontal bar, there is an inscription reading ORFEOS–BAKKIKOS." In 1921, Eisler wrote: "The crucified Christ on the cross, whose astro-mystical significance is made obvious through the addition of the half-moon and the seven stars – most likely Pleiades or the so-called Lyre of Orpheus. The cross should most likely be identified with the main stars from the constellation Orion, which in Antiquity was considered Dionysus' constellation." BAKKIKOS (Bacchus) is one of the names for Dionysus.

"For religions it has never been important how real individuals die, but rather how their public images do."

They again fell silent. Vera whispered, "They must be looking for it, too, right?"

"For what?"

"The truth. Why else would those men keep us here just to get you to date some piece of stone? They could be members of some secret society!"

"The White Brotherhood,[62] no doubt!" Franz Werder said sarcastically, forcing out a desperate laugh.

"Why not? They could be loyal guardians of the Christian faith, fighting to preserve a history stitched together with white threads. A stolen history. They gather up all the evidence that contradicts their version and destroy it. Just imagine! A centuries-old brotherhood whose duty is to preserve the white threads of faith. How original is that?! I'll have to include it in my book."

"I'm sorry," he whispered.

"For what?"

"It's my fault you're here. You were a innocent witness in the wrong place at the wrong time."

"Do you think they'll kill us?"

"God only knows."

"Which god?"

---

[62] The White Brotherhood is an esoteric Christian sect that was founded by Bulgarian mystic Peter Konstantinov Deunov, also known as Master Beinsa Douno, in the early twentieth century.

SENSES OF DOUBT

Page 441 began with an Orphic quote from one of the oldest Hellenic scrolls:
"We go into the oracular shrine in order to ask, on behalf of those seeking oracular answers, if it is right... the terrors of Hades, why are they distrustful? Not understanding dreams, nor any of the other real things, on the basis of what kinds of examples would they have trust? For overcome both by fault and by something else, pleasure, they neither know nor trust. For distrust is the same as ignorance."

The Derveni Papyrus, Col. V, translated by Andre Laks and Glenn Most

Ariman was alone. He had sent the others to look for the equipment and chemicals the historian had asked for.

He slowly climbed the stairs to the upper floor. He closed the middle door and continued down the hall. His echoing footsteps tapped out a steady rhythm. After a dozen steps, he stopped. Had he heard something? The lamps were buzzing like a nest of wasps. The light at the end of the hall was broken and crackled like a dying television.

Not hearing the noise again, Ariman walked on. He reached the room and unlocked the metal door. He went inside and closed it behind him. He took off his boots and placed them next to the door frame, feeling a throbbing relief in his toes. He looked around the room carefully as though he expected something to have changed.

He went over and sat down on the bed. It was made – which wasn't how he had left it. He saw the black sweater rolled into a ball and realized that the girl must have used it. He picked it up and brought it to his face for several seconds, closing his eyes to fully inhale the scent.

Ariman set it back down and ran his hand over the bedspread lightly, as if frightened that it might catch fire. He wanted to feel the warmth of the body that had been lying on it. When he reached the end of the bed, he made a fist to catch the buzzing mosquitoes. Actually, they weren't mosquitoes, but flies. He hadn't noticed them before. He lay back and relaxed, alone on the bed. He breathed deeply and stared blindly at the ceiling.

Only now did he feel the pain in his shoulder. He had been grazed by a bullet as he fled from the second museum guard, who had heard Ariman execute his co-worker. He put his hand beneath his shirt and felt the wound, which was crusted with dried blood.

He undressed and stood in front of the mirror. He turned to the sink next to it and opened the tap, releasing a gush of rusty water. Ariman took a sponge from the side of the sink and soaked it with water. He wet the wound, letting the water wash away the blood, which began trickling down his arm and chest. He mopped up the rivulets with the sponge and rinsed it in the sink. He washed the wound a second time. His face was expressionless, as if he were washing someone else's wound. Only his chest muscles clenched and relaxed. His skin was so white that the pink drops looked like blood spattered on snow.

After washing his wound, he examined it in the blackened mirror. He decided there was no need for stitches and put his shirt back on. He fastened the buttons, concentrating on every movement. Then he went back to the bed, stretched out fully and closed his eyes.

Next month he would be thirty-four years old. Most people in the underworld were younger than he was, yet they hardly ever left it. The Incorporeal One usually sent Ariman on missions.

Ariman personally believed that he had been born Above. He somehow felt at home here, yet had no clear memory of his childhood. Time has a way of changing the shape and color of the past until you are not sure what is real and what is invented.

No one had ever told him where he had come from. And where he had grown up, questions were never asked. There was only the set order of things, which had to be maintained.

All he could remember from before was that he had lived with a woman in a wooden house. She must have been his mother, since he had no memories of any other woman. The house was surrounded by reeds and rice paddies. They both worked in one of them. He never saw his father in his visions.

The place seemed to have been very bright. When there is lots of light, you hardly notice it. But you remember it very well once you've lost it.

He could see himself laughing. He couldn't have been more than four years old.

Only the memory of his last day there stood out from the rest. It was seared so deeply in his mind that it had become part of his body. When he was sick or in pain, the memory itself ached, while when he was content, the nightmare fell silent.

It always began with him feeling like he was asleep, only to be awakened by screams.

It was his mother.

He leapt out of bed and ran down the wooden stairs to the kitchen. She was still screaming. A man was sitting on top of her, pummeling her. She screamed again. Then the man hit his mother so hard that she didn't make another sound. She stopped moving. The man turned around. Their eyes met. Ariman knew him. He was the foreigner who lived in the white house in town. The foreigner ran away, while Ariman stood frozen on the stairs between the lower and upper floor for a whole day and night, the tears streaming down his cheeks. He surely would have died, too, if a stranger hadn't arrived, a man who hid his face in a cloak, as if fearing the sun would burn him to ashes. He was strange, but Ariman had no way of knowing it then. And now after so much time had passed, he was used to the man in the cloak, so that his strangeness no longer made any difference. In the beginning Ariman simply called him "Sir." There was nothing else he could call him, the stranger wasn't his father or master. And the strange man called the boy "Ariman."

The next day Sir brought a gun and gave it to the boy. Everything was clear without a single word. Ariman went and shot the foreigner in the white house.

Then Sir took the boy away from the rice paddies and the light.

Today Ariman was no longer certain how much of the story was true and how much was invented. He had even forgotten the smell of the rice paddies, until he saw them at the edge of the Burmese lake. However, he had been taught that even when you know the truth, the only thing that matters is what you believe.

Most of the boys in the underworld rarely ascended to the Sun People's world, especially those who had been born below. They were too pale and too different. If they did venture out they always had to wear a cloak, like the Teacher. Even in the moonlight. And this raised suspicion and fear in the inhabitants of the upper lands.

There were times when he thought of not returning. Yet when he imagined it, everything lost meaning and the life drained from his body. He could not fathom any existence without the missions to give it meaning, just as he could not picture his life without the familiar order. It was the only thing that gave him the strength to wake up in the morning and the solace to fall asleep at night. It was the reason he stopped at nothing. It was why he always went back.

Although he was still asleep, clammy beads of sweat dotted his forehead and dripped onto the pillow.

His eyes flew open. He leapt up abruptly like a soldier on duty. He looked at his watch – he had slept for almost an hour. "The boys should have returned by now," he thought. "They've been gone too long." Or perhaps they hadn't dared to wake him. They were no good for this kind of work.

He pulled on the boots standing sentry by the door and went back down the hallway towards the warehouse.

His steely eyes reflected the light of the flickering, icy-yellow lamp, while his tireless shadow followed closely on his heels.

Redemption

Page 442 said:

"'He granted him the strength of the silver-eddying Aheloy, (Orpheus named the river 'Aheloy') and of the moon, which showed itself to many on the endless earth' (Orphic words from the Derven papyrus). If the moon exceeds its bounds, existing things can be seen more clearly than before. But Orpheus did not mean this when he used 'showed itself'; because if he did mean this he wouldn't have said 'showed itself to many,' but rather 'to all.' Because without the moon people would not be able to measure the seasons or the winds... or any other things."

From **Hellenic Orphic Witnesses** by M. Aleksieva, p. 188

She heard it again. The scratching sounded like fingernails scraping sandpaper. It was getting louder and closer. This time Vera was convinced it was not her imagination – people have an amazing ability to hear and see what they are afraid of.

Vera sat up and stared blindly into the darkness, as if surfacing from an abyss. She had dozed off in the chill of the empty warehouse. Sleep was the best thing she could hope for here. Her hands were still tied. Her back was propped against the cold pillar. The rays of sunlight peeking through the boarded up windows had grown thin and grey. "It'll be dark soon," she thought. Then she realized that it didn't matter.

Suddenly she heard light scraping and tapping on the floor, like sparrows scuttling over a tin roof.

The noises were real.

"Did you hear that?" she whispered.

At that instant, the tapping stopped.

"Rats. I saw them here last night."

"Rats!?" Vera shouted.

"They'll come out as soon as the light fades. They're attracted by the crumbs from the sandwiches they bring us."

"I'm scared of mice!" she exclaimed, flailing her legs helplessly.

"They haven't bitten me at all since I've been here."

"I'm scared!" Vera tried to stand up, but tumbled back to the floor.

"They've only tied our hands," the historian noted. "Are they afraid we might escape?"

"How could we? There's only one door… and that's locked. The windows are boarded up and too high."

"But there are the rats."

"So?"

"They must come from somewhere. There must be an opening somewhere…"

Vera didn't reply, unsure of where he was going with this.

"I have an idea," Dr. Werder continued. "If we sit back-to-back we might be able to untie our hands."

"If they catch us they'll be even angrier."

"We could at least try. They're going to kill us anyway."

Vera didn't believe this last statement. That man, whoever he was, couldn't kill her. She had felt something – they both had – while they were dancing. Or perhaps her confidence stemmed from the naïve belief that death is something that happens to other people. In any case, she staggered to her knees and crawled towards Werder. She propped her back against his as he had suggested. They felt the ropes, searching for knots or loose ends.

Vera's rope was tied so tightly that Werder could not budge it. She groaned in frustration. She tore her nail to the quick but continued clawing at the knots binding the historian's hands. She finally felt one of the loops give slightly. After much persistent tugging, she finally forced her slender fingers through the coils.

"You've loosened it!" Werder exclaimed.

He rubbed his hands against each other until the noose around his wrists slackened completely. Werder stood up and unwound the remaining rope. In the darkness he felt around on the floor with his foot, searching for something.

"What are you doing?"

"I kicked a piece of glass yesterday – or something that sounded like a piece of glass. I might be able to cut your ropes."

"My dearest Dr. Werder, wouldn't there be more glass under the windows?"

"I don't want to frighten the rats."

"Are you crazy?"

"Please, call me Franz. I think we've spent enough time together to be on a first-name basis. The rats might show us the way out."

Something clinked under Werder's foot. He had found the piece of glass amidst the grime. The linoleum floor obviously hadn't been cleaned in years. The historian dragged the fragment towards him with the sole of his shoe.

"I've got it!" he cried.

He went over to Vera and began rubbing the rope with the glass' sharp edges. Eventually one of the strands snapped and her hands sprang apart. She pressed her wrists to her chest to dull the pain.

"And now what?" whispered Vera.

"Quiet. We've frightened the rats."

Vera had no choice but to trust Werder's crazy idea. The three days spent in the dark warehouse without regular food and in constant fear must have wreaked havoc on their psyches. However, she would rather chase mice than sit there doing nothing.

Werder told her to squat down. They stayed like that for a few minutes, silently listening to the echoes of distant noises.

"I hear them! At the back of the room, to the left," Werder broke the silence. "Follow me!"

Vera obeyed. The rays of sunlight had dissolved into the dark, leaving only shadows. Listening for Werder's footsteps, she followed him, trying to match his long strides. The indeterminate scratching gradually became the sound of hundreds of unseen paws and claws scampering along the linoleum, tin and concrete. Frightened, the little animals fled from the people's threatening movements.

"Watch out for the wall!" Werder warned.

She squinted and stretched her arms out as far as she could. She felt the rough, cold barrier and stopped for a moment. The historian was going to the left, along the wall. Vera followed him with her back pressed to the wall so as not to get lost in the darkness. She could feel the rough patches of plaster hooking her coat and pulling her back, like the talons of a bird-of-prey. Her outstretched fingers felt something soft and warm. It was Werder's back.

"They're hiding somewhere here…. There must be a hole out into the drains," he muttered, first in German, then when he realized that Vera was close by, he repeated his words in English.

"What can we do?"

"We'll have to look for it. They came from all directions and disappeared near the wall. Let's try to lift up the linoleum."

They bent down in the dark and found the edge of the floor covering. After a brief hesitation, Vera poked her fingers between the rubber and the concrete. Werder had done the same. Together they strained to lift the huge slab of linoleum. Over the years it had fused with the concrete floor in some places. Vera felt some soft, slimy balls between her fingers – and realized that they were moving. The underside of the linoleum was covered with hundreds of dormant slugs and many-legged bugs, swarming everywhere. One of them crawled over her fingers. She dropped the rubber edge and jumped backwards, shaking her hands and shrieking.

"Now's not the time to behave like a girl," Werder said crossly. "They won't eat you. We have to lift it up. I can't do it alone." His choked voice reflected the tremendous effort it took to lift the heavy, shapeless sheet of linoleum.

"But… it's covered with slugs and centipedes."

"I know. That means we're close to the drains."

226

Vera's face wrinkled in revulsion, but she bent down and picked up the edge of the linoleum again.

She accidentally squashed some slugs, but tried to focus on the weight in her hands. They managed to lift the linoleum a couple feet off the floor.

"I'll try to hold it. You go underneath and look for an opening," Werder said, gasping.

"No way."

"I would do it myself but you haven't got the strength to hold the linoleum."

"There's no way I'm crawling under there…"

"Those men will be back at any moment, don't you understand? We've made a lot of noise!"

Vera didn't reply. She knelt down, gritted her teeth and closed her mouth tightly. Praying not to swallow any centipedes, she began crawling. Grimaces of disgust contorted her face. As her hands explored the damp surface, she tried not to think of what the lumps and bumps she could feel were. Sharp stones stung her hands. Several centipedes crawled up her arms, but she shook them off. She kept her eyes tightly shut, since it was too dark to see in any case.

Finally the concrete under her fingers gave way to a cold metal surface. Vera felt it carefully. It was round with four symmetrical holes in the middle.

"I think I've found the cover to the drains!" she shouted.

"Try to open it," the doctor hissed through his teeth. The linoleum was starting to slip from his hands.

"It's really heavy!" she complained.

"You don't have any choice!"

Vera yanked at the drain cover with both hands, but barely managed to lift it. She wedged one of her shoes into the narrow crack she had created and managed to lever it up a bit further. Then she pushed it to one side. The heavy metal clanging broke the silence.

"There's a channel down there… and running water!" she shouted.

"Try to prop up the linoleum with the cover. I'll crawl down there, too."

Summoning all her strength, Vera managed to force the iron lid upwards until it propped up the stiff linoleum.

"Quick, someone's opening the door!" Werder shouted in terror.

Pale electric light flooded the empty warehouse, its fleshless tentacles reaching into the hole where Vera was lying and illuminating the damp bodies of the hundreds of little creatures aroused from their torpor. Without a thought for the consequences, Vera jumped into the drain pipe. She hung by her fingertips in the cold black void for a second and then let herself fall.

"Freeze!" She heard a rasping male voice shout as footsteps quickly approached.

Werder jumped in after Vera. When you have no choice, even the most repulsive decision is easy to make.

They landed with a splash in the stream and let its current drag them along. Vera heard two distant, muffled gunshots, whose echo thundered through the drainpipe.

Finally, between the vaulted stone roof and the water's sparkling surface, a blue hint of moon appeared through an iron grate where the drain flowed into the river.

"Oh my God! There's a grate! We can't get out!" Vera sobbed.

The water bubbled around the ancient rusted metal bars and disappeared out into the vast currents of the Moscow River. Werder grabbed the grate and started pushing and pulling at it. Its rotted base began to give way. Bracing his arms against the walls of the drainpipe for support, he kicked the metal barrier. The dark, dirty water swept it away. Werder grabbed Vera's hand as they let the current spit them out into the river.

Across the water they could see the city with its millions of lights glowing on the opposite shore. Its kaleidoscopic reflection shimmered on the churning black river, transforming it into a living watercolor. Directly above Vera and Werder, the full moon draped the sky in a filmy veil. The falling sleet threatened at any moment to turn to snow.

The two of them scrambled to their feet in the knee-deep muck and tried to climb up the muddy bank. The river was far too cold for swimming – otherwise it would have been the ideal escape route. Their shoes slipped in the sticky mud, while the weight of their drenched clothing pulled them back towards the water. Grabbing at trees, branches and weeds, they managed to haul themselves up onto a flat path and took off running, leaving the old warehouse behind them.

Vera glanced back. Their captors were fast on their trail and had almost caught up with them.

Ariman was closest, followed by the other two. Werder squeezed Vera's hand, dragging her along. He pushed her in front of him, shouting, "Don't stop! We have to cross the bridge!"

About twenty yards in front of them an iron railroad bridge linked the two banks of the river. Completely deserted and dark, its heavy metal body hunched over the river.

The moon, larger than ever in the Moscow night sky, nipped at the two fugitives' heels. It lit up the thunderclouds attempting to swallow it up.

"I was wrong about him," Vera whispered as they ran.

"Pardon?" Werder asked in confusion.

Two more shots rang out. Werder yelped in pain and fell to the ground. Vera stopped and knelt down by him, staring in dumb amazement, trying to grasp the harsh truth that bullets could hit anyone, even her. She could be the one lying facedown on the ground.

Like a half-crushed insect, Werder made a desperate effort to stand. He dug his fingers into the mud and strained, yet his strength failed and he crumpled back to the ground. Vera squeezed his hand and tried to lift him, but he moaned in agony.

"There's nothing you can do to help me… Run for the bridge." His words dissolved into the cold March wind.

Vera looked in confusion first at him and then at the men, who were getting closer. They were only a few yards away and holding their fire. Perhaps they wanted them alive. Or perhaps they just wanted to avoid the messy evidence of another pool of blood in the mud.

"Run, for God's sake, run!" Werder hissed, without the strength even to lift his head.

His words hit her like a slap in the face. She let go of his shoulder and whispered, "I'm sorry!"

"In Rome… look for the *Parchment Maze*… In the library at the end of the oldest street near Quo Vadis," he spluttered.

Vera could hear the men's footsteps. She sprinted for the bridge without even registering his words. She was terrified, tired, freezing, barely able to breathe – she felt nothing, not even her legs moving below her or her arms fighting their way through the icy rain. If a bullet were to hit her now, she doubted she would even feel it.

She reached the bridge. Another shot pierced the damp night air, followed by a powerful metallic crash. The bullet had hit one of the iron girders of the bridge. Vera turned around. Ariman was only a couple steps behind her. He would catch her at any moment. She stepped onto the bridge and began sprinting even faster. She jumped over the high railings and continued running along the outside of the bridge, hoping this might hinder her pursuer. But the ledge was so narrow and slippery that she had to slow down and cling to the iron railings. The strip she was walking along was no wider than a man's foot. Beneath her the churning Moscow River rushed towards the centre of the city.

"Stop right there!" the man shouted at her.

Vera stopped and looked into his eyes. His stare had lost its muted veneer. It had been replaced by something else, she wasn't sure what. His eyes seemed more alive, more earthly, perhaps more terrified.

"Stop or I'll shoot!" he repeated.

He walked slowly towards her until they were separated only by the iron railing. The gun was pointed at her forehead. They stood in silence for a few moments, staring like old friends trying to recognize each other after many years, rather than like a victim and a cold-blooded assassin.

The rain turned to snow. The drops became light snowflakes dancing in the air, twinkling with the city lights.

This is the bridge which Vera jumped off to escape from Ariman.

Those few seconds were all Vera needed to decide. Still facing the bridge, she slid her feet to the edge of the ledge. Her heels were over the open water. Her hands squeezed the iron railing. The man didn't move. He kept the gun pointed at her forehead, confident that she could not escape and that everything was under his control.

They did not take their eyes off each other. At that moment she was not thinking so much about the black water below her, but about his expression, which she could not read.

Vera slid back a few more inches and plunged off the bridge.

The frigid water engulfed her body, so icy that she could not feel the cold, just a terrible pain piercing her brain. Within a fraction of a second it coursed through her nerve endings like an electric shock and hammered into her consciousness like dozens of nails.

The swift current swallowed her up. For the first few moments she tried thrashing around with her arms and legs, but she was powerless against the river's might. As her body began to stiffen, she realized there was no point in struggling. She rolled onto her back and watched as the iron bridge and the motionless figure of the man by the railings disappeared into the distance.

Then she closed her eyes.

THE BROADLY FLOWING OCEAN

Page 443 began with the words of Orpheus:
"He possessed the enormous might of the broadly flowing Okeanos...
This verse has been made misleading and it is unclear to the many, but to those who understand correctly it is clear that Okeanos is the air and air is Zeus... But those who do not understand think that Okeanos is a river, because [Orpheus] added the epithet 'broadly flowing.' But he indicates his meaning in current and customary expressions. For they say that the very powerful among men 'flowed great'..."

From the Derven Papyrus, Col. 23, translated by Gabor Betegh

The day was quiet and clear. A young woman hurried down the sidewalk along the river. Her high heels rhythmically tapped the paving stones. She folded her arms across her chest and bowed her head to protect her face from the stinging wind. Her body was wrapped in a thick beige coat.

The walkway along the river followed the curves of the empty boulevard. Out of habit, when she reached Christ the Saviour Cathedral,[63] she went down the steps of the stone parapet. She

---

[63] The cathedral is one of the most important symbols of Moscow and one of the most impressive Orthodox churches in Russia. Construction on the original Christ the Savior Church began in 1839 and lasted more than 40 years. It was meant to express Russians' gratitude to God for saving them during the

breathed in the fresh air and stretched her neck towards the sky like a turtle. She blinked and let the pale sun caress her frozen face.

Below street level there was a wide landing where the river's waves crashed and broke. In the summer tourboats docked here to unload curious foreigners in front of the cathedral, the pride of Moscow. Like ants let out of a jar, they scurried up the steps and down the boulevard to the white cathedral whose majestic golden dome glittered in the light like the sun fallen to earth.

The woman had already reached the last step when she saw a lifeless body. Screaming, she ran back up the steps and bolted across the boulevard in a panic – luckily, there was little traffic early in the morning so she did not become a casualty herself. She ran into the church across from the steps waving her arms wildly and yelling for help like a mad woman driving away evil spirits. Two priests who were just putting on their robes for the morning service ran towards the woman to find out what the ruckus was about.

The woman led them to the body and stayed with them to watch. Despite their terror, onlookers are always fascinated by drowning victims.

A web of long, wet hair hid the girl's face. However, her chest was still moving slightly, almost imperceptibly. One of the priests peeled away a few blond locks of hair from her cheeks to get a better look at her. Putting his fingers to her jugular vein, he whispered, "She's alive."

The two men lifted the fragile, wet body and carried it into the golden-domed church. The dozens of stone angels, warriors and saints lining the windows and doors of the cathedral dispassionately watched the unfolding tragedy.

War of 1812. In 1931, Stalin ordered the church to be demolished in order for a monument to socialism, The Palace of Soviets, to be built on the site. After years of unsuccessful construction, the gaping foundation hole was eventually converted into a huge swimming pool. At the initiative of Moscow Mayor Andrey Luzhkov, the cathedral was rebuilt during the 1990s.

Vera could feel arms carrying her, but could neither move nor speak. Suddenly it was dark and she caught the scent of incense, smoke and candles. The men in dark robes had carried her into the church. They laid her down in front of an exquisite chapel in the center of the cathedral on a dusty red carpet upon which the higher clergy had recently processed with chants, crosses and incense.

One of the priests knelt down next to her and held her hand as if to hear her final confession. The other man ran off to call an ambulance. Vera could feel the fingers touching her palm but could not move. A warmth settled over her body, which nevertheless remained heavy and stiff, as if her senses had been locked up in a dark box. Yet the box was hollow, with only her heart inside, thumping against the walls.

Her eyelids fluttered open and she glimpsed seven auburn angels dancing in a circle. Smiling indifferently from the dome of the cathedral, they were looking down at her with the sort of eyes that follow you everywhere. The enormous nave was lit up by dozens of flames perched like fire flies atop long, slender wax columns. They danced rhythmically, weaving a pale veil of light. Above them, huge electric chandeliers gave a resplendent glow to the gilded wood carvings and plaster ornaments adorning the cathedral's vaulted ceilings.

Something brighter attracted her attention in the dark depths of the sanctuary – a round bright yellow light was shining in the darkness like an invisible tunnel opening up in her soul. Vera squinted to get a better look. It was the sun. In a cave.

She felt a pleasant tickling sensation, just where she had felt the warmth a moment earlier. The symbols were following her even here – although she was probably imagining it.

Yet the yellow circle continued blazing like the sun, the supreme divinity according to Orphic beliefs. Also, the Orphic mysteries were usually performed in caves where followers believed the Mother Goddess had conceived and given birth to the deity. But what was the solar god doing in an Orthodox Cathedral? The sun was not usually depicted in Christian churches.

"I must be dying." The thought stung her.

She squinted even harder to try to see, almost closing her eyes. She realized it was not the sun, but a mural depicting the birth of the infant Jesus. A white, sun-like halo surrounded the Christ child – who was also born in a cave.

The day's most impatient tourists and worshippers were beginning to enter the church. Many were lighting candles, filling the sanctuary with a buzzing flurry of movement.

Utterly soaked, Vera was shaking. She still had no control over her body. Black-clad men leaned over her anxiously, coming between her and the auburn angels. As in a dream, their mouths were moving and she heard the words, yet could not grasp their meaning.

She closed her eyes and again saw the man with the gun. He was standing frozen on the bridge only a few feet from her. His eyes radiated a strength that pierced her body like the bullet he had yet to fire. He stared at her without moving, as if unsure of what to do. The muzzle was trained on her head. A second later the icy water swallowed her…

Vera coughed violently, as water painfully squeezed from her lungs tried to find its way out of her throat. One of the men turned her head to the side, so she would not choke as she spat out mud from the river bottom.

When she opened her eyes again she saw a tall white tabernacle with gilded ornamentation, topped by a large cross. Symmetrical scenes of the Virgin Mary and the Christ Child were painted on either side of it. Inside the tabernacle was another, darker fresco with a rare depiction of the Last Supper. Jesus was calmly sitting in the center of the table with a bright halo around his head. In front of him was bread and a glass of wine. His disciples were listening to him, entranced.

The nave was incrusted with gold equilateral crosses. Crosses… she kept seeing them ever more frequently. In the modern world this symbol had many meanings, bequeathed from antiquity and from all corners of the world.

Vera sensed she was on the verge of passing out. The images disappeared one after another, as if they had been merely figments of her imagination. First the fiery haloes died away, then the light itself began to fade, extinguished by the weight of her eyelids.

The crowd of murmuring tourists gathered around the wet body. They gawked at the motionless figure for a moment, then continued on to the candle stands to add their own little flames to the collection. Afterwards they rushed off to the next tourist attraction. The smoke imbued the air with a somber melody, harmonized by the echo of whispers and shoes scraping the scuffed floor.

The song faded into a distant rumble and finally dissolved into silence.

THE MESSENGERS

"Anyone who sees a depiction of the Egyptian pharaoh Echnaton immediately wonders whether he was really human or not." **Page 444** *began with these words. "The elongated face with its serpentine expression, the oval head that bulges at the back. His skull has a capacity one and a half times larger than a normal person's. His fingers resemble a spider's antennae. His feet are like flippers, his belly is huge, and he has female breasts. This is how he was described by his contemporaries, yet he married the most beautiful woman, Nefertiti, and is likely the father of the famous pharaoh Tutankhamen. And like all the greats before him, he carried out religious reforms, imposed a cult dedicated to a new supreme deity – the sun god, Aton. In the generation after him, other unforgettable figures came to earth: Orpheus and Moses. It is not known whether they were really human; however, they taught people knowledge of unprecedented power, as well as a belief in the single God. Much wisdom was needed to see the True One amidst the multitude.*
Later the Virgin Mother, John the Baptist and Jesus appeared – they too were only half human…"

Yet another generation lived out their nights in expectation.
The last man to set out for the Upper World had not returned, while for centuries no one had descended to the Lower World. It was as if they could no longer find the path back to the First People. Legend had it that at least one person in every generation was born with the gift for reading the clues, yet no one came down anymore – despite

237

all the messengers who had been sent to the Upper World of men to bring knowledge and warn them of the final day.

Could nothing have changed in the Upper World?

Were people still doomed to the realm of shadows, while the shades wandered in Hell on Earth?

None of this mattered. All they needed was a bit more patience. Because everything that began in this world would sooner or later come to an end.

So they readied yet another messenger and escorted him to the exit beneath the eighth waterfall. He knew he was doomed, but this merely freed him from fear. He did not know what to expect in the Upper World. The prophecy claimed that if the time had come, then he would know it. If it had not, he mustn't return, so as not to bring the poison back with him.

He was to bring the new humans the next piece of knowledge that would draw them closer to the day when they would be ready to accept the truth – and that which the truth would restore to the Earth. This is what every messenger before him had done, perhaps those who came after him would continue the mission. The Prophecy written by their forefathers stated that some day humans would be ready to accept the knowledge – without it causing their destruction yet again. Some day they would be able to understand the message and not repeat the mistakes made by those who had gone before them.

Knowledge can help, save, redeem, but also kill those who are not ready to use it.

Before leaving his world, he turned around one last time to see his people.

An endless sea of incorporeal shadows gazed into the darkness with blind eyes. A multitude staring into the blackness, yet hearing, breathing, knowing, waiting, dreaming… They were hopeful, since a few humans had nevertheless managed to find their way to the Lower World – and each subsequent newcomer was closer to the First People. Perhaps the legend would come true.

At that moment someone was surely looking for clues to uncover the path…

There were also visitors who happened upon them by chance. They were not released, however, for fear that they would give the First Ones away.

Their race had been among the last to see the Earth in peace, when men did not know weapons and war.[64] They had used their knowledge to further love and life.

However, when the Seven Stars formed an arc in the vault of the heavens a second time, they knew they had to abandon their lands because the world would change again. Just as it had opened its doors for them the first time, the second time it would close them.

Some of them decided to hide from the world before it changed, so as to be able to influence it in secret.

During this age, new people would arrive, people who did not remember their creator. And along with them would come weapons, greed, godlessness, intolerance, war. They would turn any knowledge or god they touched into a machine for revenge and wealth.

---

[64] Archeological research on the vanished Eneolithic civilization in the Balkans has shown that its people did not know weapons, aggression or war. Centuries after they left these lands, new inhabitants arrived during the Bronze Era. Their culture, which is preserved in their ceramics, is fundamentally different than that of the earlier inhabitants. Their knowledge of life, religion and science had regressed to a basic level of development, while they had weapons and waged war. There is no evidence of continuity between the two cultures.

QUESTIONS

Page 445 began with the words:
"[Orpheus wrote] a hymn saying sound and lawful things... And the true nature of the words cannot be said even though they are spoken. The poem is an alien one and riddling for human beings. But Orpheus intended by means of it to say not contentious riddles, but rather great things in riddles."

From the **Derven Papyrus**, translated by Andre Laks and Glenn Most.

On this particular day, Vera was in no state to think about blossoming crocuses, but was flipping through a newspaper instead. She read about a miraculous hermit who had turned up in Ancona, Italy, and who could not remember the last time he had had contact with other humans. He had no name but bore a message. His body was also very strange. "There are still people who believe in that sort of thing, and charlatans who exploit them," she thought to herself. Yet Vera wanted to believe, too.

The police arrived to question her again.

"I thought I'd told you that already... in detail," she insisted, her amazement at the absurdity of the situation written clearly on her face.

"Why you didn't tell us anything about this?" the policeman showed her **page 445**.

"Because I don't know anything about it."

"The Moscow police told us they found this torn-out page in the room where the kidnappers had been holding you. It must be written in some secret terrorist code..."

240

Vera was propped up in bed against three pillows. She had pulled the covers up to her chin like a child who thinks the quilt will protect her from ghosts. A short policeman was sitting on a wooden chair next to the bed. His eyes tracked the young woman's every move like a hunting dog. His bushy moustache completed his canine appearance, as any suspicious statement set it quivering beneath his nose. He had put his hat in his lap to serve as a makeshift writing desk as he took down Vera's new testimony in a fresh white notebook.

The Russian police had already questioned Vera extensively at a Moscow hospital. She had spent two days and two nights there, but at her father's insistence, the Bulgarian embassy had expedited her return to Sofia, where they put her in the best ward of the Military Hospital. The Russian police still had not found any trace of the kidnappers, despite the fact that the disappearance of the Orphic amulet had made their capture that much more urgent. Now they were hoping for any new clues their Bulgarian counterparts might be able to give them.

"There are a number of discrepancies in your statement," another man who had been staring blankly through the window said. He was obviously a higher ranking officer than the man taking notes, since he always seemed to do nothing when he was there. He was dressed in civilian clothes. "You said that the suspect's name is Ariman."

"That's what he told me."

"He could have told you anything. But no one with that name has entered or left Russia."

"What if I told you that Ariman means Satan? Or the Devil, if you prefer."

The plainclothes detective looked at her questioningly, then furrowed his eyebrows, frowning.

"Are you making fun of us?" he asked.

"No, of course not! Satan has many names. Ariman is the ancient Persian one. But the question of why and when people invented the Devil is still open for debate. If you ask me, the Devil just serves to explain everything that God cannot accomplish."

The policeman with the notebook looked at his boss, blinking rapidly, as if sending a request for help in Morse code. The plainclothes officer, motionless in front of the window, was trying to swallow his irritation.

"Did you notice any other identifying features?" he asked.

Vera thought hard, closing her eyes and going deep inside the memories she usually chased away like annoying flies.

"He looked serious," she began after a pause. "Too serious to be a common criminal. That's what threw me... He was talking to the guests at the official dinner as if he knew them all – and most of them were world-famous professors and researchers. Yet at the same time he was constantly looking around as though he was waiting for someone..."

"Who?"

"How should I know? But he had strange eyes... I can tell you that for certain."

"Strange in what way?"

"Not typically Caucasian. They were shaped like elongated almonds or tears. Yet I wouldn't exactly call him Asian, because his facial features were very definitely European," Vera fell silent for a moment. "They were like Keanu Reeves' eyes."

"But isn't he American?" the man with the notebook asked.

The plainclothes officer looked daggers at his junior. He then glanced at Vera, his exasperated glare quickly fading into a look of desperation. He crossed the white room and again took up his post by the window. As his eyes roved over the metal bars outside the window, he continued.

"What did he call his assistants?"

"Nothing, as far as I recall."

"What do you mean 'nothing'?"

"They didn't speak to each other."

"Did they communicate via telepathy?"

Vera smiled for the first time since she had been pulled out of the Moscow River. "They didn't really speak in front of us, except to give us orders or ask us questions..."

"What did they ask you?"

"Well, for example… they wanted information about the stolen amulet. They made Dr. Werder judge whether it was a fake or not… and so on."

"How could he tell without the proper equipment?"

"They were going to bring the equipment when we escaped. Now I remember… the man had a tattoo."

"Where?"

"On his neck."

"Lots of people have tattoos there. Can you be a little more specific?"

Vera took a sheet of paper and pencil from the nightstand. She chewed on the eraser and stared at the ceiling. After pulling her thoughts together, she hunched over the paper and tried to draw it.

"I assume that it must be an ideogram… a symbol," she explained. She finished her sketch and showed it to them. "But I have no idea what it might mean."

"He must belong to a cult. Or a terrorist cell," the policeman with the notebook said.

"We'll run your drawing through the international criminal database. Something might come up," the other man added from the window.

They gathered up their things and wished Vera a pleasant day. She waved goodbye and looked away. Then, as if suddenly remembering something important, she sat up abruptly and called after them: "He had the chance to kill me… The gun was pointed right at my head… but he didn't."

"He must have been new at the game. He was too scared."

As the uniformed officer jotted this down in his notebook, the door to the room opened. A man came in, half-hidden behind a bouquet of flowers and balloons. The two policemen waved to Vera again and edged their way past the forest of flowers blocking the doorway.

"How are you today, darling?" The new arrival asked Vera. It was her fiancé, Kaloyan.

He placed the flowers on the table and let go of the balloons. The colorful, helium-filled spheres floated to the ceiling. Vera watched them with irritation. Kaloyan ran his hand through his gelled hair. He brushed the pollen off his expensive suit and sat down on the bed next to her, where a moment earlier the uniformed policeman's satchel had made an indentation. Kaloyan took Vera's weak hand from the covers and pressed it between his.

"Who were those guys?"

"Police... they're gathering evidence about the kidnapping and robbery."

"Good. I got brochures about the house in the south of France. It's just like you imagined it," he continued cheerfully.

He bent forward, opened his shiny leather briefcase and took out a couple of brochures. He brushed back a strand of hair that had fallen in front of his eyes.

Kaloyan had soft, light-brown hair that caught the sun like amber. It was so fine that without gel it lay shapeless, forming a wide white part down the middle. He was tall and thin with warm, chocolate eyes. His features were sharp, as though sculpted in plaster and further accentuated by his matte complexion. Vera liked his hands, which were as elegant as a pianist's, yet strong. Because everything was so perfect about him, she was convinced at their very first meeting that she would fall in love with him. When they went out together, she was proud to be with him. Gradually this anticipation of love became a substitute for love itself and habit took care of the rest.

"You didn't tell me that we were going to have a house in France," she cut him off.

"You didn't ask. But the fence is too white and ordinary, I don't think you'll like it. I've brought you the catalogue so you can choose for yourself."

"But I don't want to live in France."

"Southern France... perfect for a family with children."

"Kaloyan, I'm an archaeologist. I study Thracian culture. What will I do in France?"

"You can dig there as well!"

Vera lay back helplessly on her pillows and looked up at the familiar blotches on the ceiling. It was useless to argue. How could she expect a man who sold armchairs and bathroom tiles to understand the point of digging in rocky mountainsides and damp holes? It had occurred to her recently that he was so blinded by his own conception of the world that he hadn't even noticed how Vera had been avoiding him.

"Visiting hour is over." A nurse poked her pink nose and white hat around the door.

"But I just got here," Kaloyan protested.

"Do as they say, darling. They play by the rules here."

Vera felt relieved that she would be left alone. At the same time, a stifling sense of guilt seized her chest. Kaloyan was so sweet and kind, yet she was hurrying to get rid of him.

She squeezed his hand and sat up to kiss him, since otherwise the remorse would be unbearable until their next meeting. Thank God for the nurse, though – Vera wouldn't have been able to put up with a conversation about fences for very long. Thoughts ricocheted in her head, trying to escape the room and slip out through the iron bars to the freedom beyond.

Her fiancé took another fence catalogue out of his briefcase, left it on her bed and kissed her on the cheek. She watched him until his shadow disappeared beyond the door.

HIDDEN SO AS TO BE FOUND

Page 446 *began with the quotation:*
"The Underground Kingdom is the final aim of human existence after a series of wanderings and rebirth, according to Orphic beliefs."

From the documentary film **The Truth about Orpheus**

One of the most unpleasant things about any hospital stay is how every morning, when the first rays of sunlight shatter the darkness and your dreams are most vivid, some chattering nurse rushes into your room faster than the speed of light and pokes a thermometer into your armpit – or worse. Order is supposedly the heart and soul of medicine, hence the rules are rarely questioned.

Although it was perfectly obvious that Vera was not running a fever, the woman in white with a thick, greasy layer of moisturizer on her face stood next to her for a full five minutes. The nurse watched the hands do laps around the face of her watch, her rapid-fire complaints sprinting right along with them: traffic jams, the miserable state of public transportation and how every morning she had to get up earlier and earlier to get to work on time. Just to poke patients with thermometers. Vera let the stream of words roll off her and concentrated instead on recollecting every detail from her dream, which had been so enchanting that she wanted to re-submerge herself in it. When the short round nurse finally waddled back towards the door, Vera closed her eyes but the dream would not return.

There had been a man in her dream, someone she didn't know. She only knew that she was attracted to him. She also sensed his interest in her. He approached her, yet didn't touch her. Furious impatience took over her thoughts. But out of nowhere fear cropped up like an unexpected wind, filling her with panic...

The dream only reminded her how much she missed the feeling she had lost. The feeling she had forgotten without having had a chance to experience it.

When it got so bright that the white light began filtering through her eyelids, she finally sat up in bed. She felt small and paralyzed, just like when she had entered the cold box of a room at the Bulgarian hotel in Moscow.

On her nightstand there was a cup of tea and a sheet of paper covered with a few symbols. She had copied them the previous evening from the photographs of the golden tile on her cell phone. The tile she had seen in that room... in the warehouse by the river.

It was an absolute miracle that the telephone was still working, after everything she and it had been through. As she ran towards the bridge from which she jumped into the river, the telephone had fallen from her pocket. The detectives had found it and after carefully examining the area for clues, they had returned it to her in Bulgaria. If it had remained in her pocket when she plunged into the water, she would not have the pictures – the only copies of the unique golden artifact with its hieroglyphics and ideograms.

The symbols engraved on either side tirelessly danced in front of Vera's eyes, taunting her thoughts. Last night she had fallen asleep staring at the pictures from her telephone. She hated this stage, the beginning of an investigation when the fragmented clues are still utterly chaotic. And the more cryptic they are, the more infuriated you become. They possess you like a drug, plowing through your mind, yet when the eureka moment comes, you realize that every moment was worth it.

The golden tile's overall appearance resembled dozens of other Orphic tiles discovered in excavations. What made it unusual were the unknown symbols and hieroglyphics on the other side.

The meander could be clearly seen on both sides of the tablet – almost as if Vera's conscious mind was fixating on it because of the significance she herself had ascribed to it.

The cream-slathered nurse, her jiggling arms straining her white uniform, once again darted into the room. She quickly waddled over to Vera with slices of buttered toast and jam. After announcing that it was delicious and it was all there was on the menu, the nurse left.

Vera looked at the toast, hesitated for a moment, then opened her laptop. Kaloyan had brought it to her a couple of days earlier, hoping it would distract her from her morbid thoughts. She logged on to the Internet and began searching. She had learned of the meander's most surprising meaning at her own lecture in Moscow. She wanted to use this bit of evidence in her book, but first she had to double-check it. She spent hours surfing until she found what she was looking for.

She had pulled up a table showing the Coptic pronunciation of various letters and hieroglyphs, each accompanied by a transcription. She immediately recognized the hieroglyph for "temple," which was also one of the Meandrites' most frequently used symbols: the meander. The Thracians considered it a magical symbol as well. Orpheus' followers used it to encode their secret messages, while the Greeks regarded it as their own invention. And it really was pronounced "Erphei" or "Orphei," depending on the dialectal variations.

Was this the reason why the symbol always accompanied scenes showing the mythical hero Orpheus? Was it possible that it had preserved the Meandrites' original meaning? If so, then the question arose: How and why did it reach Thrace and Egypt? Was its transmission accidental or deliberately intended to preserve prehistoric ideas?

Vera got out of bed to stretch her legs.

She decided to call Professor Doychinov, a leading Bulgarian expert on ancient texts and undeciphered symbols in Bulgaria. She searched for his number in her cell phone and was about to dial

248

when she thought better of it. He was so full of himself that he would probably pass off the tablet as his own discovery and write scholarly articles about it, hoping to achieve the worldwide fame that always seemd to elude him. Even if he did manage to read the strings of symbols, he wouldn't share his discovery with Vera until he had made sure he had copyrighted it for himself. He had dedicated his life to following the totalitarian system's sclerotic rules for career advancement within its institutions. Now, having reached the top by crushing countless victims along the way, making sacrifices and rewriting history to his own ends, Doychinov needed to convince himself that the struggle had been worth it. Seeing his name in the newspapers reassured him.

Vera, of course, wanted to save the fame for herself. Yet she still needed to consult someone who knew more about ancient symbols than she did. She realized that a large part of her analysis consisted of her own guesswork and interpretations, adapted to suit her own hypothesis. She needed to find someone who had studied the topic purely for intellectual enjoyment, rather than to build up an ego and an academic career.

Her thumb unconsciously pressed the menu button on the phone and scrolled down the names on the display.

Futch…

"Futch" was old-fashioned Bulgarian slang for "trash." The guy's real name was Asen Litovski, but no one ever called him that. Some people didn't even know he had a real name at all.

Vera had last seen him at their graduation from the university. He hadn't gone on to graduate school – he didn't need to. He didn't even need his college diploma, which he had only gotten for his parents' sake. Their fellow archeology students whispered that after graduation he had gone over to the "dark side" – joined the *imanyari*, or illegal treasure hunters who searched for antiquities to sell on the international black market. It was not surprising that a talented young archeologist would be tempted into treasure hunting, as it offered opportunities to strike it rich and use fancy excavation technology that honest scholars sifting dirt for the state-run institutes and universities could only dream about.

Futch had had a crush on Vera since their freshman year. His awkward bumbling whenever she was near had given him away, as had his kind, gentle face. He was easy to spot, not just because of his rather full figure, but because he was the only boy who would sit in the front row during lectures. In fact, not too many girls sat there, either. He often bought chips and soda for Vera during the break, which she accepted graciously, concealing her irritation that he didn't seem to realize how fattening they were. In any case, she didn't like eating such a blast of salt and sugar. She always turned down the soda on the pretext that the carbonation irritated her stomach, after which he would sheepishly tuck it back in his enormous bag. During their student years he had been excruciatingly shy, perhaps because he was still not good at wearing a mask. Now he tried to put on a confident and amusing air, quite successfully. Yet his eyes would still dart around nervously if you looked into his for too long.

"Futch? It's Vera."

"Vera! It's been ages!"

"A year."

"A year?"

"You disappeared. I haven't heard anything about you."

"That's for the best…"

"What are you up to? Are you in Sofia?"

"Nope, I'm busy digging a hole in the mountains. I'll be back in Sofia tomorrow. What about you?"

"I'm writing my master's… I want to see you."

"Those are words I've been waiting for five years to hear!"

"I'm serious."

"I know. You've always been too serious."

"Give me a call when you get back in town. This is my number…"

"There's no way I'll forget."

Vera hung up and stretched out on the bed. She lay unmoving for a few seconds, then opened the pictures of the golden tablet again, looking for any details she might have missed. Most of the hieroglyphics and pictograms were familiar to her, which made her all the more furious with herself for her inability to combine them into words. Mysteries are most dangerous right before you solve them.

Vera put on her white hospital slippers standing like sentries beneath her bed. She walked over to the heavily barred window. She could feel the warm blood moving through her veins. Her gaze sank into the narrow street that wound around the back of the hospital.

A Truth Few Dare to Utter

Page 447 featured the following quotation:

"If the Rulers of the world do exist, there is nowhere else for them to be found apart from below the earth. This is a truth which everyone can guess at but few dare utter. Perhaps the only person who has had the courage to say it in black and white is Marquis Alexandre Saint-Yves d'Alveydre. It was he who spoke of Agartha, the Underground domicile of the Kings of the World... But all who followed him publicly were removed since they knew too much."

From **Foucault's Pendulum** by Umberto Eco, p. 309

Some relics of the fearless Saint George are said to be preserved in the small chapel bearing his name in the center of Rome. The eternal fragments are supposedly from his hip bones. Other bits of him can also be found elsewhere. Churches holding relics, no matter how miniature they might be, are more popular with the laity. Perhaps this is because in the past Christians frequently dismembered their saints' remains, once they realized that rotted holy flesh does not stink. Afterwards the parts were distributed among many churches to be revered. Legend also has it that when Orpheus was killed, he was also dismembered, like the god of the Bacchanalia, Dionysus.

A pale shadow flitted past the narrow gates of St. George's Church, passing so quickly that you could take it for a phantom, if you didn't catch a glimpse of the man it belonged to. His husky

At the end of the street, part of St. George's Church can be seen, while the Roman Arch stands to the right

figure continued up the street, which wound between the solitary stone block of the Roman Arch on the left and a crumbling stone wall on the right. Ariman stopped at the end of the wall and poked at the soft limestone bricks until one of them moved. He pulled it out carefully and looked into the empty space. Finding nothing, he put the stone back and continued on his way.

He turned right onto another small, deserted street. His footsteps echoed dully against the high, centuries-old walls. Two crumbling yellow churches kept a lonely watch on either side of the lane. Their tall doors, which looked built for giants, were tightly shut. It was very early; the sun was just peeping above the Rome's eastern rim. However, no locals had ever seen the towering doors even slightly open.

Ariman crossed the cobbled street and went up the steps to the building on the left, which looked as if no one had crossed its threshold for centuries. Besides this main entrance, the church had another door, as well as two frosted glass windows looking out onto tiny Carita Street. A passerby peering through them at just the right moment might glimpse shadows moving around on the ground floor.

The little street was named after a medieval brotherhood that modern Romans suspected still existed. An image of a decapitated head on a platter had been painted above the church's main entrance more than a century earlier. Christians drew the head of John the

253

Baptist like this. However, the Thracians had depicted the head of Orpheus in the same way.

Two white doorbells gleamed beneath the head. Ariman pressed the lower one and stepped a few feet back from the door. The recently changed lock was the only sign that people still lived here. A man in a brown hooded cloak appeared at the door. His eyes shone in the hood's shadow, neither welcoming nor hostile.

Ariman entered the gloomy stone building and went down a steep staircase. His skin sensed the familiar dampness and dank cold. He heard the thunderous tolling of a heavy bell somewhere above him.

He descended the spiral staircase slowly, as the stone steps were wet and slippery, and reached a wide open space. There was almost no furniture apart from a few wooden tables with roughly cobbled benches around them. The only decorations were the stone figures on the ceiling and walls, which Ariman was so used to that he didn't even notice them. As a child he had often gazed at them, imagining what they could mean. Now he was oblivious to the monstrous creatures' snarling fangs and their vengeful stares. He had always wanted to ask why these unearthly beings lurked on the ceiling. When he grew up and began to go out, he learned that they were devils. He found this out from the people Above, who had made hundreds of similar sculptures and drawings and put them everywhere. Yet Ariman still did not understand why these creatures were eternally stalking him.

Stone snakes slithered along the walls, amidst scenes of men and women, as well as a man with a lyre in his hand, animals, angels and devils. Ariman no longer noticed them, since they had been there as long as he could recall.

Two pale men walked past him and nodded. Another man was sitting off to the side on a wooden bench, mincing herbs with a knife and putting them into a glass bowl. A small boy was mopping the stone floor.

At the far end of the room, a dozen men were packing up ragdolls in cardboard boxes as the Incorporeal One looked on in silence. When he saw the newcomer, he started towards him. He waved to the boy to stop cleaning to let him by. As he approached Ariman, he said in a deep voice: "It's too bright up there, isn't it?"

"Sometimes."

"You are very late in returning this time."

"The circumstances of the last mission changed…"

"Come along, Ariman, I would like to stroll to the basilica."

The pair started down a hallway whose end trailed off into the dark. The Incorporeal One, as everyone here called him, was dressed in a coarse cloak that covered his entire body. His head was hidden under a hood that cast a shadow over his face. He never uncovered it except when praying or introducing initiates to the mysteries. Ariman had never witnessed such rituals. He had only heard the rumors which swirled from mouth to mouth like wind at night when the devotees prepared to encounter their dreams. If there was one person on Earth whom Ariman feared, it was the Incorporeal One. Perhaps because he was forever a stranger, even though he was Ariman's closest companion. No one knew who he was, where he had come from and when. He was called the Incorporeal One because he always concealed his body, while the little part of him that was visible was white and anemic. He was a relatively small man, his thin and hunched figure standing just over five feet.

Whoever or whatever the Incorporeal One was, he was all Ariman had. He still knew nothing about his parents. However, in the world he now inhabited, parents didn't exist – at least not in the sense understood by people Above.

Here everyone had his duty, which he doggedly carried out. The society was as ingeniously organized as an anthill, where each individual fulfils the job he was born into and never imagines wanting to do anything else. The individual's task is simple, while the whole mechanism is complex, too perfect to be an earthly creation.

The white, almost transparent hand of the Incorporeal One rose slowly and settled on Ariman's shoulder, resting there for a few minutes. His dry, bony fingers wore a heavy ring with a stylized figure of a woman holding a circle with a small dot in the center in her arms. This was the ancient ideogram of the Mother Goddess and her son, the Solar God. Ariman had seen a similar image in Christian churches, which people called the Virgin Mary and the Christ Child. However, the Christian frescoes contained much more detail than a stone engraving could. The goddess on the ring had no head.[65] The Incorporeal One had explained that if anyone were to depict her face, they would draw it in their own image, while in truth, we do not know who she is. One thing is certain, however: that she was not human, since man begets man, not the sun.

As they walked along the narrow corridors, Ariman recounted what had happened in Moscow and the jungles of Burma.

"You allowed yourself to look in the mirror!" the Incorporeal One said bitterly.

"I don't understand…"

"That woman," he sighed, continuing after a short pause. "Up there on earth, the sun rises every morning, does it not?"

Ariman thought for a moment. What was the Incorporeal One getting at with this simple question? Of course the sun rises.

"Yet people don't always see it. There are days when the sky is heavy and grey, or sometimes even black. It descends so low that you feel it might crush you. The sun is still there, but it can't be seen. Or the sky might be clear, but there are mountains or forests above us, blocking out the sun. Yet sooner or later the light breaks through, it tears obstacles apart, every one of them, until it reaches its goal. Because it is constant and persistent. As is life. As is knowledge."

Ariman nodded, but he still could not grasp the point.

---

[65] The oldest such pictogram was discovered on the bottom of an 8,000-year-old clay vessel found in the village of Gradeshnitsa, Bulgaria. It is kept in the History Museum in Vratsa, Bulgaria.

"You will go back up and complete your mission," the Incorporeal One added. "This time without any mistakes. The woman has seen too much. You have to get rid of her before her words destroy us!"

"What could she do?"

"She could reveal the return path to the people Above… It is too early. We have to preserve the Last Paradise. Despite everything we have done… they will destroy it. We, too, cannot return to it, since we also must not break the supreme law. However, we can protect it from here, since it is our only hope."

Ariman matched the Incorporeal One's pace and stared gloomily into the darkness ahead. He couldn't understand what the Teacher was talking about. The old man had never spoken with such frankness or specificity before. For this first time, he had revealed his vulnerability. And it was this that caused Ariman to doubt him like never before.

"But why can't we let the light in?" asked Ariman.

"Because we must not let it change us. The light is part of the Upper World, eternal and powerful. Nothing must stop us now. We are so close to erasing all earthly traces." The Incorporeal One fell silent for a moment, before asking in a quiet, calm voice, "Do you like the light?"

"Why are you asking me?"

"Once you grow to like it, you will never return to us."

"But you worship the Sun!"

"The Sun comes and goes. It is both good and bad, both ours and theirs. We learn from it, yet we do not follow it. It is an illusion and a reminder of the omnipotence of the Creator… But only the embrace of the Mother Goddess is eternal and pure."

The Incorporeal One opened a heavy, wrought-iron gate and stepped across the threshold. They continued along a corridor unfamiliar to Ariman, who silently followed his teacher, as was the accepted order.

"The amulet is a very important piece of evidence. It might lead the enlightened to the truth. It is the last clue before the eight waterfalls," the old man continued, "if you have the knowledge allowing you to read it."

The Incorporeal One frequently used combinations of words that Ariman found hard to follow. Yet when he asked basic questions like a child, the answer was always the same: "Everyone finds out for himself someday."

"The woman saw it. She knows the amulet has been stolen, and when you replace it with a substitute, she will realize this. Until you finish your mission, **page 447** will not be the last one."

Ariman clenched his fists and stayed silent.

"But first you must purge the light from yourself. It will prevent you from seeing."

They reached the last gate, a heavy wooden portal with elegant iron ornamentation, hinges and a decorative lock. The Incorporeal One held out his bony hand. Ariman opened his backpack and took a tin. It contained the golden tablet with the unknown symbols and the Orphic amulet. He placed it in the white palm.

The Incorporeal One closed the heavy gate behind him.

GODS AND DEMONS

The truth about the Lower Kingdom was the main topic of page 448:
"Since everyone believes in the torments of Hades which are clearly not true, we can not accept that gods exist merely because everyone believes in them... if souls continue to exist, then they are the same as demons, but if demons exist, then gods also exist, since their existence is not hindered by the preconception of what is said to happen in Hades."

Protagoras

Vera gathered her things from her hospital room, slipped on the nurse's uniform that Iliana, the laboratory assistant, had given her, and walked past the security guards, who paid her no attention at all. Thanks to Futch Litovski, a car was waiting for her outside. He was the only person she could ask for such a favor, so it was worth the risk of him sticking to her again like gum on her shoe.

When she reached the rendezvous point, Vera parked the car and took off running down the street. To the right, beyond the apartment blocks' concrete torsos, the final rays of sunlight filtered through the snarl of the chestnut trees' leafless branches.

Trying to catch up with them, she sprinted towards a clearing. The moment brought her back to one of her favorite childhood games: chasing the sun as it tirelessly galloped through the sky to reach its hiding place beyond the city. She had thought of nothing except the shafts of living light caressing her face and warming her body.

In those days she was not yet racing against her father's shadow, which made her feel small and shapeless. Now his oppressive presence grew ever more threatening, no matter how hard she tried to outrun it. Things had become even more complicated once she had to struggle against her fellow students as well. She became obsessed with building her own reputation within archeological circles and gave herself over to her obsession with new discoveries. Major success takes a lot of work – Vera was prepared to do whatever it took to fuel her need for recognition and respect. And to erase the shadow hovering over her. She didn't realize that this need had ensnared her in its nets to the point that she was willing to erase everything else in her life. Vera had disguised her needs in the traces of the vanished Meandrites.

Back then, there hadn't been any Kaloyan with his suffocating expectations of marriage and kids, which Vera nevertheless believed would help her escape from the shadow.

As a child, when chasing the sun's rays and inhaling the scent of the wild crocuses, Vera had simply been herself. She had been filled with the courage and passion of youth, which the years had since burdened with heavy castles in the sky and undermined with labyrinths, until she found herself imprisoned in her own uncompromising plans and illusions.

She continued running down the street until she reached a long brown building and stopped in front of it, out of breath. She looked into the narrow open space between the buildings. It was deserted, quiet. In the silence of her mind, a fragile memory surfaced. Lost, forgotten… no, she only thought it was lost. It had always been there, she simply had not looked for it.

Vera saw her mother slowly approaching her, taking her time. She was on her way home, like every day at the time. Her mother was carrying a shopping bag in one hand, holding their old poodle's leash in the other. When she saw Vera, she smiled quietly and calmly, as only a mother can, with her face, eyes and heart. She came closer. Dressed in blue jeans and a cardigan, she was completely ordinary, yet so precious. She was now so near that Vera could almost touch her. Her eyes were filled with tears. She reached out, but the image disappeared. She was too close…

Memories. What people turn into when they leave us.

Vera started running further down the street. There used to be a little park there, with grass, trees, paths and a little hill.

Now there was nothing but apartment blocks. Vera ducked between them, looking for some green remnant of the park. She found only the hill, spared because it insulated the new residents from the noise of the boulevard. The wealthy citizens who had built their homes on the old park wouldn't jeopardize their sleep by plowing it down.

She walked up to the top of the hill and sat down, as she had as a child. She closed her eyes and saw what she was looking for; however, empty holes gaped here and there. She couldn't remember what used to be over there. But she caught a glimpse of the little house. Except it wasn't house, but rather a trailer, and Ginka lived there, along with her parents, brothers and sisters. All in one trailer. Some kids said she was a Gypsy, but Vera only remembered her smile. They were in the same class at school. Ginka and Vera became friends in first or second grade. When Vera had new crayons or notebooks, Ginka always wanted them. Vera gave her what she wanted.

Once she had invited Vera into the trailer. There was no furniture, just beds and lots of rags. People have different ways of living…

Memories. The trailer disappeared. The gardens dissolved in the dusk, along with her mother and the little dog. The old neighborhood evaporated like froth, taking the familiar world with it. Sitting on the hill Vera felt like there was nothing left in the world that mattered to her. The engine of time had taken it all away without giving anything back.

The sun set.

"I can't give up now," Vera whispered in the dark.

She had allowed herself to get scared and lose heart. The shadow had grown to frightening dimensions. Vera could not understand the gods and demons inside her. She knew only one thing – as long as she chased the story she believed in, the shadow could not catch her.

Vera had let herself to forget. Her mother had frequently told her, "If you don't know why you are here, the present is wasted, while the past and the future lose their shape."

She stayed the night in the apartment where she had lived with her mother after her father had left them.

Vera didn't dare go into her old room. She was still not ready to face down the ghosts.

She left early in the morning, too impatient to sleep. She wanted to see the traces of the First Civilization with her own eyes. She had to do that before she could continue. It was the only way she could know whether she was really on the path to discovering anything more than evidence invented by a ravenous imagination.

BEFORE THE END
OF THE WORLD

Page 449 told of the Final Days:
"The myth about the end of the world (the end of habitation) in our lands is in all probability linked to the idea of the gods leaving the world of men. The reason for this seems to be the serious culpability of the human race, which was punished by the goddess who (...) holds in her right hand a temple with the bas-relief engraving of terrible monsters and in left hand a mace with zoomorphic representations. It seems the signal to abandon the lands in the Central Balkans was expected and presaged by important changes in the stellar maps."

From the Doctoral Dissertation Synopsis by
Professor Ana Raduncheva, p. 23

It only took Vera an hour and a half to reach the city of Vratsa, north of Sofia. In the early morning the highways were empty.

She had planned this trip from her hospital room. Her impatience had grown so intense that she had decided to escape the white room with its barred windows. At first glance, the clay vessels in the Vratsa museum had little to do with her studies of Christianity's roots in Orphism. She knew this all too well, but this didn't stop her from trying to convince herself that the subjects were somehow connected. If she didn't try to tie this trip to her research, she would have to admit that she had run off to find the answer to the burning questions: what was the golden tablet in the Moscow warehouse and who was the man whom it belonged to? Her curiosity was further piqued by the fact that there were Thracian words on one side of tablet, while on the other there were prehistoric pictograms used by the Meandrites, who had disappeared as if fleeing the apocalypse. The same symbols decorated the clay vessels discovered in the abandoned Swiss chateau. However, this provincial museum housed the largest collection of such artifacts.

Vera parked the car near the Vratsa Historical Museum and crossed the central square, which was lorded over by evergreen mountain peaks and majestic white cliffs. The museum was hidden behind a medieval tower.

It looked so deserted, dark and cold that for a moment Vera feared it might be closed. She pushed open the shabby front door and was greeted by a handful of smiling young men who materialized out of the gloom.

"Are you open?" she asked uncertainly.

"Of course!" one of them answered, his face lighting up. Another young man ran to the end of the marble-floored room and switched on the lights in the ticket office. They looked delighted to have a visitor. "They probably don't get many!" Vera thought.

"Are you interested in anything in particular?"

"I'd just like to have a look around."

"That'll be two leva! Go right on in."

Vera's gaze fell on a small glass case holding a dozen or so books, including two volumes by the archaeologist Bogdan Nikolov from 1975.[66] Their shabby, yellowing jackets contrasted sharply with three glossy books with the name "Dr. Stephen Guide" emblazoned on their covers. A number of posters in the lobby also advertised the younger scholar's books. "If Dad were here, he'd probably try to shut the museum down over that," she mused. Her father was an old school archaeologist, a strict adherent to the post-war German approach. After the field had suffered under the

---

[66] Senior Researcher Bogdan Nikolov discovered and studied the artifacts from Gradeshnitsa. His name was later associated with the Thracian Rogozen Treasure, which is also housed in the Vratsa Historical Museum.

Nazi's perverse distortion of historical facts, scholars in the post-war period advocated a strict adherence to artifacts. They carefully avoided subjective interpretations, even banning any differences of opinion. Decades later a post-modern movement backed by young archaeologists challenged them, arguing that they could never reach the truth by clinging narrowly to history. Instead, they argued that the more opinions there are being tossed about, the easier it is to zoom in on the center.

"I'd like to have a tour guide," said Vera.

"That'll be five leva extra."

One of the young men leapt to his feet. Dressed simply, he was short with a dark complexion and patchy stubble, yet he seemed likeable and eager-to-please.

"Could we see the Gradeshnitsa artifacts?" asked Vera impatiently, as they descended the marble staircase to the prehistory display.

He stared at her inquisitively for a moment, as if this would help him understand who the young lady was.

"Yes, of course," he responded after a pause. "Let me switch on the lights."

The young archaeologist ran down one of the side hallways. Vera heard a click followed by humming and buzzing. A green fluorescent light illuminated the basement, making the darkness engulfing the rest of the museum seem that much more impenetrable.

"It's very cold here," the man said to break the awkward silence. "We're trying to save on electricity and heating." His voice faltered. He bowed his head, embarrassed at his confession.

"Don't worry, I won't be staying long."

Standing next to an enormous pair of petrified jaws, the tour guide proudly announced: "Well, this is our prehistory display. People have lived in what is now Bulgaria for 40,000 years. These items here" – his outspread arms swept across two display cases – "are from the Gradeshnitsa culture. The first civilization."

The display cases were about three yards long and contained a number of large clay vessels, a few smaller ones and at least fifteen figurines of the mother goddess and men. The sign in front of them read: "Clay figures of people and animals."

"These artifacts date from around 5,000 B.C. Did you know," the young man continued tentatively, "that the symbols you now see before you are the oldest known…"

"Writing system," Vera interrupted.

"Oh, so you do know," he smiled and started chattering away happily. "So few people have actually heard of this alphabet. To tell you the truth, nobody knows besides the scholars who come here to study these finds. But they don't usually comment on it."

"Do many scholars come to see them?"

"Yes, from all over the world. But it's as if we Bulgarians ourselves don't realize that we hold the first traces of human civilization."

"It's actually a matter of some dispute in official academic circles… And in any case, they're pictograms rather than an alphabet," Vera corrected him exactly as her father would have.

"But it's been proven," the young archaeologist insisted, before adding timidly: "We've got some books upstairs."

"I've read them. Leading scholars have disputed them, calling such theories occultist nonsense. One researcher even said on TV that there should be a special law against such hypotheses."

"How typically Bulgarian…" From the young man's words, Vera could see that he had been following the debates on Internet forums.

"From here to here is the Zaminets culture," he continued, pointing to adjacent display cases. "In this culture, the figurines of the Mother Goddess are more detailed, while the vessels have fewer symbols on them. Then at some point in history they disappeared just like that – poof!" As he said this, the young man clapped his hands and looked up.

"Excuse me?"

The Prehistory Section of the Vratsa Museum

"Human habitation in these territories just vanished for at least a thousand years. No one knows why. The Eneolithic cultures to north and south of the Balkan Mountains just evaporated. As though they were fleeing from the end of the world. Yet despite that, the symbols they used began appearing in Europe, Egypt and Crete. Isn't that amazing?"

"The unexplained is always intriguing. But the fact remains that no one knows what caused this anomaly. Some say that it was a barbarian invasion, others blame it on climate change or a mini-ice age… However, such changes usually take place gradually, but the Meandrites, as I like to call them, just disappeared all of a sudden."

"You seem to know a lot about this topic. What do you do for a living?"

"Archaeology is my hobby," she lied.

People treated her differently when she told them who she was – or rather, who her father was. Better to let the young man think she was a harmless tourist so he would keep telling her everything that crossed his mind.

"Do you want to see the Rogozen Treasure?" he asked her. "It's our biggest tourist draw."

"I've come to see the clay artifacts… but I don't see the house."

"What house?"

"The clay model of the Gradeshnitsa house," Vera explained.

"Oh! You mean Orpheus' ark." The young man smiled. "That's our most valuable piece. It's on the third floor. Let me show you."

The young archaeologist raced up the stairs, jabbering away at his visitor.

"Are these the originals?" Vera asked when they arrived.

The guide was taken aback by Vera's unexpectedly serious expression. She hadn't even seemed to be listening to his explanation of how a scholar had proven the existence of Orpheus' ark and covenant. Yet while he had been carried away with his speech, Vera had surreptitiously taken her notebook out of her bag and was carefully noting down his words. Vera knew very well that there wasn't much truth in them. However, the search for the lost ark of Orpheus might be an interesting storyline for her book – the general public snapped up stories of lost arks.

"Of course! Everything you see is authentic: the ark, the tablet and the Mother Goddess."

The display case contained a clay box that historians had officially dubbed "the Model House," as well as a Mother Goddess figurine, and the famous Gradeshnitsa tile with its undeciphered symbols on either side. Archaeologists had discovered it next to the box. After decades of disputes, Bulgarian scholars had come to agree that the tablet contained the oldest known written symbols in the world.[67]

---

[67] The Gradeshnitsa Tablet was discovered by the archeologist Bogdan Nikolov, who identified the twenty-four underlined written symbols on it. Official academic opinion recognizes these symbols as the oldest proto-writing system in the work, dating back 7,500 years. The tablet is slightly concave. A stylized image of a human figure praying, also surrounded by symbols, decorates the

"Can I take pictures of them?"

"If you want, I can give you the phone number of the person in charge of them. He can take them out of the case so you can get some professional photographs. Unfortuantely, he's not here today."

"Would I be able to have a few minutes alone?"

"Of course!" The young man walked away.

"There's nowhere else on earth where the guides would politely offer to take a priceless, 7,500-year-old artifact out of its display case, just so you could take a picture of it," Vera thought. Life was on a whole different plane in Vratsa – the rules of the capital city and its scholars just didn't apply here.

The guide wandered around on the lower floor, punctuating his thoughts with an outstretched index finger while waiting for Vera to call him when she had finished. She examined the fragile display case holding the clay artifacts. Alongside the historical objects were a number of posters by Dr. Guide explaining that Egyptian hieroglyphs were based on the oldest form of writing created by the proto-Thracians and that the ark and covenant of Orpheus had also been created by this prehistoric culture. Next to his books stood the research works by the historian Nikolai Panaiotov, who claimed that the First Civilisation were in fact Jews, who had originated in ancient Bulgarian lands.

"I hope my father never comes here," Vera thought to herself and smiled. Such theories made him apoplectic.

As soon as she finished taking pictures, she called out to the young man, "Are you still there?"

The guide quickly came upstairs to join her.

---

tablet's reverse side. The Vratsa Historical Museum collection contains more than 100 artifacts with similar symbols. Nikolov considered them primarily religious symbols. Professor Vladimir Georgiev theorized that the symbols belonged to the oldest proto-writing system in the world. The archeologist Professor Vasil Nikolov suggested that the tablet describes a schematic model of the lunar cycle. He claims that the mysterious object is most likely connected to the prehistoric inhabitants of Gradeshnitsa's calendar system.

"I'd like to go downstairs and take pictures of the first clay finds," she said.

"No problem. Come on down and I'll turn the lights on for you again."

Vera went down to the display of clay artifacts from before the "End of the World." The museum staff left her alone for hours, taking photographs. She couldn't get enough of them. She also marveled at the rickety glass cases used to hold priceless objects that just might prove to be of vital significance to the history of global civilization and that could radically transform our understanding of its genesis.

Vera considered telling the museum staff about the objects they had found at Chateau Jacques, but decided against it. The museum would hardly appreciate this information – especially if it meant they would have to verify the authenticity of all their artifacts.

Anthropomorphic clay figures from Gradeshnitsa Culture. Their upper bodies show the V-shaped sign made up of "mirrored hooks," while their lower bodies are covered with meanders and rhombuses.
Their backs show anatomically accurate depictions of the human heart.

SHADOWS

Page 450 was entitled *"Shadows"*:
"It is the old story of the cave in Plato's Republic. Socrates compares this world to a cave in which people sit fettered with their backs to a fire. They see only shadows cast on the wall of the cave before them made by objects moving between them and the fire that is behind them. One of them escapes and makes his way to the outside world. When he returns and tries to describe the real world to the prisoners of the cave they think he is mad. To men of our world, the real world is illusion. To men of the real world, our world is illusion. The views are incompatible. They are mad from our viewpoint. We are mad from their viewpoint."

"The Orphic Allegory: The Comedy of Errors" by Mather Walker

The Incorporeal One came back out, the heavy door slamming behind him. Ariman stood frozen, staring at the barrier's outlines. He had never passed through it – only the Incorporeal One was entitled to do so. The Teacher frequently carried various objects inside, only to come back out again without them. Sometimes he quoted to them the Legend, which stated: "Until humanity finds the way back to the First Ones within themselves, the return path must remain hidden. While we ourselves, who also cannot return because we have been changed by the Upper World, must do everything we can to keep the last hope alive."

The key to the room hung on his chest.

Ariman felt eyes on him. The boy with the mop had reached him and was staring at him in silence. "He has probably never gone outside," Ariman thought.

Why was he thinking about that? Because he was uncertain and angry, as if poison was seeping through his body. He had never before been dogged by questions and had performed his missions coldly, seeing them as part of the existing order. He had never wanted anything, because he had never received anything. Yet now that he wanted the girl to live, and he felt the change intensely.

The same thing had happened with the light. A graying memory swam before his eyes...

He was six or seven years old, locked in the Black Room, alone with darkness and silence. He had dug a hole in the wall with the sharp end of his belt. When he left the room he plugged it with a stone. When he was sent back to the room to "cleanse his thoughts," he would remove the stone and let a shaft of white light into the room, gazing at it in wonder. Ariman didn't know what it was. He didn't ask, for fear it might be taken from him. Back then he didn't know anything about the outside world, but he liked to dream.

The light showed there was another life, different from the one he knew.

Then he found a fly.

Or rather, the fly found him. The hole which he had made in the wall was the only source of light in the underground room. Only he knew about it.

The hole must have attracted the fly. It had come in from somewhere and gotten lost in the darkness. When it found the shaft of light, it would land near the hole. Ariman would stand motionless, too. Only the thin beam of light assured him he was still alive whenever he was closed in the Black Room.

He couldn't see the fly, but could hear it. The buzzing was the only sound that reached him down below, besides his own thoughts. The insect was too large to escape through the tiny hole and buzzed around it.

272

Ariman somehow found himself striking up a conversation with the fly one day. Letting himself relax, he began to tell it his feelings and thoughts, his loneliness and fear. He had been silent for so long that before he began talking to the fly, he almost believed his tongue was knotted up and would no longer be able to form words....

Somehow his thoughts about the fly brought his dance with the woman to mind. He felt weakness as well as astonishment that after such lengthy darkness he could see a ray of light.

Ariman reluctantly traced his way back along the long corridor. The questions needled him more insistently than ever, like skewers pricking his brain. The gloomy tunnel opened out onto the refectory with its wooden benches. The memories pursued him here, too.

Metal spoons clattered against bowls, quickly, then even more quickly. As the food in his bowl disappeared, he gobbled up the remainder that much more frantically. It was always the same thing. They were hardly ever given meat. Fifteen thin boys with closely cropped heads...

He reached the staircase and descended to a lower level. The Black Room was there. The Incorporeal One had ordered him to go there whenever he was overwhelmed by undesired thoughts. Or when he had failed to complete his mission. He had to stay there at least one night. And Ariman always did it because he had always done it.

He had to do it now as well.

Ariman opened the door and entered the darkness. He sat down on the stone floor and buried his head in his hands.

UNSPOKEN

Page 452 began with an Orphic verse:
"In the belief that this god proclaims oracles,
they come inquiring what they should do.
After this [Orpheus] says:
'She proclaimed an oracle about all that was right to
him to hear.'"

From the Derveni Papyrus, Col. II, translated by Gabor Betegh

Vera got back to Sofia from the Vratsa Museum in the evening. Even though most of her things were now at Kaloyan's apartment, she preferred to stay at her mother's place. She didn't want to analyze the reason for this – she was too tired. She decided to leave thinking for the morning and began climbing the tiled staircase to the fourth floor.

As she reached the landing in front of her mother's apartment, she saw a shadow move. Fear gripped her for a moment, but when she reached the top step, she recognized Kaloyan and forced a smile.

The instant he saw her, he rushed over and hugged her, like a sailor greeting his beloved after an endless absence.

"Where did you disappear to? Your father's worried sick," he started in once he was certain that the woman in his arms was real and unhurt.

"Why are you so concerned about me all of a sudden?"

"We were worried… You disappeared from the hospital. We thought you must have been kidnapped again."

"I need to be alone."

"You should have called."

"Well, now you know."

Vera walked past him and started to unlock the apartment door.

"Wait!" He grabbed her hand, his eyes reflecting the fear that she might disappear again.

"What?"

"Let's go out... like we used to."

"I'm too tired."

"Just for ten minutes. A stroll around the neighborhood."

Vera put the key back in her pocket. She owed him that much.

They went outside in silence and walked along the first path they came across. Neither of them spoke.

Kaloyan took his hand out of his pocket, let it dangle for a few minutes like a clock's pendulum and then timidly touched Vera's fragile palm. Her fingers stayed still, motionless. He took them in his hand and squeezed them. His eyes followed the edge of the pavement. They walked on in silence. Every now and again Vera would look at him out of the corner of her eye, studying him, hoping to find something to grab hold of. She tried to discover what had attracted her to this man years ago. Everything would be so much easier if she could just go back to him. If she could feel desire again, instead of guilt over her indifference towards him.

"I want to stay at my mother's place for a while," she whispered, her eyes following the pavement's edge as well, as if it had become the center of the universe.

Kaloyan didn't ask her why, but still Vera felt obliged to explain.

"After everything that's happened… I'm confused. I need time to find myself again."

"I'll miss you," he replied, his words sounding long rehearsed.

Vera felt a heaviness in her chest, a weight that only sleep would remove.

She could have touched him, held him, made love to him. She wanted him, or rather wanted to want him, yet her body rebelled against his closeness. Not a single fiber of her body trembled at his touch. Suddenly she felt like crying. She wanted to have a family. The warm, close family she herself had never had. The one she had dreamed about ever since she was a little girl. She thought her father had taken it away from her. Had time erased these feelings, or had she never had them in the first place? Just illusions, whose details crumbled to dust.

The loss of yet another dearly held illusion was so painful that she had been putting it off as long as she could. Like most people, she figured if she didn't think about them, bad things would disappear on their own. Just this sort of mass deception steals so much of our brief time on this earth.

Vera knew that she had to accept the fact that things always did and always would turn out this way. Her realization that it was all impossible was worse than her actual separation from Kaloyan. Because the impossible killed her hopes and dreams that someday everything would turn out the way she wanted it to.

And he was perfect. Vera looked at him again from the corner of her eye. Kaloyan was handsome, very good to her and other people, he had a successful business, took care of her, did his best for her. Yet these thoughts would not make her fingers move within his hand.

Was the problem with Vera or with the accepted order of things? Was she repeating some twisted model she had inherited from her parents? It was the only model she knew…

When they reached the apartment block, Kaloyan kissed her and said as he was leaving, "I'll wait for you."

And Vera knew he would.

UNKNOWN LATITUDES

Page 452 began with an Orphic text written in the year 320 B.C.:
"The man who alters what has been laid down ... [so as to right wrongs and not do evil... he does not allow the world to accept the vagaries of fate.] Is it not for these reasons that the cosmos possesses order? In the same way, Heraclitus, changing the common views, overturns his own, he who said, speaking in the same way as a myth-teller:
'The sun according to its own nature is a human foot in width, not exceeding its boundaries. For if it goes outside its own width, the Erinyes, helpers of Justice, will find it out.'"

From The Derveni Papyrus, Col. IV,
translated by Andre Laks and Glenn Most

One day they discovered the hole in the wall and took away his shaft of light. Then they left him alone for three days as punishment. He had kept this painful memory tightly locked away. Since that incident, he had not wished for anything forbidden. Over time, the established order had turned him into a cog in its mechanism...

Ariman had been standing for hours in the dark, yet the questions would not cease. The Incorporeal One used confinement in the Black Room to intimidate people and make them believe. Who was he? Who were they? Why were they doing all this? Why did no one else ask questions as he did? Why was he different? The queries buzzed in his head.

The church whose cellar houses the Incorporeal One's crypt

Ariman jumped to his feet and started pacing around in a circle. The Incorporeal One wanted the woman dead. Ariman had not been able to kill her on the bridge in Moscow. He had never before rebelled against a mission. Now the uncertainty was crushing him.

He couldn't stay here. He pounded the stone, furious that he could not stop thinking forbidden thoughts. He paced around the Black Room a few more times, tracing a path he knew by heart. Finally, he couldn't stand it any longer.

Ariman opened the door and ran up the stairs. When he reached the refectory, he slowed down and bowed his head, hoping to hide his thoughts. Going up another floor, he reached the front door, lit by glowing wings of sun seeping through its cracks. The devils' heads watched him from the ceiling, more ferocious and prying than ever.

Ariman opened the door and dashed down the narrow street. He passed St. George's Church and continued on by the Roman Forum, losing himself in the mute streets whose ancient paving stones had embraced thousands of events, people and history.

He was weak, confused and angry. Lost in the dark, he started sprinting as fast as he could.

Ariman kept running even when he could no longer feel his legs. He couldn't catch his breath. Despite his panting, he couldn't seem to get enough oxygen.

He ran, not knowing where to, not seeing or hearing. All he knew was that he had to escape the emptiness that had seized him in its powerful jaws.

Painful memories flooded his mind. The tiny woman – was she his mother? – was holding out her arms, calling his name. Not the name he was known by now. Tears slid down her cheeks. Was she a dream or had she really existed?

The stranger was taking him away. They were on a train, then a ship. Locked in a tiny cabin, he didn't see the sun for two weeks. Then they got in a truck. The trip was a blur, but he had a clear memory of seeing the Roman Coliseum for the first time. His eyes had filled with tears, not of joy, but because he realized that everything had changed. Irrevocably. They entered the underground world beneath the rust-colored walls of the ancient church.

There were other children there.

Ariman pushed himself, running even faster.

Yet the unwanted memories strangled him, squeezing his soul in their steel tentacles, trying to drag it to Hell. No, this wretched underground labyrinth *was* Hell.

He jogged down the stone steps to the Tiber. Reaching the manmade stone bank, he continued running downstream. He hadn't been here for twenty years – not since the last time he had tried to escape the underground labyrinth.

A gap in the stone quay caught his eye. He had gotten that far last time, before being sent to the Black Room for two days as punishment. Since then he had wanted to believe that there was nowhere else he could go.

This time, however, Ariman leapt over the gap in the concrete and kept running. This was new territory for him. His breath still eluded him, but he didn't care. Only the living needed air. He had long since ceased to be one of them.

Could he kill the woman, as the Incorporeal One wanted? If he could not, he would have to leave the only world he knew. The uncertainty sapped his strength, while fury tightened his sinews. He wanted to put an end to all this. Yet inside him the fly was buzzing ever more insistently and angrily.

His legs were growing weaker, yet the canal seemed endless. Perhaps there really was no where else he could go. He would just have to accept this.

Ariman stopped, his heart hammering in his chest.

He took refuge under an ancient sycamore tree. The tree was clinging to the concrete at the very edge of the bank. Its soaring, solid branches canopied the river, reaching the opposite bank.

Ariman doubled over, his forearms leaning heavily on his knees. Exhaustion pulled his eyelids into a painful squint. He focused solely on breathing, on sucking oxygen into his lungs, yet he seemed to be inhaling only gusts of empty air. Dizzy, he dropped down onto the concrete bank, dangling his feet above the yellow water. Night was falling.

Gradually his pulse regained its natural rhythm and his breathing normalized. His body kept shaking, however.

He sat there for over an hour. Only the steady rising and falling of his chest showed he was not a wax figure.

Was he going blind or learning to see?

THE HIDDEN ONES

Page 453 began with a quotation:
One of these men is Genius to the other.
And so of these, which is the natural man,
And which the spirit? Who deciphers them?
A Comedy of Errors by William Shakespeare

"Kaloyan told me what you're cooking up... As your father, I beg you not to do it. It's suicide!" The normally reserved Professor Kandilov sounded extremely agitated.

"It's only suicide in your mind!" Vera replied hotly. "And the minds of all those other bigwig scholars moldering away in their libraries, writing books no one will ever read. Their only goal is to immortalize themselves in the academic pantheon!"

"There's no point in arguing over this."

"That's right. I've made up my mind. What happened in Moscow made me realize that I'm on the trail of something huge. And I nearly died before I could tell anyone."

"People will think you're crazy."

"That's their problem. At least my conscience will be clean."

Vera turned off her cell phone and dropped it into her bag. A woman met her at the entrance to the television studio and took her to the make-up room. Once Vera was sufficiently caked and powdered, she had to wait in a narrow, windowless hallway with only a couch and a television broadcasting the station's evening talk show.

An assistant peeked around the door and told Vera that she had ten minutes to get ready before going on. Alone between the orange walls, Vera started feeling nervous. Her breath quickened and her hands trembled. All her words seemed to desert her, scattered amidst her fragmented thoughts.

"My father can't be right," she thought. "He's just another academic dinosaur on the verge of extinction. They claim that only their ideas are true, while letting their books gather dust in libraries, instead of applying their theories to real life, where they might actually mesh with other ideas and give rise to new interpretations."

On the television screen, the talk show host was interviewing a female singer who seemed absolutely at home in front of the camera. Vera envied her, knowing that when she took the singer's place she would be trembling in her socks. "Enough of these jitters!" she commanded herself. After surviving the kidnapping, she realized she had to publicize what she knew as soon as possible. However, she still had not found a publisher for her book, which was delaying its release. Public awareness of her work would guarantee her safety – or so she hoped.

"You're on!" a short man in a baseball cap hissed, coming towards her with a wireless microphone. He unceremoniously snapped the receiver box to the back of her pants, ran the cord under her blouse and clipped the microphone to her lapel. Then he ushered her into the studio towards the interviewer and cameras.

The studio blazed with spotlights. The interviewer looked shorter than he did on screen, while his heavily powdered face resembled a crumpled rubber mask. His ridiculous appearance somehow reassured Vera and cheered her up.

She approached the interviewer and shook his hand – in the studio people always greet each other enthusiastically and smile pleasantly at each other.

"One minute and we're on the air!" he informed her.

The host stared expectantly into the camera's lifeless face, clutching a sheet of questions the editor had just given him. He teetered on the edge of his seat, as if ready to blast off at any moment.

"Everybody's nervous," Vera mused. She looked at her watch anxiously – several times. It was ten past seven. Perhaps her father was sitting in front of his television. She didn't dare look at the live audience, who were all staring at her in expectation. Feeling their eyes, she tensed up. The assistant had warned her that they would be inviting journalists and historians to make the debate livelier and to air as many opinions as possible. Of course, none of the big-name scholars deigned to appear – television debates that watered down science for the masses were beneath them. Vera braced herself for hostile questions. Even though very few people believed in the Son of God, everyone loved getting riled up over blasphemy, as if this brought them closer to God.

Vera glanced nervously at the hands of her watch again and took a deep breath. The show's theme music began. The interviewer strafed out a few brief introductory sentences about her, but Vera didn't catch a single one. Then he dove straight into the story: "You were almost killed in Moscow. Don't you think it might be time to change your profession?"

"I still want to be an archaeologist. What happened in Russia merely convinced me that my research is on the right track. The people who kidnapped Dr. Werder and me are trying to hide the truth."

"And what truth is that?"

"As far as the late Dr. Werder and I could determine, we were kidnapped because of a small amulet, which is one important clue hinting at a scandalous connection between Christ, Orpheus and perhaps an even earlier culture's god. I believe they wanted to destroy any trace of it. Ever since the amulet was first discovered centuries ago, it has continually disappeared, only to be found again, like all other artifacts showing this same connection."

"And just what is this connection you're referring to?"

"The connection between the First Civilization and all subsequent Sons of God – including Jesus Christ."

"Does such a connection really exist?"

"Absolutely, but it's very inconvenient. The 'Son of God' story is an eternally plagiarized, recycled tale, which people today call the story of Jesus, but which until yesterday was known as the myth of Orpheus, Dionysus, Mitra and Osiris and who knows who else. We still don't know how it might appear in tomorrow's truths."

A wave of whispering and shuffling rippled through the audience. Some of the spectators could not contain their indignation at Vera's claims.

"Can you give us some specific examples?" the interviewer asked.

"As we know, people invent religions to explain the unexplainable and to attain the unattainable. The fact that we no longer create gods today and hence find it difficult now to believe that people in the past invented them is another question entirely."

A buzz of consternation again filled the room, but Vera went on.

"The theft of the Orphic amulet was no coincidence. Nor is it an accident that there are hundreds of obvious yet still unrecognized links between various prophets and Sons of God from all over the world – dozens of thinkers and scholars have discussed just these connections. And it is not only the deities that are similar, but the basic religious tenets as well. Have you ever wondered why the major ideas driving the world appear on earth in regular cycles? They always have a similar ideological nucleus, reminiscent of the First Civilization's teachings, which disappeared mysteriously from Thrace, scorching all traces of its own existence. It is clear that all these ideas have to have a common source. Take, for example, Ehnaton, Orpheus and Moses, Christ, the Virgin Mary, Mitra, Buddha, John the Baptist, and even Pythagoras, Einstein, Shakespeare, Leonardo and a hundred more like them. They appear on earth unexpectedly with their great ideas, as if out of nowhere, but with such revolutionary knowledge that they transform the people who come after them like a series of strong waves. Dust to dust down through the generations. To this very day, we wonder whether they were humans, shades, gods or something else. One thing is certain, however: they all push civilization in a specific direction, yet we show our gratitude to them by condemning them, spitting on them, persecuting them, killing them, ripping them apart, deifying them... Yet we don't know who they are. So before anyone steals my theories, I want to share them with people who will understand them."

A young voice laughed loudly in the audience. Embarrassed, Vera raised her head to see dozens of pairs of eyes watching her. She glanced down at her watch again. There was still enough time to complete her presentation.

"Can you show us some evidence to back up these fantastic claims? What is the First Civilization you've mentioned?" the interviewer interrupted.

"There won't be enough time during this interview, but I'll try to explain briefly... I argue that the oldest version of the 'Son of God' story can be dated back 8,000 years. Evidence for its existence comes from pictograms discovered in the Central Balkans written by the First Civilization, whom I call the Meandrites. I believe they first came up with the idea. The most popular 'Son of God' today is Jesus. But Dionysus was a much earlier son of god, as his name shows: in Greek *dio* means 'God' and *nysa* means 'son.' As you can see, the last letters in Dionysus – ISUS – also spell out the name of the most recent Son of God: Jesus. The civilization that invented this idea for some inexplicable reason disappeared, or went into hiding, in the fourth millennium B.C. No one has any idea what happened to it or whether their ideas are still alive today," Vera scratched her nose, tossed back her hair and plunged ahead. "But let's pause for a moment on the two most recent Sons of God: Orpheus and Christ. Here is a picture of the ill-fated amulet, which combines the images of Orpheus and Christ."

A rustling filled the studio again. Vera signaled to the assistant to show the first slide, which featured a picture of a stone medallion with traces of rust, as well as a sketch of what at first glance appeared to be the same amulet. Yet there were differences between the two.

A hush fell over the studio.

"The very first researchers to study this small talisman, Freke and Gandy,[68] suggested that the image of Christ was based on ancient Thracian myths of Orpheus. Judging from the T-shaped crucifixion with the knees to the right, we can conclude that the amulet is most likely a medieval, rather than ancient, creation. However, the most puzzling thing is that no one can explain why there are seven stars over the figure's head, as well as an unusual crescent moon and two symmetrical wedges at the foot of the cross. These wedges are not exactly symmetrical in the sketch, while in the original they are thicker and identical, creating what looks like

---

[68] Freke and Gandy suggest that certain pagan religions, including the cults of Osiris, Dionysus, Atis and Mitra, were variants of a cult based on the myth of the death and resurrection of a "Divine Human," whom they call Osiris-Dionysus. The authors also argue for the idea that Christ did not actually exist as a historical individual, but rather was inspired by a syncretic reinterpretation of the fundamentally pagan "Divine Human" in Gnosticism, which was the original Christian sect. According to Freke and Gandy, orthodox Christianity was not the precursor of Gnosticism, as many scholars believe, but instead a later offshoot, which then rewrote history to make it seem as if Christianity preceded Gnosticism. They call their hypothesis "The Theory of the Mysteries of Jesus."

an arrow pointing downwards. For nearly a century no one has been able to explain their significance."

On the screen Vera showed a number of images of crucified men from Antiquity, along with several more stylized and dynamic images from the Middle Ages.

"But what interests me is the message the artist has tried to encode with this unique combination of symbols."

One of the audience members at the back of the studio raised a hand. Vera waited for the question in silence.

"So you're trying to convince us of the connection between Orpheus and Christ – solely on the basis of a picture on a stone that has now disappeared?"

"This is by no means the only evidence! I simply began with this artifact because it was the reason why I was kidnapped."

Vera signaled for the assistant to project the images from the Roman catacombs in the black book which she had found at Chateau Jacques.

"But this is nothing more than simple syncretism!" objected a voice from the first row.[69]

"Is it really so simple? Is it pure chance that there are so many coincidences between these artifacts – which, by the way, are disappearing one by one while we sit here arguing about them?"

The studio guests were staring at the interviewee's delicate figure. She had known that statement would win their attention and approval – for the time being, at least.

"Moses is the most famous prophet, right?" Vera continued. "But how many believers know that during his time there, was another prophet called Orpheus who also studied in Egypt? The two of them later sowed similar ideas amongst their peoples."

The studio audience grew restless and started whispering. The cameras cut to the host, who gleefully announced: "What

---

[69] "Syncretism" is the mixing of symbols from two or more religions when a formerly dominant religion is dying out and being replaced by a successor.

a wonderful statement to end our discussion on! Thank you for your time... And now, let's turn to a documentary film about the Bogomils!"

An ad for laundry detergent flashed onto the monitors as Vera exclaimed in indignation: "The Bogomils?! What do the Bogomils have to do with anything?"

"It's the only film on this stuff that we've got," the interviewer replied as he removed his microphone. "The audience will get a kick out of the Bogomils, too. Relax, nobody will notice the difference."

At that moment, the man in the baseball cap came up to Vera and took off her microphone. As he leaned over her, he said, "The boss wants to see you backstage right away!"

Vera looked at him with an astonishment that immediately changed to fury. She stood up quickly and walked towards the stage exit.

A man really was waiting for her. He was in his fifties and introduced himself as the producer.

"Have you got half an hour to spare?" he asked.

"Well, obviously I do... I thought I was going to be the main guest."

"I stopped the interview."

"Why?"

"Because it was absolutely criminal!"

"Oh God, are you starting in on me, too? Unless you're a religious fanatic, you should realize that my theory isn't a crime."

"I don't mean your idea, but your presentation. You can't bleed it dry like that on the air. It has to be given the proper treatment."

"Who are you?"

"I told you... I'm the producer – but I also own a publishing company. I want to offer you something more than half an hour on TV."

They reached the end of the hallway.

"They make good coffee here. Why don't we sit down?"

"Look, I don't want to disappoint you, but I've already offered my idea to two publishing companies. They rejected it."

"Because they thought you were a lunatic."

"And what do you think?"

"I know more about you than other people. Kiril, the journalist who went on the expedition to Switzerland with you, has told me quite a bit about you…"

CONDEMNED

Page 454 *quoted the "Wisdom of Solomon,"*
wherein it is written:
"'For God created man to be immortal, and made him
to be an image of his own eternity.
Nevertheless through envy of the devil came death
into the world: and they that do hold of his side do
find it.' (2:23-24) St. John Chrysostom explained this
in the following way: upon hearing that man would
be returned to the earth, the devil thirsted to see this
decision fulfilled and yet more – to see the son's end
precede the father's, the murder of brother by brother,
untimely and violent death. The devil heard that man
was condemned to death and to return to earth, and he
could not wait for the time when this sentence would be
fulfilled."

Night was falling over insomniac Rome. Ariman was only now beginning to feel the cold. He had nothing warm to put on. The river lapped at his feet.

For the first time, he heard the angry howl of loneliness, weakness and fear echoing inside him. He knew the only way to restore his life's familiar order and meaning was to complete his mission. Like the Incorporeal One wanted.

Before the questions had cropped up, everything had been quite simple, free of pain and fear. Where had these feelings come from? Did they hound him because he was different from the others? Ariman believed that he had been born in the Upper World. Few of them were.

Or had everything changed when he refused to kill the woman? She had stolen his peace of mind. Many people Above believed that a woman was responsible for the loss of Paradise.

No answers came, just the gnawing misery of the unknown.

In the darkness, he heard a faint buzzing sound and turned to see a small black fly flitting recklessly close to him. Ariman watched it carefully. The insect landed next to him on the concrete bank, its translucent wings fluttering. Tapping the cement with its feet, the fly looked for a comfortable spot to settle down. It finally stopped fidgeting and spread its wings wide to catch the last sigh of light. The wings glistened with all the colors of the rainbow.

Ariman slowly reached out for it. Spreading his fingers, he caught the fly. A quiet smile appeared on his face.

Holding his fist to his ear, he felt its legs churning frantically against his palm. He loosened his fingers slightly to give it more space.

The bank of the Tiber River, where Ariman was standing

Now he could feel its wings. Bringing his fist even closer, he heard the buzzing. He closed his eyes, concentrating fully on the sound. The fly skittered around his palm, flapping its wings helplessly, trying to find an escape route, buzzing all the while.

Ariman lay back on the cold concrete bank, still holding his fist to his ear. The buzzing calmed him, helped him order his thoughts and brought him back into his body. Just as the fly in the Black Room had – as long as it had shared his underground prison.

Ariman had chattered to the fly as it took comfort in the pale shaft of light. One day the Incorporeal One heard him talking to someone. Bursting into the Black Room, the teacher had discovered the fly and killed it. He had wanted to teach Ariman to be alone, because pain and weakness can only hurt those who nurse the secret hope of sharing them with someone.

Finally the fly in his hand stopped moving. It was probably exhausted – or had despaired of ever escaping. But how could insects despair, since they can't hope? They can't dream either – or at least that's what those thick encyclopedias said.

Ariman opened his fist. The little creature flew away.

Perhaps the Incorporeal One had been trying to protect him? "Pain and weakness can only hurt those who nurse the secret hope of sharing them with someone," he repeated to himself.

Ariman wanted to put an end to his anguish. The only way was to find the woman and complete his mission.

TRACES OF THE SAVIORS

Page 455 *stated:*
"In his book, The World's Sixteen Crucified Saviors (1875), Kersey Graves mentions more than a dozen mythical saviors and miracle workers from around the world who all supposedly died on a cross or a tree. They include Krishna, Buddha, Dionysus, Hercules, Hesus/ Eros, Attis, Tammuz/Adonis, Mithra, Quetzalcoatl, Odin, Horus, Prometheus and others."

"That stuff you talked about during the interview – do you have it in writing?" the producer asked.

"Well, most of it, but I need more evidence."

"I want to know more," he added, settling into his seat. "Kiril mentioned you had some strange ideas about Shakespeare."

"Well, they're not mine, but a scholar named Mather Walker's. He argues that Shakespeare described the solar gods' transformation and that he was one of the first to establish the connection between Orpheus and Christ. He encoded such messages in his plays."

"Finding hidden messages is a time-honored mania. It even gave rise to the science of Kabbalah. So I don't suppose it would be too difficult to find a solar deity in the works of Shakespeare," the producer mused.

Vera shot him a disapproving look and declared, "Shakespeare was an enlightened Orphist."

"Wasn't Shakespeare a Knight Templar as well?"

Vera's cheeks flamed. "Well, to be completely frank, he didn't actually exist!"

There was a moment of silence before the producer said, "Tell me about the solar deities in his plays."

Vera hesitated, but went on.

"Walker makes a number of arguments... He first asks why the two Shakespeare plays containing Orphic messages both premiered on Christmas, Christ's birthday. His explanation is that this further emphasizes the undeniable connection between Christ and Orpheus. According to him, the Orphic/Dionysian concept predates Christianity by at least 1,000 years; however, the stories told by both religions overlap. Dionysus was the son of the mightiest god, Zeus, and a mortal woman. The Titans then viciously killed the young man-god and ate him. The traces of this old legend, especially the part about him being eaten, show up in Christianity. For example, on the night when Christ was betrayed, he took bread, broke it and gave it to his disciples saying, 'Take this and eat it: this is my body given unto you.' Then he took a glass of wine and gave it to them with the words, 'This cup is the new testament in my blood, spilled for you and all men, for the forgiveness of sins.'"

"I'd never thought about it before, but now that you mention it, I suppose that is quite a coincidence..."

"No one discusses these similarities, they don't want to. Yet there are countless examples of such parallels. For example, the Orphists discovered the ritual of communion thousands of years before the Christians. The Orphic god also suffered, died and was born again. They believed that through the mystery of communion they could become one with their god. Let's just recall for a moment what's written in John 6:55-56, 'For my flesh is true food and my blood is true drink. Those who eat my flesh and drink my blood abide in me, and I in them.' The Greeks considered Dionysus the god of wine and vines, right? In the New Testament, John 15:1 claims that Jesus said, 'I am the true vine, and my Father is the vine-grower.' Orphic theology also tells of a miracle with wine, just like in the New Testament when Jesus turns water to wine. Even heaven is older than the Christian church – an early historian,

St. Justin the Martyr, claims that Dionysus was torn to pieces at his death, but was resurrected and ascended to heaven."

"That's interesting, but these are just general similarities. I can't believe that there are such strong similarities between Christian and Orphic teachings," the producer objected.

"Well, then you should brush up on your theology. The Orphists were the first to spread the idea that the world is in the clutches of evil and that the body is a burden that imprisons the soul, whose destiny is to escape to a holy and eternal life. The Christians later preached the same concept, so today everyone has heard of it. Shall I go on?"

"You've certainly aroused my curiosity."

"There are other arguments: Dionysus was both man and god – that is, he was fathered by a god and born to a mortal woman. The Christians believe the same about Christ, don't they? Dionysus was cruelly persecuted and put to death, only to be triumphantly reborn. Sound familiar? That's Jesus' story, too. According to the myths, Orpheus and Dionysus descended into Hell and came back. Christians also believe that during the three days when Jesus was dead, before the resurrection, he descended into Hell and prayed for the souls imprisoned there… Go ahead and double check everything if you doubt my arguments."

"Not in the least. I'm impressed."

"I can point out some other interesting parallels. Dionysus was also known as 'Bacchus.' Some myths say that Bacchus was raised by panthers; he was even frequently depicted with them. However, the panther is also tied to Jesus. In the Talmud he is referred to by a variety of names, including ben Pantera, ben ha Pantera, Yeshu ben Pantera. This name is indisputably very old. The philosopher Celsus in 178 heard Jews saying that Jesus' parents were Miriam and Pantera, which is where the moniker 'ben Pantera' came from.[70]

---

[70] According to Dr. Ivan Panchovski, when passing along this epithet, the early Christian scholar and theologian Origen explained that it had its source in the fact that Jacob, the father of Joseph and grandfather of Jesus, was called "Panther." From this, Origen further reasons, the Jews called Jesus the son of

Christ and Orpheus also shared similar nicknames. For example, Orpheus was called the Fisherman[71] and the Shepherd, epithets that were also used later for Christ. Orpheus was also frequently depicted with sheep, doves, panthers and peacocks, which later became Christian symbols."

"If I'm not mistaken, weren't Dionysus and Jesus born on the same date?"

"Yes. Many solar deities share the same birth day: December 25. But here's something even more interesting: the solar god has twelve followers, represented by the twelve signs of the zodiac. Christ had precisely the same number of followers – his disciples."

"Have you laid this all out in your book?"

"Hundreds of academics have presented dozens of similar hypotheses. In short, my idea is that Christ may have been just the most recent 'divine son,' one of many Sons of God who have appeared to humanity throughout the ages. Or maybe there really was only a single son, and the story has simply been told and retold with different names."

"I like the idea of God having several sons," the producer said. "So if you're right about this story… I mean if it really was not invented by the Christians, then is it Orpheus' story?"

"Oh, no! He merely retold it to the Thracians."

"Retold it? So whose idea was it in the first place?"

"I'm still working on that part of the story. I need more clues."

"But you must have some idea – you can't hunt for clues unless you know what general direction to look in."

Joseph, using the name of his supposedly human grandfather Ben Panthera, or "Son of the Panther." The scholars Nich, Black and Keller suggest a different, more probable explanation for calling Jesus "Ben Pandera." They argue that it is an inexact Jewish borrowing of the word *parqu, noj*, i.e. "virgin." The Jews, upon hearing the Christians' claims that Jesus was the "son of a virgin" (*ui'o,j th/j parqe,nou*), mockingly called him "Ben-ha-Pantera" or "son of the panther."

[71] In the early twentieth century, the German scholar Robert Eisler wrote his lengthy work *Orpheus the Fisherman*, which traces connections between Orphism and Christianity, as well as between Dionysus and Jesus.

"That's true. I came across some artifacts that made me believe that the original 'son of god' idea came from a prehistoric Balkan civilization that disappeared two millennia before Orpheus appeared. But I still can't figure out why it was precisely Orpheus who resurrected some of their ideas."

"How do you know that he resurrected these ideas and didn't just come up with them on his own?"

"By the key symbols used to encode them." Vera leaned forward and sketched a few symbols on a napkin: something that looked like a V with wings, a meander, a cross and a few other signs. Then she added, "These symbols were created 8,000 years ago by the civilization, which then disappeared in a puff of smoke. After a long absence, these symbols once again started showing up on ancient ceramics."

"Impressive!" The producer's pupils widened. "Orpheus must have found some hidden knowledge like the Knights Templar did! This is going to be a great story – especially if there is an Ark."

"I'm working on the Ark… but the truth might turn out to be very simple. New ideas are very rare. We normally borrow old ideas from other people, even if we don't always know from whom…"

"Don't tell anyone about this! And finish the book!"

"You're the first person who's encouraged me."

"How many people have you told this story to?" His face sharpened impatiently.

"My father and a historian. But the historian's dead now."

"Excellent."

"Let me be frank. I don't believe in this story."

"I don't either. But it'll make a wonderful book."

KNOWLEDGE

Page 456 told of hidden knowledge:
"The material published in 1956 appeared in a variety of forms. Part of it came out in the form of popular books, even best sellers, to a greater or lesser extent irritatingly mysterious... In addition to the multitude of books, including many which were printed at the personal expense of the authors, a huge number of articles began to appear in newspapers and magazines... The information began to surface in documents and brochures which were deposited at the National Library in limited editions... Through mysterious insinuations, handwritten comments and footnotes... each of the brochures expands and adds to the others."

From **The Holy Blood and the Holy Grail** by Michael
Baigent, Richard Leigh and Henry Lincoln, p. 112–115

After everything she had lived through that week, Vera was trying to reestablish a daily routine. She went to a few lectures at the university. She sat through a silent dinner with Kaloyan. She didn't dare call her father after her stint on television, though.

Yet nothing could distract her thoughts from circling around the mystery, whose ramparts she continued reinforcing on a daily basis. Yet she had inexplicably stopped seeing the signs. Even the connections she had discovered between the symbols had begun to fade. It was as if part of her had been left behind in Moscow – and she kept going back in her mind to look for it. The magic of discovery had evaporated. Inertia alone maintained the rhythm of everyday life.

Vera opened her eyes every morning with the expectation of learning something new, some spark that would re-enchant her daily routine, transforming it into the life her imagination envisioned. She longed to again be under a spell that could not be broken, even by exhaustion or hours of blind staring at screens and books, or by melancholy and loneliness.

The days passed, but no new clues turned up, while the old traces still did not lead to any concrete conclusions. Vera felt obliged to give Futch the pictures of the golden tablet that she had taken in Moscow, despite her deep reluctance to share her secret with the insatiable treasure hunter.

Yet another new day slipped into Vera's bedroom uninvited. She glanced at the bedside clock. It was twenty past eight, a few minutes before the alarm was set to go off.

She forced herself to get up. Raising the heavy metal window shades, she let her sleepy gaze rest on the treetops outside. Scenes from her last dreams were still spinning through her head, talking and moving as if alive. She closed her eyes and tried to capture them, knowing that in a few hours they would disappear into a blank fog of oblivion.

First she saw Futch, who kept asking her where the golden tablet had come from. She refused to tell him. He disappeared, and Vera felt the black, icy water of the Moscow River. She was swallowing it, spitting it out. It washed over her. She tried to breathe, but sucked water into her lungs. She tried to scream but couldn't. She was alive – in dreams, you're always alive. "Will you come back for May 30?" "What happens on May 30?" Why was her father asking her that over and over? The water again, but she was swimming against the current, not moving downriver with it. Dr. Werder's face appeared. He had been shot in the back. He looked up at her and told her to run. Blood dripped from his mouth into the mud. He whispered to her, "Go to Rome, to the library at the end of the oldest road... look for 'The Parchment Maze.'" Was the historian talking about a real book or just babbling? His body *went limp, yet his eyes bored into her. Unmoving, they still held her in their gaze... How easily life slips away. **456 pages** are not enough...*

Werder's final words were the last thing Vera remembered from the dream. They had woken her from her sleep yet again this morning.

She lifted her elbows from the windowsill and went into the bathroom, yawning and rubbing her eyes. She was deeply relieved not to be in that river. Yet Werder's words hounded her. "Did he mean a real book?" she wondered. The German historian had said: "In Rome... look for the *Parchment Maze*... In the library at the end of the oldest road near Quo Vadis." He probably meant the ancient Roman Via Appia, which was the oldest road in Europe. As far as Vera knew, the Quo Vadis Church was at the beginning of the road, on the spot where St. Peter had met the resurrected Christ. She couldn't remember whether there was a library there. The historian had not mentioned its name.

She washed her face, brushed her teeth and went into the kitchen to make coffee. Then she called airport information.

"Yes, hello. When is the next flight to Rome?"

"Today. There are seats available on the 2:10 flight, if you'd like."

"Great, thanks."

Vera got dressed and caught a taxi to the airport. She impatiently switched on her laptop in the cab and Googled the "Parchment Maze." Nothing came up. She tried in English, German and Italian, again with no results – just as she had suspected. She almost asked the driver to turn the car around, but the thought of the historian's eyes and words haunting her dreams indefinitely stopped her. It was worth the 600 euro for the flight and hotel to finally get a good night's sleep.

Her cell phone buzzed in her bag. Kaloyan's number came up on the display. She turned it off. The glistening airport complex loomed up ahead like an enormous flying saucer. Vera closed her laptop and paid the driver.

As the plane rolled up to the gate in Rome, she switched her phone back on to check for missed calls. After a few minutes a text message appeared: "Your father is having emergency surgery. I'm waiting for you in front of Tokuda Hospital."

It must have been sent hours ago.

Vera immediately called Kaloyan, even though she hadn't yet gotten off the plane.

"What do you mean, he's having surgery? What's going on?"

"He had a heart attack. Where are you? I waited for you in front of the hospital for more than an hour!" Kaloyan sounded angry and frightened.

"A heart attack?"

"It was completely unexpected. He was at a committee meeting discussing applications for new doctoral students… That's all I know."

"How is he? Is he going to make it?"

"He hasn't woken up from the anesthesia yet."

Vera switched the phone off, as if scared that they would all realize where she was at such a critical moment. She followed the crowd mechanically as it filed off the plane toward customs. The sounds of conversation, coughing, children crying, the squeaking of wheels and shoes bubbled up around her. It was finally her turn. After going through passport control, Vera blindly followed the crowd threading its way into the baggage claim area. She grabbed her bag from the conveyor belt and walked towards the glass doors which were streaming sunlight.

She stood in front of the airport exit for a moment, then whirled around and went back in. After taking a few steps, she clutched her bag in her slender fingers and stopped. She turned around and walked towards the exit again. Her thoughts screamed: "A heart attack! He could have died. And I wasn't with him!" Or perhaps her father and Kaloyan were trying to test her? No, they would never think to do something like that…

Vera saw an information booth. Pressing her lips to the crack in the glass, she asked in a quavering voice when the first flight to Sofia was.

"Tomorrow, May 31, at eight A.M."

Vera froze. Wide eyed, she asked in amazement, "So it's the 30th today?"

"Yes," the woman inside the information booth replied curtly.

"Today is May 30! That's why Dad kept asking whether he would see me today. The committee was interviewing new PhD applicants." Vera thought to herself, before again turning to the woman in the booth.

"How do I get to the library on the Via Appia?"

The woman looked up at her in surprise. "That's not something tourists usually ask about."

"I'm not a tourist."

The woman unfolded a city map and started hunting around. After a moment she asked, "What part of the street is it on?"

"At the beginning of the street, near the San Sebastian gate."

"I don't see any libraries in that part of the street."

"So how can I get to the San Sebastian gate?" asked Vera irritably.

With a highlighter, the woman drew yellow lines leading to the dot marking the gate. Then she handed Vera the map.

As Vera stepped outside, she was met by a warm breeze blowing off the sun-baked city. Rolling her suitcase behind her, she reached the taxi stand. She grabbed the first cab and settled in comfortably to see the city whose ancient ruins preserved much of the soul of ancient European civilization.

"There aren't any libraries along this road." The taxi driver rudely interrupted her thoughts.

"So just drop me off at the start of the Via Appia."

"The place where Christ met St. Peter?"

Fields and castles along the Via Appia

She nodded.

Their route took them past huge stone monuments, squares, castles, cathedrals and fairy-tale fountains, as well as living statues posing for tourists. Yet Vera's thoughts kept returning to Sofia, searching for a justification for being in Rome right now. There was no way she could have known, she kept telling herself. In any case, she was already here. She may as well find the library and finish what she had come to do.

She fished her sunglasses out of her purse. Their large round lenses hid half her face. Leaning her chin in her hand, she stared through the glass.

They passed soaring pines, orange and lemon trees exploding with blossoms, olive groves and grassy parks. Far away on the horizon rose the magnificent contours of the Coliseum.

The cab stopped in front of a wide green field. In the distance she could see the ruins of an old castle. Despite her archeological training, Vera had no idea what it was. The crumbling stone seemed unreal, like something from the set of a historical film. The sun was scorching. Unbuttoning her jean jacket, she walked along the sandy path towards the olive grove.

The path followed the Via Appia's curves and led her to the San Sebastian gate. Vera knew that the ancient road ended here –

The section of the Via Appia from which the entrance to the library is visible

or began, depending on your point of view. But she still didn't see any library. The thought again flashed through her mind that Dr. Werder might have sent her on a fool's errand, but she immediately dismissed it. People don't lie when they are dying. Perhaps he had meant the other end of the road, which was far away in Brindisi? No, he had definitely said Rome.

While she was juggling all sorts of thoughts in her mind, Vera spotted a wonderful orange grove on the other side of the ancient road. A caramel colored building stood in the middle of it, the weathered paint peeling from its façade. Against the bright blue sky, the fruit hanging in the trees stood out like spots on a green ladybug. The place seemed like something straight out of a fairytale, so she stopped to take a photograph and indulge the illusion of capturing the moment for posterity. In fact, she never looked back at her pictures years later.

As she focused the camera lens and zoomed in, her breath caught. A narrow path led from the caramel building towards the Via Appia. Above the ancient iron door in the stone wall dividing the garden from the street, she saw the word "Library."

History's Memory

Page 457 *featured a photograph with the following explanation written beneath it:*
"Byzantine Theological Texts is a manuscript containing anti-western Byzantine theological ideas. It is thought to have originally contained 329 pages, but ends on page 220. A note on page 220 reads, 'Sunt in hoc volumine folia scripta 329, videlicet folia scripta cccxxviiii.' According to Mercati the rest of the text was burned by a Vatican librarian by the name of Sirleto."

"Your permit?" the man at the entrance barked.

"I don't have a permit," Vera replied. "I'm just writing a master's thesis in archeology and I'm looking for a book..."

"Everybody who comes here is looking for some book or other. Your ID, please."

Vera gave him her passport. The man nodded and handed it back to her along with a visitor's pass.

"Up the stairs at the end of the corridor."

Vera dashed up the stairs and found herself staring down a long corridor. Thinking the security guard must have made a mistake letting her in so easily, she hurried down the hallway before he had a chance to change his mind.

Her footsteps reverberated along the checkered marble floor, which bore witness to the library's centuries-long existence. The sign above the entrance said it had been built in the fifteenth century, at the same time as the Vatican Archives.

Vera hurried through the forest of sunbeams streaming through the stained glass ceiling, whose colorful scenes teemed with stylized biblical scenes, saints, crosses and morose images of Christ. There were very few people. Dusty shelves crammed with books lined the walls.

It was one of those places where Vera could sense time grinding to a halt and everyday life losing its significance.

The door at the end of the corridor opened onto a reading room.

"How can I help you?" asked a man at the circulation desk. He was wearing a cap. Under his hooked red nose, a wart quivered on his upper lip like a pink bumblebee.

"I'm looking for a book..." Vera hesitated for a moment before saying the title. "*The Parchment Maze.*"

The moment she said it out loud, she remembered that she had seen that very same title written in pen inside the dusty book they had found at the Chateau Jacques. Her mind started racing.

The librarian's eyes examined the newcomer's face like a detective hunting for a case-breaking clue. His skin was as dry as his voice; deep wrinkles rutted his face and neck. He was so skeletal that his eye sockets sank into his skull. Vera fully expected him to reply that he had never heard of the book. However, he merely stared at her, studying her in silence, until finally asking: "How do you know about it?"

She wasn't sure how to answer. "I read about it... somewhere."

The man gazed at her again in silence, the wrinkles tugging at his parched face like a bridle.

"It's just been returned," he finally declared.

He disappeared down a side hallway, leaving Vera alone and confused. About ten minutes later he reappeared carrying a heavy book. It was not particularly thick, yet its oversized pages were bound between hard leather covers that were faded and ragged with age. The pages resembled parchment covered in handwritten inky scrawls. The man jotted something on Vera's pass and put it in the drawer beneath his desk. He looked at her questioningly and hesitated for fraction of a second before shoving the book into her hands.

"Row three, desk ten," he muttered.

She walked in silence to her assigned seat, which was made of heavily varnished wood. The holes eaten away by woodworms were visible beneath the lacquer. She sat down and carefully ran her fingers over the dusty cover. She had never held such an old manuscript. She traced the raised symbol on the book's front cover, as though trying to convince herself that it was real. It seemed incredible that this book, the one Dr. Werder had mentioned in his dying breath, could actually exist. She had been starting to think that everything would turn out to be no more than a figment of her imagination.

The librarian did not let her out of his sight. Vera felt his intrusive gaze and tried to hide her excitement, but her glowing cheeks gave her away.

The Orphic meander – the symbol she had been searching for – was engraved on the manuscript's cover. So this was why Dr. Werder had been so interested in discovering its meaning. He had seen it here. Although Vera thought she knew a lot about the symbol, here in the library she realized that it held far greater significance than she herself had guessed.

The librarian tracked her every movement. Trying to ignore him, Vera flipped open the book. She began turning the pages, which were permeated with centuries of history. The paper smelled of the dried ink of ancient history.

The letters were not printed, but handwritten in spindly cursive. As she turned the yellowing pages, she noticed that the numbering was jumbled. After flipping through no more than 20 pages, she found herself on page 218. She went back to the first page and looked at the top right corner where the page numbers were and saw that it read "198." She then turned to the last page and saw the number 457. The last sentence trailed off incomplete – but the most shocking thing was that the ink appeared to be completely fresh.

Vera slammed the book shut as if burned and hurried over to the librarian. Ignoring his gaping stare, she exclaimed indignantly: "This manuscript begins on page 198! And it looks like the last pages are missing as well... Do you think someone might have stolen them?"

"It's possible. It happens quite frequently. I'll make a note of it," he replied, completely unperturbed.

"You'll make a note of it? But I have to see the beginning!"

"Sorry, I guess today's not your lucky day. There was no way you could have known..."

"What do you mean, not my lucky day?"

"These things happen, even in the Vatican Library. Ten years ago they caught an American art history professor, Anthony Melnikas, who had been going there for years and stealing priceless pages from manuscripts. For years! Can you imagine?" The librarian continued, "They prosecuted him for it and managed to get part of the archive back. But it looks like he wasn't the only one."

"How could a professor do that?"

"Hundreds of precious manuscripts in Rome have also been completely or partially destroyed because of their content. Or sometimes due to plain carelessness... You never know what you might come across." He was silent for a moment, then added, "Like I told you, the book you asked for had just been returned by someone else."

"Who borrowed it?"

"That's confidential information."

The librarian's indifference infuriated Vera.

"Can you check to see whether you've got the book on microfilm?"

"We don't."

His gaze lingered on her face for a few seconds. Then his head bobbed forward as if toppling from his shoulders. He began to rifling through a box full of what looked like card catalogue files. Vera kept standing there, watching him expectantly.

"Do you no longer wish to use the book?" he asked her after a short time, as though nothing had happened.

"Do you have any idea how the manuscript ended up here? There was no information in the card catalogue."

"It doesn't say here either. There's no information."

"How can there be no information?"

"It must've been burned."

"Burned? When?"

"I can only assume that the book's file was destroyed at least one or maybe two hundred years ago. But there's no one who can confirm or deny that..."

"And only a single card catalogue entry was destroyed?"

"Who knows?" The librarian began breathing heavily, his nostrils shuddering like an old exhaust pipe. "Until recently I worked in the Vatican Archives, where I liked reading the library's chronicles. I found out that under the librarian Sirleto[72] a number of one-of-a-kind volumes and files were burned. He also destroyed the last hundred pages or so of the priceless manuscript *Byzantine Theological Texts*. I'm convinced they were very important. If such crimes were taking place in the fortress like the Vatican, we can only imagine what was going on in a little local library like ours! And Lord only knows how many switches and substitutions have been made."

Unsatisfied, Vera pressed him further. "So now no one knows who deposited this manuscript here or why?"

"That's what it looks like. But not many people ask for it. How did you find out about it?"

"Like I said, I read about it..."

---

[72] Guglielmo Sirleto was a cardinal who was born near Calabria in 1514 and who died in Rome on October 6, 1585. The son of a physician, he received an excellent education, made the acquaintance of distinguished scholars at Rome, and became an intimate friend of Cardinal Marcello Cervino, who later became Pope Marcellus II. Sirleto worked in the Vatican Library for years and compiled a series of valuable catalogues of the unique manuscripts held there. During his tenure the incidents in the archive occurred in which pages and whole manuscripts disappeared.

The librarian nodded and repeated his earlier question: "Are you going to use the manuscript or not?"

"Yes, of course I will."

Vera picked up the book and went back to the wooden bench in the third row. She opened the faded cover once again. The first 197 pages had obviously been ripped out. Tiny scraps of the missing pages poked out of the binding.

Something buzzed by her ear. Vera jerked her head up to see a brown butterfly flying chaotically around the reading room, looking for an escape. It flew up and dived down, crashing into the walls. Then the insect darted towards the window at the far end of the reading room. Shooed away by the librarian, it veered back in the direction it had come from, finally landing on the desk in front of Vera – where the librarian unceremoniously smacked it with a fly swatter. The butterfly slowly hugged its writhing legs to its body and went still. The librarian picked up the dead insect and tossed it into the trash can as Vera looked on in amazement.

"They get in through the rotted roof," he explained when he caught her glance.

Vera turned to look through the window to clear her head. Outside she could see the crown of a tall cypress. That is what the butterfly was trying to reach, she thought.

Vera looked down at the first remaining page, which began with a detailed description of a stone tablet found on Crete. The author wrote that it had been used to cover a tomb from the third millennium BC. The text inscribed upon the table spoke of people who had survived after the "End." However, Vera had never come across such a tablet in all her archeological studies. If such a thing really existed, why had no other historian written about it? The page ended with the sentence, "Eradicated in the Basilica in 1898."

Her astonishment grew when she turned to the next page and saw a picture of a stone temple in the Rhodope Mountains in Bulgaria, accompanied by a text that told of *their final traces before they went into hiding.*

Vera impatiently thumbed through the following pages, which were filled with similar descriptions and drawings, recently inserted photographs or sketches of statuettes and ritual tiles, pictures of icons, churches, frescoes, seals, bracelets, even family trees. The handwriting differed, as did the color of the ink. Further details had been added in pencil and ball-point pen. Scraps of other manuscripts, publications, brochures and articles accompanied by cryptic and fragmented handwritten explanations were interwoven between the manuscript's pages. Yet they all were tied in some way to an ancient civilization, "a hidden paradise" and "carefully preserved knowledge that will fulfill the Prophecy." There were even references to the "Son of God," although no particular deity was mentioned. There was quite a bit written about Orpheus, Dionysus, secret writing systems and codes, solar symbols, stolen evidence, unknown signs and hieroglyphics. Yet at first glance all the handwritten notes seemed unconnected.

The hodgepodge of texts, facts and pictures reminded Vera of something she'd read about: books and encyclopedias used by secret societies over the course of centuries to exchange information, ideas and notes. Kept in various libraries around the world, only the societies' initiates knew where to look so they could add to them, take things out, amend them and share information. They even existed up until the present day, although they were primarily associated with the Knights Templar and the Masons – since other secret societies were not considered as interesting.

What worried Vera most was the fact that she had not heard of any of the artifacts described in the book. Only the last items described there were familiar to her: the Orphic amulet, a number of murals from the catacombs and the double-sided golden tablet. Vera learned from the book that the tablet had been found in Burma. The manuscript's final pages piqued her curiosity, so she copied the descriptions of twenty or so unknown items into her notebook, intending to do more research on them later. She didn't have time to makes notes on all of them.

One of the oldest libraries in Rome, which houses manuscripts, some of which are more than five centuries old

Some of the descriptions in the manuscript were in Latin, while others were in Old Italian. Some words were unfamiliar, while others Vera recognized as coming from a little-known Thracian dialect. There were Old Bulgarian words as well.

She was the only person left in the library. The librarian shuffled over on his bony legs and informed her that it was closing time. He took the manuscript and gave her a note saying she had returned the book. She wouldn't be able to leave without it. He told her to exit through the door to the right and disappeared into the stacks.

The hallways were no longer as bright or welcoming as they had been on her arrival. She felt as if the faces and shadows the old masters had painted on the walls and ceilings were watching her. Despite the colorful murals, the corridor felt deserted and lonely, filled with a silence that was broken only by Vera's heels tapping along the marble floor.

A vague noise made her stop and turn around. She thought she heard the echo of footsteps that were not her own. She didn't see anything, but spooked nonetheless, she ran towards the exit. The feeling that she was being followed did not stop until she had reached the paved road outside.

The sun was already hidden beyond the coils of the seven-headed serpent,[73] leaving a wide orange trail in its wake. The empty sky was preparing to greet the white disc of the moon. Shapes were losing their outlines, while the air filled with the freshness of night.

Studying her map, Vera saw that there was a bus stop beyond the bend in the road, right near the entrance to the San Callisto Catacomb. She set out along the narrow pavement, her suitcase rumbling along behind her. The streets teemed with tourists and lovers lost in their own worlds.

While on the bus, Vera tried to make sense of what she had read in the manuscript. Why had Franz Werder thought it was so important that he mentioned it with his dying breath? How had he come across the mysterious book in the first place? The answers had died with him.

Her head now swam with more questions than ever, even though she had come to Rome hoping to discover an answer that would explain everything that had happened to her over the past few months.

The Parchment Maze was not even a book in the proper sense, but rather a collection of unconnected, perhaps even non-existent, artifacts and explanations. Yet why would anyone describe these items so painstakingly if they did not exist? Vera was impatient to find out more about the objects whose details she had managed to copy down.

The symbol on the cover, the meander, had made a particularly deep impression on her. Was it pursuing her or was she pursuing it?

---

[73] In his *Revelation*, St. John describes Rome as a "seven-headed serpent," referring to the city's seven hills.

Vera recalled that only a couple of hours before they were kidnapped in Moscow, Werder had asked her repeatedly about its significance. It was the most widespread woven decorative pattern in the world, which everyone assumed was a Greek invention. This was a ridiculous claim – but believable since the Greeks had plastered it all over their country. It was human nature to be satisfied with obvious explanations.

However, since that night in the Chateau Jacques when Vera had recognized the meander among the other prehistoric symbols, it had continually reappeared in the most unexpected places, like a premonition she could not escape. Yet its meaning seemed to change constantly. Which of these myriad meanings was the true one? Perhaps the oldest one, carved into the ceramic vessels and figurines created 7,500 years ago.

The bus wound through the streets of Rome for an hour or so. Vera looked at the photographs on her mobile telephone, scrolling through them until she found the two-sided golden tablet. She remembered seeing the meander there, too.

She finally found her hotel and checked in. Even before taking off her coat and shoes, she switched on her laptop and started searching for the artifacts described in the manuscript on the Internet, the only source available at this late hour.

In the middle of the night she decided to call Futch.

THE PARCHMENT MAZE

Page 458 *spoke of a secret document:*
"Of all the materials deposited in the National Library,
the most important is the collection of documents entitled
'Dossiers Secrets.' It had been copied to microfiche.
Until recently, however, it was no more than a ragged file
with hard covers containing individual sheets of paper
and many other apparently unconnected things, as well
as extracts from newspapers, letters glued to sheets of
papers, brochures, family trees, and pages from other
publications. Some of the pages disappeared from time
to time. Others appeared in their place. In other places
amendments and additions were added by hand."

From **The Holy Blood and the Holy Grail**, by Michael Baigent,
Richard Leigh and Henry Lincoln, p. 115

"Futch, it's me. I'm calling from Rome."

"You never cease to amaze me..." he replied with forced cheerfulness. "How are things there?"

"I haven't seen anything of the city. I've been looking for a book."

"Did you find it?"

"Yes, but it's not what I expected."

"Well, what did you expect?"

"I thought I'd discover something..."

"So was it blank or what?"

"No, it was just a manuscript full of jumbled up topics. Like a scrapbook full of pictures, newspaper clippings, descriptions..."
Vera wasn't sure whether to tell him all her theories and suspicions.

"That sounds like quite a lot, actually."

"It's just a bunch of made-up nonsense whose beginning and ending pages have been ripped out."

"What makes you think it's nonsense?"

"None of the things described in the manuscript actually exist. After copying down what I could, I've spent all night searching the Internet. The book refers to hundreds of artifacts, places, historical names, family trees, events and theories, but there is no hard evidence that any of them actually existed. Or else they're completely entangled in myths and legends."

"If your father knew you were doing research on the Internet he'd disown you."

"I didn't have any choice and besides he's..." Vera was about to say that he'd already disowned her, but when she remembered what had happened to him, the joke seemed tactless. So instead she said, "Every generation has its own methods."

"What's the book called?"

"It's not a book, but an unedited manuscript. I couldn't even figure out what the main topic tying it together was."

"Doesn't it have a name?"

"No, just a catalogue number. The librarians who accidentally discovered it have dubbed it *The Parchment Maze*. There's only one copy. And that's all I know about it."

"Does it at least have some kind of illustration on the cover?"

"Yeah, sort of like a maze. Or rather, a meander. A squared-off spiral with eight corners. 'Hell' is written above it, 'Heaven' below it, and in the middle it says 'The Taenarian Gate.'"

"That's more than enough."

"What do you mean?

"It makes sense. The contents are encoded – for the purpose described on the cover."

"How did you figure that out?" Vera asked suspiciously.

"The word 'meander' is used for the complex twists and turns a river makes as it flows along its course. The term originally comes from the Ancient Greek name for the Maiandros River – now known as Buyuk Menderes – in Asia Minor. Put more simply, a meander is the complex winding form a river takes, as if twisting through a maze. The symbol on the cover might indicate a road or a river, maybe even a labyrinth. But most likely it points toward a *river-labyrinth*," Futch, thinking aloud, emphasized these last words. "But if it is on the middle of the front cover, like you say, and is labeled 'The Taenarian Gate,' then the river has got to be the Styx, which divides the Upper and Lower Kingdoms. The gate must be somewhere between them. You did say the meander was eight-cornered, right?"

"Yes."

"Well then, it all fits together! So it has seven flat sides. The Styx goes around Hades exactly seven times. That's your labyrinth... and there's something hidden in its center. The only thing I can't figure out is why Heaven and Hell are inverted..."

"Okay, but I still don't get..."

"Most people believe heaven is up above."

"Come on, Futch, I do know at least that much. But back up a second: what do you mean by the Upper and Lower Kingdoms and some gate?"

"The Taenarian Gate is not just any old gate, but has been known since ancient times as the entrance to the Other World."

"Yes, except for there is no Other World. I know you don't believe in it, either. So why don't you tell me straight out what you're getting at."

"As far as I can tell from what you've told me about the manuscript, I figure it's a labyrinth-book. A couple such books have been around since the Middle Ages. The center of the labyrinth is the answer."

"But what's the question?"

"Judging from your description of the cover, I would guess it's a maze made up of clues, some sort of map leading to a specific place. If you take it at face value, then the place it's leading to would seem to be underground."

"But the supposed 'clues,' the artifacts the book describes, don't exist. Like I told you, I've checked them."

"Of course they don't – it's a secret map, after all. If you were to make a map to a hidden treasure, you wouldn't use obvious signs, now would you? You also wouldn't label it 'Treasure Map,' either! These maps are for select eyes only. People who know the code can decipher the meaning and recognize the clues."

"A secret code!" Vera laughed out loud. "I forgot that you're a diehard treasure hunter. You see treasure maps everywhere you look."

"I've got a nose for it – and experience. This is a puzzle and we're going to crack it. People create riddles for others to solve. Although we may not believe it, in the end we all think more or less alike. Particularly today in this world of matrices..."

As she listened to him, Vera began to understand why Asen Litovski – or "Futch" as his colleagues called him – was so sought-after not only in the underground world of illegal antique smuggling, but also in academic circles.

Futch was one of Bulgaria's most famous treasures hunters, perhaps because he was different. He didn't dig only for the money, but also for the thrill. For the excitement of solving a thousand-year-old riddle and discovering something that had stayed hidden for centuries. He was also called "Radar" in underground circles for his uncanny knack for locating caches even where there were no obvious clues.

Archaeologists, even eminent professors, hired him to lead their digs. They paid him travelling expenses, daily fees and a salary – yet their budgets always referred to him vaguely as an "expert." He personally preferred being on the "good" side. Archaeologists proudly whispered to one another that Futch had helped them. Yet his work was all hush-hush.

"So?" Vera asked after a short pause.
"Like I said, I figure the book is some sort of encoded algorithm that shows the path to somewhere... the Styx, the Taenarian Gate. They're some sort of metaphors. Maybe there's a treasure hidden in the labyrinth! And from everything we've

said it must be underground. Don't worry, digging down deep is no problem for me."

"So why couldn't it be interpreted literally as 'The Path to the Lower Kingdom?'"

"Do you believe the Lower Kingdom really exists?"

"No."

"Well, that's why."

"But how do you explain the jumble of made-up details that don't seem to be interrelated?"

"You said that the artifacts you looked up don't actually seem to exist and that the book talks about their destruction... Perhaps the person who described these traces in the manuscript also destroyed them, so that no one else would find them. When you follow the walls of a labyrinth, you get to its center. But if you destroy the existing walls, you also destroy the path to center. If the clues described in the book have already been destroyed, then the only way of getting back to whatever they were pointing towards is through the manuscript. Or I guess you could stumble into the labyrinth's center accidentally. Weren't there any artifacts that you recognized?"

"Only the last few."

"Well, something is better than nothing! Even two artifacts are enough to let us know that the maze of clues is not just a haphazard jumble. The traces were deliberately destroyed after being encoded in a secret list. As a result, the manuscript is the only map to the place where..."

There was a silence as if the line had gone dead. Vera's uncertain voice finally broke the stillness.

"You sure know your stuff!"

"Everyone's got their trade..."

"Well, I'd better go, I am phoning from Rome, after all."

"Hold on a second. I've just remembered. The symbol on the cover should hint at the direction, towards the center of the labyrinth. From what we've said, it seems like the clues in the manuscript lead to a gate," his voice trailed off for a moment before continuing. "I'm just thinking out loud. But if the book really is a maze of hidden clues, then you should go back tomorrow and copy down everything in it, real and unreal, in detail."

"I can't. I'm going back to Sofia early tomorrow morning."

"But..."

"I have to go back urgently. I don't want to argue. I'm going to bed."

"Good night!"

THE FISH

Fig. 1
FISHING SILEN.
FIFTH CENTURY RED FIGURED WINE-CUP IN
THE BRITISH MUSEUM.

After Hartwig, *Meisterschalen Stuttgart, 1893, p. 39, fig. 5.*

Page 459 *spoke of fish:*
"If people were not fish, the Apostles would never have been called the 'Fishers of Men.'[74] Such fish feed the Almighty's omnipotence, such fish can swim in the baptismal stream, such fish can be caught on the hook of faith and in the nets of holy teachings."

St. Bruno Signiensis, Matthew Iv., page 18

From the moment she got out of bed, Vera could clearly hear the fishtails flapping in the air. Even though she knew that they had already set out for the silent depths.

She turned the door handle slowly so it wouldn't squeak and peeped through the half-open door of the hospital room.

At first she thought her father was sleeping. His face looked calm, his eyes were closed and his body relaxed. Quietly, almost tiptoeing, she entered the room and sat down next to the bed. His hands lay to either side of his body, pale, wrinkled and covered with small brown spots. His fingers would occasionally flex mechanically. She wondered whether to touch them and even raised her hand, but then lowered it back down onto the bed. She was uncomfortable touching her own father. She hadn't done it for such a long time.

---

[74] Since ancient times, perhaps even since before Babylon, people have been imagined as fish and their deities as fishermen. Since early Christianity, Christ has been called the Fisherman. The same epithet was also used for Orpheus.

The empty room with its bare walls looked sad and lonely. It would almost have seemed like a morgue if it weren't for the monitor beeping rhythmically above his head.

Vera closed her eyes and quietly hummed a tune to him.

Her father's lips moved slightly. "You sing nicely."

"I hate singing."

"Why?"

"Mom used to sing so beautifully... whenever I was afraid or alone or hurting. So when I sing, I hear her. And I relive her death over and over..."

As she uttered these last words, tears stung her eyes and her cheeks blazed. The professor hadn't seen her cry since she was a child. Vera had learned to hide her emotions behind a cold mask of indifference. She hadn't even cried at her mother's funeral. He felt around on the light blue bedspread, found her slender fingers and squeezed them.

"We all have to go... someday. If it makes you feel better, just imagine that we're going to a better place."

"That's nonsense!" she cried, jerking her hand away and stepping back from the bed angrily. "That's bullshit invented to manipulate the masses and prevent them from creating problems for the system. To help people swallow their misfortunes instead of struggling to overcome them. Since you like biblical quotations so much, here's another one for you: 'The horse is made ready for the day of battle, but victory rests with the Lord!' Religions take away man's will to fight. Everything is in our own hands, dad – in our own hands. We determine the outcome. The earlier you realize that, the more you can do for yourself."

She was venting her anger not so much at her father's words but at the fact that so many people meekly accept their fate, rather than trying to change it. In the last few months of her life, her emaciated mother had spent hours on church pews kissing the priests' fat fingers, fasting, sick with hunger, leaving coins at the painted icons' feet. She cried and prayed. Once when her mother had trouble lighting her candle, she took it as a sign that the end was near – and nearly gave up the fight prematurely. During that time, something changed inside Vera. She turned her back on religion and never again lit a candle in a church.

Vera paced around the hospital room nervously. She eventually stopped in front of the window, staring out like a caged animal. In the distance below tiny, barely visible human figures scurried in all directions.

"And we don't go anywhere. We're here now, and that's it," she added.

"Vera, often the only thing we can control is our own attitude towards life."

"I know. That's all we have here on earth." She turned to her father and looked him in the eye. "You're an archaeology professor. We both know that Christianity was imposed on civilization because it offered a convenient way of enforcing authority. It's a hastily cobbled together hodgepodge of half-forgotten pagan legends that were preserved in the people's consciousness and later adapted into a form of government."

"Even if that is the case, religion still works for many people. For some it's their last hope. Why steal warmth on a soulless day? And I happen to like the idea of redemption. I actually do want to believe."

Her father's nascent smile changed to a grimace as his entire body shuddered.

"Ooh, ouch!" he moaned.

Vera shrugged helplessly. "You've just had a serious operation, it's probably quite normal to still be in pain." Comforting one's own parents is always terrifying.

She felt her cell phone vibrating in her pocket. It was Futch. She answered it in a whisper. "I'll call you later."

"I just wanted to let you know about the tablet... It might be far more important than you think."

"Pardon?"

"The golden tablet you gave me to decipher and date."

Vera remembered that a few days ago she had sent him the pictures of the gold tablet that she had taken with her phone in the

Moscow warehouse. She went out into the hallway with the phone pressed to her ear.

"Did you manage to read it?" she whispered, as if afraid the nurses might steal her secret.

"Not exactly, but I'm getting warmer."

"So what's the big news then?"

"You have to come and see something... I think it might turn out to be one of the most valuable Thracians objects ever found."

"What are you talking about?"

"The tablet is some kind of Thracian Rosetta Stone,[75] something experts have spent centuries searching for to help them interpret unknown languages including Linear A and Thracian."

"Will you be in your workshop tonight?" Vera asked him.

"I'll be waiting for you."

She hung up and slunk back to her father wearing a guilty expression.

"You look worried. Who were you talking to?" he asked.

"A friend..."

"It hurts me that you don't trust me."

"You've never supported my work."

"You're just too willful to survive in the world we live in. Society always chews up and spits out people like you – you're too tough and indigestible for them to swallow."

"I have no problem with that; I've always liked being different. Only little kids want to be the same as everyone else."

---

[75] The Rosetta Stone is one of the most important archeological discoveries ever made. It was found in 1799 during excavations near the port city of Rashid (Rosetta) on the Nile. The black slab of stone dating from 196 BC weighs nearly 750 kg and bears three translations of a single passage: two in Egyptian language scripts (hieroglyphic and Demotic) and one in classical Greek. Comparison of the Greek with the Egyptian texts allowed scholars to decipher Egyptian hieroglyphics for the first time. Since 1802, the Rosetta Stone has been housed in the British Museum, where it is still on display . Today it has become synonymous with any key to decoding an unknown language.

"You can't function outside the society you live in – even if you don't like it. Otherwise you're like a beautiful flower blooming in the dark. You grow, live and die like everyone else, but your life is pointless."

They fell silent. Vera pretended to look for something in her purse. Then her eyes began roaming around the room. Her father, who knew her better than she cared to admit, knew what this meant. "You want to ask me something."

"Not now."

"Go ahead and ask. It'll distract me from the pain."

"I'm still looking for evidence of the disappeared civilization... the Meandrites."

"You mean the Eneolithic population that vanished from the Balkans after destroying its own lands?"

"Exactly... I've recently been thinking that it might not have disappeared completely. They were the first and most highly developed civilization that we have evidence of! They knew too much to let themselves disappear just like that".

"So you think you might have found a Thracian Atlantis?"

"Don't make fun of me. I haven't found anything yet... I just think that scholars are completely wrong when they say that this culture simply vanished at the beginning of the fourth millennium BC, that it appeared out of nowhere and then disappeared back into nothingness... I'm sure they survived. You can tell from their ideas, which have been preserved and passed down to us through time, especially their symbols, which can be found in neighboring civilizations."

"Vera, the processes of human migration and cultural transfer normally leave far more tangible traces than merely a dozen or so symbols."

"But we're talking about their most significant symbols, the key signs of their knowledge." Vera bit her bottom lip, thought for a moment, then added: "But there was something else I wanted to talk to you about. I feel like I'm being bombarded with countless facts and signs... I don't believe in secret codes but after seeing so many coincidences..."

"Why don't you just tell me straight out what you're getting at?"

"I have the feeling... I've got the strangest feeling that the Meandrites have survived somewhere in Bulgaria. Untouched for millennia. Those who didn't flee."

"But where?"

"I don't know... But if they are still here that would explain why there is no record of a mass migration of people."

"But there is no archaeological evidence that they were slaughtered en masse, apart from two or three burned out houses."

"Those who survived are still alive."

"How could you hide an entire race for millennia?"

"Either very high up or deep down," replied Vera, who didn't seem to believe her own words.

YET MORE EVIDENCE

Page 460 recorded these facts:
The German scholar Adam Falkenstein, an expert on Sumerian language and literacy, supports arguments made by Dr. Nicolae Vlasa, who conducted excavations on the Vinca culture, that the engraved tablets from the Balkans contain symbols reminiscent of Mesopotamian and Cretan signs. In 1967, Sinclair Hood, director of the British Archaeological School in Athens, wrote in the leading academic journal Antiquity: "The symbols on the Vinca tablets are so similar to those on earlier tablets from Uruk that one can be sure that objects from both sites are borrowings… In addition to this the tablets' shape and the system of dividing the symbols with carved out lines are analogous." Hood also noted that dozens of the symbols have analogies within the Cretan writing systems. Two years later, more than one hundred objects covered with similar symbols were found in Bulgaria. The world was shocked when radiocarbon dating proved categorically that the symbols from Vinca and Bulgaria are at least 2,000 years older than the Mesopotamian or Cretan symbols. For decades no one dared speak again of the First Civilization's writing system.

It was getting dark. Only a fading purple streak of sunset interrupted the monotonous gray sky. The sun was now hidden beyond the city, already warming the lands beyond the horizon. The moon and the stars had not yet risen.

Vera looked around. After making sure she was alone on the dusty street, she pushed open a gate, which yowled like a tomcat as

327

she quickly slipped into the courtyard. She had the feeling someone was following close on her heels, trying to catch her shadow. She had felt this way ever since her narrow escape from the Lower Kingdom, when she had been pulled out of the Moscow River.

She ran skittishly along the side of the house to the end of the yard where another door led to Futch's workshop. She jiggled the handle, but it was locked. Not seeing a doorbell, she knocked. No one answered, so she knocked again. The metallic pounding echoed dully in the silence.

Her telephone rang. It was Futch.

"Where are you?" she asked angrily.

"Is that you out there hammering away like a lunatic?"

"Are you expecting anyone else?"

"You can never be too careful!"

Vera heard a rumble like an iron giant sighing. The door opened, revealing a yawning brick stairwell. She started down it, following a string of feeble electric lights and trying not to touch the grimy walls or ragged cobwebs hanging in the corners. When she reached the bottom step she stopped, gaping in surprise. Futch had not let her come this far into his lair last time.

The doors to his workshop stood open. Now she realized why he kept it so well-hidden. In the middle of the large room under a low, unfinished ceiling, two metal tables stood side-by-side like in a veterinarian's office. They were covered with clean newspapers upon which Futch had placed antique objects and coins still caked with dirt and mud from excavations. Powerful lamps hanging from the ceiling illuminated them. Shelves full of archeological finds lined the walls – these objects had clearly already been processed and recorded. Some of them were in clear plastic bags with the date and place of discovery carefully noted, like in a forensic laboratory; here, however, the clues were not evidence of crimes but traces of history. Undated antiquities were less valuable, thus it was crucial to record information about the place of discovery, the excavation site and the soil depth. In addition to coins and jewelry, larger items such as altars, plates, silver candlesticks, even weapons, fragments of chariots and chainmail were spread chaotically around the floor and in the corners. The lighting was soft, while the air was dry and de-ionized as in a museum to help preserve the fragile objects.

Futch smiled when he saw her. Then, afraid that his self-satisfaction was far too obvious, he bent over and fumbled with his shoelace.

"Expensive hobby you've got here!" Vera commented.

"This is nothing. Don't forget that my grandmother's voice is travelling in outer space, up there on the *Voyager*![76] Just imagine the intergalactic royalties."

Vera shot him a puzzled glance.

"Yeah, right!" she replied suspiciously. "Every five-year-old in Bulgaria knows whose voice that is."

"Maybe they do, and maybe they don't. You can always go and look it up."

She frowned and continued scrutinizing his workshop.

"It's an investment – and it repays every penny," he added. Two twenty-one-inch monitors lit up the desk in front of him. He was staring at pictures on the screen.

"Aren't you afraid I might give you away?"

"I'm sure you won't, because I know about your Rosetta Stone." He pressed a key on the keyboard and the pictures on the screen disappeared. Futch turned to Vera. "I can find a buyer for that tablet right away, if you want." He hesitated before adding, "People have been looking for a bi-lingual Thracian artifact like that for centuries. It could be the key to deciphering the pre-historical writing system used by the extinct Eneolithic-Chalcolytic civilization from the Balkans."

"Are you talking about the Meandrites?"

"Oh sorry, I forgotten you'd come up with that nickname for them during our course in pre-history." Smiling, he continued,

---

[76] The two *Voyager* spacecraft launched in 1977 carried sounds and images selected to portray the diversity of life and culture on Earth. The musical recordings included a Bulgarian folk song from the Rhodopes, "Izlel e Delyo Hajdutin," performed by the singer Valya Balkanska.

"Call them what you will, the connection to them makes the tablet three times as valuable."

"Futch, I'm not looking for a buyer... Tell me what you've found out about it."

Vera looked at her watch. It was already a quarter past eight.

Futch was obviously enjoying her impatient curiosity. He reached down to the mountain of bottles under his desk, grabbed an open beer and took a couple of leisurely swigs.

His nose was his most striking feature, not because it was particularly prominent, but because the once-broken bones formed a slight, yet eye-catching bump in the middle. His round eyes often bulged wide open, staring. His beard grew in patches, speckled with bald spots.

"So where is this golden wonder right now?" he asked.

"I don't know."

Futch's eyebrows gathered into a scowl, while his eyes stared at the computer screen.

"My comparative analysis indicates that this is one of the world's oldest golden tablets with engraved symbols," he announced.

"Why should that surprise you? After all, it's already been proven that the Meandrites, especially the ones who inhabited the Varna Necropolis, were among history's first goldsmiths."

"Of course I know that. Yet it sounds so astonishing that it hardly seems possible."

"Astonishing or no, it's a fact."

Futch's fingers marched around the keyboard, pressed "Enter" and waited.

Several windows popped open on the screen, each containing about a dozen ceramic and stone objects: engraved tablets, human figurines, seals and vessels. All the objects bore symbols and pictograms unfamiliar to modern man. Vera immediately recognized artifacts from the Vinca, Karanovo, Gradeshnitsa and Lepenski Vir civilizations, but there was also a vessel inscribed in Linear A from Yambol. She had been studying these photos intensely after asking Futch to send them to her via email a couple of days earlier. Many of the symbols were the same as Egyptian hieroglyphs, while others almost completely coincided with dozens of symbols from the undeciphered Cretan writing system, Linear A.[77] Some academics explained away these amazing coincidences, arguing that there was a physical limit to the number of combinations between lines and circles that the human hand could create, which was why the symbols in various unrelated writing systems occasionally resembled each other. But if this were the case, why did the prehistoric symbols from Ancient Europe have nothing in common with Chinese or Mayan symbols, which contain almost infinite combinations of lines and curves? Why did the Balkan symbols precisely resemble Egyptian and Cretan symbols, which appeared a thousand years after the mysterious disappearance of the Meandrites?

Futch sat motionless in front of the screen, staring at the symbols. Only his eyes moved, darting from object to object. Occasionally he would drag a frame around one of them with the mouse, separating it from the other clay artifacts. Using special software, he arranged the images into a table on the left-hand screen and then turned back to the right-hand screen and opened a new file. Vera recognized her own pictures of the golden tile, but said nothing. She was waiting to see what Futch would do next.

He highlighted a number of symbols in the unbroken rows of characters engraved on the golden tablet. Once he had arranged them in the table on the left, it became quite clear that each golden symbol had an analogue among the ceramic and stone symbols.

"That's amazing!" Vera exclaimed. "Do you think they could be written in the same script? As far as I can tell, that golden tablet can hardly be older than the second millennium BC."

---

[77] Harald Haarman from the University of Helsinki discovered more the 50 common symbols shared by Linear A and the Balkan linear symbols from the Vinca, Gradeshnitsa and Karanovo culture, which led him to conclude that such numerous similarities could not be the result of chance.

"More precisely, it dates from between the twelfth and fourteenth century BC."

"How can you be so sure? The symbols you just put in the left-hand table were created 7,500 years ago by the Meandrites..."

Her voice was lost in a torrent of rushing thoughts. Using this software, Futch had organized Vera's carefully collected evidence and uncovered links which might otherwise have taken her years of careful analysis to discover. Now she realized the reason for Futch's euphoria over the past few days: the golden tablet proved that during Orpheus' time, someone in Thrace had been using the writing systems and symbols created by the Meandrites thousands of years earlier! This was proof that the Meandrites did not simply disappear without a trace – and confirmed what she had been trying to tell her father earlier that day.

"I'm still not totally sure," replied Futch, shaking his head and staring wide-eyed at the screen in excitement. "But in my opinion the same text is written on both sides of the tablet, using two separate writing systems from different eras: once in the symbols of the lost First Civilization and again in Thracian. If that's the case, then it is just like the Rosetta Stone. I would guess someone was trying to show the connection between them. But like I said, I'm still not sure. Maybe the tablet was supposed to be read by both cultures… But how could that be, since one of the cultures disappeared twenty centuries before the other one even appeared?"

A Golden Orphic Book, the Bulgarian National History Museum

Vera followed his train of thought warily, still not convinced she could trust Futch and his software. Yet the similarities between the symbols were clear to the naked eye, further confirming the coincidence between a few of the pictograms that she'd noticed in Moscow.

Futch changed the images on the left-hand monitor. Now instead of pictograms etched in clay, he lined up a series of letters in unbroken rows. Some had been carved into golden tablets and others into stones, cliffs, altars or ceramics.

Among the artifacts Vera spotted golden Orphic tablets and an undeciphered gravestone bearing a Thracian inscription from the sixth century BC, which was now on display on the ground floor of the Archaeological Museum in Sofia. Another picture showed an engraving on a fifth-century-BC golden ring from the village of Ezerovo, which was also in undeciphered Thracian.[78] The letters were clear and in most cases Greek, with a bit of early Slavic and Coptic mixed in. Although the symbols were familiar, the words they spelled out remained cryptic. However, the most remarkable artifact was a stone tablet containing 929 letters found near the village of Gela,[79] a hamlet in the Rhodope Mountains in southern

---

[78] From *Orpheus the Thracian*, by V. Fol, p.31.

[79] N. Gigov has described and studied this inscription in detail in his book *Orpheus and Letters*. In his opinion, Orpheus lived in the 13th century BC and was the ruler of a huge Thracian kingdom. He attempted to unite the remaining tribes, but was unable to come to terms with their leaders, for which reason he was eventually murdered. During his lifetime, however, he along with four close followers supposedly invented the first alphabet. Gigov argues that the Greek alphabet is actually a copy of the Orphic one, which is also the source of present-day Cyrillic. It is probable that Orpheus brought it back with him from one of his legendary travels, perhaps to Egypt or the Lower Kingdom.

Bulgaria that is considered the birth place of Orpheus. There were also two golden Orphic tablets known as A3 from Turii and B1 from Magna Grecia. She did not recognize the others.

Vera realized where Futch was going with this. All the Thracian inscriptions he had lined up in the table had not yet been deciphered by historians. Various interpretations existed, none of them satisfactory. Scholars assumed these inscriptions were Orphic messages written in alphabets borrowed from neighboring cultures, such as Greek, Coptic and a number of local adaptations. Other academics went so far as to claim that the inscriptions had been written before the invention of the Greek alphabet and thus the symbols could not have been created by the Greeks.[80]

"Looks like you support the theory that the Thracians had their own writing system," Vera joked.

"I've seen enough to know that the only theories worth supporting are my own. In any case, I doubt we'll ever learn the truth."

On the right-hand screen, Futch brought up Vera's photo of the back side of the golden tablet, which was covered in symbols reminiscent of Thracian and Ancient Greek letters. He dragged a frame around the symbols and transferred them into a separate table, which once again highlighted the similarities between the symbols on the two screens.

"OK, let's think for a second," Futch mumbled to himself and sipped his beer. "The tablet is made of two gold sheets soldered together. The writing on the one side is quite clearly and categorically Thracian, while the pictograms on the other side are Neolithic."

---

[80] Despite the discovery of numerous artifacts bearing inscriptions that have been found in formerly Thracian lands, scholars still officially claim that the Thracians did not have a writing system. Dozens of inscriptions have been found on gold Orphic tablets, rings, cliffs, altars, gravestones and vessels; however, they have been ignored due to the fact that they have not yet been deciphered. Legends from the Rhodope Mountains in southern Bulgaria tell of a library that the Thracians hid in the cliffs (or which was destroyed by their enemies). Some claim in was located near Belintash, an ancient Thracian sanctuary in the Rhodopes.

"Can you decipher its meaning?"

"Since we can translate a few of the Thracian words, we might be able to guess the meaning of some of the pictograms in the unknown writing system."

"Even though scholars have already deciphered a few hundred Thracian words, picking them out of the jumble of letters on the tile will be tough," Vera declared. "We don't even know what direction the text is supposed to be read in."

"Don't worry, I've already figured all that out. That kind of thing is child's play for my software."

"Just what program are you using?"

"SoftArchei – but don't go looking for it in stores. It was developed by a few programmer friends of mine... for people like me, if you know what I mean."

"Why do you always end up with the best stuff?"

"Destiny! It just smiles down on me!"

Vera couldn't help but laugh along with him, despite her exasperation. Sensing her impatience, he explained more seriously: "The software allows me to quickly compare thousands of combinations of words and symbols. When I entered the symbols on the tile, here's what it spit out:

The stars of death determine the end/ the heart of the mountain (earth)/ behind eight throats beneath the river/ time of eight suns/ the place will preserve the map beneath the stars/... in the white shadows/ good (or Paradise) you will know.../ the temple of the soul.

"It's just gibberish!" Futch said disappointedly. "The software got overloaded because too many of the words and symbols don't match up with any known meanings."

THE ARK

Two hours later

Vera had not felt time passing – something that had happened only rarely in recent days. She was usually breathing down time's neck, counting each tick of the clock's hands, so as to reassure herself she was still in control.

Vera and Futch had been trying to decipher the Thracian text and the Neolithic pictograms from the golden tablet for hours. After trying hundreds of combinations of words and concepts, they finally came up with translations for a few groups of Neolithic symbols which, unfortunately, didn't make very much sense.

Anthropomorphic clay figure from Gradeshnitsa Culture. Her stomach has been engraved with the hieroglyphs for "speech" and "house" (their connection with Egyptian hieroglyphics has been postulated by Dr. S. Guide), which Vera and Futch are discussing in detail at his laboratory. A V-shaped sign made of "mirrored hooks" can be seen on the figure's chest.

"That's the Egyptian hieroglyph for 'temple' and 'guardian,' isn't it?" Futch asked, pointing to a squared-off spiral.

"Right, that's a meander, a symbol invented by the Meandrites. I recently read that in Coptic it was pronounced *Erphei*."

"Well, what do you know!" Futch smiled. "Yet another happy coincidence. Hold on a second, the software will search for other similar symbols."

He pressed "Enter" and waited a moment. "There you are. The oldest known meanders were found in Gradeshnitsa and on stones discovered in Lepenski Vir, which date back to the sixth millennium BC... So you're quite right that the Meandrites created this symbol. It was later used as a hieroglyph by the Egyptians and in Cretan Linear A, as well as in Meroitic hieroglyphs."[81] He added with a smile, "The software has also found matches with the Abbott and Givenchy logos!"

---

[81] Meroitic hieroglyphs are the oldest writing system from Sub-Saharan Africa, created by the Nubian culture, which reached its peak in the 16th century B.C. in what is now northern Sudan and southern Egypt.

"Very funny," Vera retorted. "Let's check the next symbols." She stared at the signs on the screen, nodding her head in satisfaction.

"Look, here are the signs for 'house' and 'mouth' or 'throat.'" The symbols she pointed out looked like: [graphic]

"How do you know what they mean?" Futch asked in amazement.

"That's what their Egyptian equivalents mean. Didn't I tell you my theory – that the meanings remain the same despite metamorphoses in the symbols?"

"Egypt? But these same symbols were used two millennia earlier in the Gradeshnitsa culture. They were even found on figurines of the Mother Goddess, with the 'mouth' engraved inside the 'house' on her belt," Futch marveled. He was very familiar with this civilization since such artifacts were highly sought after on international markets.

"That's right!" Vera replied. "The mouth is the symbol for 'word and knowledge.' Its combination with the 'house' sign is probably a hint that this knowledge is kept in some kind of 'home.' Remember what the Thracian text said: '*Preserved/the word kept/the truth about something in the mountains or in the earth.*' That must be the meaning of the pictograms if we read the next hieroglyph as 'mountain.'" [graphic]

"I agree. And look... next to it is the symbol for 'eternity,'" Futch pointed out excitedly.

The sign in question was a circle with a dot inside it: [graphic], which was flanked on either side by the modern-day infinity symbol, a sideways figure-eight. Futch waited for the computer to call up other equivalents of this pictogram before continuing.

"The oldest analogue was again found in Gradeshnitsa on a clay vessel, which is now housed in the Vratsa Museum.[82] But the

---

[82] The symbol consists of two concentric circles (most probably symbolizing the sun) and two spirals resembling the DNA molecule on either side of it (signs of infinity).

338

most famous version of this symbol was discovered in the tomb of Nefertari, one of the wives of the Egyptian pharaoh Ramses II, dating from 1310-1235 BC."

"The golden tablet was created during that period, wasn't it?"

"Right!" Futch replied. "Just look at the other side of the tablet – you can see the Thracian word for 'eternity' at the same place in the text!"

"I must be dreaming. You're absolutely right – this really might be a Thracian Rosetta Stone. The tablet translates pictograms from the world's earliest writing system devised by the Meandrites. It's absolutely priceless. No wonder I found it hidden in the backpack of that..."

Vera snapped her mouth shut as if trying to reel her final words back in. She stared at the terra cotta tiles.

"Whose backpack?"

"Nobody's."

"Fine, that's your business... Listen, I've just thought of something. The Thracian text on the tile is written in Greek letters, isn't it?"

Vera nodded.

"But most evidence suggests that the Greek alphabet came into prominence in the seventh century BC."

"Yet you think that the tile is from the thirteenth or fourteenth century... oh my God! Could the Greeks have borrowed their alphabet from the Thracians, rather than the other way around?" Vera hesitated for a moment, before adding: "But we might be wrong. That gold tablet might have been engraved just a hundred years ago. Until we get it tested there's no way we can know!"

"You have to show these pictures to archaeologists... even I would."

"But what can I show them? All I've got is a couple of photos taken with my cell phone. You yourself said the quality is really bad."

"But you've seen it with your own eyes!" He objected. "This artifact could change the entire history of human civilization!"

"You can't change anything with four photographs. Like I said, I have no idea where that scratched-up lump of gold is now or where it was found. They'll just call me a fanatical nationalist who believes that everything began in Bulgaria."

"Yes, because everybody constantly repeats the fact that writing and civilization first appeared in Mesopotamia and Egypt – end of story. But that's a hypothesis, not a law of nature, and every human hypothesis is open to error. The dominant theory might just be a misconception due to the lack of excavated information. However, since this idea has been repeated ad infinitum, it has become a fact and no one dares to argue that writing first arose in the Balkans, because only a few hundred examples have been discovered. And to make matters worse, the little evidence that exists has started disappearing inexplicably…"

After another hour of chaotically staggering amidst the web of symbols and searching through archeological reference books and the Internet, Vera and Futch reduced the letters and pictograms to the following string of disconnected concepts:

Temple or Orpheus; coffin/ark of knowledge/truth or burial/ word or hidden truth; heart/soul of the mountain; eternal map beneath the stars; divinely protected for eternity /the soul; 8 and river/water, the Earth and its Shadow (equivalents of Heaven and Hell) and so on.

Most of the pictograms had at least two meanings, which made their task even more complicated. Also, they couldn't find a satisfactory interpretation for the final pictogram, which resembled

a coiled snake: In the ancient world the snake was considered a guardian spirit. This one zigzagged like a meandering river.

Suddenly Vera remembered the serpentine meander tattooed on the neck of the stranger who had kidnapped her in Moscow. Futch also thought that the hieroglyph on the cover of *The Parchment Maze* symbolized a meandering river that led to the center of the maze.

She shook her head as if trying to shoo away uninvited thoughts. "I'm starting to get tired... all sorts of ridiculous ideas are popping into my head."

"There's got to be a way to make sense of this. If our logic isn't totally off track... the inscription is talking about an eternal map and ark of truth... and some mountain." Futch continued thinking aloud before suddenly exclaiming: "That's it!"

He jumped up and darted over to his bookshelves. Vera had never seen such a huge personal library, full of all sorts of unique editions that would have made even the university envious. Futch grabbed a book and started flipping through the pages. When he couldn't find what he was looking for he put it back angrily and took out another, muttering to himself the whole time, "Map beneath the sky, ark and gold..."

Vera looked at her watch anxiously. Another fragment of time had flowed past unnoticed.

"God, it's late! I promised Dad that I'd go see him at the hospital."

"You can go tomorrow."

"But he needs me."

"Then what are you doing here?"

Vera put her coat on and left.

An attempt by the archaeologist Bogdan Nikolov to systematize the written characters used by the Gradeshnitsa Culture.

Extinguished Like Embers

Page 462 began with the words:
"Analysis has shown that all the structures of the late-Neolithic society [of the Central Balkans] were marked by exceptional stability and synchronicity, which guaranteed the normal functioning of all systems. Nothing in the conduct and public activities of institutions or the population foreshadowed the impending end of settlement in this territory. The only indications were the filling in of old mine shafts and the erasure of manmade 'wounds' on the earth."

From Professor Ana Raduncheva's **Dissertation Summary**, p. 39

"I didn't think you'd come back again today." Vera heard her father whisper.

Vera opened her eyes and realized that she was in his hospital room. The dark Moscow street she had been running down breathlessly was just a dream.

She had come straight from Futch's workshop – not so much because she had promised, but because she was scared of being home alone, of the ghosts slipping from the walls of her mother's house and knocking on the door of her room, ever more insistently. Perhaps Vera's subconscious fear of losing her father brought such phantoms to life.

Her father had been asleep when she had crept into his room during the night. She wouldn't have been able to wake him if she had wanted to, since the nurse had given him a sedative. Vera asked the nurse for something to help her sleep as well, afraid that her excitement would overpower her need for sleep. Sleeping pills were a good thing. They gently spare you terrible nights of insomnia – but like all good things, they had to be used sparingly.

"Do you really think I'm that flakey?"

"You never do what's expected of you."

"On the contrary," she geared up for an argument, then decided to leave squabbling for another time, asking instead: "How are you today?"

"My arm and leg... I can't move them. It's terrifying to realize how vulnerable you are."

"Don't worry, you'll be better before you know it." Vera smiled soothingly.

"How do you know?"

"Bad things only happen to other people."

"We are 'other people.'" The professor studied her face, as if wondering whether he really knew the young woman sitting by his bed. "Vera, why did you sleep here?"

"I'm afraid of being alone."

"But you always want to be alone," her father said in surprise. "Isn't that why you put off the wedding? Kaloyan is worried."

"After what happened... fear follows me everywhere. There are more noises, shadows, voices and footsteps than ever before... My life has changed beyond all recognition. I don't want this new life."

"That's inevitable. Everything has a beginning and an end. The sooner you accept that, the more you'll be able to enjoy what's in between. Life happens in the momentary pauses. But the beginning is the most beautiful part..."

"It would be so much easier if we could see life as a series of beginnings," Vera finished his sentence for him. "Not endings. But philosophizing can't fill life up, only the past and the future can."

Her father's words brought back an unexpected rush of memories. Vera got up quickly to hide her tears. The professor watched her, not knowing what was happening, yet sensing her fear and confusion – and the fact that he had never really known her.

For a few minutes she stared into space, not saying a word. Finally, she hunted around in her bag for her notebook. She pulled her chair towards her father's bed and stared at him. She broke the silence as though someone had wiped away what had just been said with an invisible eraser.

"I have to ask you something." She formed the words slowly and quietly, as though uncertain of her question. "Those clay objects, the ones we found at the Chateau... Were they authentic?"

"Yes. All the tests and dating proved it."

"So the ones in the Vratsa museum are copies?"

"No. Only two of them are replicas. The others are real."

"So they have authentic duplicates?"

"Is that why you came? To ask me about the symbols?"

"No. I promised to come and see you."

"You also promised not to talk about your theory on television. At the university no one wants to hear about you anymore."

The professor tried to sit up in bed, but his body was half-paralyzed. He flopped back down, his face creased in a painful grimace.

"Take it easy, Dad!"

Vera went over to the sink near the door. She glanced in the mirror and tried to brush away the tear-streaked make-up beneath her eyes. She smoothed down her hair and tied it into a pony tail.

"That's interesting... So there are more clay artifacts than we thought," she added casually.

"So you really didn't come here just to see me." The professor smiled, despite the effort it cost him.

"Would you feel better if that were the case?"

"I was just like you... Could you give me a glass of water? Since you're here, you may as well help me," he replied.

Vera could sense his bitterness, which seemed to be drowning any vital signs of hope. She silently did as he asked, then announced that she was going to look for coffee and something to eat.

As she walked down the hospital's empty hallways the questions from the previous evening began to surface from the silt of their nocturnal repose. They set on her like a swarm of wasps, having waited until she was alone again to throw off their invisible cloaks. They invaded her mind, blustering furiously in all directions, not allowing her to think about anything else or expel them. She knew that she would be powerless until she found the answers.

Last night with Futch, she had finally come up with a satisfactory interpretation for most of the unconnected facts she had been gathering. The mysterious disappearance of the Meandrites' entire ancient civilization still loomed unexplained, however. This wasn't just any civilization, but the first known civilization in the history of humanity. Another puzzle was why their ideas had survived for millennia, even though the civilization had vanished from the face of the earth. Something made Vera believe that the answer to this question would also be the key to deciphering the riddle she had created for herself.

These thoughts still buzzing in her head, she returned to her father, who seemed calmer. He was browsing day-old newspapers, turning the pages with one hand. The nurse had helped him sit up in bed.

"Dad, will you let me ask you just one more question? I can't get it out of my mind."

"I was just joking before," he smiled. "Of course you can ask me, that's why they made me a professor, after all."

His words sounded so convincing that Vera believed them.

"A friend and I have been trying to develop this new hypothesis..."

"You're up to something again!"

"It's only for our own research; no TV this time, I promise... tell me about the hiatus layer discovered in Bulgaria.[83]"

---

[83] Numerous archeological studies have shown that something occurred in the Central Balkans which forced the population to destroy all traces of its own civilization and to flee from its homeland. There is still no unanimously accepted opinion about the nature of the massive disaster that could force wholesale migration

"The hiatus layer? What about it?"

"What do you think happened to the first civilization? Why did no one else settle in these lands after they disappeared?"

The professor smiled. "You mean the Central European Chalcolythic civilization?"

Vera nodded.

"You know I love this subject – it's one of the greatest mysteries in history. I'm even convinced that the legends of the Great Flood and the Apocalypse originate from the catastrophe which befell them."

Vera's skin prickled with goose bumps.

The professor shifted to get more comfortable, as if settling in to give a lecture. "What I know for certain about their end is that at some point in the fourth millennium something terrible happened to them... Their priests arranged all their temples in a very particular way and burned them. They very carefully destroyed certain parts of their altars, placed statuettes of their prophets and their god in a recumbent posture, wrote out magical symbols and then destroyed the engravings themselves. They hid their most valuable objects in a few temples, as if intending to come back for them. Then they set fire to the temple complexes. They performed their last sacrifices and left the territory.[84] The rulers and leaders led the population away in groups, going in different directions. We believe that most of the population headed south. The hiatus you asked about shows that for more than a thousand years, no one lived in their lands, the center of which is modern-day Bulgaria. An incredible story."

---

of an entire civilization. The hiatus layer indicates that for nearly 1,000 years, no other human culture inhabited the abandoned territories. In her dissertation, Professor Ana Raduncheva notes, "Attempts have been made to determine the fate of those who built and later destroyed the earliest and one of the most brilliant civilizations on the European continent. Special attention has been paid to the existence of stratigraphic hiatus layers on hills inhabited after the end of the Stone-Copper Age."

[84] Professor Ana Raduncheva points out: "Such a scene can be observed everywhere. More than ninety percent of the inhabited hills were set on fire by their own inhabitants and abandoned. For that moment on, the territory's elegant social organization ceased to function."

"Like the story of Atlantis," Vera whispered. "Except that the Meandrites' existence has been archaeologically proven beyond a doubt; anyone who wants to can actually touch the evidence. The most curious thing is that they were the first civilization. It's a crime that we Bulgarians have not pursued this story."

"But we still don't know anything about what happened," her father interjected in self-defense. "The real reasons for their flight have not been clarified. We assume that the population was not massacred, since archaeologists have found no evidence of that. From that point of view, the Meandrites, as you call them, were also unique. They had no weapons, they didn't go to war, and apparently their sole aim in life was to develop as individuals and as a society. They left because they believed the end was imminent. And the most interesting thing about it is that only when they disappeared did weapons and war appear on the continent. As if harmony and peace disappeared along with them." The professor paused for a moment, straightening his spectacles before going on. "More moderate scholars claim that climate change was the reason. Personally, I find that explanation frivolous and too simple. My colleague, Professor Ana Raduncheva, has a radical theory: she claims that the reasons they left were religious. More specifically, she argues that their exodus was linked to a certain alignment of stars in the heavens, which formed a sign that was taboo for the population, forcing them to abandon their homeland. She believes that this very same civilization had migrated from Asia Minor to settle in the Central Balkans for the same reason millennia earlier.[85] Then the constellation of stars chased them back out again."

"Do you believe that?"

---

[85] Raduncheva argues that the Balkan Neolithic-Chalcolythic civilization fled from its lands after seeing a taboo alignment of stars. "Arguments suggest that the most likely reason [causing them to flee] was the position of stars and constellations, which prehistoric man carefully observed. According to archeological astronomers, even a large formation like the Milky Way has changed its orientation in a line parallel to the horizon."

"I'm trying to be objective. Many of my colleagues think her idea is too extreme. But that's what they said when they heard claims that a Neolithic population had lived in Anatolia. The climate there had been considered too severe for prehistoric peoples. Yet in the middle of the twentieth century, scholars discovered evidence of a human population there ten thousand years before Christ. In any case, it will be a long time before we learn the truth... The most important thing is that something clearly frightened them enough that the people with the first knowledge fled. And the curse on their lands lasted for more than a millennium. Later in the Bronze Era, a culture appeared in the region, bringing with it weapons and war. It had absolutely nothing in common with the vanished civilization."

"As far as I know, during the Bronze era ceramics and other aspects of culture reverted to a very primitive level, while interest in temples and religion almost completely disappeared," Vera added. "The first followers of the Meandrites in a cultural and religious sense in this territory were the Thracians."

"Correct!" Her father replied contentedly. Vera could hardly suppress her excitement at his praise. He had just confirmed her boldest assumptions, transforming her invented story into reality.

He broke off his lecture, as Vera searched through the plastic bag she had brought with her.

"Look what I found in the attic!" She announced gleefully, taking out a dusty box and putting it on the bed next to her father. "Our old Monopoly set!"

The elderly man's face lit up.

"You made it for me, because we couldn't buy it anywhere back then, remember? I was only five but I've never forgotten... We used to play every day."

She unfolded a piece of cardboard, revealing a homemade Monopoly board. The squares were decorated with clippings from magazines showing jewelry, banks, a prison, restaurants, even a bar – the original game itself didn't have that final touch. A paper envelope held money, each bill carefully drawn by her father with colored felt-tipped pens. A pair of dice and a few game pieces

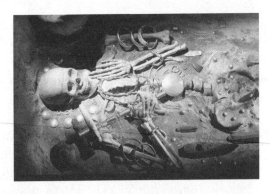

This is only one of hundreds of graves containing worked gold that have been discovered in the Varna Necropolis. The worked gold found there is the oldest known in the world, dating back to the fifth millennium B.C. and testifying to a highly developed culture. More than 3,000 gold objects have been found in the Varna Necropolis alone. The Varna Culture is also the first to have developed salt works, at a time when salt was more precious than gold.

rattled around in the envelope as well. The effort he had put into the Monopoly set made Vera reconsider whether her father had really wanted to be so far away from his wife and daughter.

The professor laughed out loud. He searched his daughter's face for something – and seemed to find it this time.

"You go first!" she proposed.

He stared at her, making sure that this was really happening. Then he shook the dice and moved the red piece. Vera had the yellow one. That's how they had played when she was a child.

"A factory! I'll buy it!" She exclaimed.

"That's not fair. It's the biggest one!"

"Don't worry, you'll catch up!"

They both laughed. Concentrating hard, the professor moved his piece. As he put it down, a forgotten thought came to him. "There is another hypothesis about the Meandrites' disappearance: migration. Dozens of scholars[86] have been studying the symbols

---

[86] The most prominent include Maria Gimbutas and Harald Haarmann.

discovered in the Vinca, Karanovo and Gradeshnitsa cultures. They disappeared for good 3,500 years ago, with the last traces found in what is now Thrace."

Vera put the dice down and cupped her chin in her hands. She could hardly contain her excitement and curiosity.

"And what do they think happened?"

"Those scholars champion the theory that this occurred during the most significant stages of the Great Migration of Peoples. They ascribe the destruction of the first civilization to persistent invasions by Indo-European hordes. The First Ones fled towards the Aegean Sea and beyond. One wave reached the island of Crete. Another wave gave rise to the Cycladic cultures which appeared around 3200 BC.[87] Many of them reached Egypt. For that reason, many of their written symbols and knowledge survive on amulets, stones and ceramics."

Vera jotted these last statements down in her notebook and put it back in her bag, grinning with satisfaction. Her father impatiently tapped the Monopoly board with his game piece.

"Hold on," she said with a sly smile. "You still haven't paid your fine. Don't forget I'm the bank as well!"

"You always want to be the banker!" He laughed, before adding quietly: "Thank you."

"For what?"

"For today."

Vera looked away. Suddenly serious, she said, "Roll. It's your turn."

The professor shook the dice and threw them.

They played all morning. For the first time in many years they laughed, joked and rolled dice together.

---

[87] This is Harald Haarmann's explanation for the movement of pre-Indo-European culture.

A THEORY OF LETTERS

Page 463 *spoke of letters:*

Letter	Unicode	Name	Pronunciation	Numerical Value	Greek Variant	Cyrillic Variant
+	□	Az	A	1	Alpha(A)	A

"The question of the Old Bulgarian alphabet's origin, which was raised more than 160 years ago, has still not been answered. The truth is constantly being sought.... It was first referred to as the Pliska-Preslav alphabet. History cannot tell us much about it. Only material evidence remains. Our observations and conclusions are based on these facts...

In the enormous territory of northeastern Bulgaria around the old Bulgarian capitals of Pliska and Preslav, as well as far from them – close to the Black Sea and the Danube – several peculiar inscriptions and individual symbols have been found, which remain undeciphered even today. The majority of them were etched in plaster walls, construction materials, clay vessels, columns and statues, while others are raised inscriptions."

The Pliska Alphabet, Cyrillic and Glagolitic *by*
Professor Vasil Yonchev, pp. 7 and 11

The next day Vera visited her father again. She wasn't sure whether she was doing so because his presence reassured her or because of the questions that multiplied with every answer she found.

The hospital continually forced her to think about life, which was galloping mercilessly onwards, destroying all hope of defying time. One by one, it cast the days back into history. The hallways felt gloomy and sad. Even if lit by all the lamps in the world, they would still seem dreary. Perhaps it was because of the feeling that within these walls, people pass away, coming face to face with pain, realizing their own brevity and vulnerability – after which everything else seems pointless.

People struggle all their lives to improve themselves until the day comes when they realize that death is an inescapable reality, at which point the struggle is to leave something behind. Usually people leave only grief and memories. Sometimes actions. Since this is too slippery to grasp, people have an urgent need for faith to take them through their earthly path and to ease their journey into oblivion.

Modern people are extremely vulnerable. In this world of science and advanced technology, God is becoming more and more impossible. Man has experienced an almost hysterical need for new miracles, searching for them everywhere. Because faith cannot be found in holiday feasts, Christmas carols, a wilting evergreen, Easter bread or painted eggs.

Vera had begun to suspect the hallway was endless when a female voice pierced the armor of her daydreams: "Who are you looking for?"

"Professor Kandilov. His room was somewhere here."

"Come with me, I'll take you."

The professor was staring through the window, watching the sun climb the sky to illuminate another day on the earth. A day on which a little of everything would happen.

"Vera," he smiled when he saw her. "Have a seat."

She sat down on the bed, but couldn't touch his hand today. Her hands stayed tightly clasped together. The only good thing about hospitals is that people forget the bad blood between them and try to give only love, warmth and support.

"The nurse tells me you haven't been eating."

352

"This is the best place to be if you want to lose a few pounds. I've been meaning to slim down for a while now. Are you up for another game?"

Vera smiled. Her father still could not move his left hand. She filled his water glass and carefully handed it to him. At that moment she felt so close to her father that she decided to confide in him.

"Dad, do you remember that symbol? The meander that was all over the clay vessels we found in the Chateau Jacques?"

The professor nodded.

"I've got the strangest feeling that it's following me... I've started seeing symbols everywhere I go. They're hounding me, screaming their story out to me – which is such a fascinating story that I suddenly realized that I've begun looking for it everywhere. And now I can't think about anything else..."

Her father sighed deeply, letting his lungs fill fully before exhaling. "You've caught it from me. And I tried so hard to protect you..."

"What are you talking about?" Vera asked anxiously.

"The explorers' disease! It's merciless. Incurable. And you've got all the symptoms."

"Come on, Dad, I'm being serious... I've made an important discovery. I've got evidence."

"Incurable, except perhaps during the fleeting moments when you realize how brief and transient life is."

"Dad." Vera smiled like her father did whenever she tried to outwit him. "The doctors said you aren't going to die just yet!"

"Listen to me, Vera. You're still so young. Forget about the symbols. If you follow them you'll lose the way back to yourself! It's far too early for you to get lost..."

"Will you at least hear me out?" Her voice and expression were insistent. "I've been investigating a third branch."

"What third branch?" He asked, confused.

"You told me yesterday about the Great Migration of Peoples and the theory that the apocalypse could have forced the Meandrites to flee."

"Yes, it's quite an impressive story, like I said."

"I didn't tell you, but when I was in Moscow I found new evidence that convinced me that some of the Meandrites actually did remain in their lands and preserved part of their civilization…"

"Of course, some of them stayed. However, we have no way of knowing where and how they developed."

"Actually, we do – we can follow the signs. The symbols! You never listen to me!" Vera shouted and her father gestured to show he wouldn't interrupt her anymore. "I think I've found the evidence."

"A few symbols?"

"Not just a few. The old Pliska and Preslav alphabet… You yourself told me that no one knows where it came from or when. But as it turns out, it contains dozens of symbols from the Meandrites' pictograms. Most surprising of all, the alphabet starts with a cross – the basic symbol within the vanished civilization's pictographic system. Besides that, the Ancient Bulgarian alphabet is the only one where I've found an equivalent for the mysterious symbol on the chest of the clay figurines from Gradeshnitsa. Similar letters have been found in Perperikon on a stone tablet. Professor Ovcharov called them Linear. As far as I'm concerned these clues are quite convincing…"

Professor Kandilov patted the bed, inviting Vera to sit a little closer. He took her hand and peered into her face anxiously.

"Vera, darling, no discovery can ever fill the emptiness, the gaping hole in your soul where there is no love. No one can live without it, without passion. And you're so pretty… Why have you followed my path?"

"Scholarly research gives me a feeling of satisfaction and completeness. Isn't that the point of everything we do?"

"No, it's only a false rhythm that you fall into when there's nothing else. You like it because it lets you forget your pain. But we are not given life to forget about it or ignore it. Quite the contrary – we have to feel the moment!"

"Words, words, words. I don't want to argue. Especially when you're in the hospital." She folded her arms irritably across her chest. "You think you know everything!"

The professor looked out at the yard in front of the hospital. A dozen magpies were marching across the grass, pecking through the fallen leaves and branches. Some were dancing, others looking for worms or fighting – each doing its own thing, yet all interwoven together in one unintelligible flurry. The professor remembered that when she was small, Vera used to call them "blue magpies."

"Okay, okay, tell me more about the symbols," he relented.

"I'm sure you know that Konstantin – also known as Kiril – the Philosopher created the Glagolitic alphabet on the basis of the Module Figure.[88] However, he came up with the figure after studying an undeciphered writing system inscribed in the fortress walls, ceramics and plaster in Pliska, Preslav and Madara. We still don't know who created that writing system." Vera shook with excitement as she took a sheet of paper out of her bag and unfolded it.

"Take this row of symbols. It looks familiar, right? The cross is the first letter, pronounced 'Az' in the Old Bulgarian alphabet. Now look at this Neolithic cross. They're identical. Now look at the Old Bulgarian symbols 'La' and 'Ra,' which look similar and convey a common idea. If you connect them with a line underneath, you get the symbol from the clay figurines. The Old Bulgarian alphabet began with an equilateral cross, marking the beginning of the Word. But why a cross if they weren't Christians yet? And

---

[88] In *The Pliska Alphabet, Cyrillic and Glagolitic*, Professor Yonchev notes: "When we traced the path of development, we noticed that these alphabets do not use random basic graphic elements, but rather everything is subordinated to a single, consecutive construction of forms. These forms are produced according to a unified internal connection and they strive towards one particular basic geometric module. We later established that this Module Figure is the same one upon which the symbols of the Pliska alphabet is based... The creator of this geometrical scheme imbued it with an important idea about the universe and all that has happened within it" (p. 7).

Orpheus' symbol – the meander – also starts being combined with the cross... Don't you see, Dad, that these are clues left by the surviving Meandrites who stayed in our lands?"

"Those are pretty words, but there's no science behind them. Like I said, a few symbols won't change history. Vera, we can always find convincing proof for what we want to believe. Logic is a tool, not evidence in and of itself. We are surrounded by countless facts. Every one of us picks out the facts that best serve our logic."

"Okay, so none of us is going to change history – but that shouldn't stop us from interpreting it in the way that suits us best!" she replied.

They both laughed. The professor said gently, "Dearest Vera, I know that any setback when you're on the verge of a discovery can be really demoralizing, but many of the signs you're talking about aren't anything unique. You'll even find versions of them in Scandinavian, Talasian, Orkhon[89] and Yeniseian[90] runes. You can't possibly think your 'hidden' Meandrites gave this 'knowledge' to the whole world, can you?"

"There you go, making fun of me again."

"I've made the same mistake myself – you get caught up in the details and lose sight of the bigger picture."

"Sometimes not knowing everything helps you see more clearly."

"Things are what they are, however difficult it may be for you to accept that."

"When I start thinking like you, I'll lie down in bed and never get up again. What would be the point?"

"Vera, my dear, I'm just trying to help you. A great archaeologist is one who overcomes his own vanity for the sake of history. However, many people make the mistake of pushing history aside for their personal glory. That's why history is so full

---

[89] Orkhon runes are an old Turkic script used by various khanates beginning in the eighth century A.D.

[90] A script from central Siberia.

of mistakes and half-baked ideas. Many people have tried to carve out their own niche within the immortality of history."

"You'll never admit that I might have discovered something where you couldn't find anything, will you?"

"Those are yet more symptoms: denial, anxiety, anger. Then you dig yourself in deeper and deeper until nothing matters except feeding the greedy logic of your theory. It's a sickness that infects every cell in your body and overwhelms reason until it completely subordinates the conscious mind. And then you find yourself utterly alone. I am alone."

"You're disillusioned. Why do you want to disillusion me, too?"

Vera couldn't find the strength to admit he was right. She had never been able to. Yet her father's words were so true that they pierced her flesh, drawing blood.

A True Fantasy

Page 464 began with the lines:
"These 'notes' are... the result of desperation and the need to share my joy and pain with someone... My last reading of the book caused me concern – do I sound too much like an embittered lone wolf? I actually do have many true friends I can count on."

Tombs, Temples, Burial Mounds: Notes from a Tomb Raider
by Georgi Kitov

Seared by the truth, Vera gunned her car's engine and peeled out, driving fast with no thought of where she was headed. She slammed on the brakes at green lights and hit the gas at red lights. The faster the car went, the harder it was to hear her thoughts. Yet they kept swooping out of the clouds like birds of prey, pecking at her mind hungrily until they found something shiny. The glittering thought would take flight, searching for sense amidst the hopelessly scrambled meanings. But there were also moments when her thoughts comforted her soul, sweeping her up in a dream-drenched veil spun from webs of imagination.

Despite her emptiness, Vera felt that the storm raging inside her would explode and destroy her if she was unable to smother it, the nameless anger.

She was no longer the same person who had entered the hospital that morning – tired, depressed, scared, chasing thoughts through the maze of memories and unspoken desires. No trace of the morning's melancholy and helplessness remained.

Vera reached the gym and parked in the lot, which was nearly deserted at that time of the day. The changing rooms were empty as well. Vera mechanically opened her locker, changed into her tracksuit and tied her hair back. The four young men in the gym watched her with curiosity. Not many women liked kick-boxing, while the ones who did were all rather strange characters. Vera went over to the punching bag and began pummeling it with her fists and feet for several minutes without stopping. She could feel eyes on her back, but was in no mood for chitchat.

After wearing herself out, she took a shower and changed back into her street clothes.

She raised her eyes to the mirror above the sink. Her long, shaggy hair, left uncut for months, was tied back with an elastic band. Her nails were trimmed to the quick, her simple make-up already smeared by the morning's events, her baggy T-shirt faded. She was alone. The suffocating weight she had been ducking suddenly pressed down on her like the giant's foot.

Vera glanced at her phone and noticed two missed calls, from Kaloyan and Futch. She thought about calling Kaloyan but changed her mind. All she would hear from him were the same painfully familiar, sappy words strung together by habit.

What had happened? She used to like him.

She remembered a conversation she had had with her father just before going to Rome.

"You've been avoiding Kaloyan recently."

"It's not the same as it was. Something's missing…. He's gotten too possessive."

"He's just trying to prove that you mean something to him."

"But when I'm with him I don't feel anything any more. All his maudlin romantic clichés, his smothering attention and letters filled with descriptions of kids and white picket fences… It's just too complicated. I need a break. Time will tell."

"Time won't tell you anything. Your relationship is simply entering another phase, which you are subconsciously not ready for yet."

"I miss the excitement and suspense."

"They're most intense when your illusions are still blooming, fed by the little you know about each other. At that point, all possibilities could become real. It's only after you've learned more about each other that your beautiful invention takes on a solid, earthly form. And that's how it should be – the family is created on earth."

"We'll see," Vera whispered to the mirror.

She was still engaged to Kaloyan, but the fear and emptiness had overwhelmed her like an avalanche. She was trying to distance herself from him, hoping that time would rekindle her old feelings. She also wanted to convince herself that she couldn't find anyone better. Yet this did nothing to heal the cold, black void in her soul, nor did it calm the fear that yet another of her precious fantasies would come crashing down around her.

They had dined together a couple of times that month. They argued more frequently, as she was constantly irritated by his annoying habits, trite phrases and predictable reactions. She avoided his advances, but delayed making any final decision until it was inevitable. Sometimes she suspected that the basic problem wasn't rooted in a fear of loneliness but in Vera herself. Was she incapable of loving someone and sustaining a long-term relationship? She fled from loneliness only to bury herself inextricably in it again. Vera had thought being engaged would cure her, but it only sharpened the illusion's outlines into the form of a concrete slab, which fell and crushed her.

Perhaps the mistake had nothing to do with love, but with the illusion that an eternal union was possible. Why do people always seek long-term relationships when they don't seem to exist – except in other people's lives, which are deceptive. We want to be like other people, yet their lives always remain beyond our grasp.

Vera slammed her locker shut and removed the key. She was tired of thinking.

It was precisely at moments like these that the Meandrites became the most important thing in her life. However, thinking of them now, she was scared that her father might have been right about the disease...

Was she on the path to illness or to a real discovery? When she started her research, she had adapted many of the facts to fit her logic – but now that logic no longer needed her. It was living a life of its own, driven by invisible forces that Vera was blindly following.

She brushed her hair and looked at her watch. It was already nine-thirty in the evening.

Vera put on some light lipstick and turned around to survey the changing room, which seemed eerily empty after the chaos it had witnessed during the day: women rushing in and out, undressing, dressing, showering, working off the day's stress, and then going back to their daily routines. So much weight had been unburdened there that there was a danger it might explode in the air. But now, the only reminders of the chaos of the day were the used towels strewn across the floor and the gaping locker doors, suggesting the presence of people.

Even if her father was right and everything was simply a figment of her imagination, what did it matter, as long as it gave her a feeling of wholeness and helped her forget? Even if she was using the story of the hidden first civilization to heal her own empty soul, today the puzzle was more real and more tangible than it had ever been. Which was why Vera was determined to see it through to the end.

RETURNING

Page 465 spoke of clues carved in stone that hinted at the First Ones and the ones who came after them:
"New Rhodope rock temples (created after the disappearance of the Eneolithic population from the Central Balkans in the fourth millennium) are being discovered and dated to the second millennium BC. The return of religious belief to Bulgarian lands, albeit largely transformed, appears to have accompanied the arrival of new populations during the Bronze Age. This period is known to us as the Orphic tradition in later religion. Only then did the rock-temple worshippers return to the mountain heights and use the older sacred sites. They rarely created new ones."

From Professor Ana Raduncheva's Doctoral Thesis Summary

Vera looked through the peephole in her door. She wasn't expecting anyone. She had just finished breakfast and was getting ready to go to the Archaeological Museum to submit the necessary paperwork for her thesis.

She recognized Futch's silhouette in the dark staircase. He was nervously tapping his thigh with a rolled up sheet of paper. Vera hesitated, not sure she wanted to open the door. He would hold her up and probably ask for some breakfast. His tousled hair made it look like he had just rolled out of bed – or that he hadn't been to bed at all.

Vera opened the door warily and asked what was going on. Futch's unshaven face with its bald patches resembled leopard skin, while the bluish circles under his eyes further emphasized his hooked nose.

"I've found the answer! Get your stuff. We're leaving!" He announced gleefully, breezing past Vera into her apartment. He was very worked up and waved the sheet of paper as if swatting flies.

"Where to?" She asked in amazement, following him with a somber expression.

"Let's go and get the treasure!"

"What…"

"Please don't make things any more difficult," he interrupted. "It was hard enough for me to invite you as it is. I was this close going alone."

Struggling to contain her anger, Vera didn't answer immediately.

"So what have you found?" She asked once she'd calmed down.

"I've proved the legend. It's true!"

"Which one of all the legends?"

"The one about the Orphic ark. It really does exist!" As Vera stared at him in confusion, he went on. "There's an ancient myth in the Rhodope Mountains about how Orpheus gathered his most valuable possession, his power, in an ark, and hid it in the heart of the mountain. Since then no one has been able to find it, even though the legend claims that his followers still know the secret." In his excitement Futch could hardly splutter out the words. "Some of the symbols we translated on the golden tablet referred to an 'ark' and 'Orpheus,' 'eternal map' and the 'heart of the mountain.' Everything points to the legend of Belintash![91]"

As soon as he said it, Vera realized that Futch had been up all night. Indeed, after endlessly reshuffling the unconnected words

---

[91] One of the legends about Belintash (also called Belentash) says that Thracian books and teachings are hidden somewhere there. This most likely refers to Orphic manuscripts. As Viktor Fol notes in *Orpheus the Thracian*, "According to the ancient Greek literary tradition, Orpheus was the founder of the Dionysian, Eleusinian and Samothracian astrological mysteries and was famous for working miracles. Ancient sources also mention poems and books written by him."

and meanings, he was convinced he'd found the answer people had spent centuries looking for, a riddle that history had turned into legend. He had read that Orpheus' followers believed their prophet and teacher possessed something which made him invincible and that his knowledge could work miracles. They said that he had been killed by envious enemies who wanted to steal his power and destroy his influence. Yet to this day, it was still disputed whether anyone had managed to learn the secret that protected Orpheus even from wild animals, whether it was still hidden, or whether it was nothing but a fanciful myth. His followers supposedly hid the secret in the ark of Orpheus, while knowledge of the ark was passed down only to those initiated into the Orphic mysteries. For centuries, amateurs and scholars alike had been scouring Thrace for the ark, but had found no trace of it.

Today few people believed the story. One place this treasure was allegedly hidden was Belintash. At the foot of this rocky plateau, archeologists discovered the only known silver plate bearing the image of Sabazios – the Thracian equivalent of Dionysus.

As Futch spilled out his rambling, chaotic theories to Vera, she started tossing whatever she could think of into a small bag, even though she hadn't decided whether she would go with him or not.

"Hurry up!" Futch urged. "The Mercedes is waiting outside!"

"What Mercedes?"

"Haven't you seen it?" Futch smiled. "Brand new! The latest model – from fifteen years ago."

Vera laughed. Futch was always joking.

"Listen, Futch, I've heard about that place, but frankly, I don't know what exactly…"

"Get your stuff," he demanded impatiently. "It's a huge rock formation in the Rhodope Mountains, one of the natural wonders of Bulgaria. The plateau on top is so flat that it looks like a huge white cake sliced with a knife. It's three hundred meters long and dotted with a pattern of 300 perfectly round holes dug into the rock surface. No one knows when and how they were made or by whom. Some scholars have suggested that the plateau is one of the world's most ancient observatories. From this peak, our forefathers carefully studied the heavenly bodies… Some people think the system of holes is a stellar map, while others claim it's a map of a geographical location. Whatever it is, it's the oldest and only eternal map I've heard of. The ancient legend also says that somewhere there, around or beneath the rock, the ark of Orpheus is hidden. The local people believe that the ark holds the Thracians' secret library, while others think it's full of gold. If you don't believe me, look it up for yourself."

Vera stopped packing and stared intently at the leopard-bearded man.

"I don't have time to look things up. So you want us to go and look for the answer in the rocks?"

Futch noisily scratched the back of his head. "It would be easier to go back to Rome and get that manuscript you told me about and copy down the clues to the center of the mysterious labyrinth… but I've got a funny feeling that it'll lead us right where we're already headed."

"I told you the manuscript doesn't give any answers, just a jumble of unrelated descriptions… and why do we need clues if we've already found the trail?" she laughed.

"It'll save time. The manuscript might be an encoded map, like I said." "It's not a map, because there wasn't any X marking the spot."

"Don't forget it might be the map to a maze. Then the X marking the spot would be visible only to a reader with the necessary knowledge."

"Are you going to pay for the flight and hotel?" She added seriously: "Futch, I think there's something you're not telling me."

He scratched his head again and smiled.

"Something popped into my head last night. You said that *The Parchment Maze* mentions the Orpheus Peak, the Taenarian Gate, Orpheus the man and the ancient writing system discovered in Thrace."

Vera nodded.

"All these clues point to the heart of the Rhodope Mountains. At the same time, we have to think logically about what we are looking for: traces of an ancient civilization that disappeared thousands of years ago and traces of Orpheus, who was the leader of the first significant culture to arise after the unexplained disappearance of the Meandrites. There must be a link between them. Then the golden tablet turns up, hinting at some 'map' and a specific place. It's written in the Meandrites' language as well as the language Orpheus himself spoke. That's a lot of coincidences. I found yet another curious link. The Meandrites, as you call them, disappeared once-and-for-all in the Rhodope Mountains, hence the most recent traces of them are there, like those found in the Trigrad Gorge."

"And just what was found there?"

"You don't need to know… it's already been sold abroad. But some of the most curious finds are from a cave in the Haramijska Gorge."

"Okay, you've convinced me. Tell me how you think the Meandrites and Orpheus might be linked."

"The last Meandrites disappeared in the Rhodope Mountains, precisely where Orpheus and the Thracians appeared two thousand years later."

"Right. And those are the two cultures whose writing is on the golden tablet… But what do you think happened?"

"I don't know… Just imagine if something important had survived from the First Civilization, which was a very advanced culture, the first to invent a writing system, mathematics, goldsmithing, glass-making, they even developed science and astrology… it gives me the goose bumps when I think that all this happened not on Mars but in Bulgaria! I'm going crazy trying to wrack my brains to figure out what the First Civilization could have left behind that would allow the Thracians to develop so quickly after they discovered this secret."

"Hold on… we still don't know whether the Thracians have anything to do with all this."

Futch didn't hear her. He had already grabbed her bag, flung open the door and was heading down the stairs. Vera hurried after him so as not to miss what he was saying.

"Just think about it, archaeological digs have shown that before the Meandrites disappeared, they systematically blocked off the entrances to their underground mines and buried their most valuable religious objects. They had a perfect understanding of the earth and what lies underground. What if we discover a gold mine?"

After loading their luggage into the car, Futch asked Vera to drive. He leaned back in the passenger seat and closed his eyes. He was too tired to drive, yet his mouth was wound up like a spring.

"The Orphic ark has to be the biggest treasure ever hidden in Thrace. Why didn't I think of it before? 'The heart of the mountain,' 'the eternal map'…"

"Listen, I don't want to get dragged into any illegal activities," she cut him off.

"Hold on just one second! It was you who dragged *me* into this!" Futch laughed, his eyes still closed.

"Just tell me where we're going!"

"Drive towards Kardzhali. When we get to Asenovgrad we'll have to look for the turn-off. The golden tablet said: 'The place is marked beneath the skies on the eternal map…' There's no place like that except the Belintash plateau." His torrent of words ended in a wide yawn.

"Do you think that this story would make a good doctoral dissertation topic?"

"It sure looks that way. But we haven't found the treasure yet!" These were Futch's last words before falling asleep.

THE SIGN OF THE APOCALYPSE

Page 446 was about signs of the End:
"Other clues hinting at the impending end of our forebears' settlement in these lands include the creation of a system of rock temples – observatories where active study of the changes in heavenly bodies could be carried out – and the gradual completion of a full cycle of ritual activities in the temple complex near the village of Dolnoslav. We can conclude that the reason for the forthcoming end of the era was the documented change in position of certain celestial configurations, which was considered a sacred symbol imposing a taboo on the habitation of certain territories."

From Professor Ana Raduncheva's Dissertation Summary, p. 39

Belintash[92] is thirty-five miles from Plovdiv, close to the town of Asenovgrad, but the only way to reach it is through the village of Vrata or "Gate." Perhaps the villagers in Vrata always kept their own gates closed, not just that afternoon. There was no one on the narrow cobbled streets, no people, no ghosts, only cattle the color of burnt caramel lumbering homewards after grazing in the nearby fields – and hundreds of crickets and birds singing to the mountains.

Vera and Futch parked the car at the foot of a steep hill and started the trek to the rocky peak. The weather forecast predicted heavy rain and thunder storms, but having slept for two hours in

---

[92] The name "Belintash" is thought to come from the Turkic for "wise stone," "stone of knowledge" or "white stone."

the car, Futch's internal clock was rewound and ticking like new – nothing could stop him from reaching his goal now. He was unfazed by the locals' warnings that the rock plateau attracted lightning like a magnet and that many people had met their end there, burned to ashes. Instead of losing his nerve, Futch took their ominous words as yet another clue to the hidden map. Vera could either stay back and miss out on the chance of discovery or risk the thunderstorm herself.

She chose the latter.

They went to a few houses looking for a guide, but the locals refused to help, claiming a stone Sphinx fiercely guarded the ancient temple. However, the centuries-old legends about this creature were all but forgotten, leaving only fear. The only thing people knew now was that the rock was dangerous. History books had little to say about the plateau. Some of them contained a few pictures, without offering any real idea about the overall form of the rocks, and thus only further fed the imagination.

From the little information Futch had found, they knew that the mountain was called either the "bad stone" or the "wise stone." Those not frightened of it worshipped the rocky outcropping, believing that it held secrets hidden by the Bessi, a Thracian tribe. The legends that had survived the centuries also said that the unique and massive rock

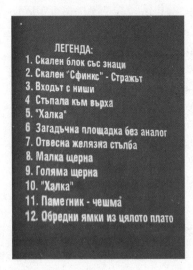

ЛЕГЕНДА:
1. Скален блок със знаци
2. Скален "Сфинкс" - Стражът
3. Входът с ниши
4. Стъпала към върха
5. "Халка"
6 Загадъчна площадка без аналог
7. Отвесна желязна стълба
8. Малка щерна
9. Голяма щерна
10. "Халка"
11. Паметник - чешма
12. Обредни ямки из цялото плато

A sign on the path to Belintash

The meadow before the plateau and the "Head of the Sphinx"

formations were home to the ancient Thracians' secret library. They also told of cryptic books and hidden messages, even the existence of the Bessi Bible. At the same time, official academic opinion categorically denied that this tribe had possessed a writing system.

The legends had attracted innumerable treasure hunters, who had gradually eaten away at the massive rock formations. They had also dug into the surrounding areas so much that it looked like a war zone. Anything they had found had been long since been exported from Bulgaria. It was nothing short of miraculous that scholars had stumbled across one of these illegally excavated, uncatalogued ritual tablets, which turned out to be the only silver tablet in the world bearing the image of Sabazios.[93]

Besides treasure hunters, Belintash also attracted hundreds of tourists and telepathic mediums who were convinced that the massive rock formations were a site of powerful energy flows. Others believed the plateau was a landing site for flying saucers. Scholars agreed that the white stone mesa was most likely the oldest map of the celestial sky or a solar observatory, as it had been known in ancient times. There

---

[93] Sabazios was one of the Thracian names for the god Dionysus, the god of nature's cycle of birth and death, as well as the solar aspects of Thracian mythology. Sabazios was the ancient Thracians' supreme deity.

were even some who argued that it was the Temple of Dionysus, which archaeologists had spent more than 130 years searching for.

Without a guide, Vera and Futch had to rely on their own imaginations and scanty research about the place – however, stumbling around on your own is often better than having other people's beliefs pressed on you. Research has long shown that unprejudiced eyes can often see what the most experienced academics cannot.

On their way to the peak, Vera told Futch about what happened between her and Kaloyan. He listened to her carefully, raising a bottle of beer to his lips from time to time. In the end he asked, "So who's the Australian?"

Vera looked at him in surprise. "What Australian?"

"Not that it matters…." Futch replied calmly and tucked the empty bottle into his bag.

The sun was climbing the sky, only to be swallowed up by a smoky cloud before reaching the peak. Lost in thought, Vera followed Futch up the steep path. To the right, a dense pine forest cast a shadow. The narrow trail wound around the edge of a smooth, sloping gorge. There was no dirt beneath their feet, just white stone covering the earth like a sugar coating. The entire mountain seemed to be one enormous rock formation, perfectly polished by the elements over thousands of years.

The distant, muffled metal bells and chimes wafted from the pines, jingling in a lively dance.

"I didn't know the locals let their cattle graze so high up in the mountains," Vera said in surprise.

"Those aren't cows. I know that sound – it's *kukeri*.[94]"

---

[94] *Kukeri* are costumed men who perform a traditional Bulgarian ritual to scare away evil spirits. The costumes, which vary from region to region, are usually made of animal skins and typically include decorated wooden masks, towering headdresses, horns, and large bells attached to the belt. Around New Year and before Lent, the *kukeri* dance through the village to drive off evil spirits with the costumes and the sound of the bells, as well as to provide a good harvest, health, and happiness to the village during the year.

"*Kukeri*? What are they doing up here?"

"They've always been here. Historically speaking, the *kukeri* originated deep in the Rhodopes. But no one knows exactly where."

"What are they doing up here in the mountains?"

"They might be rehearsing… They're getting ready for the summer solstice."

"You know too much about this place."

"I told you I've been on a few digs here."

"I've never heard about excavations around here."

"A few… unofficial digs." Futch blinked. Then he added, "I've never been up to the rock itself. I'm curious to see it."

"Did you find anything?"

"Mostly ceramics… a little gold and silver, but nowhere near as much as we expected."

As they wound their way upwards through the green tunnel of branches and bushes, they saw dozens of trenches left by treasure hunters, puckering like wounds in the earth. They must have been looking for the legendary Thracian treasure, too.

When they finally emerged from the woods, a vision appeared before them that Vera wanted to cement in her memory, anchoring it unchanging for eternity. The sky was dark and low, set to topple onto the circular meadow before them at any moment. The sun's pale disk was rolling down the peaks on the horizon. In the green field in front of them, nine black and one white *kukeri* were swaying in a circle in rhythm to the bells hanging from their bodies.

Catching sight of the interlopers, the costumed men immediately froze and stared at them. At that time of the day, especially with thunderclouds threatening, few people dared climb the mountain.

Even though Vera knew that they were no more than men in goat skins, towering headdresses and painted masks, she felt icy shivers run through her body. Ten hirsute monsters, three heads taller than a normal man, with long horns and sharp teeth, stood before them, eying them inquisitively. They resembled devils or yetis, but something set them apart from both such creatures.

372

Kukeri (mummers') costumes from the Rhodope Mountain region, Smolyan Museum

Vera and Futch timidly skirted the masked dancers. She even got up courage to give a friendly nod, which was not returned. The bells began swaying again, ringing as the *kukeri* made their way single file down the path towards Vrata.

Futch stopped and took a shiny metal flask out of his pocket. Having finished his beer, he unscrewed the cap and took a couple of swigs, smiling contentedly. Then he climbed onto a low standing rock and called out to Vera: "Take a couple of steps towards the edge of the gorge. I want to get a picture of you with the Sphinx!"

In front of them in the distance, Vera spotted a huge outcrop of rock shaped like a human head with an aquiline nose, chin and neck. With a little imagination you could also make out its eyes. The locals called it the Sphinx, which marked the beginning of the Belintash plateau.

"Don't be ridiculous. I'm not some moronic tourist wanting my picture taken with every puddle," Vera replied, stony-faced.

"Come on, everybody wants their picture with the Sphinx!"

"I don't. It's just three rocks sticking out from the cliff face at different angles."

She walked on confidently towards the plateau. Futch followed her, saying, "Sometimes people need to see certain things."

"What things?"

"Things that link harsh reality to their fantasies."

"You're getting too philosophical for me... Is this the path to the top?"

"It's the only one there is."

Their silhouettes disappeared up the steep metal steps to the summit.

THE ETERNAL MAP

*This quotation was scrawled on **page 467**:*
"Our forefathers created the first geographical map in the world!
It is interesting to note, however, that this map is not kept in the St. Cyril and Methodius National Library, nor is it preserved in a specially climate-controlled subterranean archive. No, this map is in the open air, exactly where it was created at least three millennia ago, if not longer. The map is part of the Belintash plateau in the Rhodope Mountains – one of the holy mountain's many undeciphered mysteries."

Petar Zagorski on Belintash in **Forum**

"What do you think we'll find?" Vera wheezed, winded from trudging up the steep slope.

"I don't know about you, but I'm looking for treasure."

"I need more clues," she replied.

"There's all sorts of clues up here... Has it ever occurred to you that you might be chasing a figment of your imagination? That happens to lots of academics."

"If so, clues for a story like that are the easiest to find."

"Even if you're looking for a Thracian Atlantis?"

"Atlantis is no more than a metaphor for scholarly desires to discover the undiscoverable."

The wind rose, blowing off Vera's straw hat. She tried to grab it from her precarious perch on the iron staircase, but missed. It was her favorite – but Vera had many hats. She liked seeing them in shop

The devil's face with symbols.
A clearer image can be seen
at www.parchmentmaze.com

windows, she even liked looking at them on other women's heads. She thought they looked cute when she tried them on in the store, but when she got home she usually decided they looked funny.

After reaching the top of the steps, they found themselves on a cream-colored plateau. It looked like a piazza of ivory, unnaturally flat and smooth, as if leveled by man. The surface was pocked by numerous holes, furrows, carved lines, and even three wells that were more than five feet across and six feet deep, with absolutely smooth walls. Vera recalled that she had seen similar but larger cisterns at Perperikon. "Perhaps they were made at the same time," she thought. Futch explained that the holes and furrows – which were perfectly straight when seen from the air – formed what was known as the "eternal map."

"I don't see anything particularly mystical about these holes," she replied.

"Their perfect roundness and smoothness is impressive; that would've been extremely difficult to do in ancient times".

376

"But look, they're all filled with water, which drains off and evaporates very slowly, while at the same time burrowing deeper into the stone. As you know, no human hand can replicate the smooth curves formed by the gentle but persistent effect of water."

"Then how do you explain the fact that there are exactly three hundred holes, which corresponds to the exact length of the plateau in meters?"

Vera hesitated for a moment before replying. "I'll have to think on that one."

Futch took the metal flask out his pocket and raised it to his lips with a sigh of relief. They were alone on the mountain top. They each went their separate ways, looking for clues.

Vera saw three perfectly parallel lines, like a set of triple rails. A fourth line beneath them was made up of several equidistant, square holes. Water clearly had not carved out these shapes, but she said nothing to Futch, knowing he would seize the chance to tease her.[95]

The plateau sloped gently to one side, where three massive outcrops loomed above Vrata. Vera crossed the four lines and headed towards one of the jutting rocks. Another strange hole caught her attention. This time, however, it looked like the outline of a diabolical face crowned by a number of smaller holes that seemed to represent a constellation. For a moment Vera thought it might be a link with the stars on the Orphic amulet, but quickly dismissed the idea.

She sat on the edge of the outcrop and gazed into the distance. Beneath her feet, pine forests ringed a gaping canyon of white stone. The wind brought the smell of distant chimneys and the faint tinkling of cowbells.

Suddenly she gasped, as she caught sight of the rocky outcrop to her right. A rectangle had been carved in the center of its smooth vertical surface, like a giant picture frame. Inside the frame stood a

---

[95] Everything the characters are seeing can be viewed by readers on the book's website in the "Belintash" folder.

The small devil's head – arrow

single human figure with arms raised to the heavens in prayer. She was not surprised so much by the fact that someone had engraved a picture into the rock face, but that the silhouette inside the frame closely resembled the praying figure etched into the clay tablet from Gradeshnitsa. The same figure appeared 2,000 years later as a hieroglyph in Egypt. Later it decorated a Trojan seal, which read: "The bearer of this symbol shall be protected by God."

THE DEEPEST DARKNESS

Page 468 spoke of the darkness:
"More modern etymologies compare the old Indo-European root for 'obscure' with the ancient Greek words orphnos and orphnaios, which also mean 'dark' and 'gloomy,' or with the Semitic Erebos, which means 'cosmic night' or 'the deepest darkness.' But it is possible that the deep darkness is connected to the fundamental concepts of solar Orphism. At the same time, it could also hint at Orpheus' journey to the deepest and darkest world under the earth: the Lower Kingdom of pale shades.... where he could not easily identify with his main enemy, the ruler of Hades' eternal darkness, also known as the 'Invisible One' or the 'Incorporeal One.'"

From Orpheus the Fisher *by Robert Eisler*

While he was waiting, hidden like a shadow, Ariman's thoughts once again returned to the rocky underground hideaway. They picked up details, recognized words and ceaselessly sought the hidden answers. Even though he had decided to complete his mission, the poison that was changing him day by day had worked its way through his flesh and into the bone. His need to know who he was and why he was different had warped into rage and hysteria.

Yet he still went back, and still kept searching…

He had grown up here in the underground lair. His memory pictured a cold, damp and dark place, but today it seemed somehow different. Because the meaning was gone. All of these questions and his fury at his own weakness had eaten away at the meaning. And when you lose hold of it, you also realize your own insignificance. But for now he was the only one who knew this. No one else suspected the questions raging inside him.

Thin young men with ashen skin lined the long wooden benches. They took apart and sewed back up singing rag dolls, whose song said:

> *Fear and ego are your masters,*
> *yet without them even God would be unnecessary.*
> *Close your eyes and you'll wake up,*
> *having searched deep within yourself.*

The boys on the benches were workers. Ariman had never done that.

The young men still didn't know that they were free. This was probably for the best. They were not tormented by questions and poison.

He was the only one who was trying to follow the trail of clues back to the beginning.

He bounded up the stairs towards the exit. He went outside, slamming the door behind him. Nearby there was another, smaller gate with a severed head carved above it. The same grisly image watched over the mailbox. Over the centuries it had almost faded into the wall, but it was still visible to those who knew to look for it. Or to exceptionally observant tourists who by some strange chance found themselves in front of Mercy Church.

He wanted to believe that it was not too late to set the past to rights and to purge himself of this nameless thing that was eating him up inside.

His eyes glittered with redemptive resolve.

He would wait to catch the woman alone…

THE LOST PARADISE

*A deep cave was sketched on **Page 469**,
and under the drawing, this text was scrawled:
"…the traces of the First Ones were scattered throughout
Egypt, Crete, Europe and Thrace, but their Knowledge
survived only in the Lower Kingdom. Because their
prophets knew that when shadows covered the earthly
world, the only safe refuge was the place from whence
they had come. Until the seven stars once again aligned
in an arc. When Orpheus descended to them in search for
his beloved, they gave him the symbols. He brought them
back to earth through the cave, where he and his followers
adapted them to the new world. In order to preserve the
secret, he told everyone that Down Below was the realm of
the shadows and Hades. Since then people have drawn and
told tales of the Devil and Pan, who comes from the caves.
However, in the hidden library it is written that Orpheus
returned from the bowels of the earth with letters."*

*A wall painting
of "Judgment
Day," the Smolyan
Museum*

The Trigrad Gorge with a view towards the Haramiyska Cave

When they reached Trigrad, Vera and Futch found a small rural hotel. They had to share a room, since there were no others available. During the summer, the gorge was a popular destination, even for foreign tourists.

Dusk was falling. The two of them sat down to dinner at the guesthouse's restaurant. The courtyard barely had room for the three hastily cobbled together tables. However, the spot offered a bird's eye view of the entire region.

Trigrad was a small village cozily nestled between the steep white cliffs. Jutting up into the sky, the stone seemed to keep it from falling. The mountain ridges bristled with evergreen forests, the trees themselves like spears, sharpened and ready for Judgment Day. If you watched long enough, you could even glimpse a falcon swooping through the heights, the wind's sole master.

Today Futch wasn't talking much, devoting his energy to drinking instead. Vera also had a drink to calm her anxious thoughts.

"You're hiding something," he announced suddenly. He set his empty brandy glass on the table and locked eyes with Vera.

"What are you talking about?"

"I don't know, but I can feel it. I don't think you've told me everything about that manuscript in Rome."

"You mean *The Parchment Maze*?"

He nodded. Her face tightened, reddening slightly, as if the desire to spill her secret was wrestling with her conviction that it was better to stay silent.

"Swear that you'll keep it a secret!"

"I swear!" Futch said with a hiccup.

"It's really strange. I myself don't even know how it happened, but… most of the conclusions and theories in the manuscript resembled the argument in my book, my research book. If I'd seen the manuscript earlier, I could say that I'd been influenced by it. But now? Maybe the reason is simple. Even though there's billions of people on Earth, we can't think up too many different things and sooner or later, our ideas start overlapping. Maybe that's even the reason for the similarities across cultures and civilizations in the symbols I've been researching. Especially when they start off on equal footing. But we're used to thinking that an idea belongs to the first one…"

"What idea are you talking about? I haven't read your book."

"Like I said, I was describing traces of the Meandrites, the oldest civilization, which disappeared thousands of years ago. Later I came up with the idea that its rebirth was connected with Orpheus, which is most likely the reason that his symbols are none other than the meander and the cross – both created by the vanished ones. Orpheus was brutally murdered due to the power of his knowledge, which he brought back from Somewhere. Later, the ones who came after him stole it. And the manuscript calls that Somewhere the 'Lost Paradise.'"

"Paradise? So where is this paradise?" Futch livened up.

"It doesn't say. It must be in the first part of the manuscript or the end. But they were ripped out."

"Since the ideas are similar, why don't you cite *The Parchment Maze* in your book? You can use as a source to prove your theory."

"No way! If I did that I'd be giving away the most valuable thing about it – the originality of the idea. I don't want anyone to find out about that manuscript… If I had the guts, I'd rip out the remaining pages myself. Besides, it won't make a good source since it's anonymous."

Her face darkened, while her gaze hovered between the white cliffs and the night sky. Futch ordered yet another brandy from the waiter, who frowned and disappeared into the kitchen.

"I want to see that manuscript," Futch announced.

"You don't need to. The anonymous author was far trickier than I am. He based his theory on artifacts that don't exist. It's genius. You don't have to waste time searching for them; you can just pick what you need. And in the end only a few readers will bother double-checking them. But I double-checked them. Like I told you, there was no trace of most of them, while for others there were only hazy legends, but not a bit of hard proof. Only the last few were an exception."

"The amulet, the golden tablet and the frescoes?"

"You swore not to tell, right?"

"Not to tell what?"

"Well, there's one more real artifact: an ancient clay tablet with an inscription similar to the one found in Gradeshnitsa. And I am the last person lucky enough to see it, so that's how I know it exists."

"Wait, back up and tell me the whole story!" Futch pleaded.

"The final surviving page of *The Parchment Maze* talked about it. I know you'll be shocked, but the tablet in question had already disappeared from my father's study the night before we left for Switzerland. My father barely survived the loss." Notes of sorrow in Vera's eyes gave away her regret. "He guarded it so carefully. We were at the Chateau Jacques when they told him…"

"The manuscript's authors must have stolen it!" Futch guessed. "I haven't heard anything about it…"

"Nobody has. It was a gift from a Bulgarian tycoon, a notorious collector of antiquities. Of course, he didn't say where it was found – he didn't want to give away his team of treasure hunters. Without information about where it was found and the characteristics of the soil layer where it was discovered, it doesn't have much historical value. However, comparative analysis shows that it belonged to the Meandrites."

"And you were the last one to see it?"

"Keep your mouth shut. Remember, I've seen that coin collection of yours down in the basement."

"Dirty traitor," he smiled. "Wait a second. You're not hinting that you took it from your father?"

Vera didn't answer. She lifted her glass of wine, drank it down and asked: "So you still think we'll find something here, huh?"

"Of course. All the signs leading us here were real. You discovered them, I confirmed them."

"My dearest Futch, if you're convinced, that means my book will be a huge success. Want to know what happens from here on out? We'll discover the ark down there, just like you're hoping. Do you know what we'll find inside?"

"Do you know?"

"Yes. Unfortunately lots of treasure hunters have passed through here before us, so there won't be much left. But we'll discover my father's ancient clay tablet, which will turn out to be extremely important, because it will prove my whole theory. It clearly shows a text of ancient pictograms similar to the ones we used to reach this place."

"But how can you know all that?"

"Like I said, I made it up. And the tablet will be the same one that disappeared from my father's study. I stole it myself."

"You kill me." Futch's smile disappeared into his brandy glass. He ordered another one.

"We're closing," the waiter replied rudely.

"So give me the whole bottle and go ahead and close up!"

"I'm not doing anything illegal," Vera protested. "I've simply arranged a few authentic artifacts, linked them up with a unique story and confirmed a legend to boot. Besides, that clay tile is too important for history to sit in my dad's closet. After our discovery, it will have the status of a real find and will hold a place of honor in the Archaeological Museum's collection."

"But won't your dad recognize it?"

"Of course, but he won't be able to figure out what happened. He won't suspect me at all. Besides, why couldn't there be two identical tablets?"

"That's unheard of! They've never found two identical clay tablets with ancient pictograms."

"That's where you're wrong. At the beginning of the year, my father and I stumbled across just such a collection in Switzerland."

"Why are you telling me all this?"

"You've been my accomplice from the beginning. I won't be able to do it alone. And we'll share the glory."

The waiter turned off the lights and locked up the kitchen. He was the only employee left in the restaurant. On his way out, as he passed by Futch and Vera's table, he said, "You're quite a drinker, sir."

"Worse than the local drunks?"

"There aren't many of those around. People here get up early to work."

"I guess that means I'm different. My old man always told me that was important."

EIGHT WATERFALLS

Page 470 began with a poetic verse:
"Now you die and you are born,
three times blessed upon this morn!...
And the same mystery awaits you below the ground
As the other holy men have found."

**Orphic text from a golden plate shaped like an ivy leaf,
from the fourth century B.C., discovered in Thessaly**

They set off for the cave early the next morning.

"Why do we have to go and waste our time in there if we already know what we'll find?" Futch grumbled.

"Everything has to look as authentic as possible. Sooner or later we'll have to talk to the press, as well as scholars, and they'll want to know every tiny detail about our discovery."

Vera and Futch waited outside the entrance of the Devil's Throat Cave with about a hundred other tourists. The cave had become such an organized tourist attraction that the only way to get into it was through the manmade entrance, accompanied by a guide who unlocked the door once an hour between 9:30 AM and 5:30 PM.

"We'll have to explain exactly where we made the discovery and what clues led us to it."

"Now I know why you stole your father's tablet – you believe this story. It's more than obvious. But I believe in it, too. The clues that led us here were real!"

Vera started to cry and tried to hide her tears behind her sunglasses.

"What are you crying for?"

"You wouldn't understand."

"Try me."

"I feel so mixed up inside. Every single day I dream of being like all the other archaeologists. I want to go to my dig at seven o'clock in the morning, and then record and describe all my artifacts. I want to be treated like a colleague and not like the professor's spoiled daughter." She paused before adding angrily, "You're right, I do believe in it! I have to. I want to discover something that will get me out of this whirlpool. But if this theory doesn't pan out, the disappointment will be so agonizing that I'll need to make up some other story to fool myself into thinking everything worked out. I've lost everything else... Like I said, you wouldn't understand".

"Actually, I do. I'm the same, except for I didn't even graduate from college. Ambition is infectious."

The guide known as "Kotseto" rounded up the tourists near the entrance and began his spiel. However, the group was so large and the thundering waterfall so deafening that those at the back of the crowd couldn't hear a single word.

"This cave is called the Devil's Throat," he explained, "because whatever goes into it never comes out. We can only imagine its enormous underground galleries and the huge caverns hidden deep in the earth. Its only natural link with the Upper World is the river with its eight waterfalls. The cave also has another claim to fame: for centuries it has been believed that Orpheus descended to Hades – also known as the Underworld or the Kingdom of the Incorporeal Shades – through the Devil's Throat. It is low water season at the moment," the guide continued, "but during the high water season the river sweeps hundreds of tree trunks, dead animals and all sorts of trash into the 'throat,' yet no one knows where it ends up. The Devil's Throat is the deepest cave in the Balkans. In 1970, two divers named Siana and Evstati tried to follow the underground river into the cave. As far as we know, after the eight waterfalls, there is a whirlpool – which is where the two divers are believed to have met their death, taking with them the secrets of what they saw in the Underworld. Since then no one has dared retrace their steps.[96]"

"Eight waterfalls!" Vera whispered in disbelief.

The crowd of tourists entered the cold underground tunnel leading to the cave.

---

[96] Excerpts from the explanation given before entering the cave by Kostadin "Kotseto" Hadzhijski, the most famous guide to the Devil's Throat and the Haramijska Cave.

DAY ZERO

Page 471 *began with an ancient calendar:*

THE STRUCTURE OF THE YEAR IN THE ANCIENT BULGARIAN CALENDAR

	Period	Length (Days)	Ancient Bulgarian Name
New Year's	The shortest day of the year (December 22)	1	Sur, Eni, Ignazhden
First Trimester	Month 1	31	Alem
	Month 2	30	Tutom
	Month 3	30	Chitem
Second Trimester	Month 4	31	Tvirem
	Month 5	30	Vechem
	Month 6	30	Shechtem
Third Trimester	Month 7	31	Setem
	Month 8	30	Esem
	Month 9	30	Devem
Fourth Trimester	Month 10	31	Elem
	Month 11	30	Elnem
	Month 12	30	Altom
Day Zero	The longest day of the year (June 22)	1	Ba(e)khti

An hour later, Vera and Futch came out of the cave through its natural entrance, which was in fact the beginning of the enormous waterfall that could be heard thundering throughout the whole

cavern. Vera's face had been somber and expressionless as she wandered through the underground canyon. Futch knew why, but said nothing. Vera spoke first once they'd gotten away from the noisy crowd of tourists.

"Nothing. Not a trace. This is where the trail of clues ends."

Dejected, they walked up the asphalt road towards the village.

"Perhaps we're not looking in the right place," he suggested.

"Or maybe it's just not our day."

"Not our day!" Futch shouted. "That's exactly right. We need the right day! How could we expect to find ancient symbols in a cave on any old day of the year!"

Vera looked at him with confusion, so he explained: "All rituals and symbols left by pre-historic cave people, and by Thracians as well, were connected with a specific day and event. Especially in the caves! Well done, Vera. We need the right day!"

Just then they heard dozens of hollering voices, stamping feet and clattering bells behind them and whirled around to see another band of *kukeri*. The group of young men wearing masks and furry costumes quickly passed them by, shouting in explanation that they were rehearsing for the upcoming summer solstice festival, which marked the beginning of the Orphic mysteries. In July, the festivities culminated in thousands of people from Bulgaria and abroad gathered in the Trigrad Gorge for torch-lit parades, *kuker* dances and horse races. The event's bravest guests went into the

Devil's Throat where, according to legend, Orpheus had descended into black Tartarus to look for his beloved Eurydice. The torch-lit parade was called "Orpheus in the Underworld" and supposedly resembled Greek tragedy with a chorus of mourners, criers and singers.

"Oh no, not more *kukeri*?" Futch moaned. Then he stopped frozen in the middle of the road, thunderstruck.

"That's exactly right! The Orphic mysteries… Orpheus, Bacchus and the summer solstice. That's it! The Orphic mysteries and the Bacchanalia," he babbled incoherently.

"What's that about Bacchus?"

"Give me a sheet of paper and something to write with!"

"What's going on?"

"Hurry up before I lose my train of thought!"

Vera handed him her notebook.

"What's the date today?" Futch asked her.

"The twenty-third of June."

"Everything's falling into place. The answer is Day Zero! Perhaps *Bakhti* is the root of the name Bacchus." He scribbled on the sheet of paper while rambling on. "The name Bacchus hints at the day, *Bakhti*. Oh my God, today must be Day Zero![97] So if there's a sign, it can't be seen on Day Zero. That's why we didn't find anything. According to Ancient Bulgarian beliefs, this day is outside time. But tomorrow is June 24th – the day of the Twin of the Beginning."

"I can't understand a word you're saying… Slow down and tell me what you're talking about," Vera was losing patience at her friend's ecstatic gibberish.

Futch was sketching out some sort of table. He wrote numbers, dates and names in the boxes, yet Vera still couldn't grasp the meaning.

---

[97] The calendrical elements cited here follow the works of Petar Dobrev. The leap years in the Gregorian and Ancient Bulgarian calendrical systems do not coincide, for that reason when converting from one to the other, the dates might be off by a day.

"The facts fall into place far too perfectly – as if I made it all up. You know about the Ancient Bulgarian calendar, right?" He asked.[98]

"Of course. What about it?"

"It's the most accurate calendar system in the world according to UNESCO. Most recent studies have shown that the calendar begins in the year 5505 BC. In other words, according to the Ancient Bulgarians, that date is the beginning of history."

"But how is that possible?... Right around 5500 BC, the first encoded symbols appeared, messages from the Meandrites. The tablets and the figurines from Gradeshnitsa date from then... I never made the connections that the most perfect calendar in the world began during that same period! How could the Ancient Bulgarians, who flourished in the seventh century AD, have known what had happened millennia before their existence, without archaeologists?"

"Someone might have told them," Futch smiled, but then continued more seriously. "I have no idea. Perhaps they somehow inherited the First Ones' knowledge. But since we're collecting coincidences, here's another one for you: around 5500 BC, the Great Flood described in the Bible supposedly occurred, causing catastrophic changes to the Black Sea basin."

"You're right, there are just too many coincidences... You'll have me believing in the stars before long!" Vera smiled. "Tell me more about Day Zero."

"I knew it – you really do believe the story. Otherwise we wouldn't be here." Futch waved her closer and showed her the table he had drawn. "I'll skip the details about the calendrical system and just explain the most important elements. In the Ancient Bulgarian calendar, St. Ignatius' day is the shortest day

---

[98] The ancient Bulgarian calendar is considered the most accurate in the world, according to UNESCO. Recent studies show that the calendar began in 5505 B.C. With its twelve-year cycles, the calendar resembles the Chinese one, however it is more ancient and is most likely the latter's original source.

in the year and is a separate month in itself. It's also not counted as a day of the week. So a year is made up of three-hundred and sixty-four days plus one. The first day of the year, *Alem*, always falls on a Sunday, which is the first day of the week. During leap years, after the twenty-second day of the sixth month, a "Day Zero" is added, called *Bakhti*, which is the longest day of the year. If it isn't a leap year, this day falls on the twenty-third of June, known as the shadow of *Bakhti*. So according to the Old Bulgarian calendar, today is Day Zero, which also marks the beginning of the Orphic mysteries and the festivities of the cult of Dionysus or Bacchus. What's more, in the local dialect the consonants 'k' and 'h' sound the same, so *Bakhti* can be read as the root of *Bahtikos*, or Bacchus."

"You're a master sleuth!" Vera exclaimed.

"That's how I make my living!"

"Okay, okay… But why should we go back to the Devil's Throat tomorrow, June 24? I don't see that anywhere in the Ancient Bulgarian calendar."

"All it takes is a simple calculation." Futch wrote "Orpheus" in Latin letters, then in the Greek transcription. "If we write down one of the names of John the Baptist and Orpheus, we can see that they have the same cipher code."

IOOANNES = ORFAS (Orpheus) = 72

"Numerology was very important for both early Christianity and Orphism," Vera commented.

"True. And the fact that iconographers and artists, including Leonardo da Vinci, painted John the Baptist as Christ's twin. After the Virgin Mary, John was the second half-human to be immaculately conceived, six months before Christ," Futch added. "John the Baptist was born on June 24, the summer solstice, exactly six months before the longest night of the year and the Nativity of Christ on the winter solstice. Some people even interpret John the Baptist as the Christian projection of Orpheus, pointing to the common cipher code and the fact that John the Baptist, like Orpheus, was decapitated and is often depicted with a severed head. The transcription IOOANNES means the 'deity of fish and sea creatures' or the 'Fish God.'"

"Many philosophers during the nineteenth and twentieth centuries, including Jung and Eisler, claimed that Orpheus was the original Fisherman," Vera added. "Now I get what you mean – today is Day Zero, so tomorrow is the birthday of the first twin."

"That's exactly right! So if there is anything in that bat-infested thunder hole, tomorrow is the only day we can see it…"

THE EIGHT-POINTED SUN

Page 472 opened with this quotation:
"The Roman catacomb of San Domitilla has a unique mural painted on the ceiling. It contains a depiction of Orpheus in the center of an octagonal shape, within which Christians are sometimes baptized. The octagon has eight corners, which divide eight scenes from the Old and New Testaments. Orpheus is surrounded by animals which are considered to be symbols of the Christian conception. It is also interesting that in the New Testament and without any apparent reason, Immanu-el (God is with us) begins to be called, "Emmanuel." It will also be interesting for the reader to note that according to numerological connections between Orpheus, the Pythagoreans and Jesus, there is another connection: Emmanuel ΕΜΜΑΝΟΥΗΛ = 96: ΟΡΦΕΥΕ (Orpheus) = 96. Such an argument is convincing evidence that the Messiah in the ancient Jewish texts is the reborn mythical Orpheus."

From **Orpheus the Fisher** by Robert Eisler, page 51.

"Are you asleep?" Futch whispered in the darkness.

"No, I'm thinking about tomorrow. There's got to be something down there…"

"Of course there is! If nothing else, then I'm convinced there must be secret underground galleries at the bottom; after all, it is the deepest cave in Eastern Europe. But as the experts say, no one who has gone in has ever come back out."

Vera sat up in bed and switched on the bedside lamp. They looked at each other, and she whispered.

"Except Orpheus? All these clues can't just be pure imagination."

"You know, there is one detail that is still nagging at me."

"What's that?"

"You once mentioned that on the cover of that labyrinth book, there was an eight-pointed meander, while a lot of the pages had a seal with an eight-pointed star," Futch reminded her.

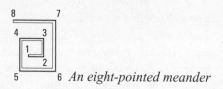

An eight-pointed meander

"Yes, that's what I said," Vera replied distractedly.

"I don't think all these eights are purely coincidence... Maybe it has something to do with the star of the Sumerian goddess Ishtar?"

"That seems a little farfetched."

Futch leapt out of his bed and started pacing the room. After a few laps, he went into the bathroom to get a beer. Since the room did not have a refrigerator, he kept a few bottles in cold water in the bathtub – as if gearing up for a rough night. Beer in hand, he resumed his brainstorming.

"The eight-pointed star is the rarest star form used in modern times. Didn't the manuscript say anything about it? Or at least about the number eight?"

"I don't remember seeing anything, although I did read through it pretty quickly. The librarian kept giving me these strange looks."

"Well, you are a pretty blonde. He was probably just ogling you."

Vera frowned.

Futch grabbed his dictionary of symbols and began searching for everything he could find on the number eight and stars, muttering to himself. "Symbols of hope, no, that's lame... 'man's striving to go beyond the boundaries of his own world'... blah blah

blah!" He flipped through more pages until he came to the entry for the number eight. After reading a bit, he exclaimed, "At last something makes sense! Eight is the symbol of universal balance, rebirth and resurrection, which fits in with our idea that all these clues are tied to Orphic teachings."

Futch dragged his index finger along the glossy paper as he scanned the lines. It suddenly stopped, as if his fingernail was stuck between the letters.

"Check this out!" He said. "In early Christianity, the ritual baptismal fonts were octagons, just like the octagonal fresco of Orpheus from the San Domitilla catacombs that you showed on TV. Isn't this yet more proof of your crazy idea about the fusion of Christianity and Orphism?"

"It's just a hypothesis."

"Well, perhaps this mystery we've got ourselves mixed up in is encrypted with some sort of code to protect it from busybodies. We've just got to find the symbol that will unlock the cipher..." he thought for a moment. "The eight-pointed star can't have been chosen randomly."

Futch's eyes widened, revealing a web of bursting capillaries. The dark shadows beneath them sagged to his cheekbones, while the veins in his neck bulged.

A golden Orphic mask. A series of eight-pointed meanders have been inscribed on the forehead, while the beard is made up of the sign meaning "eternity," "infinity" or interwoven figure-eights

"In all the years you've spent fiddling around with Orphism and the Thracians, haven't you ever come across any link between Orpheus and the number eight?"

"I'm not sure," Vera struggled to recall some connection, no matter how fleeting. "Besides the frescoes in the catacomb, there are the eight-pointed meanders decorating Orphic scenes and ritual items."

"Wait! In the fresco, Orpheus is in the centre of an octagonal sun! And one of the meander's most ancient meanings is the sun."

Futch's words reminded Vera of the ring worn by Monsieur Marten, the caretaker at the Chateau Jacques, which showed an eight-pointed star with a meander inside it. Perhaps Futch was right about the connection between the two symbols. Kiril might have been right that the octagonal star was indeed the sun.

Futch drummed his fingers on his laptop impatiently, waiting for a file to open.

"I've recorded all the meanders that we've come across up until now. Along with the cross, they're the most common signs in this maze of symbols you've pulled me into."

Futch began studying the meanders one by one, looking for some connection between the symbols that he had missed. Something linked with the number eight.

"That's it. The number eight must be the code to the cipher!" He cried unexpectedly.

"How did you work that out?"

"Most of the meanders used in the Orphic message really have eight corners or points. My hypothesis will be confirmed if the first symbols created by the Meandrites are also eight-pointed."

Futch opened the file where he had collected the symbols from hundreds of pre-historic clay and stone objects left by the Meandrites, along with a description of the nameless stone tile found by Professor Ovcharov, which also appeared to be from the same period. Indeed, the most commonly used hieroglyphs really were eight-pointed meanders.

*A cult scene, clay, 5th millennium B.C. Village mound in Ovcharovo,
near Turgovishte. All the figures and objects are inscribed with
meanders and suns.*

At that moment Vera realized why Dr. Werder had constantly
referred not simply to the meander, but to the eight-pointed meander.
He, too, must have been obsessed with learning the truth about the
Roman labyrinth book, just as Vera was now. Franz Werder had
studied much of the manuscript in detail without managing to lift
the veil of its mystery even an inch. In the end he had come to
Vera in the Hotel Metropol to plead for more information about
the secret sign on the cover. He must have been desperate since he
asked her, a complete stranger. Or perhaps he had tried everything
else, to no avail.

The meander he had scribbled on a piece of paper had eight
points, but at that time Vera had not paid any significance to the
number of corners. Moreover, the excitement of the celebratory
dinner had deadened her desire to dig through other people's
fantasies. The number of points on the meander seemed to her
unremarkable, even when she saw them again on the cover of the

book. She had no idea back then that the symbols were distinguished by the number of corners.

"What you're saying makes sense," she admitted quietly, as though anxious not to wake anyone in the dark night. "But if you're right, then that blows my theory of a link between the Neolithic meanders and the Egyptian hieroglyphs created millennia later, since the Egyptian ones have six points."

"Don't rush to conclusions. Most hieroglyphs used today in dictionaries and reference books are stylized. We have to find out what the hieroglyph looked like when it first appeared in Egypt," Futch reassured her and started pecking at the keyboard. "I'll send an email to a friend of mine in London who is obsessed with symbols. But we probably won't get an answer for an hour or two."

Futch sent the message and continued looking through the files. The crickets' song wafted through the open window, unfazed by the cold night air.

"The most common ancient meanders have eight or six points," he commented. "But the meanders accompanying the figure of Orpheus mostly have eight corners. That's why I'm convinced that the number is the key to the code!" he added with excitement.

"Better not jump to easy conclusions. Let's wait for your friend to reply."

Futch, convinced they were on the right track, continued comparing other symbols, as if he hadn't heard her. Whenever came across something remarkable, he would whisper to himself.

"There are ancient Orphic meanders with thick equilateral crosses next to them. Jesus, they've got eight points, too. That must be why the cross accompanies Orphic scenes and messages. Even the Orphic amulet you told me about contains the same code, but in the form of seven stars plus one moon, which still equals to eight. And again, there's a cross beneath them. But why should there be any six-pointed meanders then?"

Futch's last words made Vera shiver. If he was right that the number eight was a code, then knowledge of it must be handed down only to the enlightened. The octagonal meander and the cross were most likely used only by certain schools, which passed on their message through art. Was this the code referred to in the labyrinthine book? It frequently spoke of the "solar code."

Even Kiril, the reporter, had discovered a similar meaning in the eight-pointed star in the octagonal sundial at the Euxinovgrad Palace. If the cipher truly existed, the enlightened must have tried to encode secret Meandrite messages within their art. Then other artistic schools had merely copied the pretty pattern without realizing its meaning, giving rise to five, six, seven and even nine-pointed meanders.

"Has your friend replied yet?" Vera asked impatiently.

"Give him time."

"It's late. I want to get some sleep."

She turned away and pulled the sheets over her head, as if hiding from irritating thoughts – but they were stronger then she was. Her euphoria grew with every minute. Vera's mind buzzed with symbols, words and numbers. Futch was right about the stolen Orphic amulet with its seven stars – which were themselves small equilateral crosses – with a single inverted moon beneath them. It was a formula: 7+1. The amulet contained 7+1 heavenly lights. Only now did she realize that the Orphic cycle consisted of 7+1 phases: seven levels plus one which itself was the rebirth of the soul. The eight-cornered meander had seven sides plus a single centre, just like river Styx, which formed seven circles to bring souls to the center of the Lower Kingdom…

Vera's heart pounded wildly and she knew any thought of sleep was hopeless. All she could do was to wait for the first rays of the sun. So she could put her plan in motion.

THIEVES OF FAITH

Page 473 *began with a verse:*

"Without faith I wander aimlessly
And lose myself in fear and wrath.
'What do you believe?' He asked.
'It doesn't matter,
as long as you don't stop...'"

The white sunlight seeped through the curtains like sand through a sieve. As soon as she felt its first rays Vera sat up quietly in bed. She looked at her watch. Six o'clock. "Great," she thought. "I can be in the cave by eight. If that number is really so important, then eight o'clock will be the moment of truth." She smiled to herself.

She got up and dressed quietly. Futch seemed to be exhaling boulders rather than air. She didn't wake him – he wouldn't be opening his eyes any time soon. Next to his bed stood three empty, sour-smelling wine bottles.

Vera wanted to take this final step alone. If she found anything, she would owe it to Futch, but she wanted to keep the thrill of discovery for herself.

Before leaving the room, she unplugged the laptop and tucked it under her arm. She took the clay tablet she had stolen from her father's study and packed it into her backpack, which she tossed on her back. She tiptoed out of the room and put her shoes on outside the door.

The guest house's owner had already gotten up and was bent over the fireplace, beginning her daily chores. Her graying hair was skillfully braided and a red apron was tied tightly around her waist. When she saw Vera, she offered her breakfast, which Vera didn't refuse. She needed the energy, especially after a sleepless night. She felt exhausted.

While sipping her coffee and dipping her fried doughnuts in sugar, she switched the computer on and logged on to Futch's mail – there was a new message from someone named James in London. "That must be the answer," she thought and opened it.

"The hieroglyph you asked me about was first used in Egypt around 3000 BC," the brief letter began.

"That's a few centuries after the Meandrites disappeared from Thrace," Vera thought to herself and continued reading.

"It was used to mean 'guardian' and had either eight or seven points. Over time its shape became noticeably stylized and simplified to make it easier to chisel into stone tablets. It is most frequently written with six or seven corners. It also means 'temple' and eventually transformed into the hieroglyph for the letter 'H.' If you're particularly interested in the number eight, you may want to know that it is considered a symbol of the god of wisdom, while the eight-pointed star is the ancient symbol of the rising sun.
Let me know if there's anything else I can help you with.

James"

A lump of fried doughnut stuck in her throat.

"Of course, the Sun! The inspiration for all gods!" Vera whispered to herself.

She took a huge gulp of coffee, jumped up from the table and ran down the road towards the entrance to the cave. The sky was swollen with imminent rain, while a wet fog hung over the gorge.

The streets were empty, sunless and quiet, as they should be when a town is still sleeping. The guesthouse was at the far end of the village where its windows could look out over the green meadows and the craggy jaws of the white cliffs. The road wound past the

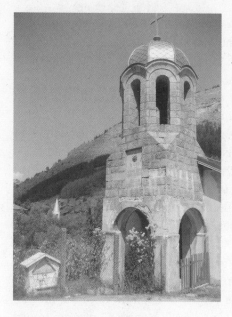 village church at the end of a thick spruce forest. The church gradually appeared over the hill – first the metal cross, next to the minaret of a silver mosque, came into view, then the copper cupola peeked out, followed by the stone bell tower holding it up to the skies. Finally, the ramshackle sanctuary completed the picture. Above the entrance to the church, there was an iron cross within a star – whose entire form was eight-pointed.

On the glass pane in the church's front door hung a faded black silk bow, like unfurled bat's wings, signifying that someone had recently died.

In her haste, Vera might not have noticed the church if it hadn't been for the little boy huddled in the doorway. His thin figure was curled up on the threshold. He looked so tiny and vulnerable against the looming cliffs and rocks that Vera felt compelled to stop and go over to him. She asked him what he was doing there alone. He replied that he was praying and talking to his mother and sister who had died in a fire in their hut.

"But why are you here so early in the morning?"

"I had a really bad dream," the boy replied, stretching out the word "really." "Daddy told me that the church brings us closer to God and to the people we love who have died... he said they're looking down on us from heaven and that one day we'll go up there to be with them. And then we'll be together again."

"What was your dream?"

"I dreamt that mommy and my sister had left heaven, so they couldn't see me any more and I couldn't hear their voices like usual."

An invisible hand grasped Vera's throat and squeezed. She wanted to hear her mother's voice, but she knew that Up Above there was nothing but clouds and air currents. She knew that her mother's body had decayed in the ground and that her own body would rot there, too, some day. "It's nice to be able to believe in heaven," she thought. She stroked the little boy's hair.

"When they open the church, you can go and light a candle for them," she said, although she never did so herself. Yet she knew this was something the little boy needed to do.

"But they'll throw me out of the church," he replied.

"Why? I'm sure they won't."

"I beg from people. Daddy gathers herbs. And the priest gets angry and says that I annoy the tourists."

The boy was staring intently at her, forcing Vera to look away. She wanted to say something to ease his pain.

"My mommy's dead, too," she whispered.

Vera had not uttered these words out loud before.

"So where's your mommy now?"

"What?…. In the graveyard," Vera replied in surprise.

"My mommy's in heaven. It's better there. What are you doing here?"

"I'm writing a book."

"What about?"

"It's very complicated."

"Tell me anyway."

"I'm trying to find out the truth about the First Civilization and the ancient roots of the story of the Son of God, which came before the story of Christ…"

"You shouldn't write about things like that!" The boy shouted. He stared at the cross on the roof of the church.

"Why not?"

"Because if you take heaven away, there'll be no place for mommy and Bozhura!"

"Yes, there will…"

"Where?"

Vera couldn't reply.

"Isn't your mommy in heaven?" The little boy insisted.

"I don't know…"

"Perhaps she hasn't gotten there yet. That's why you don't know. You'll have to ask her again soon. But leave the story of God alone…."

"I'm writing about the truth!"

"If that's the truth, then I won't have the strength to save daddy. And he won't be able to save me. All I know is that God looks after us and mommy is watching over us and I'm not scared about tomorrow. Goodbye!"

The little boy got up and left. And Vera's hands went cold like burned-out embers, gripping the backpack holding the tablet she had stolen from her father – because she believed it was the last piece of evidence to disprove mankind's illusions.

THE LOWER KINGDOM

Page 474 began with a quotation.
"You will go to the well built palaces of Hades:
To the right there is spring.
Next to the spring stands a tall white cypress.
This is where the souls descend to find refreshment.
Do not even go near this spring.
Further on you will find cold water flowing
From the lake of Mnemosyne.[99] Guardians stand before it
And they will ask you sternly
Why you are studying the darkness of the fogs of Hades."

From a golden Orphic tablet found in 1969 in the burial mound of Hiponion

The cool morning breeze stroked Vera's hands like a silk veil. It ruffled her hair and tugged at her clothes, yet remained as intangible as her thoughts. Vera was dressed in black leggings and a short-sleeved T-shirt. She had packed her bag with food, a bottle of water, sturdy climbing rope, a wetsuit and, of course, her notebook.

She was sure she'd planned everything perfectly. It would be another couple of hours before the area was thronged with tourists, spectators and enterprising villagers trying to make money any way they could – from telling stories and playing music to selling herbs,

---

[99] He who drinks from the waters of the Mnemosyne remembers all of his previous lives and possesses great knowledge. According to Plato, before being reborn, souls drink from the River Lethe in order to forget their past lives. Mnemosyne was the goddess of memory in ancient Greek mythology. According to Orphic beliefs, if you are thirsting for salvation in the afterlife, your soul must forget nothing, but rather must possess a supernatural memory.

honey, property and even stones. They scanned the passing herd, spotting the weak ones and sinking their teeth into them. They bit right down to the bone, not letting go until the hapless victim gave in completely to their demands. They had no choice but to prowl – this was how sixty percent of the villagers made their living. It was the only way they could feed their children, as there was no other work in the area besides the Forestry Service.

Vera left the main road and walked along a narrow path winding towards the Devil's Throat. The growl of rushing water began to grow louder until a cloud of icy steam enveloped her entirely.

Vera had never seen the place so deserted. She had even beaten the old man who sold herbal tea there from morning till night, whispering to everyone: "no one ever returned from Hell." His standard uniform was military fatigues topped with a pointy cap, his face as papery as a mummy's. He would look at you, smile, and as his blue eyes widened, he would call out: "Buy some, my child, for your health!"

Vera reached the iron bars closing off the man-made entrance to the cave, which had been built especially for tourists. Next to it was the cave's natural opening, which the roaring river rushed through before splintering into the highest waterfall in the Balkans inside the cave. The manmade entrance led to a staircase the height of a twenty-storey building. As you climbed breathlessly, enveloped in a cloud of silver mist, to the right a churning white torrent crashed

The shaft of light in the cave, whose end points to the cross and the arc of "seven stars" as on the amulet

into the depths of the earth. The blue cliffs above the throat were cut vertically like a never-ending ladder to the heavens. Between the clouds and the river hung a centuries-old spruce tree rooted in the stone and spreading its crown above the water like a pair of giant angel's wings. The view reminded Vera of the description of the path to the Underworld: "You will go to the well-built palaces of Hades: to the right there is a spring, next to it stands a tall white cypress; where the souls descend to find refreshment."

Orpheus was believed to have followed this path…

Rusty bars blocked the steep steps down to the bottomless depths of the gorge. Vera checked to see if by any chance the padlock had been left unlocked, but as she suspected, the gate wouldn't budge. Yesterday when she and Futch had examined every detail of the cave, Vera had noticed that there was a gap between the bent upper bars above the gate wide enough even for a chubby man to slide through. To make things easier, right beneath the gap, a rock jutted out, providing a convenient stepping stone, as if someone had placed it there deliberately.

Vera hung her backpack on the iron gate and climbed up towards the bars above the entrance. She hopped over the gate and lowered herself through the opening. As she stepped onto a moss-covered rock, her foot slipped, leaving her hanging over the black abyss to the right. She froze.

411

The Orpheus Amulet, which disappeared in 1945. At the base of the cross, two wedges can be clearly seen, forming an arrow pointing downward

She carefully stepped back onto the rock, making sure she had a steady foothold before jumping over the railing. She was now on the steep concrete stairway leading to the bottom of the "Thunder Room," as locals called it. She pulled her backpack through the bars of the gate and, squeezing the wet metal parapet very tightly, began her descent.

The thousands of tons of water crashing mercilessly into the rock face deafened every sound and thought. The cave was darker than it normally was since only a small fraction of the lighting had been left on in the center of the tunnel. The stairs were illuminated by only a solitary ray of light peeping through the Devil's eyes into the impenetrable darkness until it lost strength and faded in the blackness.

Suddenly Vera heard a sharp metallic clanging, like something smacking into the iron gate behind her. She listened again, but didn't hear anything else. She decided she must have imagined it. Fear creates all sorts of sensory illusions.

412

The Seven Lights within the Devil's Throat Cave, shining like stars

When she got tired, she stopped to rest. Her eyes stared at the beam of light falling like a spotlight in the darkness. The beam illuminated the rock face opposite her like a giant white pointer.

Then she saw it. The sign! It was real and clear. At the very top of the pointer, exactly at 8:00 AM on the Day of the Twin, she saw a huge equilateral cross engraved in stone. As if someone was trying to mark this as The Place. Indeed, one of the most frequent meanings of the cross in Antiquity was "place" or "city." Although the cross was astonishing in and of itself, Vera's jaw dropped even further when she saw the arc of seven stars above it.

"So that's what it must mean!" She murmured in the dark.

The cross and the seven stars were just like the ones on the Orphic amulet, which used such an inexplicable jumble of symbols that many scholars considered it a mistake. She took her camera out of her backpack and took a picture. She recalled that her father had told her about a Bulgarian professor who argued that the disappearance of the First Civilization was caused by an arc-like configuration of stars – just like the ones here and on the amulet with the crucified man.

At that moment Vera realized the significance of each individual symbol in the amulet, even the two triangular wedges at the bottom of the cross, which had stumped scholars. What she saw here made it clear that they were an arrow pointing downwards. If

413

the cross indicated the place, then the wedges gave the direction. They must be the final clue she had to follow.

Vera's blood surged in her veins, dispelling any vestige of fatigue. She was sure she was on the right path now. She continued downwards, trying to hurry before the guides and tourists arrived.

She reached the foot of the steps, jumped over the concrete wall and started down the gentle slope towards the underground lake. Dozens of cave bats fluttered around her head, whizzing past like bullets in the darkness. Large drops of water trickled from the ceiling.

She looked back towards the illuminated concrete bridge built for the tourists to see how far she had descended. The pale electric light bulbs flickered like distant stars in the night sky. They were arranged symmetrically and when she counted them, her breath caught in amazement. She counted them over and over, as though unable to believe her own eyes. There were exactly seven lamps, arranged just like on the amulet. Every single tourist visiting the site could see this for themselves.

"Did the person who wired the electricity in the cave know about this, too?" She wondered. Why not? If Vera could see it, then so could anyone else. Which meant anyone could make it to where she was. Vera glanced up at the ceiling, checking for familiar figures, but it was dark and silent.

She continued her descent. She skirted the huge jutting rocks and made her way to the end of the cave and the water's edge. The lake was so calm and clear that its surface was almost invisible. The low-flying bats, squeaking and skimming the water, created the only ripples that gave away its presence.

She dipped her fingers in the invisible liquid. It was ice-cold. The guide had said that it was only slightly above freezing. She set her backpack down and took out the wet suit she had rented for the journey. She had decided to follow the underground river as far as she could safely go. The signs that had led her here must have some purpose. There were too many of them, all so logically ordered. And as far as she could see there was no other entrance to the Underworld.

She pulled the tight black suit over her body and jammed her legs into thigh-high rubber boots.

Standing at the water's edge, Vera tried to summon up the courage to go on. The cave guides' words echoed in her head. Before letting visitors into the cave, they always warned, "Nothing has ever come out in the crystal clear water flowing from the cave. Nothing has ever come out, no living person has every returned. No one knows what lies between the beginning and end of the cave or what is hidden in the boundless depths of the earth. The water flows over eight small waterfalls before reaching a whirlpool that has never been explored. We know nothing about it, except that it is big enough to swallow everything that goes into it…"

"Eight!" she murmured. "Where did I read about the 'Eight suns between Heaven and Hell'?" Yet as soon as the words were out of her mouth, the answer came to her. "That's what the inscription on the fresco in the Roman catacombs said before it was eroded."

Vera raised her eyes to the ceiling as though searching for the heavens and a Savior watching over her from above. Her eyes automatically formed the dark spots and lines into an image, as people had been doing this since time immemorial. They seemed to need to impose a familiar shape on their visual perceptions so as to interpret them. She saw a man with unnaturally bulging eyes, an egg-shaped head and a straight nose. His arms were spread wide, as though crucified. He had a huge bulbous body, long thin arms and short legs. Immediately above his head a symbol was clearly etched out in black – two symmetrical hooks joined by a line on the bottom, just like the drawings on the clay figures from Gradeshnitsa. It was a stylized version of the sign whose meaning Vera had puzzling over for more than a year. The only difference was the small line extended from the bottom of the symbol pointing to the head of the crucified figure.

She rubbed her eyes to be certain she wasn't imagining it. But the picture did not disappear.[100] "This must be yet another sign that there are still more clues to be found," she thought to herself.

Vera stepped resolutely into the icy water. Despite her wetsuit, the cold slowly crept up her limbs. She was oblivious to it, however, since her mind was simmering with questions: what was hidden behind all these signs so carefully arranged in the ancient labyrinth of history, yet understood by so few? If the Ark of Orpheus really was hidden here, what power had made Orpheus invincible? Or was she still looking for facts to prop up a story she had invented? She would soon find out...

Suddenly she heard noises and jumped. Distant muffled sounds came from the concrete steps. Then a rock tumbled down into the water with a splash, frightening even the bats, which chaotically took flight. Holding her breath, Vera looked up and saw a shadowy male figure. He was coming towards her.

Vera grabbed her backpack and waded further into the water without a thought of the cold or the eight waterfalls. The man seemed in a hurry to follow her. He jumped over the low wall lining the tourist walkway and headed towards the lake. Vera ran as fast as she could downriver, but her feet slipped on the mossy stone river bed. She stumbled, fell, got up again and continued. The man plunged into the water, despite not having a wetsuit – a fact that encouraged Vera, who was sure that he would quickly give up the chase in the icy cold. The cave walls in front of Vera grew narrower and the calm waters began churning, surging through the bottleneck. The man was still following her. With his long strides he had nearly caught up with her. He seemed immune to both fear and cold.

Vera felt the current sweeping her towards an opening in the rocks exactly below an artificial bridge illuminated by two electric

---

[100] This image really exists. Anyone standing on the bank of the crystalline underground lake can see it (although, in principle, tourists are not allowed to reach the lake) by looking up at the ceiling. Wait for your eyes to adjust to the darkness and put together the dark parts of the picture.

416

light bulbs. She had almost reached the edge. From there the water exploded into millions of droplets before merging once again in the rapids further on. The First Waterfall, Vera thought. She hesitated and turned around. The man was coming closer. The faint light illuminated his face.

It was Ariman.

The moment she saw him, her entire body trembled with a forgotten impatience. Yet only for a moment, before her memories rushed back. He had pursued her all the way here, to destroy every trace of his crimes. Why had he let her live on that bridge in Moscow? He must have assumed she had drowned.

"You? Here?" She whispered and added in desperation. "So I really have found what I've been looking for…"

"Very few people know what they are looking for," he replied roughly. His eyebrows were tightly drawn, his jaw clenched. His eyes were furious and unhesitating.

"I'm looking for the answer, the secret knowledge…"

"The knowledge is concealed from people." As he said these words, Ariman raised his gun and pointed it at her.

"Are you going to kill me?" She whispered, trembling.

The man did not reply. He just took a couple of more steps towards her.

"Then instead of the ark I must have found the Taenarian Gate,"[101] Vera whispered ironically, surprised at how easy it was to accept death. Perhaps because she had no choice – she could wait for the man to shoot her or give herself up to the river's rapids.

Ariman in turn was surprised that the woman knew about the Secret Gateway which was depicted on one of the walls of the brotherhood's underground hideaway, in the final scene from the Prophecy. If the opening here really was the Taenarian Gate, then only humans could pass through it. That was what the Incorporeal One had told him.

---

[101] An expression for the exit toward death.

Vera was standing at the edge of the waterfall. Despite the growing speed and strength of the current, the piercing cold water and the mortal danger, Ariman kept coming closer.

In desperation she hurled her backpack at him and jumped into the underground waterfall, which greedily swept her up in its icy embrace. It seemed impatient to rescue her from the savage stranger – the pale man with the strange sandy eyes... Even if that meant dragging her through the seven circles of the Styx, through the silt of oblivion, to the gloomy kingdom of pale shadows...

Ariman rushed forward to follow her, but then remembered Teacher's words. Only humans could pass through the gate.

While he did not know quite who he was, he knew that he could not follow the woman. He could only listen to her screams echoing through the bottomless cavern.

The insurmountable tension of his desire to follow her and the impossibility of doing so raged inside him. His soul sank into the gorge, he stopped hearing and seeing. As he bent over to pick up Vera's wet backpack, the hand-sized clay tablet tumbled out. This was the final piece of evidence the Incorporeal One had instructed him to find.

He put it in his pocket and returned to Rome.

And somewhere there from the mountain,
In the haze of the distance,
The sad song of Orpheus could be heard.

THE END OF HISTORY

Page 475 began with a few blank lines about the Knowledge:

....

....

....

And continued with the words:
"These lines are to be completed by the reader who has learned the Knowledge. Because the necessary knowledge is that which everyone discovers for himself using only the evidence he or she is ready to accept. Because the Truth is that in which you have had the strength and courage to believe. And because a lack of both may lead one person to kill another, while for someone else it is may become a weapon."

When he passed the Church of St. George in the still dark yet quiet morning in Rome, Ariman remembered the hole in the limestone wall opposite the Roman Arch with its stone figures. He knew that in the shadow of the reliquary church, initiates left instructions about the mission and messages. It had been empty the last time he looked.

Ariman ran as fast as he could to check.

This time he found a note written in a long-forgotten language with directions for a meeting at the estate in an hour's time.

He would have to hurry, as the Incorporeal One's earthly estate was far away, on the edge of the city.

Angry, chaotic thoughts swarmed his head like furious flies as Ariman arrived in front of a tall metal gate. As he expected, it was

The gate with the eight-pointed star

locked. Guards with dogs were patrolling in front of it. He studied the gate's iron spikes, trying to figure out how high they were. Above them, illuminated by the first rays of the sun, was an eight-pointed star, right in the center. He didn't know what it symbolized either; it was as cryptic to him as the demonic heads flanking the gate. And the underground world, and the pale ones, the shadows and himself….

*And beyond
the gate*

*View through
the fence*

Seeing no way of getting through the main entrance, he continued along the quiet street to the right of the entrance. It gently sloped towards the rear entrance, winding around the estate walls, which were too high to scale without the proper equipment.

Ariman had always wanted to know what was hidden behind the walls besides the beautiful garden, but the Incorporeal One had never allowed him inside. He had told Ariman that it was too early, that he would be allowed to enter when he was ready. Once the Teacher had taken Ariman there to move a heavy chest, but had forbidden him from going any further than the entrance with the eight-pointed star.

Ariman continued down the street towards the corner of the walls, which met at a marble column topped by a stone creature with a dog's body and a dragon's head. As the light of day slowly began to wake sleeping Rome, this monster observed the passersby with undisguised savagery.

The stone wall butted up against the courtyard of the house next door, where several cars and a van were parked next to the wall. After glancing around to make sure he wasn't being watched, Ariman took a running jump onto the roof of the van. The alarm began to squeal hysterically, but within seconds he was inside the estate's grounds.

To avoid notice, he slipped into a small stand of trees and made his way to the back of the house. Somewhere from the ground floor of the house he could hear slow, somber music, occasionally interrupted by melodious chords before the dirge-like refrain again repeated.

Hearing voices, Ariman drew closer to listen. One of the ground-floor windows was slightly open. He could see three figures dressed in cloaks like black shadows.

The Incorporeal One was speaking, his words were calm and monotonous – yet taken together, they seemed nonsensical.

"The Idea and the Faith are eternal," he intoned.
"The form is transient.
The Idea and Belief free us from the shackles of mortal life, however false.
The form is a prison for the soul.
The Idea is One and forgetting the Idea leads to self-destruction.
But the metamorphoses of the form are as numerous as the people on Earth.
Some succeed in imposing themselves
And thrive on the eternal need of souls to believe.
And they are transformed into the Truth.
Man has the inherent instinct for self-preservation,
And hence he always finds the evidence for his belief.
And the Prophecy will be repeated!"

Ariman stepped back from the window. There was nothing he could do now. He had to wait until the Teacher was alone. He could no longer douse his internal fires with more lies – it was a blaze fuelled by the conscious awareness of his ignorance.

What was all of this for? Everything that he was doing? Who was the Incorporeal One? Who was he, Ariman? Why did he have to destroy the woman who had changed him...

He crept into the huge house, hiding in the shadows of the high ceilings and marble columns. Fast and silent as an uncatchable spirit, he searched the second floor. He entered the study and saw an iron key on the desk. Too big to be for a safe or chest, it was most probably to a door with an old-fashioned lock.

The music still echoed from downstairs. Ariman figured that as long as the music was still playing, the rest of the house would be empty. He examined the two remaining floors more quickly, checking for locked doors. The door he was looking for was next to the study where he had found the key. He put the key into the lock and turned it. The lock clicked and the door opened wide.

Ariman found himself staring into a large dark room. He could make out the outlines of hundreds of randomly stacked objects, big and small, old and new. Some were blackened with time, while other shone resplendent in their history. Stone, wood, gold and silver… Ariman opened the door wider to let more light in.

He recognized some of the objects. He himself had brought them to the Incorporeal One, having killed for them and risked his own life. Why? He did not know. He did it because he did not know anything else.

He took the clay tablet he had found in the woman's backpack, thinking that it, too, would soon join the clutter.

At the very front of the random heap of artifacts, a golden tablet glittered in the light from the door. Ariman had brought it from Burma. Next to it lay the small stone amulet from his last mission. He touched them to see if they were real. He ventured further into the room: crosses, statues, decorations, tablets with inscriptions and hieroglyphs, ritual plates… The objects were from all over the world, from all cultures and religions. He noticed that nearly all of them bore a handwritten number and a reference to pages from a manuscript called *The Parchment Maze*.

Before he could even begin to make sense of what he had found, Ariman heard heavy footsteps behind him. He turned around sharply, mechanically touching his concealed gun.

It was the Incorporeal One. As always, he was unarmed and dressed in his old faded hooded cloak. He approached Ariman slowly, his footsteps echoing beneath the high vaulted ceiling.

"How dare you enter here?" He shouted, his voice filled not so much with anger but pain.

"What are all these things? What are we? I want to know. Now!"

"Get out of here!" the old man hissed and began to strike him.

He had done so only once before, when Ariman was a child. This time, however, Ariman would not stand for it. He pushed the old man's hand away. The resolve in Ariman's eyes frightened the Teacher, as it seemed to lack any belief or thought.

Ariman took a step towards the Incorporeal One and asked in a low voice: "Who am I? Am I different?"

The Incorporeal One did not respond immediately. No one had dared ask that question.

"You're the very best!" He whispered. "I send you where no one else could go."

"Stop!" Ariman's expression was cold and angry. "I want to know who I am. Where am I from? What are we doing here? What is the point of all this?"

"Every human being looks for these answers. But they are within you."

Ariman took another couple of steps towards him. He looked like an enraged machine. His fists were tightly clenched, the sinews in his arms almost tearing his skin. His veins darkened, and his jaw hardened.

"I have to know," he said slowly and huskily.

"Knowledge burdens and confuses the conscious mind. It is always relative. And it never changes what happens…"

"Don't give me your nonsense! You keep us here like slaves. Who gave you the right to do so?"

"You are free. It has always been your choice to return. Why do you always come back?"

Ariman looked away. The Incorporeal One was right – but this realization only infuriated him all the more. The old man would not get away with his slippery words this time. He took another step forwards. Hesitation flashed across his face, but then he shouted:

"I've had enough of your lies! I want the truth... Does the Taenarian Gate exist? Why can only people pass through it?"

The old man sighed. Ariman knew. He replied in a weak voice. "It leads to the bottom of the History. Only human beings can descend through the gateway. We came out in order to guard our world. The only one of us who can return is he who witnesses people believing in the Prophecy and following their Creator. He will tell the Hidden Ones that it is time to return."

"What are you talking about? Who am I?"

The old man was silent as though his words might ignite the air itself. As Ariman stepped closer, the old man burst out: "You are my son!"

"You're lying!" Ariman retorted angrily. "That is not possible. I was born Above. You are lying to me to keep me here."

"When you are ready, you will learn."

"No, you'll tell me now."

The Incorporeal One sighed and then said quietly, "Very well... but the people must not find out. Not yet... Anyone who has learned the truth is doomed to serve the secret. Because it is humanity's last hope before God slams shut the doors of paradise forever!"

"What is this nonsense? You don't believe in any god!"

"I want you to believe. Here, Above, there is no existence without God."

"Without fear there is no belief."

"When you learn my secret, you will give yourself up to it willingly. Because humans are doomed without it. Yet when you realize its burden, you will be sorry, but it will be too late – because you will have lost your freedom."

"Are you the one who protects humans?"

"I have dedicated my life to the task of hiding the path back to the Paradise they lost. If humans find it now, they will only destroy it with their darkness..."

"That is complete bullshit. We are the ones living in darkness!" Ariman yelled.

"Light and Darkness are conditions of the soul. They exist only within us. As we choose."

Ariman squeezed his fists again.

"You want to deceive me. That's what you've always done... I've had enough of your words!"

The Incorporeal One shuddered and bent double as though wracked by a sudden pain. Then he slowly straightened up, whispering, "Knowledge is not always salvation. It can become a lethal poison."

"I'm not a child. You said that knowledge of the hidden Paradise will save humanity."

"But only when they are ready for it. If you tell a child that fairies and Santa Claus don't exist, then he ceases to be a child – but he is not yet an adult. Humanity's development cannot be rushed. At best, we hope it can be influenced... and for millennia, fragment by fragment we have been returning the hidden knowledge to humans to bring them closer to the day when they will be ready. However, no one had ever returned to the Lower Kingdom from here above to tell us whether the Prophecy was true. When my turn came, I saw the Upper World for myself and realized that humans continually ostracized and savagely murdered all their teachers. They condemned them, hounded them and crucified every one of our emissaries who had come to them ahead of time, bringing revolutionary ideas to the world to help them find the way. And the knowledge people had gained from the misunderstood emissaries was instantly turned into a deadly weapon or a money machine."

"Is this why you do everything you do – to hide the knowledge?"

"Like light, knowledge cannot be hidden. However, in order to return to the lost Paradise, humans have to be ready. They are still not ready. Much time has passed... and I no longer know whether they will ever be ready." The Incorporeal One wheezed, giving a deep sigh. "Don't forget that the emissaries are forbidden from returning, thus I did not return... But when I saw this world I decided to dedicate my life to protecting Paradise from humans.

And I would do it a thousand times over, just to hide the return path. With the help of those who came after me and those whom I created, we built what you see here… I have spent my life hiding the signs from humans. And I recorded the clues in a labyrinthine manuscript in the library."

"Stop!" Ariman shouted in frustration. "Don't you understand, I need to know the whole truth now!"

He glared savagely at the hooded creature. His eyebrows gathered in fury, yet every other muscle of his face was frozen. His eyes were absolutely still, as if the anger was the only thing inside him. Yet the old man's words were incomprehensible.

"Then there will be no tomorrow for you."

"There is no tomorrow now," Ariman hissed in reply.

"Never contradict me!" The Incorporeal One barked and again raised his fist to strike Ariman with all the strength his shriveled body could muster. But Ariman parried the blow, holding the Teacher's arm for a moment before returning the punch. The old man fell backwards.

"What am I?" Ariman screamed in rage. He pointed his gun at the Incorporeal One, his eyes glittering with unrestrained anger. "You were like a father to me… I can't take it anymore. What am I? What are you? Lies!"

The Incorporeal One scrambled up, turned around and headed for a side door. Ariman followed him.

"You cannot escape. Stop!" he screamed.

There was no response. The old man did not stop. Ariman's mind fogged with anger. Without feeling his fingers, he slowly squeezed the trigger until the gun finally fired. Ariman jumped back in shock as though not been expecting the shot. He threw the gun down and ran towards the old man's slumping body. The Incorporeal One crashed to the floor and lay there trembling. His lips whispered, "Guard the final hope!" – and his body went limp. He did not speak. Or make a sound. Or move.

The Incorporeal One's body law sprawled at Ariman's feet covered in the old, coarse cloak. For several minutes he did not dare touch the saintly figure. The dead old man seemed so precious to him that his death seemed to be the end to his world.

During all these years, Ariman had wanted to uncover the face he had never seen in the light. His hand lightly touched the edge of the hood. After a moment's hesitation, he pulled it back.

He jumped back at the unexpected sight. Now he realized why the Teacher was called the Incorporeal One – and why he was always hidden under thick cloth. His skin was bright, but so pale and transparent that all his muscles and arteries showed through. Instead of hair only a few thick grey strands straggled from his skull. Through the half-closed eyelids the old man's eyes were colorful. His skull was broad and elongated, his lips small and his arms and torso long… His appearance resembled animals and plants cultivated in complete darkness. Ariman wondered if this was because the Incorporeal One almost never ventured outside the underground chambers. But that in itself would not have been enough to transform him to such an extent. In the middle of his back there was a pair of small bony wings. What was he? He was gone, taking the secret with him. Or perhaps he had preserved it in the labyrinth book he had mentioned.

Ariman picked up the weak lifeless hand. The dry fingers were like fragile branches, one wearing a shiny silver ring. Ariman slipped it off. The image engraved there was familiar: the Goddess and her Son. He put it on the chain around his neck and squeezed his eyes shut against the pain.

Then he stood up and ran without turning back.

THE FINAL PAGE

Page 476, *the final page, began thus:*
"If these words are uttered by the incorporeal spirit when it has to pass through the Seven Gates and again when it has already passed through the gates, then it will not be sent back nor will it be stopped before Osiris, and only then will it be able to go to the other Blessed Ones."

From the Egyptian Book of the Dead

Before dying, the Incorporeal One had mentioned *The Parchment Maze* hidden in the library. Ariman knew where he meant, since he had accompanied his Teacher to the beginning of the most ancient road a number of times.

Ariman found the manuscript and read it. Only then did he learn what the insurmountable light was – the light which had given strength to the Incorporeal One. A light which would not allow him to search for his own peace. Now Ariman was the only person who could keep it alive. Just as the Incorporeal One had done.

Ariman now knew what he was serving and where all the destroyed clues had been leading. But this did not make his task any easier, so he continued reading – until the burden of the knowledge had grasped him between its grinding jaws.

Perhaps the Incorporeal One had spoken the truth when he had said he was Ariman's father. Even though there was no resemblance, except perhaps for the colorful eyes. Ariman's skin was pale – but not as pale as the Teacher's…

The Incorporeal One had also been right that once he learned the Truth it would burden his soul and enslave him.

Today Ariman understood where the labyrinthine manuscript was leading him – towards the gate at the bottom of History.

The Incorporeal One had also said that those who learn the Truth cannot return through the gate. The only ones who could were those humans who have deciphered the signs. Because in knowledge, some saw perdition while others saw salvation.

Thus, the Incorporeal One had to hide the signs from humanity until they were able to change or until the Seven Stars once again came into alignment in the heavenly vaults, indicating that people and shadows would change places. If the Prophecy was true.

However, the Incorporeal One knew what lay behind the gate – while Ariman did not. And he would not stop until he knew. Only then would he truly understand why he was here.

He continued preparing.

He heard a fly. Rather, he heard countless flies, wrapping around his throat like a noose. Ariman's eyes glistened with tears as he realized that the Incorporeal One had only wanted to preserve the world and humanity until humans themselves had the strength to change the direction of the End.

Before he dedicated himself wholeheartedly to protecting the hidden Paradise, Ariman had to be sure it truly existed. Perhaps during all these years, Ariman had become infected with the human poison, since he could not believe in the Truth that had guided the world since its existence. People wanted to witness miracles before they could believe, so the teachers had to perform them. Perhaps Ariman was human after all?

There was no way he could be sure, which is why he could not risk trying to pass through the Taenarian Gate. But he would wait for someone to ascend through it once again. Sometime, somewhere. And he would be there, to find out.

And so Ariman reached the end of the Manuscript.

The Incorporeal One had not managed to complete his work, which trailed off unfinished at **page 476**.

Ariman read to the end. "Could a hidden Paradise or angels really exist in this world? Or were they just another human invention, like devils?" he wondered. The Incorporeal One had left this world before he could say. Now if anyone else might know, it was the woman who had reached the end of the labyrinth – if she was alive.

Ariman turned to the next page and recorded his notes. Then he added **page 477**.

He returned *The Parchment Maze* to the library for further annotations.

And he waited…

BOOK REVIEWS

The Parchment Maze is quite unique – an archival thriller, a mystery fantasy, and an historical riddle gamebook. Vera is a young archaeologist who discovers the existence of a secret society that has been hidden from the rest of the world for six thousand years. Fiction and science combine in an intriguing novel based on real archaeological discoveries and actual icons, a daring combination of Dan Brown and Umberto Eco. Could the legend of Orpheus and his descent into the Underworld be more than just mythology?There is supernatural love, there are secrets; there is murder, there is history; from Berlin to Moscow, from Rome to Burma, Filipova's novel is sure to intrigue.

Colin Falconer, *author of twenty novels, translated into seventeen languages over the last twenty-five years*

The Parchment Maze is a carefully crafted literary work that could be both entertaining and illuminating for readers throughout the world, especially in the United States. The contribution of *The Parchment Maze* to the literature of the occult is quite significant. In my professional opinion, this novel surpasses those of both Dan Brown and Elizabeth Kostova in terms of complexity and theme.Three specific features of the novel that are noteworthy are as follows: (1) the labyrinthine structure of the story; (2) the well-drawn relationships of Vera-Ariman, Vera-Futch, and Vera-her father; and (3) the sustained journey motif that stresses the quest for illumination/faith/paradise. Finally, the mysterious ending of the novel leaves the reader hoping for more. Perhaps Vera is not dead. A sequel is certainly possible.

Joseph F. Ceccio, Ph.D., *March 2011, professor of English literature at the University of Akron*

Ancient myths from both Bulgaria and the world, historical sources along with a lot fictionalized past, quoted manuscripts with lost ends, roads that cross, and characters in whose destinies events from more than a century and a half ago come together: these are only some of the ideas behind *The Parchment Maze*. The intricate interplay of history, its interpretations and politics in the novel determines the characters' personal stories, while the author takes us through a number of genres in her writing: thriller, philosophical and historical novel, non-fictional and matter-of-fact literature. And although this technique reminds us of the voices of some of the bestselling writers of the day, such as Dan Brown and Elizabeth Kostova, and even the internationally acclaimed Umberto Eco, *The Parchment Maze* shows us that these voices are very well assimilated into the writing of its author, who, nevertheless, retains her own style, respects the readers and relies on their active interpretation of the text, while at the same time wanting her writing to be convertible. *The Parchment Maze* by Ludmila Filipova is perhaps one of the author's best books so far. Following one of the most successful literary models – especially in terms of sales and appeal to a versatile readership – the novel is perched on the border between fiction and non-fiction. Its full-blooded characters have their own personal stories and particular roles in the texture and plot of the novel, but they also come with specific ideas about the past. It is through them that Bulgarian and international myths are interpreted, the past is given a new meaning – layer over layer of interpretations get accumulated, unfinished stories are continued. The novel deals with politics, shaping of theories, demystifications and discoveries of new mysteries.To recap in literary terms, *The Parchment Maze* is a typical post-modern novel, relying on quotability, the active role of the readers' imagination in reading and interpreting the novel, and the readers' readiness to experiment with genre-mixing (thriller, philosophical novel, journalistic narrative, etc). It is a novel that thinks of the separation between fiction and non-fiction, between literature and non-literature, as surmountable and which believes in quotability's role as a fundamental principle on which our contemporary culture is based. As a result, the novel's aspiration is to overcome the regional confinements in terms of both the problems treated and the way of thinking implied.

Amelia Licheva, *professor of literature*, *Sofia University*

A novel based on mysteries and riddles – where do we come from; where are we going? Where did knowledge originate from? And who are its guardians? The story of *The Parchment Maze* takes place in the familiar, unfamiliar Bulgarian scene and in some of the largest cultural centers, such as Berlin, Moscow, Rome, Switzerland and Burma. Putting on display some of the most controversial treasures of the Old World, the author takes us to the dusty backrooms of the museums where the 'tricky' artifacts are hidden. The novel tells us the engaging story of a woman who has devoted her life to archaeology. Vera is a young scientist on the verge of a huge discovery that would completely alter our ideas about the past of our lands. At some point in the late prehistoric era there appeared a civilization that greatly impacted the development of Europe and the world. In her attempt to unravel the mysteries surrounding the history of that civilization, the heroine of the novel comes across a mysterious society, which has succeeded in keeping its secrets and knowledge hidden from the rest of the world since 4000 B.C. Who is Orpheus and who are the people who professed Orphism? When did they appear and why did they disappear? Who are their heirs and what are the secrets they are still keeping?

Science, secrets, murders, love and wounds that have left their deep marks in the souls of the characters – they all come together to make *The Parchment Maze* a novel about the past, the present and the future. The author skillfully combines fictional characters and actual archaeological discoveries, thus making the readers aware of some not-so-famous real discoveries and artifacts, most of which were made within the territory of present-day Bulgaria.

Petranka Nedelcheva, *assistant professor of archeology*

Ludmila Filipova is a young author with a few already published and successful novels. But what is important is that Ludmila is not afraid to experiment, always searching for something new; she does not strictly follow literary models and meticulously avoidd clichés; it's difficult to frame her work in literary terms.

The Parchment Maze is a wonderful experiment. The idea behind it is simple and very effective. The reader is involved in an investigation, a quest for knowledge about an ancient civilization that has disappeared. Very few traces are left behind – most of the traces have been painstakingly obliterated. The reader becomes an archaeologist, a criminologist, and a discoverer. She is given access to a database of information consisting of documents, photos, artifacts, hints implying some paths that should lead him/her to the truth. And the truth is somewhere around us. We just need to see it.

The huge amount of documentary material found and collected speaks to the author's credit. And so does the serious, thorough analysis of the facts. It is on those that the main hypothesis of the novel is based. The author has treated them very professionally, including numerous quotations, papers, photos and pictures on the pages of her novel. The clear, succinct style underlines the complexity of the main idea of the novel.

The Parchment Maze is, in fact, the only Bulgarian example of a riddle novel. The worth of such novels stems from the fact that they easily engage readers of all ages and greatly facilitate their remembering of the information shared. On top of that, in this particular example, the action is fast, while the novel is full of suspense and is, therefore, likely to keep the readers absorbed.

The very structure of the book betrays experimentalism. It mirrors the structure of the ancient manuscript around which the intrigue in the story revolves. The book comes complete with superb illustrations and a lot of photographic material. All that leaves us with a definite feeling of the documentariness.

Maria Stankova, writer, literary critic

This is not just a novel, but rather a cinematic story that will make you alter your ideas about the origins of human knowledge multiple times.

From the ever-engagingly changing "pictures," you will learn why we, the people inhabiting the territories of the earliest civilization in the world, are responsible for unraveling its mysteries and carrying into the future its ancient knowledge about the meaning of human life and the immortality of the human soul.

Stiliyan Ivanov, director and screenwriter